YOU DON'T KNOW
HOW LUCKY YOU ARE, BOYS . . .

In 1782 the Loyalists fled the American Revolution; whole regiments with their families and slaves set sail from the ports of Savannah and Charleston. In South Africa they found a new home, and built a new nation—the Domination of the Draka, an empire of cruelty and beauty, a warrior people possessed by a wolfish will to power.

1942: The Eurasian War. The fleets of Imperial Japan raid the coasts of a United States that stretches from Panama to the Arctic. The Nazi Wehrmacht storms Moscow and sweeps to the Urals. And to the south the Domination of the Draka is a giant forge, serf-manned factories pouring out tanks and dirigibles and steam cars as the Janissary legions gather for the final triumph and the ultimate revenge.

ACKNOWLEDGMENTS

To the Bunch of Seven, for criticism, role-playing, and advice which made this a better book (even from those who wanted to nuke 'em from orbit): Terri, Karen, Shirley, Louise, Marion, Mike, Tonya, and Fiona. And to Louise Spillsbury, ditto. May all your books sell.

To David Hughes, for access to his militaria and advice.

To David Kirby, for Point Ariel.

To Dave Fountain and Fred Schultz, for the software.

To Kevin Davies, for helping me carry home the computer and putting up with nit-picking on the cover.

To Erast Myrc, for helping me with the Russian.

To Dave Drake, for saying such nice things about the book, even back when it was in diapers. I needed that.

And to Jim and Betsy and all the other people at Baen, for restoring my faith in the publishing industry. Every one a true mensch.

MARCHING THROUGH GEORGIA

S.M. STIRLING

BAEN BOOKS

To Jan, with love.

Copyright © 1988 by S.M. Stirling

A Baen Books Original

Baen Publishing Enterprises
260 Fifth Avenue
New York, N.Y. 10001

First printing, May 1988

ISBN: 0-671-65407-1

Cover art by Kevin Davies

Lyrics to the song "Golden Eyes" are by Mercedes Lackey; music by Leslie Fish. From *Horsetamer's Daughter*. "Darkness is a Friend of Mine" is by Shirley Meier.

Printed in the United States of America

Distributed by
SIMON & SCHUSTER
1230 Avenue of the Americas
New York, N.Y. 10020

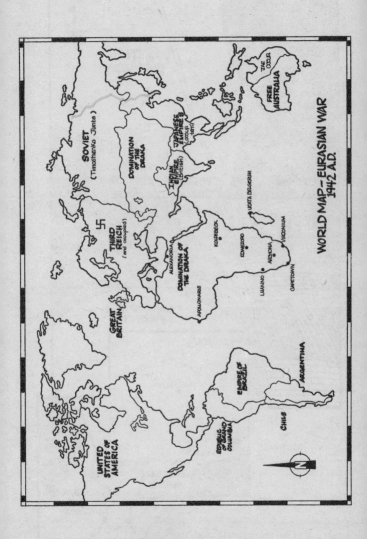

WORLD MAP — EURASIAN WAR 1942 A.D.

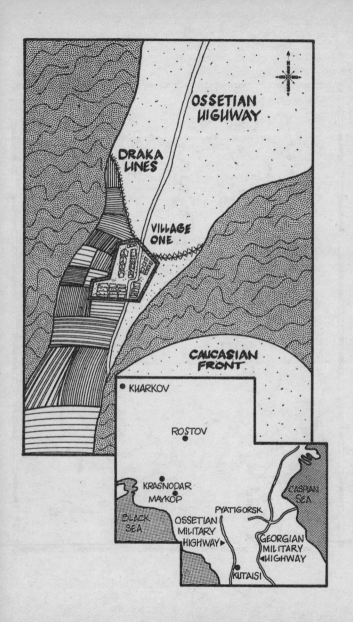

CHAPTER ONE

"... finally in 1783, by the Peace of Paris, Great Britain made peace with the American revolutionists and their European allies. However, the revival of British naval strength in the last years of the war made Spain and France ready to offer a face-saving compromise, particularly when they could do so at the expense of the weakest partner in their coalition, the Netherlands. Franco-Spanish gains in the West Indies were to be balanced by allowing Britain to annex the Dutch Cape colony, which had been occupied in 1779 to prevent its use by the French—almost as an afterthought, in an operation nearly cancelled.

Poor and remote, the Cape was renamed after Francis Drake and used as a dumping ground for Britain's other inheritance from the American war; the Loyalists, tens of thousands of whom had fought for the Crown and now faced exile as penniless refugees. As early as 1781 shiploads were arriving; after the Peace, whole regiments set sail with their families and slaves as the southern ports of Savannah and Charleston were evacuated. They were joined by large numbers of Hessian and other German mercenaries formerly in British service. Within a decade over 250,000 immigrants had arrived, swamping and assimilating the thin scattering of Dutch-Afrikaander settlers ...

> *200 Years: A Social History of the Domination,*
> by Alan E. Sorensson, Ph.D.
> Archona Press, 1983

1

NORTH CAUCASUS FRONT, 20,000 ft.
APRIL 14, 1942: 0400 HOURS

The shattering roar of six giant radial engines filled the hold of the Hippo-class transport aircraft, as tightly as the troopers of Century A, 1st Airborne Legion. They leaned stolidly against the bucking, vibrating walls of the riveted metal box, packed in their cocoons of parasail and body harness, strapped about with personal equipment and weapons like so many deadly slate-grey Christmas trees. The thin, cold air was full of a smell of oil and iron, brass and sweat and the black greasepaint that striped the soldiers' faces; the smell of tools, of a trade, of war. High at the front of the hold, above the ramp that led to the crew compartment, a dim red light began to flash.

Centurion Eric von Shrakenberg clicked off the pocket flashlight, folded the map back into his case and sighed. *0400*, he thought. *Ten minutes to drop*. Eighty soldiers here in the transport; as many again in the one behind, and each pulled a *Helot*-class glider loaded with heavy equipment and twenty more troopers.

He was a tall young man, a hundred and eighty centimeters even without the heavy-soled paratrooper's boots, hard smooth athlete's muscle rolling on the long bones. Yellow hair and mustache were cropped close in the Draka military style; new lines scored down his face on either side of the beak nose, making him look older than his twenty-four years. He sighed again, recognizing the futility of worry and the impossibility of calm.

Some of the old sweats seemed to have it, the ones who'd carried the banners of the Domination of the Draka from Suez to Constantinople and east to Samarkand and the borderlands of China in the last war. And then spent the next twenty years hammering Turks and Kurds and Arabs into serfs as meek as the folk of the old African provinces. Senior Decurion McWhirter there, for instance, with the Constantinople Medal and the Afghan ribbon pinned to his combat fatigues, bald head shining in the dim lights . . .

He looked at the watch again. 0405: time was creeping by. Only two hours since liftoff, if you could believe it.

I'll fret, he thought. *Staying calm would drive me crazy. Christ, I could use a smoke.* It would take the edge off; skydiving was the greatest thing since sex was invented, but combat was something you never really got used to. You were nervous the first time; then you met the reality, and it was worse than you'd feared. And every time after that, the waiting was harder . . .

Eric had come to believe he would not survive this war many months ago; his mind believed it, at least. The body never believed in death, and always feared it. It was odd; he hated the war and its purposes, but during the fighting, that conflict could be put aside. Garrison duty was the worst—

In search of peace, he returned to The Dream. It had come to him often, these last few years. Sometimes he would be walking through orchards, on a cool and misty spring morning; cherry blossoms arched above his head, heavy with scent, over grass starred with droplets of fog. There was a dog with him, a setter. Or it might be a study with a fire of applewood, lined with books with stamped leather spines, windows closed against slow rain . . . He had always loved books; loved even the smell and texture of them, their weight. There was a woman, too: walking beside him or sitting with her red hair spilling over his knees. A dream built of memories, things that might have been, things that could never be.

Abruptly he shook himself free of it. War was full of times with nothing to do but dream, but this was not one of them.

Most of the others were waiting quietly, with less tension than he remembered from the first combat drop last summer—blank-faced, lost in their own thoughts. Occasional pairs of lovers gripped hands. *The old Spartans were right about that,* he thought. *It does make for better fighters . . . although they'd probably not have approved of a heterosexual application.*

A few felt his gaze, nodded or smiled back. They had been together a long time, he and they; he had been private, NCO and officer-candidate in this unit. If this had been a legion of the Regular Line, they would all have been from the same area, too; it was High Command policy to keep familiar personnel together, on the theory that while you might enlist for your country, you died for your friends. And to keep your pride in their eyes.

The biggest drop of the war. Two full legions, 1st and 2nd Airborne, jumping at night into mountain country. Twice the size of the surprise assault in Sicily last summer, when the Domination had come into the war. Half again the size of the lightning strike that had given Fritz the Maikop oil fields intact last October, right after Moscow fell. Twenty-four thousand of the Domination's best, leaping into the night, "fangs out and hair on fire."

He grimaced. He'd been a tetrarch in Sicily, with only thirty-three troopers to command. *A soldier's battle,* they'd called it. Which meant bloody chaos, and relying on the troops and the regimental officers to pull it out of the can. Still, it had succeeded, and the parachute *chiliarchoi* had been built up to legion size, a tripling of numbers. Lots of promotions, if you made it at all. And a merciful transfer out once Italy was conquered and the "pacification" began; there would be nothing but butcher's work there now, best left to the Security Directorate and the Janissaries.

Sofie Nixon, his comtech, lit two cigarettes and handed him one at arm's length, as close as she could lean, padded out with the double burden of parasail and backpack radio.

"No wrinkles, Cap," she shouted cheerfully, in the clipped tones of Capetown and the Western Province. Listening to her made *him* feel nineteen again, sometimes. And sometimes older than the hills—slang changed so *fast*. That was a new one for "no problems."

"All this new equipment: to listen to the briefing papers, hell, it'll be like the old days. We can be heroes on the cheap, like our great-granddads were, shootin' down black spear-chuckers," she continued.

With no change of expression: "And I'm the Empress of Siam; would I lie?"

He smiled back at the cheerful, cynical face. There was little formality of rank in the Draka armies, less in the field, least of all among the volunteer elite of the airborne corps. Conformists did not enlist for a radical experiment; jumping out of airplanes into battle was still new enough to repel the conservatives.

Satisfied, Sofie dragged the harsh, comforting bite of the tobacco into her lungs. The Centurion was a good sort, but he tended to . . . *worry* too much. That was part of being an officer, of course, and one of the reasons she was satisfied to stay at monitor, stick-commander. But he overdid it; you could wreck yourself up that way. And he was very much of the Old Domination, a scion of the planter aristocracy and their iron creed of duty; she was city-bred, her grandfather a Scottish mercenary immigrant, her father a dock-loading foreman.

Me, I'm going to relax while I can, she thought. There was a lot of waiting in the Army, that was about the worst thing . . . apart from the crowding

and the monotonous food, and good Christ but being
under fire was scary. Not nice-scary like being on a
board when the surf was hot, or a practice jump;
plain *bad*. You really felt good afterward, though,
when your body realized it was alive . . .

She pushed the thought out of her head. The
sitreps had said this was going to be much worse
than Sicily, and that had been deep-shit enough.
Still, there had been good parts. The Italians really
had some pretty things, and the paratroops got the
first pick. That jewelry from the bishop's palace in
Palermo was absolutely divine! And the tapestry . . .
she sighed and smiled, in reminiscence. There had
been leave, too—empty space on transport airships
heading south, if you knew the right people. It was
good to be able to peacock a little—do some party-
ing, with a new campaign ribbon and the glamour of
victory, and some pretties to show off.

Her smile grew smug. She had been *very* popular,
with all the sexes and their permutations; a change from
ugly-duckling adolescence. *Men are nice, definitely,*
she thought. *Pity I had to wait 'til I reported to boot
camp to start in on 'em.*

That was the other thing about the Army; it was
better than school. Draka schooling was sex-segre-
gated, on the theory that youth should not be dis-
tracted from learning and their premilitary training.
Either that or sheer conservatism. Eight months of
the year spent isolated in the countryside: from five
to eighteen it had been her life, and the last few
years had been growing harder to take. She was glad
to be out of it, the endless round of gymnastics and
classes and petty feuds and crushes; the Army was
tougher, paratroop school more so, but what you did
off duty was your own business. It was good to be an
adult, free.

Even the winter in Mosul had been all right. The
town was a hole, of course—provincial, and all new

since the Draka conquest in 1916. Nothing like the mellow beauty of Capetown, with its theaters and concerts and famous nightspots . . . Mosul—well, what could you expect of a place whose main claim to fame was petrochemical plants? They'd been up in the mountains most of the time, training hard. She flexed her shoulders and neck complacently. She'd thought herself fit before, but four months of climbing under full load and wrestling equipment over boulders had taken the last traces of puppy fat off and left her with what her people considered the ideal feminine figure—sleek, compactly curved, strong, and quick.

Sofie glanced sidelong at her commander; she thought he'd been noticing, since she qualified for comtech. Couldn't tell, though; he was one for keeping to himself. Just visited the officer's Rest Center every week or so. But a man like that wouldn't be satisfied with serf girls; he'd want someone he could *talk* to . . .

Or maybe it's my face? she thought worriedly, absently stripping the clip out of the pistol-grip well of her machinepistol and inserting it again. It was still obstinately round and snub-nosed; freckles were all very well, enough men had described it as *cute*, but it obstinately refused to mature into the cold, aquiline regularity that was most admired. She sighed, lit another cigarette, started running the latest costume drama over again in her head. *Tragic Destiny:* Signy Anders and Derek Wallis as doomed Loyalist lovers fighting the American rebels, with Carey Plesance playing the satanic traitor George Washington . . .

God, it must have been uncomfortable wearing those petticoats, she thought. *No wonder they couldn't do anything but look pretty and faint; how could you fight while wearing a bloody tent? Good thing Africa cured them of those notions.*

*   *   *

0410, Eric thought. *Time.* The voice of the pilot spoke in his earphones, tinny and remote.

"Coming up on the drop zone, Centurion," she said. "Wind direction and strength as per briefing. Scattered cloud, bright moonlight." A pause. "Good luck."

He nodded, touching his tongue to his lip. The microphone was smooth and heavy in his hand. Beside him the American war correspondent, Bill Dreiser, looked up from his pad and then continued jotting in shorthand.

Dreiser finished the paragraph and forced his mind to consider it critically, scanning word by word with the pinhead light on the other end of the pen. Useful, when you had to consult a map or instrument without a conspicuous light; the Domination issued them to all its officers, and he had been quick to pick one up. The device was typical of that whole bewildering civilization; he turned it in his hands, feeling the smooth careful machining of its duralumin parts, admiring the compact powerful batteries, the six different colors of ink, the moving segments that made it a slide rule as well.

Typical indeed, he thought wryly. Turned out on specialized machine tools, by illiterate factory-serfs who thought the world was flat and that the Combine that owned their contracts ruled the universe.

He licked dry lips, recognizing the thought for what it was: a distraction from fear. He had been through jump training, of course—an abbreviated version tailored to the limitations of a sedentary American in early middle age. And he had seen enough accidents to the youngsters about him to give him well-justified nightmares; if those magnificent young animals could suffer their quota of broken bones and wrenched backs, so could he. And they would be jumping into the arms of Hitler's Wehrmacht; his years reporting from Berlin had not endeared him to the National Socialists . . .

He glanced across the echoing gloom of the cargo hold to where Eric sat, smoking a last cigarette. His face was impassive, showing no more emotion than it had at briefings around the sand table in Mosul. A strange young man. The eagle-faced blond good looks were almost a caricature of what a landed aristocrat of the Domination of the Draka was expected to be; so was his manner, most of the time. Easy enough to suppose there was nothing there but the bleakly efficient, intellectual killing machine of legend, the amoral and ruthless superman driven by the Will to Power whom Nietzsche had proclaimed.

He had mentioned that to Eric, once. *A useful myth,* had been the Draka's reply. That had led them to a discussion of the German thinker's role in developing the Domination's beliefs; and of how Nietzsche's philosophy had been modified by the welcoming environment he found among the Draka, so different from the incomprehension and contempt of his countrymen.

The Domination was founded by losers, Eric had said, letting an underlying bitterness show through. *Ex-masters like the Loyalists and all those displaced European aristocrats and Confederate southerners; prophets without followers like Carlyle and Gobineau and Nietzsche. The outcasts of Western civilization, not the "huddled masses" you Yankees got. My ancestors were the ones who wouldn't give up their grudges. Now they're coming back for their revenge.*

Dreiser shrugged and brought his mind back to the present, tugging at the straps of his harness one more time. Times like this you could understand the isolationists; he had been born in Illinois and raised in Iowa himself, and knew the breed. A lot of them were decent enough, not fascist sympathizers like the German-American Bund, or dupes like Lindberg. Just decent people, and it was so tempting to think the oceans could guard American wholesomeness and decency from the iron insanities and corruptions of Europe . . .

Not that he had ever subscribed to that habit of thought; it led too easily to white sheets and hatred, destroying a tradition to protect it. Or to the Babbittry that had driven him to Paris in the 1920's; the America he returned to in the Depression years was more alive than Hoover's had been, finally acknowledging its problems. Trying to *do* something about the submerged third of the population, taking up the cause of the Negro abandoned during Reconstruction, reforming the Hispanic backwaters south of the Rio Grande, where annexation in 1848 had produced states free only in name.

Dreiser ground his teeth, remembering the pictures from Pearl Harbor—oily smoke pouring to the sky from Battleship Row, the aircraft carrier *Enterprise* exploding in a huge globe of orange fire as the Japanese dive-bombers caught her in the harbor mouth . . . The United States had paid a heavy price for the illusion of isolation, and now it was fighting on its own soil, full-fledged states like Hawaii and the Philippines under enemy occupation. His prewar warnings of the Nazi menace had not been heeded; now his reports might serve to keep the public aware that Japan was not the only enemy, or the most dangerous of the Axis.

"JUMPMASTERS TO YOUR STATIONS!" Eric's amplified voice overrode even the engines; there was a glisten of eyes, a hundredfold rattle as hands reflexively sought the ripcords. "PREPARE TO OPEN HATCH DOORS."

"And step into the shit," came the traditional chorus in reply.

*   *   *

Far to the south in Castle Tarleton, overlooking the Draka capital of Archona, a man stood leaning on the railing of a gallery, staring moodily at the projacmap that filled the huge room below. He was an *Arch-Strategos*, a general of the Supreme General Staff. The floor of the room was glass, twenty meters by thirty; the relief map was eerily three dimensional and underlit to put contrast against contour marks and unit counters. The mountains of Armenia extended in an infinity of scored rock, littered with the symbols of legions, equipment, airstrips, and roads; the red dots of aircraft crawled north toward Mt. Elbruz and the passes of the Caucasus. Stale tobacco scented the air, and the click-humm of the equipment echoed oddly in the unpeopled spaces.

"Risky," he said, nodding toward the map. "Twenty legions of armor, thirty mechanized. Another sixty of Janissary motorized infantry. Six thousand tanks, twenty thousand infantry carriers, a thousand SP guns . . . two million troops, and it all depends on two legions of paratroopers. North of the mountains, in an open-field battle of maneuver, we can take the Fritz. The Ivans are still holding hard east of the Volga, the Germans took on too much; they haven't got a strategic reserve to speak of . . . But butting our heads into the Caucasus, fighting our way over the mountains, inch by inch—" He shook his head. "We can't afford a war of attrition; there aren't enough Draka; it would ruin us. And there may not be any limit to the number of serfs we can conscript for the Janissaries, but there *are* limits to the number we can arm safely."

"War is risk," the officer beside him replied. The cat-pupiled eye of Intelligence was on her collar; she had the same air of well-kept middle age as he, and a scholar's bearing. "Breaking the Ankara Line was a risk, too; but it gave us Anatolia, back in '17."

The general laughed, rubbing at his leg. The fragments from the Austrian antiairship burst had severed tendons and cut nerves; the pain was a constant backdrop to his life, and worse on these cold nights. *Pain does not hurt*, he reminded himself. *Only another sensation. The Will is Master*. "Then I was an optimistic young centurion, out at the sharp end, sure I could pull it out of the *kaak* even if the high command fucked it up," he said. "Now the new generation's out there, and probably expecting to have to scoop up *my* mistakes."

"I was driving a field ambulance in '16; all you male lords of creation thought us fit for, then."

He laughed. "We weren't quite so stretched for reliable personnel, then." The woman snorted and poked a finger into his ribs.

"Hai, that was a *joke*, Cohortarch," he complained with a smile.

"So was that, you shameless reactionary bastard," she retorted. "If you're going to insult me, do it when we're on-duty and I can't object . . ."

He nodded, and grew grim. "Well, we're committed to this attack; the Domination wasn't built by playing safe. There'll never be another chance like this. Thank the White Christ that Hitler attacked the Soviets after he finished off the French. If they'd stayed in Europe, we'd never have been able to touch them."

She nodded, hesitated, spoke: "Your boy's in the first wave, isn't he, Karl?"

The man nodded, turning away from the railing and leaning his weight against the ebony cane at his side. "Eric's got a Century in the First Airborne," he said quietly, looking out over the city. "And my daughter's flying an Eagle out of Kars." The outer wall was window from floor to ceiling; Castle Tarleton stood on a height that gave a fine view of the Domination's capital. The fort had been built in 1791, when the Crown Colony of Drakia was new. The hilltop had been for practical reasons, once: Cavalry had been based here, rounding up labor for the sugar plantations of Natal, where the ancestors of the Draka were settling into their African home.

Those had been American loyalists, mostly southerners; driven from their homes by vengeful neighbors after the triumph of the Revolution. The British had seized the Cape from its Dutch masters during that war, and found it cheap enough to pay their supporters with the stolen goods of colonial empire. "Strange," Karl von Shrakenberg continued, softly enough to make her lean toward the craggy face. "I can command a legion handily enough—by Gobineau's ghost, I wish they'd give me a field command!—run my estate; I even get along well with my daughters. But my son . . . Where do the children go? I remember taking him from the midwife, I remember setting him on my shoulders and naming the stars for him, putting him on his first pony. And now? We hardly speak, except to argue. About absurdities: politics, books . . . When did we become strangers? When he left, there was nothing. I wanted to tell him . . . everything: to come back alive, that I loved him. Did he know it?"

His companion laid a hand on his shoulder. "Why didn't you say it?" she asked softly. "If you can tell me?"

He sighed wearily. "Never was very good with words, not that sort. And there are things you can say to a friend that you can't to your blood; perhaps, if Mary were still alive . . ." He straightened, his eyes focusing on the world beyond the glass. "Well. This view was always a favorite of mine. It's seen a lot."

Together they looked down across the basin, conscious of the winds hooting off the high plateau at their backs, cold and dry with winter. The first small fort of native fieldstone had grown over the years; grown with the colony of Drakia, named for Francis Drake and heir to that ruthless freebooter's spirit. It was a frontier post guarding the ranches and diamond mines, at first. Railways had snaked by to the great gold fields of the Whiteridge; local coal and iron had proved more valuable still, and this was a convenient post for a garrison to watch the teeming compounds of serf factory hands that grew beside the steel mills and machine-works. Then the Crown Colony became the autonomous Dominion of Draka and needed a capital, a centrum for a realm that stretched from Senegal to Aden, from the Cape to Algeria.

Lights starred the slopes beneath them, fading the true stars above; mansions with roofs of red tile, set in acres of garden. A monorail looped past, a train swinging through silently toward the airship haven and airport to the west, windows yellow against the darkness. A tracery of streets, sprawling over ridge and valley to the edge of sight, interrupted by the darker squares of parkland. Archona was the greatest city of the Domination—eight million souls. Through the center slashed the broad Way of the Armies, lined with flowering jacaranda trees, framed between six-story office blocks, their marble and tile washed snow-pale in moonlight. The Assembly building, with its great two hundred meter dome of iridescent stained glass; the Palace where Archon Gunnarson had brought law into conformity with fact and proclaimed the Domination a sovereign state, back in 1919.

Karl's mouth quirked; he had been here in the Castle on that memorable day. The staff officers had raised a loyal glass of Paarl brandy, then gone back to their planning for the pacification of the New Territories and the *next* war. None of them had expected the Versailles peace to last more than a generation, whatever the American president might say of a "war to end war." Unconsciously, his lip curled in contempt; only a Yankee could believe something that obviously fatuous.

"You grew up here, didn't you, Sannie?" he said, shaking off the mood of gloom.

"*Ja*," she replied. "Born over there—" she pointed past the block of government buildings, to where the scattered colonnades of the University clustered. "In the house where Thomas Carlyle lived. Nietzsche visited my father there, seemed to think it was some sort of shrine. That was a little while after he moved to the Domination. Anthony Trollope stopped by as well, they tell me. While he was researching that book, *Prussia in the Antipodes*, back in the 1870's. He was the one the English didn't pay any attention to, and then wished they had."

They both smiled; it was an old joke in the Domination, that the British had been warned so openly of the Frankenstein's monster they had created by unleashing the Draka south of Capricorn. Their gaze lifted, to the glow that lit the northern horizon—the furnaces and factories of the Ferrous Metals Combine, stamping and grinding out the engines of war. The serfs of the industrial combines were being kept to their tasks; for the rest, there was little traffic. Mobilization among the citizens had left little of Archona's vaunted nightlife, and curfew kept the subject races off the central streets.

"Well," he said, offering her an arm with a courtesy old-fashioned even in their generation of Draka. "Shall we see if, somewhere in this bureaucrat's paradise of a city, two ancient and off-duty warriors can find a drink?"

He would face the waiting as he would any other trial; as befitted a von Shrakenberg of Oakenwald. *Even if I'm the last,* he thought, as his halting boot echoed through the empty halls of the fortress.

Thump! Eric's parachute unfolded, a rectangle of

blackness against the paling stars of dawn. He blinked; starlight and moonlight were almost painfully bright after the crowded gloom of the transport; silence caressed his mind.

Straps caught at crotch and waist and armpits, then cradled him in their padding. Above him the night was full of thunder, as hundreds of the huge transports spilled their cargos of troops and equipment into the thin air; south and east still more formations bulked black against the stars: transports and glider-tugs. Chutes blossomed, sorted themselves into formations, turned to their destinations . . . A paratrooper lost velocity fast; the transports drew ahead and above quite quickly. Above a flight of Falcon III fighters banked, their line stretching into an arc, moonlight glinting on the bubble canopies. Sharks of the sky.

This is the best time, Eric thought, as the flight of transports vanished, climbing and turning for height and home, southward to their bases. Silence, except for the fading machines and the hiss of the wind through the silk. Silence over a great scattered cloudscape, castles and billows of silver under a huge cool moon; air like crisp white wine in the lungs, aloneness. A feeling beyond the self; peace, joy, freedom—in a life bound on the iron cross of duty, in the service of repression and death. There had been a few other times like this; making love with Tyansha, or single-handing a ketch through monsoon storms. But always here, alone in the sky.

His hands were working on the lines, turning and banking; these new sail-chutes *flew* like gliders. None of the old business of dropping all over the farmyard, where the wind and fate pleased. You could jump high and sail to your drop zone quietly, with no thunder of engines to announce you. And you could land soft; that was important. Paratroopers had to carry most of their equipment—as much again as their own body weight. With a load like that you could break your back just stepping into a ditch, if you weren't careful.

The rest of the Century were forming up behind, wheeling like a flight of birds of prey; he saw with relief that the gliders, with their cargo of heavy weapons and specialists, were following. The Legion was dropping on the whole pass that took the Ossetian Military Highway through the mountains from north to south, but the bulk of it was landing at the southern end. The 2nd Cohort was the northernmost unit, and Century A was the point formation of 2nd Cohort. They would take the shock of whatever reaction force the Fritz could muster to relieve their cut-off comrades south of the mountains. Two hundred of them, to blunt the enemy spearheads; they were going to *need* that special equipment, and the thirty-odd specialists in the *tetrarchy* of combat engineers. Very badly.

Now . . . The cloud cover was patchy, light and shadow. Southward, the main peaks of the Caucasus shone snow white. Below was a black-purple immensity of scree, talus-slope, dark forests of beech and holm oak, sloping down to a valley and a thread of road winding up into the mountains. On a map it was nothing, a narrow sliver of highland between the Black and Caspian Seas . . .

Over it all loomed the great mass of Mount Elbruz; beyond it was the south slope, ex-Soviet Georgia; beyond that the Draka armored legions massing in the valleys of Armenia. The symbolism of it struck him—all Europe was in shadow, in a sense. From the Elbe to the Urals, there was a killing underway great enough to leave even the cold hearts at Castle Tarleton shaken . . . Eric had been a student of history, among other things; his mouth quirked at the supreme irony that the Draka should come as deliverers.

Still, true enough, he thought, as his body automatically leaned and twisted to turn the parasail. The rule of the Domination was cruel and arbitrary, merciless in breaking resistance. But his people made war for land and booty, killed to enforce submission. What the Intelligence reports said was happening below was madness come to earth: slaughter for its own sake, an end rather than a means.

The Fritz must be convinced they've won it all, he thought, as his eyes automatically scanned for the landing zone. *There* . . .

He stooped, a giddy exhilarating slide across the sky, a breathless joy. For a moment he was a bird, a hunting bird, an eagle. Stooping on the world, feeling the air rushing past his wings . . . *Be practical, Eric,* he reminded himself severely. Once they grounded they would have only their feet, and the south slope of the mountains was German-held.

But lightly, by the spearhead divisions of General Von Paulus' Sixth Army, itself the vanguard of Army Group South. They had fought their way across the Ukraine, through the great encirclement battles at Kiev and Kharkov, even with most of their armor up north for the attack on Moscow. The frantic Russian counterattacks had failed; the Panzers came south, ground down by a thousand miles of route-march over frozen wasteland and the costly destruction of Zhukov's Siberians. The offensive continued, on through the winter and the mud of spring; east to the Volga at Stalingrad, wheeling south and east to Astrakhan, south into the Kalmyk steppe, taking Maikop and Krasnodar, on to the Kuban.

Now . . . now they were a *very* long way from home—thousands of miles of mud trail, torn-up railway, scorched earth. Good troops, but exhausted, fought out, short of supplies. If the paradrop could hold the passes behind them, they could be crushed out of existence by waves of Janissary infantry; then the Draka armor would pour into the Russian plains, close to their bases, fresh, with superior weapons and limitless supplies, against enemies who had battered each other into broken-backed impotence.

The ground was coming up fast; he could smell it, a wet green scent of trees and spring meadow-grass and rock. This area had been swarming with Draka reconnaissance planes for months; the contours were springing out at him, familiar from hundreds of hours poring over photomaps. He banked to get a straight run at the oblong meadow. *Carefully now, don't get caught in that fucking treeline . . .* Branches went by three meters below. He hauled back on the lines, turning up the forward edge of the parasail; it climbed, spilled air, slowed. With the loss of momentum it turned from a wing to a simple parachute once more, and good timing landed him softly on his feet, boots vanishing in knee-high grass starred with white flowers.

Landing was a plunge from morning into darkness and shadow, as the sun dropped below the mountains to the southeast. And always, there was a sense of sadness, of loss; lightness turning to earthbound reality. *Not an eagle any more*, went through him. *More like a hyena*, a mordant part of his mind prompted. *Come to squabble over the carcass of Russia with the rival pack.*

Swiftly, he hit the quick-release catches and the synthsilk billowed out, white against the dark grass. He turned, clicking on the shielded red flashlight, waving it in slow arcs above his head. The first troopers of his Century were only seconds behind him, grey rectangles against the stars. They landed past him, a chorus of soft grunts and thuds, a curse and a clatter as somebody rolled. A quick check: mapcase, handradio, binoculars, Holbars T-6 assault rifle, three 75-round drums of 5mm for it, medikit, iron rations, fighting dagger in his boot, bush knife

across his back . . . That was an affectation—the
machete-sword was more a tradition than anything
else—but . . .

Dropping their chutes and jogging back by stick
and section, rallying to the shouts of their decurions
and tetrarchs, platoon-commanders, the troopers hur-
ried to form in the shadows of the trees. The mottled
grey of their uniforms was nearly invisible in the dim
light, and their faces were white ovals beneath the
rims of their wide-flared steel helmets. Sofie jogged
over to her position with the headquarters communi-
cation *lochos*, the antennae waving over her shoul-
der; she had the headset on already, tufts of bright
tow hair ruffling out between the straps. As usual,
she had clipped her helmet to her harness on touch-
down; also as usual, she had just lit a cigarette. The
match went *scrit* against the magazine well of her
machinepistol; she flicked it away and held out the
handset.

For Dreiser, leaving the airplane had been a
whirling, chaotic rush. For a moment he tumbled,
then remembered instructions. *Arms and legs straight*.
That brought the sickening spiral to a stop; he was
flying forward, down toward silver clouds and the
dark holes between them.

"Flying, hell, I'm *falling*," he said into the rush of
cold wind. His teeth chattered as he gripped the
release toggle and gave the single firm jerk the Draka
instructors had taught. For a heart-stopping moment
there was nothing, and then the pilot chute un-
folded, dragging out the main sail. It bloomed above
him, the reduction in speed seeming to drag him
backward out of his fall. Air gusted past him, more
slowly now that the parachute was holding. He glanced
up to the rectangle above him, a box of dozens of
long cloth tubes fastened together side by side, held
taut by the rush of air.

" 'The parasail functions as both a parachute and a wing,' " he quoted to himself. " 'To acquire forward speed, lean forward. Steer by hauling on left or right cords, or by shifting the center of gravity . . .' "

God, it's working. Blinking his eyes behind the goggles that held his glasses to his face, he peered about for the recognition-light. The aircraft had vanished, nothing more than a thrumm of engine noise somewhere in the distance. There it was, a weak red blinking: he shifted his weight forward, increasing the angle of glide. Cautiously; you could nose down in these things, and he doubted he could right it again before he hit.

The meadow rose up to strike; he flung himself back, too soon, lost directional control, and barely avoided landing boot-first in another chute at a hundred feet up. Ground slammed into his soles and he collapsed, dragging.

"Watch where yo' puttin' y'feet. Yankee pigfuckah," an incongruously young and feminine voice snarled as he skidded through tall grass and sharp-edged gravel on his behind, scrabbling at the release straps until the billowing mass of fabric peeled away to join the others flapping on the ground. He stood, turned, flung himself down again as the dark bulk of a glider went by a foot above his head, followed by a second.

"Jesus!" he swore, as they landed behind him and collided with a brief *crunch* of splintering plywood and balsa. Boots hurdled him, voices called in throttled shouts.

As he came to his feet, the meadow seemed to be in utter chaos, groups of Draka paratroopers dashing about, parasails still banking in, color-coded lights flashing. But visibly, the mass of men, women, and machinery was sorting itself into units, moving according to prearranged plans. Behind him the detachable nose of a glider broke free under enthusiastic hands and the ramp to the cargo-hold dropped; a pilot staggered down to sit cradling his head in his hands, while a file of troopers ran up to begin unloading crates. Dreiser walked toward the spot where the Draka commanders would be gathering, feeling strength return to his rubbery legs and a strange exhilaration building.

Did it, by God! he thought. So much for being an old man at thirty-eight . . . Now, about the article, let's see: *The landing showed once again the value of careful preparation and training. Modern warfare, with its complex coordination of different arms, is something new on this earth. Our devotion to the "minuteman" tradition of the amateur citizen-soldier is a critical handicap . . .*

Eric took the handset, silent for a moment as the gliders came in with a *shush* of parted air, guiding themselves down into the field marked with discarded parasails. Moonlight and predawn glow cast their wings in patterns of shade and light as flaps and slots opened to shed lift. Around him there was a holding of breath as the landing skids cut turf with a screeching of steel on gravel. The sailplanes slewed to a halt, the wing of one catching the other's tail with a crunch of plywood. A sigh gusted up as the detachable nose-sections fell away and figures began unloading.

Sofie gently tapped his hand. "Set's workin' fine, Centurion," she said. "Got the Cohort Sparks already, green-beepers from all the handradios in the Century . . . want a smoke?"

"Trying to give it up," he grunted, lifting the phone to his ear and clicking the pressure-button in his call sign. "You should too." He glanced at his watch: 0420 almost exactly. Forty-five minutes to dawn.

"Hey, Centurion, do I complain about your baby girls?" she replied, grinning. The rest of the headquarters tetrarchy were falling in around him: Senior Decurion McWhirter, two five-trooper rifle "sticks" who would double as runners, two rocket-gun teams and a heavy machine gun.

They both fell silent as the hissing of static gave way to voices; coded sequences and barked instructions. Unconsciously, Eric nodded several times before speaking.

"Yes? Yes, sir. No sir; just coming in, but it looks good." Reception was excellent; he could hear a blast of small-arms fire in the background, the rapid snarl of Draka assault-rifles, the slower thump and chatter of German carbines and MG 34's.

"Ah, good." Then he and the comtech winced in unison. "The armor landed *where*? Sorry, sir, I know you didn't design this terrain . . . Right, proceed according to plan, hold them hard as long as I can. Any chance of extra antitank . . . yes, Cohortarch, I appreciate everybody wants more firepower, but we *are* the farthest north . . . Yes, sir, we can do it. Over and out, status report when Phase A is complete. Thank you, sir, and good luck to you, too."

"Because we're both going to need it," he added under his breath as he released the send button. The Legion had had a Cohort of light tanks, Cheetahs with 75mm guns in oscillating turrets. Those had apparently come down neatly in a gully . . .

The gliders were emptying, stacks of crates and heavy weapons being lifted onto their wheeled carts. Paratroopers jumped with light weapons—their Holbars assault rifles, machine guns, machinepistols for techs and weapons teams, the 85mm recoilless-rocket guns that served as tetrarchy antitank. The gliders held much of the Century's fighting power—trench-mortars, the 100mm automortars, 120mm recoilless guns, heavy machine guns, flame-throwers, demolition charges, ammunition. Not to mention most of their food and medical supplies. It would

likely be all they had until the regular supply drops
started. And already the trunks of the birches were
showing pale in the light of dawn.

A sudden sense of the . . . *unlikeliness* of it all
struck Eric. He had been born in the heartlands of
the Domination, fourteen thousand kilometers away
in southern Africa. And here he stood, on soil that
had seen . . . how many armies? Indoeuropeans mov-
ing south to become Hittites, Cimmerians, Scythians,
Sarmatians, Persians, Greeks, Romans, Byzantines,
Armenians, Arabs, Turks, Czarist Russians, Bolshe-
viks . . . and now a Century of Draka, commanded
by a descendant of Hessian mercenaries, come to kill
Germans who might be remote cousins, and who had
marched two thousand kilometers east to meet
him. . . .

What am I doing here? Where did it start? he
thought. Such a long way to journey, to die among
angry strangers. A journey that had lasted all his life
. . . The start? Oakenwald Plantation, of course. In
the year of his birth; and last year, six months ago.
But that was the past, and the battle was here and
now, an ending awaiting him. An end to pain, weari-
ness; an end to the conflict within, and to loneliness.
You could forget a great deal in combat.

Eric von Shrakenberg took a deep breath and
stepped forward, into the war.

CHAPTER TWO

. . . Napoleonic wars cut off imports, and industries had to be established if only because the mines were far inland; the need for a strong military-industrial complex maintained the pressure. Lack of navigable waterways led to an early development of steam transport, and southern Africa proved to be rich in copper, iron, and coal, as well as precious metals. Gold prompted rapid expansion northward; plantation agriculture remained dominant, but increasingly, its markets were local.

. . . steam-engine pioneer Richard Trevithick was only the first of many British engineers to find Drakia welcoming. With no local entrepreneurial class, the landed aristocracy stepped in to invest, followed by the State and the free-employee guilds; the social pattern of the countryside repeated itself in the growing industrial cities of the early nineteenth century. Outright enslavement of the natives was forbidden by the British, but the proto-Draka quickly developed a system of indentured labor and debt-peonage distinguishable only in name . . .

200 Years: A Social History of the Domination
by Alan E. Sorensson, Ph.D.
Archona Press, 1983

ARCHONA TO OAKENWALD
PLANTATION OCTOBER, 1941

The airdrop on Sicily had earned Eric von Shraken-
burg a number of things: a long scar on one thigh,
certain memories, and a field-promotion to Centuri-
on's rank. When the 1st Airborne Chiliarchy was
pulled back into reserve after the fall of Milan, the
promotion was confirmed; a rare honor for a man
barely twenty-four. With it came fourteen-day leave
passes to run from October 1st, 1941, and unlike
most of his comrades, he had not disappeared into
the pleasure quarter of Alexandria. The new move-
ment orders had already been cut: Draka Forces
Base Mosul, Province of Mesopotamia. Paratroopers
were cutting-edge assault troops; obviously, the High
Command did not expect the *de facto* truce with
Hitler to last. And that would be a more serious
matter than overrunning an Italy taken by surprise
and abandoned by its Axis allies. It was well for a
man to visit the earth that bore him before he died.
He would spend his leave in Oakenwald, the von
Shrakenberg plantation, now that the quarrel with
his father had been patched up. After a fashion.

Travel space was scarce, as mobilization built
toward its climax, but even in the Draka army it
helped to be the son of an *Arch-Strategos*, a staff
general. A place was found on a transport-dirigible
heading south with a priority cargo of machine-parts;
two days nonstop to the high plateau of southern
Africa. He spent the last half-hour in the control
gallery, for the view; they were coming in to Archona
from the north, and it was a side of the capital free
citizens seldom saw, unless business took them there.
For a citizen, Archona was the marble-and-tile pub-
lic buildings and low-rise office blocks, parks and

broad avenues, the University campus, and pleasant, leafy suburbs with the gardens for which the city was famed.

Beyond the basin that held the freemen's city lay the world of the industrial combines, hectare upon hectare, eating ever deeper into the bush country of the middleveld. A spiderweb of roads, rail-sidings, monorails, landing platforms for freight airships. The sky was falling into night, but there was no sleep below, only an unrestfulness full of the light of arc-lamps and the bellowing flares of the blast furnaces; factory-windows carpeted the low hills, shifts working round the clock. Only the serf-compounds were dark, the flesh-and-blood robots of the State exhausted on their pallets, a brief escape from a lockstep existence spent in that wilderness of metal and concrete.

Eric watched it with a fascination tinged with horror as the crew guided the great bulk of the lighter-than-air ship in, until light-spots danced before his eyes. And remembered.

In the center of Archona, where the Avenue of Triumph met the Way of the Armies, there was a square with a victory monument. A hundred summers had turned the bronze green and faded the marble plinth; about it were gardens of unearthly loveliness, where children played between the flower-banks. The statue showed a group of Draka soldiers on horseback; their weapons were the Ferguson rifle-muskets and double-barreled dragoon pistols of the eighteenth century. Their leader stood dismounted, reins in one hand, bush-knife in the other. A black warrior knelt before him, and the Draka's boot rested on the man's neck.

Below, in letters of gold, were words: *To the Victors*. That was *their* monument; northern Archona was a monument to the vanquished, and so were the other industrial cities that stretched north a thousand kilometers to Katanga; so were mines and plantations and ranches from the Cape to Shensi.

Eric slept the night in transit quarters; he got the bed, but there were two other officers on the floor, for lack of space. He would not have minded that, or even their insistence on making love, if the sexual athletics had not been so noisy . . . In the morning the transport clerk was apologetic; also harried. Private autocars were up on blocks for the duration, mostly; in the end, all she could offer was a van taking two Janissaries south to pick up recruits from the plantations. Eric shrugged indifferently, to the clerk's surprise. The city-bred might be prickly in their insistence on the privileges of the master caste, but a von Shrakenberg was raised to ignore such trivia. Also . . . he remembered the rows of Janissary dead outside Palermo, where they had broken the enemy lines to relieve the encircled paratroops.

The roadvan turned out to be a big, six-wheeled Kellerman steamer twenty years old, a round-edged metal box with running boards chest-high and wheels taller than he. It had been requisitioned from the Transportation Directorate, and still had eyebolts in the floor for the leg shackles of the work gangs. The Janissaries rose from their kitbags as Eric approached, flicking away cigarettes and giving him a respectful but unservile salute; the driver in her grimy coverall of unbleached cotton bowed low, hands before eyes.

"Carry on," Eric said, returning the salute. The serf soldiers were big men, as tall as he, their snug uniforms of dove-grey and silver making his plain Citizen Force walking-out blacks seem almost drab. Both were in their late thirties and Master Sergeants, the highest rank subject-race personnel could aspire to. They were much alike—hard-faced and thick-muscled; unarmed, here within the Police Zone, but carrying steel-tipped swagger sticks in white-gloved hands. One was ebony black, the other green-eyed and tanned olive, and might have passed for a freeman save for the shaven skull and serf identity-number tattooed on his neck.

The Draka climbed the short, fixed ladder and swung into the seat beside the driver. While the woman fired the van's boiler, he propped his Priority pass inside the slanted windscreen that ran to their knees; that ought to save them delay at the inevitable Security Directorate roadblocks. The vehicle pulled out of the loading bay with the smooth silence of steam power, into the crowded streets; he brought out a book of poetry, Rimbaud, and lost himself in the fire-bright imagery.

When he looked up in midmorning they were south of the city. Crossing the Whiteridge and the scatter of mining and manufacturing settlements along it, past the huge, man-made heaps of spoilage from the gold mines. Some were still rawly yellow with the cyanide compounds used to extract the precious metal; others were in every stage of reclamation, down to forested mounds that might have been natural. This ground had yielded more gold in its century and a half than all the rest of the earth in all the years of humankind; four thousand meters beneath the road, men still clawed at rock hot enough to raise blisters on naked skin. Then they were past, into the farmlands of the high plateau.

He rolled down the window, breathing deeply. The Draka took pains to keep industry from fouling the air or water too badly; masters had to breathe and drink, too, after all. Still, it was a relief to smell the goddess breath of spring overtaking the carrion stink of industrial-age war. The four-lane asphalt surface of the road stretched dead straight to meet the horizon that lay around them like a bowl; waist-high fields of young corn flicked by, each giving an instant's glimpse down long, leafy tunnels floored with brown, plowed earth. Air that smelled of dust and heat and green poured in, and the sea of corn shimmered as the leaves rippled.

They spent noon at a roadside waystation that was glad to see him; Eric was not surprised, remembering how sparse passenger traffic had been. Most of the vehicles had been *drags*—heavy haulers pulling articulated cargo trucks—or plantation vans heading to the rail stations with produce; once there had been a long convoy of wheeled personnel carriers taking Janissary infantry toward the training camps in the mountains to the east. He strolled, stretching his legs and idly watching the herds of cattle and eland grazing in the fields about; listened to the silence and the rustling of leaves in the eucalyptus trees that framed the low pleasant buildings of colored brick with their round stained-glass windows; sat in the empty courtyard and ate a satisfying luncheon of fried grits, sausage, and eggs—not forgetting to have food and beer sent out to the van . . .

The manager had time on her hands, and was inclined to be maternal. It was not until he had sat and listened politely to her rambling description of a son and daughter who were with the 5th Armored in Tashkent that he suspected that he was procrastinating; his own mother had died only a few years after his birth, and he did not generally tolerate attempts at coddling. Not until he found himself seriously considering her offer of an hour upstairs with the pretty but bedraggled serving-wench was he sure of it. He excused himself, looked in the back window of the van, saw that one of the Janissary NCO's had the driver bent over a bench and was preparing to mount. Eric rapped on the glass with impatient disgust, and the soldier released her to scurry, whimpering, back to the driver's seat, zipping her overall with shaking fingers.

It would be no easier to meet his father again if he delayed arrival until nightfall. Restlessly, he reopened the book; anticipation warred with . . . yes, fear: he had been afraid at that last interview with his father. Karl von Shrakenberg was not a man to be taken lightly.

The quiet sobbing of the driver as she wrestled with the wheel cut across his thoughts. Irritated, he found a handkerchief and handed it across to her, then pulled the peaked cap down over his eyes and turned a shoulder as he settled back and pretended to sleep. *Useless gesture*, he thought with self-contempt. A serf without a protector was a victim, and there were five hundred million more like this one. The system ground on, they were the meat, and the fact that he was tied on top of the machine did not mean he could remake it. And there were worse places than this—much worse: in a mine, or the newly taken Italian territories he had helped to conquer, to the drumroll beat of the Security Directorate's execution squads, liquidation rosters, destructive-labor camps.

Shut up, he thought. *Shut up, wench, I've troubles of my own!*

It was still light when they turned in under the tall stone arch of the gates, the six wheels of the Kellerman crunching on the smooth, crushed rock, beneath the sign that read: "Oakenwald Plantation, est. 1788. K. von Shrakenberg, Landholder." But the sun was sinking behind them. Ahead, the jagged crags of the Maluti Mountains were outlined in the Prussian blue of shadow and sandstone gold. This valley was higher than the plateau plains west of the Caledon River; rocky, flat-topped hills reared out of the rolling fields.

The narrow plantation road was lined with oaks, huge branches meeting twenty meters over their heads; the lower slopes of the hills were planted to the king-trees as well.

Beyond were the hedged fields, divided by rows of Lombardy poplar: wheat and barley still green with a hint of gold as they began to head out, contour-ploughed cornfields, pastures dotted with white-fleeced sheep, spring lambs, horses, yellow-coated cattle. The fieldworkers were heading in, hoes and tools slanted over their shoulders, mules hanging their heads as they wearily trudged back toward the stables. A few paused to look up in curiosity as the vehicle passed; Eric could hear the low, rhythmic song of a work team as they walked homeward, a sad sweet memory from childhood.

Despite himself he smiled, glancing about. It had been, by the White Christ and almighty Thor, two years now since his last visit. "You can't go home again," he said softly to himself. "The problem is, you can't ever really leave it, either." Memory turned in on itself, and the past colored the present; he could remember his first pony, and his father's hands lifting him into the saddle, how his fingers smelled of tobacco and leather and strong soap. And the first time he had been invited into his father's study to talk with the adults after a dinner party. Ruefully, he smiled as he remembered holding the brandy snifter in an authoritative pose anyone but himself must have recognized as copied from Pa's . . . And yet it was all tinged with sorrow and anger; impossible to forget, hurtful to remember, a turning and itching in his mind.

He looked downslope; beyond that screen of pines was a stock dam where the children of the house had gone swimming sometimes, gods alone knew why, except that they were *supposed* to use the pool up by the manor. There, one memorable day, he had knocked Frikkie Thyssen flat for sneering at his poetry. The memory brought a grin; it had been the sort of epic you'd expect a twelve-year-old in love with Chapman's Homer to do, but that little bastard Thyssen wouldn't have known if it had been a work of genius . . . And over there in the cherry orchard he had lost his virginity under a harvest moon one week after his thirteenth birthday, to a giggling field wench twice his age and weight . . .

And then there had been Tyansha, the Circassian girl. Pa had given her to him on his fourteenth birthday. The dealer had called her something more pronounceable, but that was the name she had taught him, along with her mother tongue. She had been . . . perhaps four years older than he; nobody had been keeping records in eastern Turkey during those years of blood and chaos. There were vague memories of a father, she had said, and a veiled woman who held her close, then lay in a ditch by a burning house and did not move. Then the bayonets of the Janissaries herding her and a mob of terrified children into trucks. Thirst, darkness, hunger; then the training creche. Learning reading and writing, the soft blurred Draka dialect of English; household duties, dancing, the arts of pleasing. Friends, who vanished one by one into the world beyond the walls. And him.

Her eyes had been what he had noticed first— huge, a deep pale blue, like a wild thing seen in the forest. Dark-red hair falling to her waist, past a smooth, pale, high-cheeked face. She had worn a silver-link collar that emphasized the slender neck and the serf-number tattooed on it, and a wrapped white sheath-dress to show off her long legs and high, small breasts. Hands linked before her, she had stood between his smiling father and the impassive dealer, who slapped her riding-crop against one boot, anxious to be gone.

"Well, boy, does she please?" Pa had asked. Eric
remembered a wordless stutter until his voice broke
humiliatingly in a squeak; his elder brother John had
roared laughter and slapped him on the back, urging
him forward as he led her from the room by the
hand. Hers had been small and cool; his own hands
and feet felt enormous, clumsy; he was hideously
aware of a pimple beside his nose.

She had been afraid—not showing it much, but he
could tell. He had not touched her; not then, or in
the month that followed. Not even at the first shyly
beautiful smile . . .

Gods, but I was callow, Eric thought in sadly
affectionate embarrassment. They had talked; rather,
he had, while she replied in tense, polite monosylla-
bles, until she began to shed the fear. He had showed
her things—his battle prints, his butterfly collection—
that had disgusted her—and the secret place in the
pine grove, where he came to dream the vast vague
glories of youth . . . A month, before she crept in
beside him one night. A friend, one of the overseer's
sons, had asked casually to borrow her; he had beaten
the older boy bloody. Not wildly, in the manner of
puppy fights, but with the *pankration* disciplines, in
a cold ferocity that ended only when he was pulled
off.

There had been little constraint between them, in
private. She even came to use his first name without
the "master," eventually. He had allowed her his
books, and she had devoured them with a hunger that
astonished him; so did her questions, sometimes dis-
concertingly sharp. Making love with a lover was
. . . different. Better; she had been more knowl-
edgeable than he, if less experienced, and they had
learned together. Once in a haystack, he remem-
bered; prickly, it had made him sneeze. Afterward
they had lain holding hands, and he had shown her
the southern sky's constellations.

She died in childbirth three years later, bearing his daughter. The child had lived, but that was small consolation. That had been the last time he wept in public; the first time since his mother had died when he was ten. And it had also been the last time his father had beaten him; for weakness. Casual fornication aside, it was well enough for a boy to have a serf-girl of his own. Even for him to care for her, since it helped keep him from the temptations that all-male boarding schools were prone to. But the public tears allowable for blood-kin were unseemly for a concubine.

Eric had caught the thong of the riding crop in one hand and jerked it free. "*Hit me again, and I'll kill you,*" he had said, in a tone flat as gunmetal. Had seen his father's face change as the scales of parental blindness fell away, and the elder von Shrakenberg realized that he was facing a very dangerous man, not a boy. And that it is not well to taunt an unbearable grief.

He shook his head and looked out again at the familiar fields; it was a sadness in itself, that time healed. Grief faded into nostalgia, and it was a sickness to try and hold it. That mood stayed with him as they swung into the steep drive and through the gardens below Oakenwald's Great House. The manor had been built into the slope of a hill—for defense, in the early days—and it still gave a memorable view. The rocky slope had been terraced for lawns, flowerbanks, ornamental trees, and fountains; forest grew over the steepening slope behind, and then a great table of rock reared two hundred meters into the darkening sky.

The manor itself was ashlar blocks of honey-colored local sandstone, a central three-story block fronted with white marble columns and topped with a low-pitched roof of rose tile; there were lower wings to each side—arched colonnades supporting second-story balconies. There was a crowd waiting beneath the pillars, and a parked grey-painted staff car with a *strategos'* red-and-black checkerboard pennant fixed to one bumper; the tall figure of his father stood amidst the household, leaning on his cane. Eric took a deep breath and opened the door of the van, pitching his baggage to the ground and jumping down to the surface of the drive.

Air washed over him cool and clean, smelling of roses and falling water, dusty crushed rock and hot metal from the van; bread was baking somewhere, and there was woodsmoke from the chimneys. The globe lights came on over the main doors, and he saw who awaited: his father, of course; his younger sister Johanna in undress uniform; the overseers, and some of the house servants behind . . .

He waved, then turned back to the van for a moment, pulling a half-empty bottle out of his kit and leaning in for a parting salute to the Janissaries.

They looked up, and their faces lit with surprised gratitude as he tossed the long-necked glass bulb; it was Oakenwald Kijaffa, cherry brandy in the same sense that Dom Perignon was sparkling wine, and beyond the pockets of most freemen.

"T'anks be to yaz, Centurion, sar," the black said, his teeth shining white. "Sergeants Miller and Assad at yar s'rvice, sar."

"For Palermo," he said, and turned his head to the driver. She raised a face streaked with the tracks of dried tears from where it had rested on the wheel, glancing back apprehensively at the soldiers. "Back, and take the turning to the left, half a kilometer to the Quarters. Ask for the headman; he'll put you all up."

A young houseboy had run forward to take Eric's baggage; he craned his head to see into the long cabin of the van after making his bow, his face an O of surprise at the bright Janissary uniforms. And he kept glancing back as he bore the valise and bag away. Eric paused to take a few parcels out of it, reflecting that they probably had another volunteer there. Then he was striding up the broad black-stone steps, the hard soles of his high boots clattering. The servants bowed like a rippling field, and there were genuine smiles of welcome. Eric had always been popular with the staff, as such things went.

He clicked heels and saluted. His father returned it, and they stood for a wordless moment eye to eye; they were of a height. Alike in color and cast of face as well; the resemblance was stronger now that pain had graven lines in the younger man's face to match his sire's.

"Recovered from your wound, I see." The strategos paused, searching for words. "I read the report. You were a credit to the service and the family, Eric."

"Thank you, sir," he replied neutrally, fighting down an irrational surge of anger. *I didn't want the Academy,* a part of him thought savagely. *The first von Shrakenberg in seven generations not to, and a would-be artist to boot. Does that make me an incompetent, or a coward?*

And that was unjust. Pa had not really been surprised that he had the makings of a good officer; he had too much confidence in the von Shrakenberg blood for that. *What was it that makes me draw back?* he thought. Alone, he could wish so strongly to be at peace with his father again. Those grey eyes, more accustomed to cold mastery, shared his own baffled hurt; he could see it. But together . . . they fought, or coexisted with an icy politeness that was worse.

Or *usually* worse. Two years ago he had sent Tyansha's daughter out of the country. To America, where there was a Quaker group that specialized in helping the tiny trickle of escaped serfs who managed to flee; they must have been surprised to receive a tow-haired girlchild from an aristocrat of the Domination, together with an annuity to pay for her upkeep and education. Not that he had been fond of the girl; he had handed her to the women of the servant's quarters, and as she grew her looks were an intolerable reminder. But she was Tyansha's . . . It had required a good deal of money, and several illegalities.

To Arch-Strategos Karl von Shrakenberg, that had been a matter touching on honor, and on the interests of the Race and the nation. His father had threatened to abandon him to the Security Directorate; that could have meant a one-way trip to a cold cellar with instruments of metal, a trip that ended with a pistol-bullet in the back of the head. Eric suspected that if his brother John had still been alive to carry on the family name, it might have come to that. As it was, he had been forbidden the house, until service in Italy had changed the general's mind.

I saved my daugh . . . a little girl, he thought. *For that, I was a criminal and will always be watched. But by helping to destroy a city and killing hundreds who've never done me harm, I'm a hero and all is forgiven.* Tyansha had once told him that she had given up expecting sense from the world long ago; more and more, he saw her point.

He forced his mind back to the older man's words. "And the Janissaries won't have any problems in the Quarters?"

"Not unless someone's foolish enough to provoke them. They're Master Sergeants, steady types; the Headman will find them beds and a couple of willing girls."

There was another awkward pause, and the strategos turned to go. "Well. I'll see you when we dine, then."

Johanna had been waiting impatiently, but in this

household the proprieties were observed. As Eric turned to face her she straightened and threw a crackling salute, then winked broadly and pointed her thumb upward at the collar of her uniform jacket.

He returned the salute and followed her digit. "Well, well! *Pilot Officer* Johanna von Shrakenberg, now!" He spread his arms and she gave him a swift fierce hug. She was four years younger than he; on her the bony family looks and the regulations that cropped her fair hair close produced an effect halfway between elegance and adolescent homeliness.

"That was quick—fighters? And what's this I hear about Tom? You two are still an 'item'?" With a stage magician's gesture he produced a flat package.

"They're turning us out quick, these days—cutting out nonessentials like sleep. Yes, fighters: Eagles, interceptors." The wrapping crumpled under strong, tanned fingers. "And no, Tom and I aren't an item; we're *engaged*." She paused to roll her eyes. "Wouldn't you know it, guess where his lochos's been sent? *Xian!* Shensi, to watch the Japanese!"

The package opened. Within were twin eardrops, cabochon-cut rubies the size of a thumbnail, set in chased silver. Johanna whistled and held them up to the light as Eric shook hands with the overseers, inquired after their children in the Forces, handed out minor gifts among the house servants and hugged old Nanny Sukie, the family child-nurse. Arms linked, Eric and Johanna strolled into the house.

"Loot?" she inquired, holding up the jewels. "Sort of Draka-looking . . ."

"*Made* from loot," he said affectionately. It was a rare Draka who doubted the morality of conquest. To deny that the property of the vanquished was proper booty would go beyond eccentricity to madness. "You think I'm buying rubies like that on a Centurion's pay? They're from an Italian bishop's crozier—he won't be needing it in the labor camp, after all." The man had smiled under the gun muzzles, actually, and signed a cross in the air as they prodded him away. Eric pushed the memory aside. "I had the setting done up in Alexandria . . ."

CHAPTER THREE

... *maintained rapid growth in population and wealth. Immigration continued through the 1790's, first with the Icelandic refugees fleeing the great eruptions. Frenchmen followed, first from Haiti-Santo Domingo after the slave revolt, then royalists from France proper. A continued trickle came through the "legions" of European mercenaries maintained by the Colony, first mainly German, and then including many Norse ...*

... *Seizure of Ceylon from the Dutch in 1796 and Egypt from its Napoleonic occupiers in 1800 made the raising of a merchant marine and navy imperative ... Congress of Vienna made the new acquisitions permanent as compensation for the loss of Canada to the Americans in 1812–1814. Manpower resources remained extremely tight. The employment of free citizen women in the increasing number of clerical and administrative posts followed, as did peacetime conscription and the raising of the first Janissary legions. Modeled on the slave-soldiers of the Ottoman Empire, they proved a crucial innovation ...*

200 Years: A Social History of the Domination
by E. Sorensson, Ph.D.
Archona Press, 1983

OAKENWALD PLANTATION
OCTOBER, 1941

Eric woke in mid-morning. It was his old room at the corner of the west wing, a big, airy chamber ten meters by twenty with two walls giving on to the second story balcony through doors of sliding glass. The air was sharp with spring, with a little of the dew-smell yet, full of scents from the garden and a wilder smell from the forest and wet rock that stretched beyond the manor; the breath of his childhood years, the smell of home.

He lay for a moment, enjoying the crisp smooth feel of the linen sheets, feeling rested enough but a little heavy with the wine and liqueurs from last night. It was like being sick, when he was a child. Not too ill, just feverish, allowed to lie abed and read. Ma would be there, to see that he drank the soup . . .

Dinner had been better than he expected; Pa had avoided topics which might set them off (which meant platitudes and silence, mostly), and everyone had admired Johanna's eardrops, which led naturally to the hilarious story of the near-mutiny in Rome, when the troops arrived to find Security units guarding the Vatican and preventing a sack. Florence had been much better; he had picked up a number of interesting items, including a Cellini, two Raphaels and a couple of *really* interesting illuminated manuscripts. Better than jewelry, far too precious to sell.

Illegal, of course, he mused, throwing a loose caftan over his nakedness and tossing down a glass of the fresh-squeezed orange juice from the jug by the bedside. *Still, why let the Cultural Directorate stick the books in a warehouse for a generation while the museums and the universities quarreled over 'em?*

*   *   *

The baths were as he remembered them—magnificent, in a fashion forty years out of date, like much of the manor. That had been the last major renovation, in the expansive and self-confident years just before the Great War, when the African territories were well pacified and the Draka were pleasantly engaged in dreaming of further conquests, rather than performing the hard, actual work. There was a waterfall springing from dragon heads cast in aluminum bronze, steam rooms and soaking tubs and a swimming pool of red and violet Northmark marble. The walls were lined with mosaics from the Klimt workshops, done on white Carrara in gilded copper, silver, coral, semi-precious stones, gold and colored faience; his great-grandmother's taste had run to wildlife, landscapes (the dreamlike cone of Kilimanjaro rising above the Serengeti was a favorite), dancing maidens of eerily elongated shapes . . .

Soaking, massage, and a dozen laps chased the last stiffness from his muscles; he lazed naked against a couch on the terrace, toying with a breakfast of iced mango, hot breads, and Kenia coffee with thick mountain cream. Potted fruit trees laid dappled patterns of sun and shade across his body; a last spray of peach blossom cast petals and scent on long, taut-muscled arms and deep runner's chest. The angry purple scar on his thigh had faded toward dusty white. He was conscious of an immense well-being as wind stroked silk-gentle across cleansed skin.

The serving girl padded up to collect the dishes, averting her eyes; Draka of his generation had little sense of body modesty, but their serfs were more prudish. Lazily, he stretched out a hand as she bent and laid it on the small of her back. She froze, controlled a shrinking and looked back at him over her shoulder.

"Please, masta, no?" she said in a small breathless voice.

Eric shrugged, smiling, and withdrew his touch; he had never liked tumbling with a woman who didn't desire him. Not that that had ever been a problem, he being the master's son, young, handsome, and well-spoken . . .

Too young, anyway, he mused. He preferred women about his own years or a little older. *Hmmmm, I could take a rifle up into the hills and try for that leopard Pa mentioned before it takes more sheep. No, too much like work. And curse it, Johanna will already be out hawking, she said "early tomorrow"* . . . A ride with a falcon on his wrist was something that had been lacking these last few years.

He looked down and grinned; the body had its own priorities. *No, first thoughts are best: a woman.* That was a minor problem; he had been away from the estate for years now. There had been a few serf girls he'd been having, after his period of mourning for Tyansha ended, but they would be married now. Not that a serf wedding had any legal standing, but the underfolk took their unions seriously; more seriously than the masters did, these days. It would cause distress, if he called one of them to his bed.

He snapped his fingers. Rahksan—Johanna's maid. She'd have mentioned it in her letters if the wench had taken a lasting mate. Uncle Everard had brought her back from Afghanistan, one small girl found miraculously alive in a village bombed with phosgene-gas for supporting the *badmash* rebels. He had given her to Johanna for her sixth birthday, much as he might have a puppy or a kitten. They had all run tame together, and she had seldom said no, in the old days . . .

Let's see, Johanna's out with her hawk; Rahksan'd probably be in her rooms, tidying up.

*   *   *

The corridor gave onto Johanna's study; the door was ajar, and he padded through on quiet feet, leaning his head around the entrance into the bedroom. Rahksan was there, but so was Johanna, and they were very much occupied. Eric pursed his mouth thoughtfully, lifted one eyebrow and withdrew to the study unnoticed. There was a good selection of reading material; he picked up a newsmagazine with a profile of Wendel Wilkie, the new Yankee President. The speech he had given opening the new lock at Montreal in the State of Quebec was considered quite important, bearing on the new administration's attitude to the war . . .

Rahksan came through the door with her shoes in one hand, buttoning the linen blouse with the other. She was a short woman, full in breast and hip, with a mane of curling blue-black hair and skin a pale creamy olive that reminded him of Italians he had seen. Her face was roundly pretty, eyes heavy-lidded above a dreamy smile.

He stood: the serf squeaked and jumped in startlement, then relaxed into a broad grin as she recognized him.

"Why, masta Eric, good t'see yaz egin," she said, tilting her head on one side and glancing up at him; she came barely to his shoulder.

He laughed and pulled her close; she flowed into his arm, warm, soft, skin damp and carrying a faint pleasant scent of woman.

"I was looking for you, Rahksan," he said.

"Why, what*evah* fo'?" she asked slyly, snuggling. They had always been friendly, as far as different stations allowed, and occasional bedmates in the years since Tyansha died.

". . . unless you're too tired?" he finished politely.

"Well . . . ah *do* have wuk t'do, masta. 'Sides all this bedwenchin', that is." She paused, with a show

of considering. "Tonaaht? Pr'bly feel laahk it agin
bah then."

He nodded, and she jumped up with an arm around
his neck; he tasted musk on her lips as they kissed,
and then she was gone with a flash of bare feet,
giggling as she gave him a swift intimate caress in
passing. Eric shook his head, grinning.

*Another thing that hasn't changed about Oaken-
wald*, he thought. Rahksan had always had a sunny
disposition, and an uncomplicated outlook on life. It
was restful, for a man given to introspective brooding.

His sister's voice interrupted his musing. "Well,
brother dear, if you're *quite* finished making assigna-
tions with my serf wench, come on in."

Johanna was lying comfortably sprawled across her
bed amid the rumpled black satin of the sheets,
sipping at pale yellow wine in a bell-goblet and toe-
wrestling with a long-haired persian cat. She was, he
noted with amusement, still wearing his gift of ear-
drops, if nothing else; she had the greyhound build
of the von Shrakenbergs, but was thicker through
the neck and shoulders than when he had seen her
last, a year ago. Wrestling a two-engined pursuit
plane through the sky took strength as well as skill.

He seated himself and took up the second glass,
pouring from the straw-covered flask in its bed of
ice. "Glad to see you're not wasting *your* leave," he
said. "A little . . . schoolgirlish, though, isn't it?"

"Now, listen to me, Eric—" She sank back into
the pillows at his smile. "Freya, but it's always a
surprise when that solemness of yours breaks down."
Johanna paused to pick a black hair from her lip with
thumb and forefinger.

"Glad you knew I was joking; Pa might not be,
though. He's a stickler for dignity," Eric said.

Johanna snorted. "I'm old enough to fight for the
Domination, I'm old enough to choose my own plea-
sures," she said. More slowly: "For that matter, it's

like school around here, these days: no men. Not between eighteen and forty, at least. Draka men, that is; plenty of likely-looking serf bucks . . . just joking brother, just joking. I know the Race Purity laws as well as anyone, and I've no wish to do my last dance on the end of a rope. Actually, the only man I'm interested in is six thousand kilometers away in Mongolia, while celibacy interests me not at all."

She sighed. "And . . . the locho's going operational in another month, once we've finished shaking down on ground-support. Ever noticed how war puts a hand on your shoulder, and says 'hurry'?"

"Yes indeed," he said, refilling her glass. "Confidentially . . . Johanna, the Germans are getting pretty close to the Caucasus. They've taken Rostov-on-Don already, and it looks like Moscow will fall within the month. Then they'll push on to the Caspian, which will put them right on our northern border. Three guesses as to where the next round of fighting begins."

She nodded, thoughtful. The Domination had never really been at peace in all the centuries of its existence; a citizen was reared to the knowledge that death in combat was as likely a way to go as cancer in bed. This would be different: a *gotterdammerung*, where whole nations were beaten into dust . . .

Too big, she mused. Impossible to think about in any meaningful sense; you could only see it in personal terms. And seeing it that way, Armageddon itself couldn't kill you deader than a skirmish. It was the personal that was *real*, anyhow. You lived and died in person-time, not history-time.

"Funny," she said. "Back when we were children, we couldn't wait to grow up . . . Do you remember when Uncle Everard gave Rahksan to me? I was around six, so you must have been going on ten."

Eric nodded, reminiscing. "Yes: you'd play at giving orders, until she got tired of it; then she'd plump down and cross her arms and say, 'This is a stupid

game and I'm not going to play anymore,' and we'd all
roll around laughing?"

"Hmmm, well, it was a change to give anybody
orders. At that age, nurse and all the house-serfs tell
you what to do, and wallop your bottom if you don't
. . . Did you know she'd have nightmares?"

Surprised, he shook his head. "Always seemed a
happy little wench."

"At night, she'd wake up sometimes on the pallet
down at the foot of the bed, thinking she couldn't
breathe. Damn what the vet said, I think she got
some lung damage when they gassed her village. I'd
let her crawl in with me and hold her until she went
to sleep; then later, when we were both older, well
. . ." She paused and frowned. "You know, I never
did go in for the schoolgirl stuff, the real thing, roses
and fruit left at the window, bad poetry under the
door, meetings in the pergola at midnight . . . Al-
ways seemed silly, as if this was seventy years ago
and you could get in real trouble. So did what hap-
pened in the summer months-off, everyone rushing
out and falling on the nearest boy like ravening
leopardesses on a goat."

He laughed. She had always been able to draw
him out of himself, even if that humor was a little
barbed at times.

"Rahksan . . . that's just fun and exuberance, and
release from need, with more affection than you can
get in barracks. I really like her, you know, and she
me." She paused to sip the cool tart wine. "And I
miss Tom."

"I always thought you two were in love," Eric said
lightly. "From the way you quarrelled: you'd ride
ten miles just to have a fight with him."

Johanna smiled ruefully. "True enough. And I do
love him . . ." She paused, set down the empty glass
and linked her fingers about one knee. "Not the way
you felt about that Circassian wench," she continued

softly. "Don't think I didn't notice. I'll never love anyone with that . . . crazy single-mindedness, never, an I thank the nonexistent gods for it."

He glanced away. "There has to be one sensible person in this family," he said. He thought of his other sisters, twins three years younger than Johanna. "Besides the Terrible Two, of course."

"Yes; they were threatening me bodily harm if I won the war before they could get into it . . . Eric, you know the problem with you and Pa? You think and feel exactly alike."

"We haven't agreed on a goddamned thing in ten years!"

"I didn't say the *contents* of your thoughts were alike, but the *way* you think is no-shit *identical*, big brother. You feel things . . . too much: duty, love, hate, whatever. Everything's a matter of principle; everything counts too much. You both *want* too much—things that aren't possible to us mortals."

"Possibly; but even if that's true, it's no solution to our problems."

"Shit, you always did want *solutions*, didn't you? Most of the things that bother you two *aren't* problems, and they don't *have* solutions—they're the conditions of life and you have to *live* with them." She sighed at the tightening of his lips. "It's like talking to a rock, with either of you. Mind you, Pa's more often right on some things, to my way of thinking. Politics, certainly."

"You don't think I should have gotten Tyansha's child out of the Domination?"

"Oh, that—that was your business. And she was yours, after all. You could have done it more . . . discreetly, the law is intended to discourage *escape*, not a man sending his own property out. I can even see *why* you did it, not that I would have, myself; with her looks that one was going to have trouble once she was into her 'teens. Tyansha was very lucky to end up belonging to you. No, I meant the other stuff, real politics."

"Hmmm," he said. "I can't remember you ever taking much interest in party matters."

"Well," she said, sitting up and stretching. "I'm a voter now. I mean, how long has it been since the Draka League party lost an election, even locally? Sixty years, seventy? Regular as clockwork, 70 percent of the vote. The Liberals—'free enterprise'—doesn't it occur to them that three-quarters of the electorate are employees of the State and the Combines? They could all be underbid by serf labor if the restrictions were lifted, then there'd be revolution and we'd all be dead. That the Liberals get as much as 3 percent is a monument to human stupidity. Then there's the Rationalists. I suppose you support them because they want a pacific foreign policy and an end to expansion. Same thing, only slower; we're just not *compatible* with the existence of another social system. And we're unique . . ."

"The government line, and very convenient; but this war might kill us both," he said grimly. "The way our precious social system already killed our brother. I wouldn't be much loss to anyone, even myself, but you would, and I miss John."

They turned their eyes to the portrait beside Johanna's bed. It showed their elder brother in uniform, field-kit; a Century of Janissaries had stood grouped around him. It was policy that those earmarked for advancement hold commands in both the serf army and the Citizen Force. John was smiling; that was how most remembered him. Alone of the von Shrakenberg children of this generation he had taken after their mother's kindred, a stocky broadfaced man with seal-brown hair and eyes and big capable hands.

He had died in the Ituri, the great jungle north of the Congo bend. That was part of the Police Zone, the area of civil government, but there was little settlement—a few rubber plantations near navigable water, timber concessions, and gold mines in the Ituri that were supplied by airship. The rest was half a million square kilometers of National Park, where nothing human lived but a few bands of pygmies left to their Old Stone Age existence, looking up in wonder as the silvery shapes of Draka dirigibles glided past.

The mines were conveniently isolated. They were run by the Security Directorate, and used as a sink for serf convicts, the incorrigibles, the sweepings of the labor camps. The Draka technicians and overseers were those too incompetent to hold a post elsewhere, or who had mortally offended the powers that were. There had been an uprising below ground, brief and desperate and hopeless. The usual procedure would have been to turn off the drainage, or pump the tunnels full of poison-gas. But the rebels had taken Draka hostages, and John's unit had been doing jungle-combat training nearby. There was no time to summon Security's Intervention Squads, specialists in such work. Their brother had volunteered to lead his troops below; they had volunteered to follow, to a man.

Eric had never liked to imagine what it had been like; he had always disliked confined spaces. The fighting had been at close quarters, machine-pistols and grenades, knives and boots and picks and lengths of tubing stuffed full of blasting explosive. The power lines had been cut early on; at the last they had been struggling in water waist high, in absolute blackness . . . Incredibly, they had rescued most of the prisoners; John had been covering the withdrawal when an improvised bomb went off at his feet. His Janissaries had carried him out on their backs at risk of their lives, but it had been far too late.

They had been able to keep his last words, spoken

in delirium. "*I tried Daddy, honest. I tried real hard.*"

"I'm not surprised they brought him out," Eric said into the silence. "He was an easy man to love."

"Unlike you and Pa," Johanna said drily. "Rahksan was head-over-heels for him; Pa . . . took it hard, you'll remember. I thought he was going to cry at the funeral. That shook me; I can't imagine Pa crying."

"I can," Eric said, surprising her. "You were too young, but I remember when Mother died. Not at the funeral, but afterwards I went looking for him, found him in the study. He'd forgotten to lock the door. He was sitting there at the desk with his head in his hands." The sobs had been harsh, racking, the weeping of a man unaccustomed to it.

They looked at each other uncomfortably and shifted. "Time to go," Johanna said at last. "Pa wanted us down in the Quarters when the recruits get selected."

They had taken horses, this being too nearly a formal occasion to walk. The path led down the slope of the hill between cut-stone walls, through the oak-wood their ancestors had planted and patches of native scrub where the soil was too thin over rock to grow the big trees. The gravel crunched beneath hooves, and light came down in bright flickering shafts as the leaf-canopy stirred, lancing into the cool wet-smelling green air of spring. Ferns carpeted the rocky ground, with flowers of blue and yellow and white. The trunks about them were thick and twisted, massive moss-grown shapes sinking their roots deep into the fractured rock of the hill.

Like the von Shrakenbergs, Eric thought idly, as they clattered over a small stone bridge, well-kept but ancient; the little stream beneath had been channeled to power a gristmill, in the early days.

They passed through a belt of hybrid poplar trees,

coppiced for fuel, and into the working quarters of the plantation on the flat ground. The old mill bulked square, now the smithy and machine-shop; about it were the laundry, bake-house, carpenter's workshop, garage—all the intricate fabric of maintenance an estate needed. The great barns were off to one side, with the creamery and cheese-house and cooling sheds where cherries and peaches from the orchards were stored. Woolsheds and round granaries of red brick bulked beyond; holding paddocks, stables for the working stock . . . then a row of trees before the Quarters proper.

Four hundred serfs worked the fields of Oakenwald; their homes were grouped about a village green. Square, four-roomed cottages of fieldstone with tile roofs stood along a grid of brick-paved lanes, each with its patch of garden to supplement the ration of meat and flour and roots. Pruned fruit trees were planted along the streets; privies stood behind the cottages, with chicken coops and rabbit hutches. To-day was Saturday, a half-holiday save during harvest; only essential tasks with the stock would be seen to. Families sat on their porches, smoking their pipes, sewing, mending pieces of household gear; they rose to bow as Eric and Johanna cantered through on their big crop-maned hunters, children and dogs scattering before the hooves.

The central green was four hundred meters on a side, fringed with tall poplars. The south flank held the slightly larger homes of the headman and the elite of the Quarters: gang foremen, stockmen, skilled workers. The others were public buildings—a storehouse for cloth and rations, the communal bathhouse, an infirmary, a chapel where the serf minister preached a Christian faith the masters had largely abandoned. Beside it was the most recent addition—a school where he taught basic letters to a few of the

most promising children; there were more tasks that
needed such skills, these last few generations.

The green itself was mostly shaggy lawn, with a
pair of goalposts where the younger fieldhands some-
times played soccer in their scant leisure time; the
water fountain was no longer needed now that the
cottages had their own taps, but it still played mer-
rily. Dances were held here of an evening; there was
a barbecue pit, where whole oxen and pigs might be
roasted at harvest and planting and Christmas festi-
vals, or when a wedding or a birth in the Great
House brought celebration.

And on one side was a covered dais of stone, with
a bell beside it; also stocks, and the seldom-used
whipping post. Here the work assignments were given
out, and the master sat to make judgments. The son
and daughter of the House drew rein beside it, lean-
ing on their saddle pommels to watch and nodding to
their father, seated in his wooden chair.

The two Janissaries were there, with a crowd of
the younger serfs standing about them. They were
stripped to shorts and barefoot, practicing stick-fighting
with their swaggercanes, moving and feinting and
slashing with no sound but the stamp of feet and
grunting of breath. But for color they were much
alike, heavy muscle rolling over thick bone, moving
cat-graceful; scarred and quick and deadly. A smack
of wood on flesh marked the end; they drew them-
selves up, saluted each other with their canes, and
repeated the gesture to the Draka before trotting off
to wash and change back into their uniforms.

Eric dismounted and tossed his reins to a serf.
"Formidable," he murmured to his sister as they
mounted the dais and assumed their seats. "Wouldn't
care to take on either of them, hand to hand."

She smiled agreement; the elder von Shrakenberg
nodded to the crowd of young fieldhands before them.

"Not without its effect there," he said, and raised his voice. "Headman, summon the people."

That elderly worthy bowed and swung the clapper of the bell. Almost at once the serfs began to assemble, by ones and twos and family groups, to stand in an irregular fan about the place of judgment. Eric spent the time musing. This was, he supposed, the best side of the Domination. Certainly, he had seen worse in Italy; much worse, among the peasants of Sicily and Calabria—sickness, hunger, and rags. All the von Shrakenberg serfs looked well-fed, tended, clothed; there had been callous men and women among his ancestors, even cruel ones, but few fools who expected work from starvelings. A drab existence, though: labor, a few simple pleasures, the consolations of their religion, old age spent rocking on the porch. So that the von Shrakenbergs might have power and wealth and leisure; so that the Domination might have armies for its fear-driven aggression.

There would always be enough willing recruits for the Janissaries. In theory they were conscripts, but there were a million plantations such as this, not counting the inhabitants of the Combines' labor compounds. And that was well for the Domination, for it was the Janissary legions that made the Draka a Great Power, able to wage offensive war. The Citizen Force was a delicate precision instrument, a rapier; it destroyed armies not by destroying their equipment and personnel, but by shock and psychological dislocation. Its aim was not to kill men, but to break their hearts and make them *run*. Draka were trained to war from childhood, and none but cripples escaped the Forces. But by the same token, their casualties were expenditure from capital, not income; too many expensive victories could ruin their nation.

And the Janissaries . . . they were the Domination's battle-axe, their function to gore and crush and utterly destroy. Half a million had died breaking the

Ankara line in Anatolia, in 1917, and as many more in the grinding campaigns of pacification in the Asian territories after the war. Where there were no elegant solutions, where there could be no escaping the brutal arithmetic of attrition, the Janissaries would be used—street fighting, positional defense, frontal assault.

Eric was startled to hear his father speak. "Economical," he murmured, and continued at his son's glance.

"Conquest makes serfs, serfs make soldiers, soldiers make conquest . . . empire feeds on itself."

Eric made a noncommittal sound and looked out over his family's human chattel; he could name most of them, and the younger adults had been the playmates of his childhood, before age imposed an increasing distance. They stood quietly, hats in hand, their voices a quiet *shusshps* running under the sound of the wind. Most were descendants of the tribes who had dwelt here before the Draka came, some of imports since then—Tamil, Arab, Berber, Egyptian. None spoke the old language; that had been extinct for a century or more, leaving only loan-words and place names. And few were of unmixed blood; seven generations of von Shrakenberg males and their overseers taking their pleasure in the Quarters had left light-brown the predominant skin color. Not a few yellow heads and grey eyes were scattered through the crowd, and he reflected ruefully that most of his blood-kin were probably standing before him.

It occurred to him suddenly that these people had only to rush in a body to destroy their owners. *Only three of us,* he mused. *Sidearms, but no automatic wepons. We couldn't kill more than half a dozen.*

It would not happen, could not, because they could not think it . . . There had been serf revolts, in the early days. His great-great-great-grandfather had commanded the levies that impaled four thousand rebels along the road from Virconium to Shahnapur, down in the sugar country of the coast; there was a mural of it in the Great House. Oakenwald serfs had worked the fields in chains, in his day. Past, long past . . .

The two NCO's returned, spruce and glittering in the noonday sun, each bearing a brace of file-folders; these they stacked neatly on a camp table set up before the dais. They turned to salute it, and his father rose to speak. A ripple of bows greeted him, like wind on corn.

"Folk of Oakenwald," he said, leaning on his cane. "The Domination is at war. The Archon, who commands me as I command you, has called for a new levy of soldiers. Six among your young men will be accorded the high honor of becoming arms-bearers in the service of the State, and for the welfare of our common home. Pray for their souls."

There was another long-drawn murmur. The news was no surprise; a regular grapevine ran from manor to manor, spread by the servants of guests, serfs sent to town on errands, even by telephone in these times. The young men shuffled their feet and glanced at each other with uneasy grins as the black Janissary rose to his feet and called out a roster of names. More than two score came raggedly forward.

"Yaz awl tinkin' how lucky yaz bein'," he began, the thick dialect and harsh tone a shock after the master's words. " 'T be Janissary—faahn uniforms, 't best a' food an' likker, usin' t' whip 'stead a' feelin' it, an' plunder 'n girls in captured towns. Live laahk a fightin'-cock, walk praawd."

His glance passed across them with scorn. There was more to it, of course: to give a salute rather than the serf's low bow before the masters; excitement; travel beyond the narrow horizons of village or compound. Education, for those who could use it; training in difficult skills; respect. And the mystery of arms, the mark of the masters; for any but the Janissaries, it would be death to hold a weapon. A Janissary held nearly as many privileges over the serf population as a master, with fewer restraints. The chance to discharge a lifetime's repressed anger . . .

His voice cracked out like a lash. "*Yaz tink t' be Janissary? Yaz should live s' long!*" He came forward to walk down the ragged line, the hunting-cat grace of his gait a contrast to their ploughboy awkwardness. They were all young, between seventeen and nineteen, all in good health and over the minimum height. Draka law required exact records, and he had studied them with care. The swagger stick poked out suddenly, taking one lad under the ribs. He doubled over with a startled *oofff!* and fell to his knees.

"Soft! Yaz soft! Tink cauz yaz c'n stare all day up t' arse-end of a plough-mule, yaz woan' drop dead onna force-march. Shit yaz pants when a' mortarshells star' a' droppin.' Whicha yaz momma's darlin's, whicha yaz houseserf bumboys tink they got it?"

He drew a line in the sparse grass with his swagger stick and waited, rising and falling slowly on the balls of his feet and tapping the stick in the palm of one gloved hand, a walking advertisement.

The serf youths looked at him, at his comrade lolling lordly-wise at the table with a file folder in his hands, back at the humdrum village of all their days. Visibly, they weighed the alternatives: danger against boredom; safety against the highest advancement a serf could achieve. Two dozen crowded forward over the line, and the Master Sergeant grinned, suddenly jovial. His stick pointed out one, another, up to the six required; he had been watching carefully, sounding them out without seeming to, and the records were exhaustive. Their friends milled about, slapping the dazed recruits on the back and shoulder, while in the background Eric could hear a sudden weeping, quickly hushed.

Probably a mother, he thought, rising with his father. Janissaries were not discouraged from keeping up contacts with their families, but they had their own camps and towns when not in the field, a world to itself. The plantation preacher would hold a service for their leaving, and it would be the one for the dead. Silence fell anew. "In honor of these young men," the general called, smiling, "I declare a feast tonight. Headman, see to issuing the stores. Tell the House steward that I authorize two kegs of wine, and open the vats at the brewery."

That brought a roar of applause, as the family of the master descended from the dais to shake the hands of the six chosen, a signal honor. They stood, grinning, in a haze of glory, as the preparations for the evening's entertainment began; tomorrow they would travel with the two soldiers to the estates round about, there would be more feasts, admiration . . . and the master had called them "young men," not bucks . . .

Eric hoped that the memories would help them when they reached the training camps. The roster of formed units in the Janissary arm was complete, but the *ersatz* Cohorts, the training and replacement units, were being expanded. Infantry numbers eroded quickly in intensive operations; the legions would need riflemen by the hundred thousand, soon.

As he swung back into the saddle, he wondered idly how many would survive to wear the uniforms of Master Sergeants themselves. Not many, probably. The training camps themselves would kill some; the regimen was harsh to the point of brutality, deliberately so. A few would die, more would wash out into secondary arms, the Security Directorate could always use more executioners and camp-guard "bulls." The survivors would learn: learn that they were the elite, that they had no family but their squadmates, no father but their officer, no country or nation but their legions. Learn loyalty, *kadaversobedienz*—the ability to obey like a corpse.

His father's quiet words jarred him out of his thoughts as they rode slowly through the crowd and then heeled their mounts into a canter through the deserted village beyond.

"Eric, I have a favor to ask of you."

"Sir?" He looked up, startled.

"A . . . command matter. It's the Yankees. They're the only major Power left uncommitted, and we need them to counterbalance the Japanese. We *don't* need another war in East Asia while we fight the Germans, and if it does come we'll have to cooperate with the U.S. Certainly if we expect them to do most of the fighting, and help out in Europe besides."

Eric nodded, baffled. More reluctantly, his father continued.

"As part of keeping them sweet, we're allowing in a war correspondent."

"I should think, sir, knowing the Yankees, allowing a newspaperman into the Domination would be likely to turn them against us, once he started reporting."

"Not if he's allowed to see only the proper sights, then assigned to a combat unit and, ah, overseen by the proper officer."

"I see. Sir." Eric said. *Now, that's an insult, if you like*, he thought. The implication being that he was a weak-livered milksop, unlikely to arouse the notorious Yankee squeamishness. The younger man's lips tightened. "As you command, sir. I will see you at dinner, then."

Karl von Shrakenberg stared after the diminishing thunder of his son's horse, a brief flush rising to his weathered cheeks. He had suggested the assignment; pushed for it, in fact, as a way to prove Eric's loyalty beyond doubt, restore his career prospects. The Security case-officer had objected, but not too strongly;

Karl suspected he looked at it as a baited trap, luring Eric into indiscretions that not even an Arch-Strategos' influence could protect him from. And this was his reward . . .

Behind him, Johanna raised her eyes to heaven and sighed. *Maybe Rahksan can ease him up for tomorrow*, she thought glumly. *Home sweet home, bullshit*.

CHAPTER FOUR

Memo: *18/11/41*
          ref: 2sm30/Z1
From: *Security Directorate, Alexandria D.H.Q.*
             Decurion F. Vachon
To: *Stevenson & de Verre, Labor Agents*
          Attn: T. de Verre
Re: *Labor Consignment 2sm30*

*With regard to yours of the 10th Oct., please be advised that
the shipment in question is now ready for pickup at Holding Pen
#17, above address. Standard terms, net 32 aurics per head.*

*Labor units in question are category 3m72 (unsound elements,
liquidated, dependents of) and category 3m73 (unsound ele-
ments, religious cadre) from the occupied zone in Italy. Milan
District Office.*

Service to the State!

(handwritten postscript)

Here's the lot I promised: 123 of them, 12–30, wenches and prettybucks. Prime stuff, you aren't going to sell these cheap to wash dishes. The wives and children of the Fascist politicians and university professors won't give you any trouble but I advise splitting up the nuns. Their pen's right under my office, and the bitches have been singing, praying, and chanting fit to give you the heebies. Had to send in the bulls with electroprods twice last week to shut 'em up.

Anyway, you owe me for this one, good buddy. The bureaucratic bunfights I had to go through! First, Tech Section tried to grab 'em for that hush-hush uranium refining thing out by the Quattara, then that greasy immigrant Lederman in Forces Morale Section wanted them for his knocking-shops ...

Edgar sends his regards to you and Cynthia. Still on for tennis Saturday?

Love Felice

as quoted in:
Under the Yoke: Postwar Europe
by Angleo Menzarotti
Cuba State University Press, Havana, 1977

OAKENWALD PLANTATION
OCTOBER, 1941

The car pulled into Oakenwald's drive three hours past midnight. With a start, William Dreiser jerked himself awake; he was a mild-faced man in his thirties, balding, with thick black-rimmed glasses and a battered pipe tucked into the pocket of his trench coat. Sandy-eyed, he rubbed at his mustache and glanced across at the Draka woman who was his escort-guard. The car was a steam-sedan, four-doored, with two sets of seats facing each other in the rear compartment. Rather like a Stanley Raccoon, in fact.

It had been two weeks' travel from Washington. By rail south to New Orleans, then ferryboat to

Havana. The Caribbean was safe enough, rimmed with American territory from Florida through the Gulf and on through the States carved out of Mexico and Central America a century before; there were U-boats in the South Atlantic, though, and even neutral shipping was in danger. Pan American flying-boat south to Recife, then Brazilian Airways dirigible to Apollonaris, just long enough to transfer to a Draka airship headed south. That was where he had acquired his Security Directorate shadow; they were treating the American reporter as if he carried a highly contagious disease.

And so I do, he thought. *Freedom.*

They had hustled him into the car in Archona, right at the airship haven. The Security decurion went into the compartment with him; in front were a driver in the grubby coverall which seemed to be the uniform of the urban working class and an armed guard with a shaven head; both had serf-tattoos on their necks. The American felt a small queasy sensation each time he glanced through the glass panels and saw the orange seven-digit code, a column below the right ear: letter-number-number-letter-number-number-number.

Seeing was not the same as reading, not at all. He had done his homework thoroughly: histories, geographies, statistics. And the Draka basics, Carlyle's *Philosophy of Mastery*, Nietzsche's *The Will to Power*, Fitzhugh's *Imperial Destiny*, even Gobineau's turgid *Inequality of Human Races*, and the eerie and chilling *Meditations of Elvira Naldorssen*. The Domination's own publications had a gruesome forthrightness that he suspected was equal portions of indifference and a sadistic desire to shock. None of it had prepared him adequately for the reality.

Archona had been glimpses: alien magnificence. A broad shallow bowl in the edge of the plateau. Ringroads cut across with wide avenues, lined with flowering trees that were a mist of gold and purple. Statues, fountains, frescoes, mosaics: things beautiful, incomprehensible, obscene. Six-story buildings set back in gardens; some walls sheets of colored glass, others honeycomb marble, one entirely covered with tiles in the shape of a giant flowering vine. Then suburbs that might almost have been parts of California, whitewashed walls and tile roofs, courtyards . . .

The secret police officer opened her eyes, pale blue slits in the darkness. She was a squat woman with broad spatulate hands, black hair in a cut just long enough to comb, like the Eton crop of the flappers in the '20's. But there was nothing frivolous in her high-collared uniform of dark green, or the ceremonial whip that hung coiled at her belt. One hand rested on her sidearm; he could see the house lights wink on the gold and emeralds of a heavy thumb-ring.

He was almost startled when she spoke; there had not been more than fifty words between them in any day of the six they had been together, most just last evening, when she had tried to draw the curtains as they ran parallel to a train for half an hour. There were tanks on flatcars, hundreds of them, *Hond III* class—massive, low-slung, predatory-looking vehicles, broad tracks and thick sloped armor, the long 120mm cannon in travelling-clamps . . .

"We're here," she said. His mind heard it as *we-ahz heyah*, like a Southern accent, Alabama or Cuba, but with an undertone clipped and guttural.

I'm on automatic pilot, he thought, and tried to flog his responses into alertness. He had always been a man who woke slowly, and now he felt sluggish and stupid—a not-quite-here feeling, cramped muscles, stomach burning from too much coffee and too many days of motion. Travel fatigue . . .

The silence of the halt was loud, after the long

singing of tires on asphalt, wind-rush and the *chuff-chuffchuff* of the engine. Metal pinged, cooling. The driver climbed out and opened the front-mounted trunk to unload the luggage. The policewoman nodded to the dimly seen building.

"Oakenwald Plantation. Centurion von Shrakenberg's here; Strategos von Shrakenberg, too. Old family; very old, very prominent. *Strategoi*, Senators, landholders, athletes; pro'bly behind the decision to let you in, Yankee. Political considerations, they're influential in the Army and the Foreign Affairs Directorate . . . You're safe enough with them. A guest's sacred, and it'd be 'neath their dignity to care what a foreign scribbler says."

He nodded warily and climbed out stiffly, muscles protesting. She reached through the window to tap his shoulder. He turned, and squawked as her hand shot out to grab the collar of his coat. The speed was startling, and so was the strength of fingers and wrist and shoulder; she dragged his face down level with hers, and the square bulldog countenance filled his vision, full lips pulling back from strong white teeth.

"*Well, it isn't 'neath mine, rebel pig!*" The concentrated venom in the tone was as shocking as a bucketful of cold water in the face. "You start causin' trouble, one word wrong to a serf, *one word*, and then by your slave-loving Christ, you're *mine*, Yankee. *Understood?*" She twisted the fabric until he croaked agreement, then shoved him staggering back.

He stood shaking as the green-painted car crunched its way back down the graveled path. *I should never have come,* he thought. It had not been needful, either; he was too senior for war-correspondent work in the field. His *Berlin Journal* was selling well, fruit of several years observation while he managed the Central European section of ABS' new radio-broadcasting service. The print pieces on the fall of France were probably going to get him a Pulitzer. He had Ingrid and a new daughter to look after . . .

And this was the opportunity of a lifetime. The Domination was not sealed the way Stalin's Russia had been before the war, but entry was restricted. Businessmen, a few tourists prepared to pay dearly for the wildlife or a tour of Samarkand or Jerusalem or the ruins of Mecca, scientists . . . all closely watched. Since 1939, nothing: the attack on Italy had come like a thunderbolt in the night. Who would have expected the Domination to come into the war on the Allied side? Granted, there had been little fighting with the Germans yet, but . . . And it was important to keep the American public conscious that the war was still going on; that there was more to it than a defeated Russia and an England growing steadily more hungry and shabby and desperate behind the Nazi submarine blockade.

If Roosevelt had run for a third term . . . well, no use dreaming. Wilkie's heart was in the right place, but he was a sick man and his attention was on the Japanese menace in the Far East. The United States was going to have to hold its nose and cooperate with the Draka if Germany was to be stopped, and a newsman could do his bit. His meek-and-mild appearance had been useful before; people tended to underestimate a man with wire-framed glasses and a double chin.

He glanced about. The gardens stretched below him, a darkness full of scents, washed pale by moonlight; he caught glints on polished stone, the moving water of fountain and pool. The house bulked, its shadow falling across him cold and remote; behind loomed the hill, a smell of oak and wet rock; above wheeled a brightness of stars undimmed by men's lights. It was cold, the thin air full of a high-altitude chill like spring in the Rockies.

The tall doors opened; he blinked against the sud-

den glow of electric light from a cluster of globes
above the brass-studded mahogany. He moved for-
ward as dark hands lifted the battered suitcases.

Dreiser found Oakenwald a little daunting. Not as
much so as Herman Goering's weekend parties had
been at his hunting lodge in East Prussia, but strange.
So had waking been, in the huge four-poster bed
with its disturbing, water-filled mattress; silent im-
passive brown-skinned girls had brought coffee and
juice and drawn back the curtains, laying out slippers
of red Moorish leather and a grey silk caftan. He felt
foolish in it; more so as they tied the sash about his
waist.

The breakfast room was large and high-ceilinged
and sparsely furnished. One wall was a mural of
reeds and flamingos with a snow-capped volcano in
the background; another was covered with screens of
black-lacquered Coromandel sandalwood, inlaid with
ivory and mother-of-pearl. Tall glass doors had been
folded back, and the checkerboard stone tiles of the
floor ran out onto a second-story roof terrace where a
table had been set. He walked toward it past man-
high vases of green marble; vines spilled down their
sides in sprays of green leaf and scarlet blossom.

Irritated, Dreiser began stuffing his pipe, taking
comfort from its disreputable solidity. There were
three Draka seated at the table: a middle-aged man
in the familiar black uniform of boots, loose trousers,
belted jacket and roll-topped shirt, and two younger
figures in silk robes.

Good, he thought. It made him feel a little less in
fancy dress. All three had a family resemblance—
lean bodies and strong-boned faces, wheat-colored
hair and pale grey eyes against skin tanned dark. It
took him a moment to realize that the youngest was a
woman. That was irritating, and had happened more
than once since he had entered the Domination. It

wasn't just the cut of the hair or the prevalence of uniforms, he decided, or even the fact that both sexes wore personal jewelry. There was something about the way they stood and moved; it deprived his eye of unconscious clues, so that he had to deliberately *look*, to examine wrists and necks or check for the swell of breast and hip. Baffling, that something so basic could be obscured by mere differences of custom . . .

The elder man clicked heels and extended a hand. It closed on his, unexpectedly callused and very strong.

"William Dreiser," the American said, remembering what he had read of Draka etiquette. Name, rank and occupation, that was the drill. "Syndicated columnist for the Washington *Chronicle-Herald* and New York *Times*, among others. Bureau chief for the American Broadcasting Service."

"Arch-Strategos Karl von Shrakenberg," the Draka replied. "Director of the Strategic Planning Section, Supreme General Staff. My son, Centurion Eric von Shrakenberg, 1st Airborne Chiliarchy; my daughter, Pilot Officer Johanna von Shrakenberg, 211th Pursuit Lochos." He paused. "Welcome to Oakenwald, Mr. Dreiser."

They sat, and the inevitable servants presented the luncheon: biscuits and scones, fruits, grilled meats on wooden platters, salads, juices.

"I understand that I have you to thank for my visa, general," Dreiser said, buttering a scone. It was excellent, as usual; he had not had a bad meal since Dakar. The meat dishes were a little too highly spiced, as always. It was a sort of Scottish-Austrian-Indonesian cuisine, with a touch of Louisiana thrown in.

The strategos nodded and raised his cup slightly. Hands appeared to fill it, add cream and sugar. "Myself and others," he said. "The strategic situation makes cooperation between the Domination and North

America necessary; given your system of government and social organization, that means a press policy as well. You have influence with ABS, an audience, and are suitably anti-German. There was opposition, but the Strategic section and the Archon agreed that it was advisable." He smiled thinly.

Dreiser nodded. "It's reassuring that your Leader realizes the need for friendship between our countries at this critical juncture," he said, cursing himself for the unction he heard in his own voice. *This is a scary old bastard, but you've seen worse*, he told himself.

Johanna hid a chuckle behind a cough. The elder von Shrakenberg grinned openly. "Back when our good Archon was merely Director of Foreign Affairs, I once overheard her express a fervent desire to separate your President from his testicles and make him eat them. Presumably a metaphor, but with Edwina Palme, you never know. That was in . . . ah, '38; she must have meant that Roosevelt fellow. I sincerely doubt that friendship for anything American has ever been among her motivations. She's a mean bitch, but not stupid, and she can recognize a strategic necessity when we point it out."

He crumbled a scone and added meditatively: "Personally, I would have preferred McClintock, or better still Terreblanche, particularly in wartime; he could have made the General Staff if he'd stayed in uniform. Just not on, though; the Party wouldn't have him."

Dreiser blinked in surprise. "Ah," Karl von Shrakenberg said. "Apologies . . . you probably find Draka frankness a little unexpected. I read your articles on Germany, by the way; very perceptive, given the limits to your information. Remember, though, the Domination is not a totalitarian dictatorship of the Nazi type; we practice . . . oligarchical collectivism is probably the best term. The citizen body as a whole is our idol, not the State or its officers; they merely execute and coordinate. And citizens all have the same fundamental interests, which means that criticism—*tactical* criticism—can safely be allowed. Which makes for greater efficiency."

"Now, if we could only get the Security Directorate to agree," Eric said dryly. Johanna laughed.

"One institution among many," Karl said, waving a dismissive hand.

Dreiser laid down his knife. "To be frank, general, if you hope to convert me, this is scarcely the way to go about it."

"Oh, not in the least. We don't generally proselytize . . . except by conquest, to be sure. Our present goal is, at most, a temporary alliance of convenience, which requires some manipulation of your public opinion. How did Oscar Wilde put it, after he settled in the Domination? The rest of the Anglo-Saxon world is convinced that the Draka are brutal, licentious, and depraved; the Draka are convinced that outlanders are prigs, hypocritical prudes, and weaklings *and both parties are right . . .*"

Dreiser blinked again, overcome by a slight feeling of unreality. "The problem," he said, "will be to convince the American public that Nazi Germany is more dangerous than your Domination."

"It isn't," the Draka general said cheerfully. "We're far more dangerous to you, in the long run. But the National Socialists are more dangerous *right now;* the Domination is patient, we never bite off more than we can chew and digest. Hitler is a parvenu, and he's in a hurry; wants to build a thousand-year Reich in a decade. And he's been very lucky and very able, so far. He's on the verge of making Germany a real World Power, just as the Japanese are in East Asia. As I said, the strategic situation—"

Dreiser leaned forward. "What *is* the strategic situation?" he asked.

"Ah." Karl von Shrakenberg steepled his fingers. "Well, in general, the world situation is approaching what we in Strategic Planning call an *endgame*. Analogous to the Hellenistic period during the Roman-Carthaginian wars. The game is played out between the Great Powers, and ends when only one is left. To be a Great Power—or World Power—requires certain assets: size, population, food and raw materials, administrative and military skills, industrial production.

"The West Europeans are out of the running; they're too small. The British are holding on, because we allow them a trickle of supplies—we may give them more later, if it seems expedient. The Soviets had all the qualifications except skill; now the Germans have knocked them out for good and all. That leaves two *actual* World Powers—the Domination, which has all of Africa, the Middle East, Central Asia, Afghanistan, Mongolia, northwest China, and the United States, which stretches from the Arctic to Panama, and controls South America through satellite governments. We have more territory, population, and resource-base; you have a slightly larger industrial machine."

He wiped his fingers on a napkin of drawn-thread linen. "And there are two *potential* World Powers: Germany and Japan. Germany holds all of Europe, and is in the process of taking European Russia; Japan has most of China, and is gobbling up the former European possessions in Southeast Asia and Indonesia. In both cases, if given a generation to digest, develop and organize their conquests, they would be powers of the first rank. Germany is more immediately dangerous because of her already strong industrial production and high degree of military skill. This *present* war is to settle the question of whether the two potential powers will survive to enter the next generation of the game. I suggest it is strongly in the American interest that they not be allowed to do so."

"Why?" Dreiser said bluntly, overcoming distaste. This brutal honesty was one of the reasons for the widespread hatred of the Domination. Hypocrisy was the tribute vice paid to virtue, and the Draka refused to render it; refused to even *pretend* to virtues that they rejected and despised.

The Draka grinned like a wolf. "Ideology, demographics . . . If National Socialism and the Japanese Empire consolidate their gains, we'll have to come to an accommodation with them. In both, the master-race population is several times larger than ours. We're expansionists by inclination, they by necessity. *Lebensraum*, you see. The only basis for an accommodation would be an alliance against the Western Hemisphere, the more so as all three of us find your world-view subversive and repugnant in the extreme. Of course, two of the victors would then ally to destroy the third, and then fall out with each other. Endgame."

"And if Hitler and the Japanese *are* stopped?" the American said softly.

"Why, the U.S.A. and the Domination would divide the spoils between them," the Draka said jovially. "You'd have a generation of peace, at least: it would take us that long to digest our gains, build up our own numbers, break the conquered peoples to the yoke. Then . . . who knows? We have superior numbers, patience, continuity of purpose. You have more flexibility and ingenuity. It'll be interesting, at least."

The American considered his hands. "You may be impossible to live with in the long run," he said. "I've seen Hitler at first hand; he's impossible in the *short* run . . . but an American audience isn't going to be moved by considerations of *realpolitik*: as far as the voters are concerned, munitions merchants got us into the last one, with nothing more to show than unpaid debts from the Europeans and more serfs for the Draka."

The general shrugged, blotted his lips and rose. "Ah yes, the notorious Yankee moralism; it makes your electorate even less inclined to rational behavior than ours. I won't say *tell it to the Mexicans* . . ." He leaned forward across the table, resting his weight on his palms. "If your *audience* needs a pin in the bum of their moral indignation to work up a fighting spirit, consider this. You've heard the rumors about what's happening to the Jews in Europe?"

Dreiser nodded, mouth dry. "From the Friends Service Committee," he said. "I believed them; most of my compatriots didn't. They're . . . unbelievable. Even some of those who admit they're true won't believe them." Out of the corner of his eye he saw the younger von Shrakenbergs start at the name of the Quaker humanitarian group.

The general nodded. "They *are* true, and you can have the Intelligence reports to prove it. And if the Yankee in the street isn't moved by love of the Jews, the Fritz—the Germans—plan to stuff the Poles and Russians into the incinerators next." He straightened. "As to your reports—keep them non-specific, for the present, on the Domination, and the units to which you'll be attached. Then, when there's action . . . you'll be there, won't you? A 'scoop' for you, and a minor factor in our favor, at least. Now, if you'll pardon me, I have a great deal to do. As a guest, you have free run of the House; if you want anything in the way of diversion, horses or women or whatever, the Steward will see to it. Good day."

Dreiser stared blankly as the tall figure limped from the terrace. He looked about. The table faced south, over a courtyard surrounded by a colonnade. Cloud-shadow rolled down the naked rock of the hill behind, over the dappled oak forest, past fenced pasture and stables, smelling of turned earth and rock and the huge wild mountains to the east. The courtyard fountain bent before the wind, throwing a mist of spray across tiles blue as lapis. The two young Draka leaned back in their chairs, smiling in a not unkindly scorn.

"Pa—Strategos von Shrakenberg—can be a little . . . alarming at times," Eric said, offering his hand. "Very much the *grand seigneur*. An able man, very, but hard."

Johanna laughed. "I think Mr. Dreiser was a bit alarmed by Pa's offer of hospitality in the form of a girl," she drawled. "Visions of weeping captive women dragged to his bed in chains, no doubt."

"Ah," Eric said, pouring himself another cup of coffee. "Well, don't concern yourself; the Steward never has any trouble finding volunteers."

"Eh, Rahksan?" Johanna said jokingly, turning to a serf-girl who sat behind her on a stool, knitting. She did not look like the locals, the American noticed; she was lighter, like a south European. And looking him over with cool detachment.

"*Noooo*, thank yaz kahndly, mistis," Rahksan said. "Got mo' than 'nuff on mah plate, as 'tis." The Draka woman laughed, and put a segment of tangerine between the serf's lips.

"I'm married," the American said, flushing. The two Draka and the serf looked at him a moment in incomprehension.

"Mind you," Eric continued in a tactful change of subject, "if this was Grandfather Alexander's time, we could have shown you some more spectacular entertainment. *He* kept a private troupe of serf wenches trained in the ballet, among other things. Used to perform nude at private parties."

With a monumental effort, Dreiser regained his balance. "Well, what did your grandmother think of that?" he asked.

"Enjoyed herself thoroughly, from what she used to cackle to me," Johanna said, rising. "I'll leave you two to business; see you at dinner, Mr. Dreiser. Come on, Rahksan; I'm for a swim."

"This . . . isn't quite what I expected," Dreiser said, relighting his pipe. Eric yawned and stretched, the yellow silk of his robe falling back from a tanned and muscular forearm.

"Well, probably the High Command thought you might as well see the Draka at home before you reported on our military. This," he waved a hand, "is less likely to jar on Yankee sensibilities than a good many other places in the Domination."

"It is?" Dreiser shook his head. He had hated Berlin—the whole iron apparatus of lies and cruelty and hatred; hated it the more since he had been in the city in the 20's, when it had been the most exciting place in Europe. Doubly exciting to an American expatriate, fleeing the stifling conformity of the Coolidge years. *Be honest*, he told himself. *This isn't more evil. Less so, if anything. Just more . . . alien. Longer established and more self-confident.*

"Also, out here and then on a military installation, *you* are less likely to jar on *Security's* sensibilities." Eric paused, making a small production of dismembering a pomegranate and wiping his hands. "I read your book *Berlin Journal*," he said in a neutral tone. "You mentioned helping Jews and dissidents escape, with the help of that Quaker group. You interest yourself in their activities?"

"Yes," the American replied, sitting up. A newsman's instincts awakened.

The Draka tapped a finger. "This is confidential?" At Dreiser's nod, he continued. "There was a young wench . . . small girl, about two years ago. Age seven, blond, blue eyes. Named Anna, number C22D178." The young officer's voice stayed flat, his face expressionless; a combination of menace and appeal behind the harsh grey eyes.

"Why, yes," Dreiser said. "It created quite a sensation at the time, but the Committee kept it out of the press. She was adopted by a Philadelphia family; old Quaker stock, but childless. That was the last I heard. Why?" It *had* created a sensation: almost all escapees were adults, mainly from the North African and Middle Eastern provinces. For a serf from the heart of the Police Zone there was nowhere to go, and an unaccompanied child was unprecedented.

Eric's eyes closed for a moment. "No reason that should be mentioned by either of us," he said. His hand reached out and gripped the other's forearm. "It wouldn't be *safe*. For either of us. Understood?"

Dreiser nodded. The Draka continued: "And if you're going to be attached to a paratroop unit, I strongly advise you to start getting into shape. Even if it's several months before the next action."

"*Yaaaaaaah!*"

Despite himself, Dreiser flinched slightly as Johanna's nine-inch knife blurred toward her brother's stomach. That was real steel, and *sharp*. Eric swayed aside, just enough; clamped the arm between his own and his flank, and brought his knee up into her stomach. She rolled sideways with an *ooff*, came to her feet and scooped the blade from the dimpled surface of the cotton matting.

"God*damn*!" she swore, flicking the knife six feet into a hardwood block. "I *know* you're no faster than me—"

"You're still telegraphing."

"I am *not*!"

"Subliminally, then." He turned to Dreiser. "Swim, Bill?"

The American shook his head silently, still exhausted from the hour-long workout, and watched as

they shed the rough cotton exercise outfits and dove
into the great pool. He sighed and leaned back against
the padded wicker chair, reaching for the lemonade.
It was astonishing how the body craved fluids for
hours after a workout; he had never been the athletic
type, and the past week had been hard on a seden-
tary man of middle years.

*And goddamn it, I'm still not used to mixed skinny-
dipping,* he thought resentfully, watching the sleek
naked bodies arrowing through the water. He had
imagined that twenty years of Europe had worn away
the results of a childhood spent in small-town Iowa,
and lately found that not so. Not that it would raise
many brows in Hollywood circles, for instance . . .

He pulled the towelcloth robe around himself and
looked about the . . . *baths.* It was more like a
gymnasium-health club complex, filling most of a wing,
with artwork that a du Pont might have envied . . .

*If those pirates knew a work of art when it bit
them on the leg,* a New Dealer in the back of his
mind prompted. The whole thing was of a piece with
his experience of the Domination, so far: unthinkable
luxury, beauty, blood, cruelty, perversion. But not
decadence, whatever the Holy Rollers at home
thought; these might be hedonists, but it was the
sybarism of a strong, hungry people. *Quo Vadis,* his
mind continued sourly. *If de Mille had any taste,
and didn't have the Catholic Decency League on his
ass.*

Rahksan sat on a stool nearby, knitting again, with
a long-haired Persian at her feet making an occa-
sional halfhearted bat at the wool. *That* had bothered
him more than he thought it would, too—particularly
since Johanna had mentioned that she was engaged
to be married, and the serf girl seemed to be—having
an affair? Could you use that term when one party
was chattel to the other?—Whatever, with Eric.
Things got thoroughly confused around here. He

chuckled to himself, remembering how his mother had warned him about loose women when he left for that assignment in Paris, back in '22. *Little did she know,* he thought.

Rahksan looked up and met his eyes. He coughed, searching for words. He always felt so *sorry* for the poor little bitch—a combination of pity and bone-deep distaste. And on top of that awkwardness, it was always difficult to know what to say to a serf, the need for discretion aside. The tattoo on her neck drew his eyes, loaded with a freight of symbol that made it difficult to see through to the human being, the person, behind it. He'd had something of the same feeling in India back a decade ago, when he'd been reporting on Gandhi, with some of the Hindu *sadhus* he'd met; a feeling that there was simply no meeting place of experience.

"We'll be going soon," he said. It beat *my, aren't the walls vertical,* at least.

"Yassuh," she said tranquilly, and sighed. "Be a montha so, fo' Mistis Jo git perm'nant quahtahs, send fo' me." She held up the knitting, pursed her lips and undid a stitch, then giggled. "Glada tha rest; naace havin' they both heah, buta little, *strenuous-ifyin'*, does yaz be knowin' wha' Ah mean."

"Ah," he said noncommittally, lips tightening. *This is either the best actress I've ever met, or what southerners used to call the "perfect nigger,"* he thought.

The serf dropped the wool into her lap; she was looking cool and crisp and elegant in a pleated silk skirt and embroidered blouse of white linen. A slim gold chain lay about the smooth olive column of her neck, sparkling against the blue-black curls falling to her shoulders. He forced his attention back to her face; it had been a long time since he left home and wife.

"Yaz doan laahk me ovahmuch, suh, does yaz?"

The young woman's voice carried the usual soft, amiable submissiveness, but the words were uncomfortably sharp.

"No . . . what makes you think that?" He felt slightly guilty agreement, and a sharp wish he had been better at concealing it. *Goddamit, you're a newsman, act like it!* he thought savagely to himself.

"Masta Dreiser, moas' freemen tink bondfolk be foolish, which ama foolishness itself. Mebbe moah 'scusable ina Yankee, wha doan see us day by day."

She looked over to the pool. Brother and sister had climbed up on the rocks beneath the waterfall, and Eric had just pitched his sister backwards into the torrent.

"Ah doan' remembah mucha mah fam'ly," she said meditatively. " 'Cept lying undah they-ah bodies, an' being pulled out." She turned her eyes to the Draka. "They didn' do it, Mastah Drieser," she said. "Ah unnahstood that, soon's Ah stahted thinkin' 'bout things. Coulda spent alla mah taahm hatin'; what it get me? Just twisted up insaahd, laak them is what makes a life a hatin'." She smiled grimly.

" 'Sides, what Ah do remembah, is mah fathah hittin' me fo' makin' noise. An' mommah, she give th' food t' mah brothahs, on 'count they boys, leave me cryin' an' hongry. If'n the Draka hadn' come, Ah'd a growed up inna hut with the goats, been *sold* fo' goats, hadta put onna tent t' go out. *Chador*, hey? Nevah been clean, nevah had 'nuff t' eat, nevah seen anytin' pretty . . .

"So-ah." She touched the numerals behind her ear. "This doan mean Ah's a plough, oah a stove. Cain' nohow see how a man's thinkin' undah his face. Serf need that moah thana freemen." She paused. "Yo' a Godshoutah, suh?" At his blank look: "Christman, laahk somma they-ah down in t'Quahtahs. What 'jects to folks pleasurin' as they-ah sees fit?"

"No, not really." Not altogether true, but he *should*

have remembered that illiteracy was not synonymous with stupidity. "Besides, you don't have much choice in the matter."

"Oh, but Ah *does*. Luckiah than 'lotta folks, thayt way." She leaned closer. "Masta Dreiser, yo' a Yankee-man, means well, so Masta Eric tell thissun'. Say talk if'n yo' wanna, so Ah bean' talkin', not justa *Yassuh, masta*, an' *Nossuh, masta* laahk Ah could. So Ah says, keep youah pity an' youah look-down-nose foah them as needs it. Two 'tings y'otta 'tink on, masta: Ah laahks Masta Eric well 'nuff. Good man, when he-ah doan' git t'tinkin' so much. Laahk Mistis Jo lot moah; she allays been naahce t'me. Weeeell, near allays as no mattah, nobody naahce alla taahm.

"Othah ting: serf, buck oah wench *needa* good masta, good mistis. Tings diff'ren yaz contry, mebbe; heah *anytin'* can happen t' the laahk'sa me. *Anytin'*. Yaz tinks onna thayt. Ah grows up witta Mistis Jo, Masta Eric, t'othahs. Laahk . . . pet, hey? Ah knows they; they knows me, near as good. Doan't gonna laahk me if'n Ah doan laahk they, yaz see? Easy 'nuff to laahk they, so-ah? Doan't nuthin' bayd happen if'n Ah wuz ta act sullen. Ah jus end up cookin', oah pullin' spuds, milkin' cows. Thayt mah choice."

For a moment the softly pretty face looked almost fierce. "So-ah, yaz doan' hayve mah laaf t'live, mah de-cisions t'mayk, does yaz, *masta*? So, mebbe little lessa *drawin' asaahd t'skirts of tha garment*, eh, Masta Dreiser, suh?"

He flushed, slightly ashamed, feeling a stirring of liking despite himself, nodded. *Well, you always knew people were complicated,* he chided himself.

The Draka returned. Rahksan bounced up to hand them towels and began drying Johanna's back.

"Well," Eric said, pulling on a robe in deference to the guest's sensibilities. "You'll be glad enough to get where you can put the *war* back into the corre-spondent, eh?"

Dreiser nodded. "Although I've gotten some interesting background material here," he said.

"Yes," Johanna chimed in, muffled through the towel. "And even more interesting, the way you slanted it. Gives me a good idea of what the particular phobias of the Yankees are: nasty-minded lot, I must say."

"And I've been working up some stuff on the domestic angle," he said, indicating the interior with a nod. "How the Draka live at home." *Some of which won't see the light of day until after the war*, he added silently.

The two young Draka stared at him. "I hope," Johanna said carefully, "you aren't under the impression that *most* citizens live this way." She waved a hand, indicating the Great House. "Or maybe you do? I've read some American novels about the Domination that are real howlers."

"Well, most Draka are quite affluent," he replied. "And I did get the impression that most citizen families were serfholders."

"Oh, yes," Eric said. "You have to be an alcoholic or a retard to be really poor, and then they just put you in a comfortable institution, sterilize you and encourage life-shortening vices."

Dreiser blinked. Eric was a decent enough sort, but half the time he just didn't seem to *hear* the things he said.

"Yes; well over ninety percent hold *some* serfs," Johanna said, propping a foot on the plinth of a statue. It was an onyx leopard, with ivory fangs and claws.

"But . . . hmmm, last census, three-quarters held ten or less. Half five or less. Look, you know how our economy's set up?"

"Vaguely. 'Feudal Socialism'—that's the official term, isn't it?" the American said.

Eric sighed. "Carlyle popularized the phrase, back

over a century ago. Actually, it just sort of grew. To simplify . . . big industries are owned by the State, by the free-employee guilds, or by the Landholder's League."

"That's sort of like a cooperative for plantation owners, isn't it?" Dreiser said.

"Plantation *holders*. We don't have private ownership of land, strictly speaking. That's what the League started out as, yes. Branched out into shipping, transport, processing, then banking. Nowadays, hmmm, take the Ferrous Metals Combine. Iron and coal mining, steel, heavy engineering. Ten percent of the shares are owned by the War Directorate; used to be more, they started in with cannon-foundries. Thirty percent are owned by the Ferric Guild. The rest are shared by the State and the Landholder's League. The same is true in varying proportions with the others: Capricorn Textiles Combine, Naysmith Machine Tools, Trevithick Autosteam, Dos Santos Dirigibles . . .

"So instead of industry exploiting agriculture, the way it is with you Americans—well, the von Shrakenbergs get a third of their income from the League, apart from what four thousand hectares brings in."

Johanna stretched and yawned. "So these days, most citizens are city-dwellers—technicians, engineers, overseers, bureaucrats, police agents, artists, schoolteachers . . . The *salatariat* not the *proletariat*."

Eric snorted. "Feeble wit, sister dear. Actually, it's more complicated than that. There's a, hmmm, 'private sector'—small business, luxury goods, mostly. And, for example, guess who lobbies for a higher standard of living for the factory-serfs?"

"Nobody?" Dreiser said coolly.

The Draka laughed. "Actually, the League," Eric said. "Plantation agriculture means farming for sale; 91 percent of the population are serfs, after all. The better the Combines feed and clothe their workers, the more we sell. In the old days we sold abroad, but that's out of the question nowadays—we're just too *big*."

Johanna nodded and tossed her robe over one shoulder. "Adieu, Bill, Eric; see you at dinner." Rahksan rose to follow her. "You two discuss the whichness of wherefore; time enough for work when the leave-pass is up."

Dreiser watched her go. Colored light reflected off marble and fresco to pattern her skin, which rippled smoothly as she swayed across the floor. He indicated the block, with its knives, and the exercise floor. "That sort of thing is impressive as hell, especially the chucking-each-other-about part," he said, as the women left.

"Oh, you mean the *pankration*? Actually, we got most of that from the Asians, oddly enough. Despite the Greek name. Back in the 1880's, when we imported a lot of coolies. The overseer tried to touch up a lot of Okinawans with his sjambok and found out they had ways of personal mayhem . . . bought their contracts, learned it all, and set up a *salle d'armes*."

"Ah," Dreiser said again, making a mental note. "Surprising how well your sister stands up to you, considering the advantages."

Eric ran fingers through his short, damp hair. "Size and reach, or gender?" he said. "Incidentally, watch what you say on that subject when we get back to the field. Lot of women are still pretty sensitive about that sort of thing; there was a long controversy about it when I was a toddler and you still find the occasional shellback conservative. You might be able to get away with turning down a duel, being a foreigner, but there are some who'd . . . react."

"React how?" the American asked.

"They'd break your bones."

"You're serious? Yes, I see you are. Thanks, Eric."

The Draka shrugged. "You'll understand it better when we're in the field," he said.

CHAPTER FIVE

Both love and hatred can be frustrating emotions, when their object is not present. My father had sent me away. Not that I missed him overmuch; it was not he who had raised me, after all. But he had sent me away from the only home I had ever known, from those who had loved and cared for me. How could I not hate him? But I was a precocious child, and of an age to begin thinking. In Philadelphia I was a stranger, and lonely, but I was free. Schooling, books, later university and the play of minds; all these he had given me, at the risk of his own life; there was nothing for me in the Domination. And he was my father; how could I not love him?

And he was not there; I could not scream my anger at him, or embrace him and say the words of love. And so I created a father in my head, as other children had imaginary playmates: daydreams of things we would do together—trips to the zoo or Atlantic City, conversations, arguments . . . an inner life that helped to train the growth of my being, as a vine is shaped by its trellis. Good training for a novelist. A poor substitute for a home.

Daughter to Darkness: A Life
by Anna von Shrakenberg
Houghton & Stewart, New York, 1964

OAKENWALD PLANTATION
OCTOBER 1941

Arch-Strategos Karl von Shrakenberg sipped carefully from the snifter, cradling it in his hands and looking down from the study window, southwest across the gardens and the valley, green fields and poplars and the golden hue of sandstone from the hills . . .

One more, he thought, turning and pouring a careful half-ounce into the wide-mouthed goblet. One more, and another when Eric came; he had to be careful with brandy, as with any drug that could numb the pain of his leg. The surgeons had done their best, but that had been 1917, and technique was less advanced; also, they were busy. More cutting might lessen the pain, but it would also chance losing more control of the muscle, and that he would not risk.

He leaned weight on the windowsill and sighed; sun rippled through the branches of the tree outside, with a cool wind that hinted of the night's chill. He would be glad of a fire.

Ach, well, life is a wounding, he thought. *An accumulation of pains and maimings and grief. We heal as we can, bear them as we must, until the weight grows too much to bear and we go down into the earth.*

"I wish I could tell Eric that," he whispered. But what use? He was young, and full of youth's rebellion against the world. He would simply hear a command to bow to the wisdom of age, to accept the unacceptable and endure the unendurable. His tongue rolled the brandy about his mouth. *Would I have stood for that sort of advice when I was his age?*

Well, outwardly, at least. My ambitions were always more concrete. He rubbed thumb and forefinger against the bridge of his nose, wearily considering the stacks of reports on his desk; many of them were marked with a stylized terrestrial globe in a saurian claw: top secret. *I wanted command, accomplishment, a warrior's name—and what am I?* A glorified clerk, reading and annotating reports: Intelligence reports, survey reports, reports on steel production and machine-tool output, ammunition stockpile reports . . .

Old men sitting in a basement, playing wargames on sand tables and sending our sons and daughters out to die on the strength of it, he thought. You succeeded, won your dreams, and *that was not the finish of it.* Not like those novels Eric was so fond of, where the ends could be tied up and kept from unravelling. Life went on . . . how dry and horrible that would have seemed once!

Stop grumbling, old man, he told himself. There had been good times enough, girls and glory and power, more than enough if you thought how most humans had to live out their lives. Limping, he walked down one wall, running his fingers lovingly along the leather-bound spines of the books. The study was as old as the manor, and had changed less; a place for the head of the family, a working room, it had escaped the great redecoration his mother had overseen as a young bride. His eyes paused as he came to his wife's portrait. It showed her as she had been when they had pledged themselves, in that hospital on Crete, looking young and self-consciously stern in her Medical Corps uniform, doctor's stethoscope neatly buttoned over her breast and her long brown hair drawn back in a workmanlike bun.

Mary would have helped, he thought, raising his glass to her memory. She had been better than he at . . . feelings? No, at talking about them when it was needful. She would have known what to do when Eric became too infatuated with that damned Circassian wench.

No, he thought grudgingly. *Tyansha understood— better than Eric. She never tried to get him to go beyond propriety in public.*

He had tried to talk to his son, but it had been useless. Maybe Mary could have got at him through the girl. Mary had been like that—always dignified, but even the housegirls and fieldhands had talked freely with her. Tyansha had frozen into silence whenever the Old Master looked at her. Tempting just to send her away, but that would have been punishing her for Eric's fault, and a von Shrakenberg did not treat a family serf that way; honor forbade. He had been relieved when she had died naturally in childbirth, until . . .

Mary could be hard when she had to be, Karl thought. *It was a tool with her, something she brought out when it was needed. Me . . . I'm beginning to think it's like armor that I can't take off even if I wanted to.*

The Draka had made more of the differences between the sexes in his generation, although less than other peoples did. The change had been necessary—there was the work of the world to do, and never enough trustworthy hands—but there were times when he felt his people had lost something by banishing softness from their lives.

Well, I'll just have to do my best, he thought. His hand fell on a rude-carved image on a shelf—a figurine of Thor, product of the failed attempt to revive the Old Faith back in the last century. "Even you couldn't lift the Midgard Serpent or outwrestle the Crone Age, eh, Redbeard?"

A knock sounded. That would be his son.

Haven't seen the inside of this very often, since I was a boy, Eric thought, looking about his father's study. *And not often under happy circumstances then. Usually a thrashing.* There was nothing of that sort to await today, of course; merely a farewell. *Damned if I'm going to kneel and ask his blessing, tradition or not.*

The room was big and dim, smelling of leather and tobacco, open windows overshadowed by trees. Eric remembered climbing them to peer within as a boy.

Walls held books, old and leather-bound; plantation
accounts running back to the founding; family rec-
ords; volumes on agriculture, stockbreeding, strat-
egy, hunting. Among them were keepsakes accumu-
lated through generations: a pair of baSotho throwing
spears nearly two centuries old, crossed over a battle-
axe—relics from the land-taking. A Chokwe spirit
mask from Angola, a Tuareg broadsword, a Moroccan
jezail musket, an Armenian fighting-knife with a hilt
of lacy silver filigree . . .

And the family portraits, back to *Freiherr* Augus-
tus von Shrakenberg himself, who had led a regi-
ment of Mecklenberg dragoons in British service in
the American Revolution, and taken this estate in
payment. Title to it, at least; the natives had had
other ideas, until he persuaded them. Six genera-
tions of Landholders since, in uniform, mostly: proud
narrow faces full of wolfish energy and a cold, intelli-
gent ferocity. Conquerors . . .

*At least that was the face they chose to show the
world,* he thought. *A man's mind is a forest at night.
We don't know our own inwardness, much less each
other's.*

His father was standing by the cabinet, filling two
brandy snifters. The study's only trophy was above
it, a black-maned Cape lion. Karl von Shrakenberg
had killed it himself, with a lance.

Eric took the balloon glass and swirled it carefully
to release the scent before lifting it to touch his
father's. The smell was rich but slightly spicy, com-
plementing the room's odors of books, old, well-kept
furniture, and polished wood.

"*A bad harvest or a bloody war*," the elder von
Shrakenberg said, using the ancient toast.

"Prosit," Eric replied. There was a silence, as they
avoided each other's eyes. Karl limped heavily to the
great desk and sank into the armchair amid a sigh of
cushions. Eric felt himself vaguely uneasy with child-

hood memories of standing to receive rebuke, and forced himself to sit, leaning back with negligent elegance. The brandy bit his tongue like a caress; it was the forty-year Thieuniskraal, for special occasions.

"Not too bloody, I hope," he continued. Suddenly, there was a wetness on his brow, a feeling of things coiling beneath the surface of his mind, like snakes in black water. *I should never have come back. It all seemed safely distant while I was away.*

Karl nodded, searching for words. They were Draka, and there was no need to skirt the subject of death. "Yes." A pause. "A pity that it came before you could marry. Long life to you, Eric, but it would have been good to see grandchildren here at Oakenwald before you went into harm's way. Children are your immortality, as much as your deeds." He saw his son flinch, swore inwardly. *He's a man, isn't he? It's been six years since the wench died!*

Eric set the glass down on the arm of his seat with immense care. "Well, you rather foreclosed that option, didn't you, Father?"

The time-scored eagle's face reared back. "I did nothing of the kind. Did nothing."

"You let her die." Eric heard the words speak themselves; he felt perfectly lucid but floating, beyond himself. Calm, a spectator. *Odd, I've felt that sentence waiting for six years and never dared,* some detached portion of himself observed.

"The first I knew of it was when they told me she was dead!"

"Which was why you buried her before I got back. Burned her things. Left me nothing!" Suddenly he was on his feet, breath rasping through his mouth.

"That was for your own good. You were a child— you were obsessed!" Karl was on his feet as well, his fist smashing down on the teakwood of the desk top, a drumbeat sound. They had never spoken of this before, and it was like the breaking of a cyst. "It was

unworthy of you. I was trying to bring you back to
your senses!"

"Unworthy of *your blood*, you mean; unworthy of
that tin image of what a von Shrakenberg should be.
It killed John, and it's hounded me all my life. When
it's killed Johanna and me, will that satisfy your
pride?" He saw his father's face pale and then flush
at the mention of his elder brother's name, saw for a
moment the secret fear that visited him in darkness;
knew that he had scored, felt a miserable joy. The
torrent of words continued.

"Obsessed? *I loved her! As you've never loved
anything in your reptile-blooded life!* And you let me
go a month at school without a word; if my favorite
horse had died, you would have done more."

The shout bounced off the walls, startling him
back to awareness of self. There was a tinkling, a stab
of pain in his right hand; he looked down to see the
snifter shattered in his grasp, blood trickling about
glass shards. He brought his focus back to his father.
"I hold you responsible," he finished softly.

Karl's eyes held his. *Love? What do you know
about it—you're a child. It's something to be done,
not talked about.* Aloud:

"God's curse on you, boy, pregnancy isn't an
illness—she had the same midwife who delivered
you!" He fought down anger, forced gentleness into
his voice. "It happens, Eric; don't blame it on me
because you can't shout at fate." Sternly: "Or did you
think I told them to hold a pillow over her face? *She*
knew your interests, boy, better than you did, she
never stepped beyond her station. Are you saying
that I'd kill a von Shrakenberg serf who was blame-
less, to punish my own child?"

"I say—" Eric began, and stopped. His father's
face was an iron mask, but it had gone white about
the nostrils. Something inside him prompted *sayit-
sayitsayit*, a hunger to deliver the wound that would

hurt beyond bearing, and he forced his lips closed by sheer force of will. Blood kin or not, no one called Karl von Shrakenberg a liar to his face. Ever.

"I say that I had better leave. Sir." He saluted, his fist leaving a smear of blood on the left breast of his uniform tunic, clicked his heels, marched to the door.

Karl felt the rage-strength leave him as the door sighed closed. He sagged back into the chair, leaning on the desk, the old wound sending a lance of agony from hip to spine.

"What happened?" he asked dully. His eyes sought out a framed photograph on the desk—his wife's, black-bordered. "Oh, Mary, you could have told me what to say, what to do . . . Why did you leave me, my heart? This may be the last time I see him alive—John and—" His head dropped into his hands. *"My son, my son!"*

CHAPTER SIX

... decision to attack the German forces was a risk, but a calculated one. The Nazi armies were large, but their armored/ mechanized spearheads were less than 10 percent of the whole. For example, in the spring of 1942, the Werhmacht's total inventory of tanks was barely 4,000, including many obsolete light models and captured Russian vehicles; the Domination had more than 14,000, all modern Hond III types. The average German infantryman was lucky to get an occasional ride in a truck; even the Janissary units of the Draka forces had wheeled armored personnel carriers. The technological gap was exemplified by the rival powers' standard infantry weapons: a bolt action Mauser designed in 1898 versus automatic assault rifles.

Yet the Third Reich had already defeated the Soviet Union, a power with comparable superiority in numbers and materiel, if not skill. Once allowed to consolidate and exploit their conquests, the Germans could have become a terrible threat. Even as it was, the Draka troopers found "Fritz" a formidable opponent and a tricky, ruthless fighter. Particularly in the opening phases of the campaign, the decisive factor was the combat qualities of small units operating in comparative isolation ...

Fire And Blood: The Eurasian War
V. I: Tiflis to Warsaw, 1942-1943
by Strategos Robert A. Jackson (ret.)
New Territories Press, Vienna, 1965

OSSETIAN MILITARY HIGHWAY, SOVIET GEORGIA APRIL 14, 1942: 0500 HOURS

Eric stood, the steel folding stock of his rifle resting on one hip, looking downslope. The forest was mostly below eye level from the plateau where the paratroops had landed. Black tree limbs twisted in the paling moonlight, glistening with frost granules, the first mist of green from opening buds like a tender illusion trembling before the eyes. Breath smoked white before him; the thin cold air poured into his lungs like a taste of home. Yet these mountains were not his; they were huger, wilder, sharper. To the east across the trough of the pass the peaks caught rosy light, their snowcaps turning blood red before his eyes.

"Right," he said. The tetrarchy leaders and their seconds were grouped around him, squatting and leaning on their assault rifles. It had taken only a few minutes to uncrate the equipment and form the Century: training, and a common knowledge that defeat and death were one and the same.

"First, two minor miracles. We hit our drop zone right on; so did Cohort, chiliarchy, and legion." Southward, higher up the slope of the pass, man-made thunder rolled back from the stony walls. "So, they're engaging the main Fritz units farther up. Should go well, complete strategic surprise. Also, the communications are all working right for once."

There were appreciative murmurs. Vacuum tubes and parachutes simply went ill together, and fragile radios had cost the experimental paratroop arm dearly earlier in the war. Experience was beginning to pay off.

"Which is all to the good; we aren't fighting Italians anymore. In fact, there seem to be complete formed units up there, not just the communications and engineering personnel we were hoping for. Now for the rest of it. The gliders with the light armor came down perfectly—right into a ravine. Chiliarchy H.Q. says they may be able to put a rubble ramp down for some of it; take a day, at least."

"Zebra shit!" That was Marie Kaine, in charge of the reinforced sapper and heavy-weapons tetrarchy. "Sorry, sir. Look, Eric, this new recoilless stuff has its advantages. But it isn't very mobile, there's no protection for the crews, and the backblast's so bad you can't dig it in much. We needed that armor."

He shrugged. "No help for it. Right." He pointed downslope; they were high enough to catch glimpses of the road over treetops still black in the false dawn. Morning had brought out the birds, and a trilling chorus was starting up. The troopers waited quietly below, a few smoking or talking softly, most silent.

"That track, believe it or not, is the Ossetian Military Highway, half the road net over the mountains." He gestured southward with his mapboard. "The rest of the legion is up there, fighting their way into Kutaisi and points back toward us."

His hand cut the air to the north. "Down there, the Fritz armor is regrouping around Pyatigorsk. We're not sure exactly what units—the Intelligence network is shot to hell since the Fritz got here and started liquidating anything that moves—but definitely tank units in strength. If they're up to form, we should be getting a reaction force pretty damn quick."

The Centurion's next gesture was due east, to the unseen S-curve of the two-lane "highway" that hugged the mountain slope on which they stood. "And a kilometer that way is Village One. Dense forest nearly to the road. Stone houses, and a switchback starts there. Our objective. Tom?"

"I head up the road, cross above the village, spread lst Tetrarchy as a stop force."

"And *don't* let them get past you into the woods. Marie?"

"15mm's and the 120mm recoilless along the treeline; mortars back; flamethrower and demolition teams to key off you and move forward in support."

"Einar, Lisa, John?"

"Left-right concentric, work our way in house-to-house. You coordinate on the rough spots."

"Correct. Any questions?"

Tetrarch Lisa Telford shifted on her haunches. "What about locals?"

"Ignore them if they're quiet. Otherwise, expend 'em. Synch watches: 0500 at . . . *mark!* Go in at 0530, white flare. Nothing more? Good, let's *do* it, people, let's *go!*"

The Germans in the Circassian village were wary— enough to set sentries hundreds of meters in the woods beyond the fields. Eric stooped over the body, noted the mottled camouflage jacket, glanced at the collar tabs, up at the trooper who stood smiling fondly and wiping his knife on the seat of his trousers.

"Got his paybook?" he snapped.

"Heah y'are, suh."

Eric riffled through it. "Shit! Waffen-SS, Liebstandarte Adolf Hitler! I was hoping for a logistics unit, or at least line infantry." The soldier had been nineteen, and an Austrian; for a brief instant the Draka officer wondered if the Caucasus had reminded him of the Tyrol.

If wishes were horses, we'd all have lovely rose gardens, he thought. *Quickly now, Eric-me-lad, they're not going to give you time . . .* There was a field telephone beside the sprawled figure in its improvised blind of branches; someone was going to notice the lack of a call-in soon. On impulse, he reached down and closed the staring brown eyes.

With luck, there were ten minutes before the Fritz noticed; they were probably expecting attack from the south. The noise there was peaking, the narrow walls of the pass channeling a rapid chatter of automatic-weapons fire as well as the boom of heavy weapons; that would be the rest of first and second Cohorts . . . or even the legion. Heavy fighting riveted the attention. Even so, the Fritz in the village had an all-around perimeter, for anti-partisan defense, if nothing else.

Their CO is probably getting screams for help. They might pull out . . . No, too chancy.

Ducking through thickening underbrush of wild pistachio, he made his way toward the treeline. The sun was well up now, but the mountain beeches wove a canopy fifteen meters above, turning the air to a cool olive gloom. Nearer the edge of the woods sunlight allowed more growth and the thicker timber had been logged off; there were thickets of saplings laced together with wild grapevines and witch hazel and huge clumps of wild rhododendron.

He dropped to his belly and leopard-crawled forward. The support teams were setting up, manhandling the tripod mounts of the heavy 15mm machine guns into position, the long, slender fluted barrels snaking out of improvised nests of rock and bush. The heavy *snick* sounds of oiled metal sounded as the bolts were pulled back. The three 120mm recoilless rifles were close behind, wrestled through by sheer strength and awkwardness; working parties clearing the way with bush knives, others following, bent under loads of the heavy perforated-shell ammunition.

There was a swift murmuring as team leaders picked targets; the infantry "sticks" spread out, shedding their marching packs for combat load.

Carefully, Eric nudged his rifle through the last

screen of tall grass and sighted through the x4 integral scope. The view leaped out at him. Half a thousand meters of cleared fields stretched around the village, more downslope to the north, bare and brown in the spring, still sodden from melting snow. The fields themselves were uneven, steeply sloped, studded with low terraces, heaps of fieldstone, walls of piled rock: much of it would be dead ground from the town. Closer to the tumbled huddle of stone houses were orchards, apple and plum, and walled paddocks for sheep.

Distantly he was aware of his body's reaction, sweat staining the field jacket down from his armpits, blood loud in his ears, a dryness in his mouth. He had seen enough combat to know what explosive and flying metal did to human bodies. The fears were standard, every soldier felt them—of death, of pain even more. Stomach wounds particularly, even with sulfiomide and antibiotics. Castration, blinding, burns; a life as a cripple, a thing women would puke to see . . . Draka officers were expected to delegate freely and lead from the front; a Centurion had a shorter life expectancy than a private. Almost without effort, training overrode fear, and his hands were steady as he switched to field glasses.

Standard, he thought. The village might have been any of a thousand thousand others in High Asia, anywhere from Anatolia to Sinkiang: flat-topped structures of rough stone with mud mortar, some plastered and whitewashed, others raw; sheds and narrow, twisted lanes. The military "highway" went straight through, with the burnt-out wreckage of a Russian T-34 standing by the verge on the northern outskirts, the blackened barrel of its cannon pointing in silent futility down toward the plains. There was a square, and a building with onion domes that looked to have been a mosque, before the Revolution, then until last fall a Soviet "House of Culture." There were a

few other modernish-looking structures, two nonde-
script trucks in German army paint, more horse-
drawn vehicles parked outside.

Movement: chickens, an old woman in the head-to-
toe swathing of Islamic modesty . . . and *yes*, figures
in Fritz field grey. He switched his view to the
outskirts, almost hidden in greenery: spider holes,
wire, the houses with firing-slits knocked into their
walls . . . it wasn't going to be a walkover.

He reached a hand behind him and Sofie thrust
the handset into his grasp. Senior Decurion McWhir-
ter and the five troopers waited behind her. He
clicked code into the pressure button and spoke:

"Marie."

"Targets ranged, teams ready." Along the firing
line, hands clutched the grips and lanyards; a hun-
dred meters behind, she stood with her eyes pressed
to the visor of a split-view rangefinder. The automortar
crews waited, hands on the elevating screws, loaders
ready with fresh five-round clips.

"Tetrarchy commanders."

"In position."

Eric forced himself to half a dozen slow, deep
breaths. *Hell*, he thought. *Why don't I just tell them
I'm going for a look-see and start walking to China?*
Because it would be silly, of course. Because these
were his friends.

"Well, then." He cased the binoculars, hooked the
assault sling of his rifle over his head, watched
his wrist as the second hand swept inexorably around
to 0530. When he spoke, his voice was quiet,
conversational.

"Flare."

It went up from the observation post with a quiet
pop and burst two hundred meters up. Magnesium
flame blossomed against the innocent blue of the
sky, white and harsh. *Plop-whine*, the first mortar
shells went by overhead, plunging downward into

the pink froth of apple blossom along the edge of the village: *thump-crash* fountains of black earth and shattered branches, steel and rock fragments equally deadly whirling through the air. *Crash-crash-crash-crash*, without stopping; the new automortars were heavier, on their wheeled carriages, but while the ammunition lasted, they could spray the 100mm bombs the way a submachine gun did pistol-bullets. Century A's teams had been practicing for a long time, and their hands moved reloads in with steady, metronomic regularity.

From either side the heavy machine guns erupted, controlled four-second bursts arching toward the smoke and shattered wood on the town's edge. Red tracer flicked out, blurring from the muzzles, seeming to float as it approached the roiling dust of the target zone. The firing positions here at the treeline overlooked the thin net of German defensive posts, commanded the roofs and streets beyond. They raked the windows and firing slits, and already figures in SS jackets were falling.

"*Storm storm!*" the officers' shouts rang out. The Draka infantry rose; they had shed their marching loads and the lead sticks were crouched and ready. Now they sprinted forward, running full-tilt, bobbing and jinking and weaving as they advanced. A hundred meters and they threw themselves down in firing positions; the assault rifles opened up, and the light rifle-calibre machine guns. The second-string lochoi were already leapfrogging their positions, moving with smooth athlete's grace. The operation would be repeated at the same speed, as many times as was necessary to reach the objective. This was where thousands of hours of training paid off—training that began for Draka children at the age of six to produce soldiers enormously strong and fit. Troops that could keep up this pace for hours.

And the covering fire would be *accurate*—sniper

accurate, with soldiers who could use optical scopes as quickly as those of other nations did iron sights.

"*BuLala! BuLala!*" The battle cry roared out, as old as the Draka, in a language of the Bantu extinct for more than a century: *Kill! Kill!*

The return fire was shaky and wild—the slow banging of the German Kar 98 bolt-action rifles, then the long *brrrrrtttt* of a MG 34. The line of machine-gun bullets stabbed out from a farmhouse on the outer edge of the village. Draka were falling. Seconds later one of the 120mm recoilless rifles fired.

There was a huge sound, a *crash* at once very loud and yet muffled. Behind the stubby weapon a great cloud of incandescent gas flared—the backblast that balanced the recoil. Saplings slapped to the ground and leaf-litter caught fire, and the ammunition squad leaped to beat out the flames with curses and spades. But it was the effect on the German machine-gun nest that mattered, and that was shattering. The shells were low-velocity, but they were heavy and filled with *plastique*, confined by thin steel mesh. The warhead struck directly below the muzzle of the German gun, spreading instantly into a great flat pancake of explosive; milliseconds later, the fuse in its base detonated.

Those shells had been designed for use against armor, or ferroconcrete bunkers. The loose stone of the farmhouse wall disintegrated, collapsing inward as if at the blow of an invisible fist. Beyond, the opposite wall blew outward even before the first stones reached it, destroyed by air driven to the density of steel in the confined space of the house. The roof and upper floor hung for a moment, as if suspended against gravity. Then they fell, to be buried in their turn by the inward topple of the end walls. Moments before there had been a house, squalid enough, but solid. Now there was only a heap of shattered ashlar blocks.

"Now!" Eric threw himself forward. The headquarters lochos followed. Ahead the mortar barrage "walked" into the town proper, then back to its original position. But now the shells carried smoke, thick and white, veiling all sight; bullets stabbed out of it blindly. The 120's crashed again and again, two working along the edge of the village, another elevating slightly to shell the larger buildings in the square.

With cold detachment, Tetrarch Marie Kaine watched the shellfire crumble the buildings, flicked a hand to silence the firing line as the rifle Tetrarchies reached the barrier of smoke. It thinned rapidly; she could hear the crackling bang of snake charges blasting pathways through the German wire. The small-arms fire died away for a brief moment as the first enemy fire positions were blasted out of existence, overrun, silenced. The medics and their stretcher bearers were running forward to attend to the Draka wounded.

"Combat pioneers forward!" she said crisply. The teams launched themselves downhill, as enthusiastically as the rifle infantry had done; being weighed down with twenty kilos of napalm tank for a flamethrower, or an equal weight of demolition explosive, was as good an incentive for finding cover as she knew.

"All right," she continued crisply. "Machine-gun sections cease fire. Resume on targets of opportunity or fire-requests."

The smoke had blown quickly; a dozen houses were rubble, and fires had started already from beams shattered over charcoal braziers. The fighting was moving into the town; she could see figures in Draka uniforms swarming over rooftops, the stitching lines of tracer. They were as tiny as dolls, the town spread out below like a map . . .

But then, I always did like dolls, she thought. *And*

maps. Her father was something of a traditionalist; he had been quite pleased about the dolls, until she started making her own . . . and organizing the others into work parties.

The maps, too: she had loved those. Drawing her own lines on them, making her own continents for the elaborate imagined worlds of her daydreams. Then she discovered that you could do that in the *real* world: school trips to the great projects, the tunnel from the Orange River to the Fish, the huge dams along the Zambezi. *Horses and engineering magazines*, she thought wryly. *The twin pillars of my teenage years.*

It had been the newsreels, finally. There wasn't much left to be done south of the Zambezi, or anywhere in Africa—just execution of projects long planned, touching up, factory extensions. But the New Territories, the lands conquered in 1914–1919 . . . ah! She could still shiver at the memory of watching the final breakthrough on the Dead Sea–Mediterranean Canal, the frothing silver water forcing its way through the great turbines, the humm, the *power*. The school texts said the Will to Power was the master-force. True enough . . . but anyone could have power over serfs, all you needed was to be born a citizen. The power to make cultivated land out of a desert, to channel a river, build a city where nothing but a wretched collection of hovels stood —*that* was power! Father had had a future mapped out for her, or so he thought: the Army, of course; an Arts B.A.; then she could marry, and satisfy herself with laying out gardens around the manor. Or if she must, follow some genteel, feminine profession, like architecture . . .

But no, I was going to build, she thought. And here I am, destined to spend the best years of my life laying out tank traps, clearing minefields and blowing things up. Oh, well, the war won't last forever. Russia, Europe . . . we'll have that, and there's room for projects with real *scale*, there.

A trained eye told her that it was time. "Forward," she called. "Wallis, stop fiddling with that radio and bring the spare set. New firing line at the first row of houses." *Or rubble*, her mind added. That was the worst of war—you were adding to entropy rather than fighting it. *Just clearing the way for something better*, she mused, dodging forward. *Hovels, not a decent drain in the place.*

CHAPTER SEVEN

" ... saw little of my father. Home was the servants' quarters of Oakenwald, where I was happy, much of the time. Tantie Sannie fed me and loved me, there were the other children of the House and Quarters to play with, the gardens and the mountainside to explore. Memory is fragmentary before six; it slips away, the consciousness which bore it too alien for the adult mind to re-experience. Images remain only—the great kitchens and Tantie baking biscuits, watching from behind a rosebush as guests arrived for a dance, fascinating and beautiful and mysterious, with their jewels and gowns and uniforms.

A child can know, without the knowledge having meaning. We had numbers on our necks; that was natural. The Masters did not. There were things said among ourselves, never to the Masters. I remember watching Tantie Sannie talk to one of the overseers, and suddenly realizing she's afraid ... The Young Master was my father, and came to give me presents once a year. I thought that he must dislike me, because his face went hard and fixed when he looked at me, and I wondered what I had done to anger him. A terrible thought—my Mother had died bearing me. Had I killed her? Now I know it was just her looks showing in me, but the memory of that grief is with me always. And then he came one night to take me away from all I had known and loved, telling me that it was for the best. Movement, cars and boats, strangers; America, voices I could hardly understand ..."

Daughter to Darkness: A Life
by Anna von Shrakenberg
Houghton & Stoddart, New York, 1978

VILLAGE ONE, OSSETIAN MILITARY HIGHWAY APRIL 14, 1942: 0530 HOURS

Eric cleared the low stone fence with a raking stride. Noise was all around them as they ran: stutter of weapons, explosion blast, screams; the harsh stink of cordite filled his nose, and he felt his mouth open and join in the shout. The rifle stuttered in his hands, three-round bursts from the hip. Behind him he heard Sofie shrieking, a high exultant sound; even the stolid McWhirter was yelling. They plunged among the apple trees, gnarled little things barely twice man height, some shattered to stumps; the Fritz wire was ahead, laneways blasted through it with snake charges. Fire stabbed at them; he flicked a stick-grenade out of his belt, yanked the pin, tossed it.

Automatically, they dove for the dirt. Sofie *ooffed* as the weight of the radio drove her ribs into the ground, then opened up with her light machine-pistol. Assault rifles hammered, but the German fire continued; a round went crack-*whhhit* off a stone in front of his face, knocking splinters into his cheek. Eric swore, then called over his shoulder.

"Neal! Rocket gun!"

The trooper grunted and crawled to one side. The tube of the weapon cradled against her cheek, the rear venturi carefully pointed away from her comrades; her hands tightened on the twin pistol grips, a finger stroked the trigger. *Thump* and the light recoilless charge kicked the round out of the short, smooth-bore barrel. It blurred forward as the fins unfolded; there was a bright streak as the sustainer rocket motor boosted the round up to terminal velocity: *crash* as it struck and exploded. Her partner reached to work the bolt and open the breech, slid in a fresh shell and slapped her on the helmet.

"Fire in the hole!" he called.

Forward again, through the thinning white mist of the smoke barrage, over the rubble of the blasted house. That put them on a level with the housetops, where the village sloped down to the road. He reached for the handset.

"Marie, report."

"Acknowledged. Activity in the mosque, runners going out. Want me to knock it down?"

"Radio?"

"Nothing on the direction-finder since I hit the room with the antennae."

"Hold on the mosque, they'd just put their H.Q. somewhere else, and we're going to need the 120 ammo later. Bring two of the heavies forward, I'll take them over; leave the other four in the line, shift positions, direct fire support on tetrarchy-leader direction. Use the 120's if we spot major targets; keep the road north under observation. And send in the Ronsons and satchelmen—we're going to have to burn and blast some of them out." A different series of clicks. "Tom, close in. Tetrarchy commanders, report."

"Einar here. Lisa's hit, 3rd Tetrarchy's senior decurion's taken over. Working our way in southwest to southeast, then behind the mosque."

Damn! He hoped she wasn't dead; she'd been first in line if *he* "inherited the plantation."

"John here. Same, northwest and hook."

"John, pull in a little and go straight—Tom's going to hit the northeast anyway. We'll split them. I'll be on your left flank. Everybody remember, this is three-dimensional. Work your way down from the roofs as well as up; I'll establish fire positions on commanding locations, move 'em forward as needed. Over."

Eric raised his head over the crest of the rubble. The peculiar smell of fresh destruction was in the air, old dust and dirt and soiled laundry. Ruins needed time to achieve majesty, or even pathos;

right after they had been fought over there was nothing but . . . seediness, and mess. Ahead was a narrow alleyway: nothing moved in it but a starved-looking mongrel, and an overturned basket of clothes that had barely stopped rocking. The locals were going to earth, the crust of posts in the orchard had been overrun, and the bulk of the Fritz were probably bivouacked around the town square: it was the only place in town with anything approaching a European standard of building. Therefore, they would be fanning out toward the noise of combat. Therefore . . .

"Follow me," he said. McWhirter flicked out the bipod of his Holbars, settled it on the ridge and prepared for covering fire. Eric rose and leaped down the shifting slope, loose stone crunching and moving beneath his boots. They went forward, alleys and doors, every window a hole with the fear of death behind it, leapfrogging into support positions. Two waves of potential violence, expanding toward their meeting place like quantum electron shells, waiting for an observer to make them real.

They were panting, bellies tightening for the expected hammer of a Fritz machine pistol that did not come. Then they were across the lane, slamming themselves into the rough wall, plastered flat. That put them out of the line of fire from the windows, but not from something explosive, tossed out. One of the troopers whirled out, slammed his boot into the door, passed on; another tossed a short-fuse grenade through as the rough planks jarred inward.

Blast and fragments vomited out; Eric and Sofie plunged through, fingers ready on the trigger, but not firing: nobody courted a ricochet without need. But the room beyond was bare, except for a few sticks of shattered furniture, a rough pole-ladder to the upper story . . . and a wooden trapdoor in the floor.

That raised a fraction of an inch; out poked a
wooden stick with a rag that might once have been
white. A face followed it, wrinkled, greybearded,
emaciated and looking as old as time. Somewhere
below a child whimpered, and a woman's voice hushed
it, in a language he recognized.

"Nix Schiessen!" the ancient quavered in pid-
gin-german. "Stalino kaputt—Hitler kaputt—*urra*
Drakanski!"

Despite himself, Eric almost grinned; he could
hear a snuffle of laughter from Sofie. The locals seemed
to have learned something about street fighting; also,
their place in the scheme of things. The smile faded
quickly. There was a bleak squalor to the room; it
smelled sourly of privation, ancient poverty, fear.
For a moment his mind was daunted by the thought
of a life lived in a place such as this—at best, endless
struggle with a grudging earth wearing you down
into an ox, with the fruits kept for others. Scuttling
aside from the iron hooves of the armies as they went
trampling and smashing through the shattered gar-
den of their lives, incomprehensible giants, warriors
from nowhere. *The lesson being,* he thought grimly,
that this is defeat, so avoid it.

"Lochos upstairs," he snapped. "Roof, then wait
for me." He motioned the greybeard up with the
muzzle of his assault rifle, switching to fluent Circassian.

"You, old man, come here. The rest get down and
stay down."

The man came forward, shuffling and wavering, in
fear and hunger both, to judge from the look of the
hands and neck and the way his ragged khaftan hung
on his bones. But he had been a tall man once, and
the sound of his own tongue straightened his back a
little.

"Spare our children, honored sir," he began. The
honorific he used was *uork,*; it meant "Lord," and
could be used as an endearment in other circum-

stances. "In the name of Allah the Merciful, the Compassionate—"

The Draka cut him off with a chopping hand, ignoring memories that twisted under his lungs. "If you want mercy, old one, you must earn it. This is the *Dar 'al Harb*, the House of War. *Where are the Germanski?*"

The instructions were valuable—clear, concise, flawed only by a peasant's assumption that every stone in his village was known from birth. Dismissed, he climbed back to his family, into the cellar of their hopes. McWhirter paused above the trapdoor, hefted a grenade and glanced a question. At the Centurion's headshake he turned to the ladder, disappointment obvious in the set of his shoulders.

"McWhiter doesn't like ragheads much, does he, Centurion?" Sofie said as she ran antenna line out the window; the intelligence would have to be spread while it was fresh.

Inwardly, she made a moue of distaste. McWhirter was a veteran, and a man with those medal ribbons was due respect . . . but there was something about him that made her queasy, as if . . .

As if he were like that thing in the Yank magazine— what was it called, Amazing Stories? *Something eaten out of him, so that he wasn't really human anymore.* Not that she was going to say much—the old bastard was always going on about how women were too soft for front-line formations. A roar distracted her for an instant. She looked up, saw wings slash past only a hundred meters up. *Ours,* she thought: Rhino twin-engine ground attack ships, the "flying tanks." Heading north at low altitude, and three flights went over before she glanced down once more. *Going to be some surprised and unhappy Fritz down there in the plains,* she thought.

With a grunt of relief, she turned and rested the

weight of the radio on a lip of rock; the Centurion was facing her, that way they could cover each other's backs. She looked at his face, thoughtful and relaxed now, and remembered the hot metal flying past them with a curious warm feeling low in her stomach. It would be . . . unbearable if that taut perfection were ruined into ugliness, and she had seen that happen to human bodies too often. And . . .

What if he was wounded? Not serious, just a leg wound, and I was the one to carry him out. Images flashed though her mind—gratitude in the cool grey eyes as she lifted his head to her canteen, and—

Oh, shut the fuck up, she told her mind, then started slightly; had she spoken aloud? Good, no. *Almighty Thor, woman, are you still sixteen or what? The last time you had daydreams like that it was about pulling the captain of the field-hockey team out of a burning building. What you really wanted was bed.* That was cheering, since she *had* gotten to bed with *her*.

Eric stood, lost in thought. His mind was translating raw information into tactics and possibilities, while another layer answered the comtech's question about McWhirter: "Well, he *was* in Afghanistan," he said. "Bad fighting. We had to kill three-quarters to get the rest to give up. McWhirter was there eight years, lost a lot of friends."

Sofie shrugged; she was six months past her nineteenth birthday, and that war had been over before her tenth. "How come you understand the local jabber, then?" And to the radio: "Testing, acknowledge."

"Oh, my first concubine was a Circassian; Father gave her to me as a fourteenth birthday present. I was the envy of the county—she cost three hundred aurics." He thrust the memory from him. There was the work of the day to attend to.

"Next . . ."

*   *   *

Standartenfuhrer Felix Hoth awoke, mumbling, fighting a strangling enemy that he only gradually realized was a mass of sweat-soaked bedclothes. Panting, he swung his feet to the floor and hung his head in his hands, the palm-heels pressed against his eyes. *Lieber Herr Gott,* but he'd thought the dreams had stopped. Perhaps it was the vodka last night; he hadn't done that in a while, not since the first month after Moscow. He was back in the tunnels, in the dark, but alone; he could hear their breathing as they closed in on him *and he could not even scream . . .*

"Herr Standartenfuhrer?" The question was repeated twice before it penetrated. It was one of his Slav girls—Valentina, or Tina, whatever; holding out a bottle of Stolichnaya and a glass. The smell of the liquor seized him with a sudden fierce longing, then combined with the odors of sweat and stale semen to make his stomach twist.

"No!" he shouted. His hand sent it crashing to the floor; she stood, cringing, to receive the backhanded slap. "You stupid Russki bitch, how many times do I have to tell you, not in the morning! Fetch coffee and food. Schnell!"

The effort of rage exhausted him; he fought the temptation of a collapse back onto the four-poster bed. Instead, he forced his muscles into movement, walking to the dresser and splashing himself with water from the jug, pouring more from the spirit-heater and beginning to shave. Sometimes he thought she was more trouble than she was worth, that he should find a good orderly, and only send for her when he needed a woman. You expected an *untermensch* to be stupid, but it was what, five months now since he had grabbed her out of that burning schoolhouse in Tula, and she still couldn't speak more than a few words of German. His Russian was better. And she was supposed to have been a teacher!

It showed that Reichsfuhrer Himmler was right: intellectual training had nothing to do with real intelligence—that was in the blood. Or . . . sometimes he wondered if she was as dull as she seemed. Perhaps it would be better just to liquidate her. Two were enough, surely, or there were thousands more . . .

No. That was how Kube had gotten it, up around Minsk: one of them had smuggled an antipersonnel mine under the bed and blown them both to bits. Frightened but not completely desperate, that was the ticket.

Breakfast repaired his spirits; the ration situation was definitely picking up, not like last winter when they'd all been gnawing black bread in the freezing dark. Real coffee, now that the U-boats were keeping the English too busy for blockades; good bacon and eggs and butter and cream. He glanced around the room with satisfaction as he ate; it was furnished with baroque elegance. Pyatigorsk had been a health resort for Tsarist nobles with a taste for medicinal springs at the foot of the Caucasus, and the Commissars had not let it run down. Not bad for a Silesian peasant's son, brought up to touch the cap to the *Herr Rittermeister*; the Waffen-SS offered a career open to the talents, all right. No social distinctions at the Bad Tolz Junkerschul, the officer's training academy. No limits to how high a sound Aryan could rise; in the Wehrmacht he'd have been lucky to make Unteroffizier, with some traitorous monocled "gentleman" telling him what to do.

Well, piss on the regular Army and their opinion of Felix Hoth. Felix Hoth now commanded a regiment of SS-Division "Liebstandarte Adolf Hitler." The Leader's own Guards, the victors of Minsk, Smolensk, Moscow, Kharkov, Astrakhan. The elite of the New Order . . . and just finishing its conversion from a motorized infantry brigade to a Panzer division. He glanced at the mantel clock with its plump cupids. 0530. Good, another half hour and he'd roust the second Panzergrenadier battalion out—surprise inspection and a four-kilometer run. Good lads, but the new recruits needed stiffening. Not many left of the cadre—not many of the men who had jumped off from Poland a year ago. And as soon as they finished refitting they'd be back in the line—real fighting out on the Sverdlosk front instead of this chickenshit anti-partisan work.

The situation reports had come up with breakfast; they were a real pleasure. The trickle of equipment from the captured Russian factories was turning into a steady flow, not like the old days when the Wehrmacht had grudged the SS every bayonet, and they'd had to make do with Czech and French booty. The SS could improvise; if the supply lines to the Fatherland were long, seize local potential! Ivan equipment: their armor and artillery were first-rate. He winced at the memory of trying to stop that first Russian T-34 with a 37mm antitank gun.

Burning pine forest, the smell like a mockery of Christmas fires. Burning trucks and human flesh, the human wave of Russian troops in their mustard-yellow uniforms, arms linked. *Urra! Urra!* The machine guns scythed them down, artillery firing point-blank, blasting huge gaps in their line, bits and pieces of human flung through the forest and hanging from the trees . . . and the tank, low, massive, unstoppable, its broad tracks grinding through the swamp.

Aim, range 800, pull the lanyard . . . crack-*whang*! He'd frozen for a moment in sheer disbelief, the reload in his hand. A clean hit, and the thick-sloped plate had shed it into the trees like . . . like a tennis ball. Left only a shallow gouge, crackling and red as it cooled. Coming on, shot after shot rebounding, grinding over the gun, cutting Friedrich in half.

He'd lain there looking up and not even bleeding for
a second, then it had all come out . . .

Hoth looked down at his right hand; half the little
finger was missing. He had been very lucky; jumping
on the deck of a tank and ramming a grenade down
the muzzle of its cannon was not something you did
with any great hope of survival. Automatic, really;
not thinking of living, or of the Knight's Cross and
the promotion . . .

With a smile on his thick-boned, stolid face he
strode to the window and pulled open the drapes.
There they were, spread out in leaguer three stories
below, across the tread-chewed lawns of what had
once been a nobleman's park. Dawn was just break-
ing, reaching beams to gild the squat, grey-steel
shapes, throw shadows from the hulls and long can-
non. Tanks in the outer ring, then the assault guns,
infantry carriers (praise Providence, all the motor-
ized infantry on tracks at last!), soft transport. Rus-
sian designs, much of it. Improved, brought into line
with German practice, pouring out of Kharkov and
Stalingrad and Kirovy Rog, with technicians from
Krupp and Daimler-Benz to organize, and overseers
from the SS Totenkopf squads with stock-whips to
see that the Russian workers did not flag at their
eighteen-hour days.

Not really necessary to pull into hedgehog like
this, but it was good practice and the partisans seemed
damnably well informed. Suicide parties with explo-
sive charges had infiltrated more than once. *Perhaps
more hostages*, he thought, turning to the east and
taking a deep breath of fresh, crisp spring air with a
pleasant undertang of diesel oil.

The aircraft were difficult to spot, coming in low
out of the dawning sun. He squinted, his first thought
that it was a training flight . . .

The smile slid slowly off his face. Too many, too
fast, too low; at least 450 km/h, hedgehopping over

poplars and orchards. Two engines, huge radials; low-wing monoplanes, their noses bristling with muzzles, long teardrop canopies . . . *One 50mm autocannon, six 25mm,* the Luftwaffe intelligence report ran through his head. *Five tonnes of bombs, rockets, jellied petrol* . . . Draka ground-attack aircraft, P-12 "Rhino" class. The nominal belligerence of the Domination had suddenly become very real.

There was no time to react; the first flight came in for its strafing run even as the alarm klaxon began to warble. He could hear the heavy *dumpa-dumpa-dumpa* of the 50mm's, see the massive frames of the Rhinos shudder in the air with recoil. Crater lines stitched through the mud, meaty *smacks* as the tungsten-cored solid shot rammed into wet earth, then the heavy *chunk* as they struck his tanks, into the thinner side and deck armor. The lighter autocannon were a continuous orange flicker, stabbing into the soft-skinned transport. Something blew up with a muffled *thump*, a soft soughing noise and flash; petrol tanker, spraying burning liquid for meters in every direction. Vehicles were flaming all over the fields about the house, fuel and ammunition exploding, early-morning fireworks as tracer and incendiary rounds shot through the sky trailing smoke. The crews were pouring out of hutments, racing through the rain of metal to their tanks and carriers, and falling, their bodies jerking in the grotesque dance of human flesh caught in automatic-weapons fire. The attackers were past; then another wave, and the first returning, looping for a second pass.

"*Todentanz,*" he murmured. *Dance of death.* The telephone rang: he picked it up and began the ritual of questions and orders, because there was nothing else to do. And nothing of use *to* do; this was a quiet sector, and he had been stripped of most of his antiaircraft for the east, where the enemy still had some planes. The rest were *flackpanzers,* out there with the rest . . .

Engine rumble added to the din of blast and shouts;
some of the Liebstandarte troopers were reaching
their machines, and a percentage of crews were al-
ways on duty. A four-barreled 20mm opened up, one
of the new self-propelled models. The ball turret
traversed, hosing shells into the air; a Draka airplane
took that across a belly whose skin was machined
from armorplate, shrugged it off in a shower of sparks.
Another was not so lucky, the canopy shattering as
the gun caught it banking into a turn. Unguided, it
cartwheeled into a barracks; building and wreck van-
ished in a huge, orange-black ball of flame as its load
of destruction detonated. The blast blew the diamond-
pane windows back on either side of him, shattering
against the stone walls. He could feel the heat of it
on his face, like a summer sun after too long at the
swimming-baths, when the skin has begun to burn,
taut and prickling. Another Rhino wheeled and fired
a salvo of rockets from its underwing racks into the
flackpanzer that had killed its wingmate. Twisted
metal burned when the cloud of powdered soil cleared,
and now the others were dropping napalm, cannisters
tumbling to leave trails of inextinguishable flame in
their wake, yellow surf-walls that buried everything
in their path . . .
Standartenfuhrer Hoth had been a young fanatic a
year ago. Only a year ago, but no man could be
young again who had walked those long miles from
Germany to the Kremlin; who had stood to break the
death ride of the Siberian armor as it drove for
encircled Moscow; who had survived the final night-
mare battles through the burning streets, flushing
NKVD holdout battalions from the prison-cellars of
the Lubyanka . . . That year had taken his youth; his
fanaticism it had honed, tempered with caution, sharp-
ened with realism. His face was sweat-sheened, but
it might have been carved from ivory as he held the
field telephone in a white-fingered grip.

"Shut up. They are not attacking the barracks because they are at the limit of operational range and must concentrate on priority targets," he said tonelessly. "Get me Schmidt."

The line buzzed and clicked for a moment, but the switchboard in the basement was secure. *Probably overloaded, to be sure,* came a mordant thought. One part of his mind was raging, longing to run screaming into the open, firing his pistol at the black-grey vulture shapes. He could see the squadron markings as some of them flew by the manor at scarcely more than rooftop height; see the winged flame-lizard that was the enemy's national emblem, with the symbolic sword of death and the slave-chain of mastery in its claws.

Fafnir, he thought. *The reptile cunning, patience to wait until all the enemies are weakened . . .*

And another part wished simply to weep, for grief of loss at the destruction of his work, his love, the beautiful and deadly instrument he had helped to forge . . .

"Sch-Schmidt here," a voice at the other end of the line gasped. "Standartenfuhrer, air raid—"

"And Stalin is dead, is this news?" he used the sarcasm deliberately, as a whip of ice.

"No—sir, Divisional H.Q. in Krasnodar, too, and, and—reports from the Gross Deutschland in Grozny, the Luftwaffe . . ."

"Silence." His voice was flat, but it produced a quiet that echoed. The sound of aircraft engines was fading; the raid was already history. You did not fight history, you used it. He looked south, to the pass.

"You will attempt to contact Hauptsturmfuhrer Keilig in the village. There will be no reply, but keep trying."

"Ja wohl, Herr Standartenfuhrer."

"Call Division. Inform them that the Ossetian Military Highway is under attack by air-assault troops."

"But, Standartenfuhrer, how—"

"Silence." An instant. "You will find Hauptman Schtackel, or his immediate subordinate if he is dead or incapacitated. Tell him to prepare a reconnaissance squadron of Puma armored cars; also my command car, or a vehicle with equivalent communications equipment. By exactly—" He looked at the clock, still ticking serenely between its pink-cheeked plaster godlets. "—0600 hours, I wish to be under way. He is also to begin formation of a *Kampfgruppe* of at least battalion size from intact formations, jump-off time to be no later than 1440 hours today. I will have returned and will be in command of the kampfgruppe. Should I fail to return, Obersturmbannfuhrer Keistmann is to exercise his discretion until orders arrive from H.Q." His voice lost its metronomic quality. "*Is that clear?*"

"Zum Befehl, Herr Standartenfuhrer!"

He replaced the receiver with a soft click and turned from the scene of devastation; his eyes had never left it for an instant during the conversation. Turning, he saw that the girl Tina had returned. "Leave the tray, I will be finishing it," he said. A soldier ate when he could, in the field. "Fetch my camouflage fatigues and kit. Have them ready here within ten minutes."

He paused in the doorway, to give the fires smoking beyond one last glance. "My loyalty is my honor," he quoted to himself, murmuring: the SS oath. "If nothing else, there is always that."

Valentina Fedorova made very sure that the footsteps were not returning before she crossed to the folder and began to leaf through it with steady, systematic speed. Her fluent German she had learned in the Institute; almost as a hobby, she had a gift for languages. The memory that made a quick scan almost as effective as the impossible camera was a gift as well, one that had been very useful these past few months. Not that she had expected much besides a little, little revenge before she was inevitably found out, before the drum was beaten in the town square for another flogging to the death. She raised the lid of the coffeepot, worked her mouth, spat copiously. Then she crossed to the window, allowing herself the luxury of one long, joyous look before laying out the uniform. She smiled.

It was the first genuine smile in a long time.

"Burn," she whispered. "Burn."

It was odd, Eric thought, how it was easy to remember the mind's construct of a battle, the shape and direction of it, when the personal faded into a blur of shapes, sounds, smells, sharp bursts of emotion. Not what you might expect; after all, a "battle" was a thing you made in your mind, while street fighting was continuous alertness, total focus, reflexes key-triggered for the death that waited around every corner and behind every door.

The men of the Liebstandarte had outnumbered the Draka, but they had been surprised, too shaken to establish a perimeter before the paratroops were in among them—

Sofie's eyes had widened. The muzzle of her machine pistol had come up, straight at him; time froze, the burst cracked past his ear, powder grains burnt his cheek. He wheeled to watch the Fritz tumble down the steps dropping his carbine, clutching at a belly ripped open by the soft-nosed 10mm slugs.

The wounded man's mouth worked. "Mutti," he whispered, eyes staring disbelief at the life leaking out between his fingers. "Mutti, hilfe, mutti—"

A three-round burst from Eric's rifle hammered him back into silence.

Eric looked up, met Sophie's eyes. She was smiling, but not the usual cocksure urchin grin; a softer expression, almost tremulous. Quickly, she glanced aside.

Well, well, he thought. Then: *Oh, not now.* Aloud, he murmured, "Thanks; good thing you've got steady hands."

"Ya, ah, c'mon, let's get up those stairs, hey?" she muttered, leading the way with a smooth steady stride that took her up the board steps noiselessly, even under the heavy load of the backpack radio.

The resistance had been disorganized, split into pockets. But the pockets had held out, squads and sections and lone snipers fighting with a stolid determination to make their enemy pay a price for the victory, to cost him precious time that might have been used to consolidate against counterattack. The overwhelming firepower of the assault rifles and rocket guns had told, as Eric switched sticks of paratroopers back and forth in a fluid dance. Building local superiority against an opponent denied mobility by the Draka heavy weapons, which raked the streets with fire at the first sight of a German uniform.

The 15mm had hammered beside his ear; for a moment part of him wondered how much combat it would take to damage his hearing. This was worse than working in a drop-forging plant. His mouth was dry, filled with a thick saliva no swallowing could clear; there was water in his canteen, but no time for it. The rifles of his lochos took it up, hammering at the narrow slit window twenty meters away, keeping the Fritz machine-gunner from manning his post. The light high-velocity 5mm rounds skittered off in spark-trails; heavy 15mm bullets chewed at the stone, tattering it with craters.

"Damn hovels are built like forts!" one of the troopers snarled, as the ammunition drum of his Holbars emptied and automatically ejected. He scrabbled at his belt for the last replacement, slapped the guide lips into the magazine well, and jacked the cocking lever.

"They *are* forts," McWhirter grunted. "Sand coons are treacherous. Don't sleep easy without bunkers and firing-slits 'tween them and the neighbors."

Serfdom was too easy on them, he thought viciously. It was the smells that brought it back—rancid mutton fat and spices, sweaty wool and kohl. You could never trust ragheads—Afghans or Circassians or Turks or whatever; they kept coming back at you. Better to herd them all into their mosque and turn the Ronsons on them. He remembered that, from the Panjir Valley in Afghanistan; reprisals for an ambush by the *badmash,* the guerillas.

The Draka had found the drivers of the burnt-out trucks with their testicles stuffed into their mouths . . . Ten villages for that; he'd pulled the plunger on the flamer himself. The women had tried to push their children out the slit windows when the roof caught, flaming bundles on hands dissolving into flame as he washed the jet of napalm across them, limestone subliming and burning in the heat. He saw that often, waking and asleep.

One hand snuggled the butt of his Holbars into his shoulder while the other held the pistol-grip; he was trying for deflection shots, aiming at the windowframe to bounce rounds inside. Tracer flicked out; he clenched his teeth and tasted sweat running down the taut-trembling muscles of his face. *"Kill them all,"* he muttered, not conscious of the whisper. Figures writhed in his mind, Germans melting into burning villagers into shadowed figures in robes and turbans with long knives into prisoners sewn into raw pigskins and left in the desert sun. "Kill them all."

"Sven, *short bursts*, unless you've got a personal ammo store about you," he added with flat normality. The trooper beside him nodded, turned to look at the noncom, turned back sweating to the sight-picture through the x4 of his assault rifle. It was considerably more reassuring than a human voice coming out of the thing McWhirter's face had momentarily become.

Below them two paratroopers crawled, down in the mud and sheep dung of the alley. One had a smooth oblong box strapped to her back; a hose was connected to the thing she pushed ahead—an object like a thick-barreled weapon with twin grips. Four meters from the window, and she was in the dead ground below it, below the angle the gunner could reach without leaning out . . . and in more danger from the supporting fire than the enemy.

"Cease fire!" McWhirter and Eric called, in perfect unison; gave each other gaunt smiles as silence fell for an instant. Then the flamethrower spoke, a silibant roar in the narrow street. Hot orange at the core, flame yellow, bordered by smoke that curled black and filthy, the tongue of burning napalm stretched for the blackened hole. Dropped through it, spattering: most of a flamer's load was still liquid when it hit the target. And it would burn on contact with air and cling, impossible to quench.

Flame belched back out of the window. A pause, then screams—screams that went on and on. Wreathed in fire, a human figure fell out over the sill to writhe and crackle for an instant, then slump still. A door burst open and two more men ran shrieking into the street, their uniforms and hair burning; the gunner at the 15mm cut them down with a single merciful burst.

Senior Decurion McWhirter turned to curse the waste of ammunition, closed his mouth at her silent glare, shrugged, and followed the rest as they jogged down the lane and waited while the pointman dropped to the ground and peered around the corner.

"Love those Ronsons," he said, using the affectionate cigarette-lighter nickname. "Damn having women in a combat zone anyway," he grumbled more quietly. "Too fucking sentimental, if you ask me."

Eric smiled, checking the level of the rounds in

his Holbars through the translucent rear face of the magazine. He was glad of the excuse to avoid looking at the still-smoldering corpses; unfortunately, there was no way of avoiding the burnt-pork stink of it.

"Times change, Senior Decurion. Hell, we gave 'em the vote in 1832. A hundred years was enough to have the privilege without the responsibility."

"Did well enough in the last war, keeping them in support formations," McWhirter replied, turning to keep the rooftops under observation. You could never count on ground in a built-up area; it didn't *stay* taken.

"We weren't fighting the Fritz, then, either. Mostly the Abduls." He paused. "Off to Legate Kaine, if you please, Decurion; my compliments, and she's to hand over two of the 120's for deployment here on the edge of the square. We'll need something heavy to get at the holdouts in the mosque and town hall."

McWhirter grunted again. "Meier, Huff, follow me."

Sofie stuck out her tongue at his departing back. "Old fart," she muttered, then brightened. Marie Kaine did not like McWhirter, and McWhirter detested the newfangled recoilless weapons with their murderous backblast. It would not be a happy time for him. She busied herself with the radio. Reception was tricky with all this stone around, but you could usually get around it, using metal guttering or something similar as an aeriel.

The last pocket had fallen around 0600. The sight of the watch had been a shock; he was familiar with the rubber time of combat, but even so he would have expected an hour or two at least. Eric stood on the minaret of the one-time mosque, looking out through shattered stone lacework and tile. The view was excellent, except where thick columns of black smoke rose from the ruins of burning buildings; he noted absently that there had to be an observation

post here ... Very few of the *Liebstandarte* had
surrendered unwounded; it was a pity that they had
to shoot the ones who did. They fought well, but
there were no facilities.

The water was incredibly sweet; he swilled the
first mouthful about, spat it out, drank. His body
seemed less to drink than to absorb, leaving him
conscious of every vein, down to his toes. He was
abruptly aware of his own sweat, itching and stink-
ing; of the black smudges of soot on hands and face,
the irritating sting of a minor splinter-wound on his
leg. The helmet was a monstrous burden. He shed
it, and the clean mountain wind made a benediction
through the dense tawny cap of his cropped hair.
Suddenly he felt light, happy, tension fading out of
the muscles of neck and shoulders.

"Report to Cohort," he said. "Phase A complete.
Then get me the tetrarchy commanders." They re-
ported in, routine until the Sapper tetrarch's.

"Yo?"

"Seems the Fritz were using the place as some
sort of supply dump," Marie Kaine said.

"What did we get?"

"Well, about three thousand board-feet of lumber,
for a start. Had a truck rigged to an improvised
circular saw—nice piece of work. Then there's a
couple of hundred two-meter lengths of angle-iron, a
shitload of barbed wire ... and some prisoners in a
wire pen, most of them in sad shape." A pause. "Also
about a tonne of explosives."

"Loki on a jumping-jack, I'm glad they didn't re-
member to blow *that* bundle of Father Christmas'
store."

"Exactly: it's about half loose stuff—some sort of
blasting material that looks civilian. Russian mark-
ings, cyrillic. And the rest is ammunition—105mm
howitzer shells, propellant and bursting charges both.
Lots of wire and detonators, too. Must have been

planning some construction through here. And blankets, about a week's worth of rations for a Cohort, medical supplies . . ."

He turned to the south, studying the valley as it narrowed toward the village in which he stood. It was a great, steep-sided funnel, whose densely wooded slopes crowded closer and closer to the single road. His mind was turning over smoothly, almost with delight. His hand bore down on the send-button.

"Is McWhirter with you? Look, Marie, see you in front of the mosque in ten. Tell McWhirter to meet us there, with the old raghead; he'll know who I mean. Tell him *absolutely* no damage. Tetrarchy commanders conference, main square, ten minutes. Oh, and throw some supplies into that holding cage." He looked up to see Sofie regarding him quizzically.

"Another brilliant flash, Centurion?" she said. He was looking very, well, *alive* now. Some men's faces got that way in combat, but the Centurion's just went more ice-mask when they were fighting. It was when he came up with something tricky that it lighted up, a half-smile and lights dancing behind the grey eyes. *Damn, but yo're pretty when you think,* she reflected wryly. Not something you could say out loud.

"Maybe. See if you can get me through to Logistics at division." He waited for a moment for the patch-relay; the first sound through the receiver was a blast of gunfire. Whoever held the speaker was firing one-handed as he acknowledged the call.

"Centurion von Shrakenberg here. Problems?"

"No," the voice came back. "Not unless you count a goddamned Fritz counterattack and a third of my people shot up before they hit the fuckin' ground—" The voice broke off: more faintly Eric could hear screams, a rocket-gun shell exploding, a shouted instruction, *"They're behind that bloody tank hulk—"*

The quartermaster's voice returned, slightly breathless: "But apart from that, all fine. What do you need, besides the assigned load?"

"Engineering supplies, if you have any—wire, explosives, hand tools, sandbags. More Broadsword directional mines if you can spare them, and any Fritz material available." He paused. "Petrol—again, if there is any. We're the farthest element south; unless we stop them, you're going to be getting it right up the ass. Can do?"

"What are you going to do with all . . . never mind." The Draka had a tradition of decentralized command, which meant trusting an officer to accomplish the assigned tasks in his own fashion. "Will if we can—as soon as the tactical situation here is under control. It depends on how much Fritz stuff gets captured intact . . ."

CHAPTER EIGHT

" ... had been an expatriate for twenty years; I was no stranger to culture shock. For an American to live among Draka was something different: eerie echoes, visions of might-have-beens, twisted alien developments from common roots. Even the language had a disturbing pseudo-familiarity: a Southern dialect, which was not surprising considering how many of the Loyalist founders had been from below the Mason-Dixon line, but more archaic than any I had heard in the U.S., full of Dutch and French and German loan-words and turns of phrase, even of Africanisms.

That made the true differences all the harder to see, much less to accept. The environment into which I was plunged was not simply unAmerican, or even anti-American; it was an anti-America, the place where all the historical experiences which had formed my past had turned out the other way. Even in the most fetid backwaters of Mississippi or Guatemala, Americans paid at least lip-service to the ideals of Jefferson and Paine and Lincoln; even the most reactionary Roosevelt-hating anti-New Dealer couched his arguments in terms of individualism, progress, or States' Rights. The Domination showed how much in common a left-wing Democrat like me had with Chamber of Commerce Republicans, with my late employer the Colonel in Chicago, or even the small-town Daughters of *the American Revolution. At times I found myself longing even for the provincial drabness, prudery, piety, and hypocrisy that had driven me to New York and then Europe in the first place. Here were a people genuinely without bourgeois sentimentality or moralism, and I found I liked the result far less than I might have expected.*

But revulsion could never be unalloyed. Savagery and depravity, yes. An icy concentration on the means of power that both awed and disgusted me; so much human energy and intelligence, wasted. Yet, unwillingly, I also had to conceed the Domination's accomplishments. Far too many humane and rational men had neglected and despised military power, and left us helpless before totalitarian aggression. The Draka were never helpless; not simply because they were militarists, but because they refused to delude themselves to avoid effort and pain. Their aristocrats were mostly honest and honorable men by their own standards; however brutal and regressive their code, they lived by it, worked for it, were ready to die for it. They dreamed grandly, and accomplished much; if their serfs were so much machinery, so many work-animals to them, then they were carefully tended machinery and well-kept animals. There is no substitute for freedom; I kept my faith that we would solve our problems through it, but I was sometimes uneasily aware that there were some in the U.S.—sharecroppers, slumdwellers, the peons of the Guatemalan coffee fincas—who might have been willing to change places for the assurance of food and medicine and a roof. Nor was all of the surplus squeezed from the workers spent on war and repression and luxury. The Draka truly loved beauty and hated ugliness and vulgarity and waste. Much that they built and made had a haunting loveliness. In the end only this was certain: these were not my people, and I wanted to go home . . ."

Empires of the Night: A '40's Journal
by William A. Dreiser
MacMillan, New York, 1956

VILLAGE ONE, OSSETIAN MILITARY
HIGHWAY APRIL 14, 1942: 0700 HOURS

CRACK went the bullet, then spang-winnnnnnng off the stone.

Reflexively, Dreiser froze as spalled-off microfragments of stone drove into his forehead. A hand grabbed him by the back of his webbing-harness and yanked him down behind the ruined wall. He controlled his shaking with an effort, drawing in deep drafts of air that smelled of wet rock and barnyard, blinking sunlight out of his eyes. The closest he had come to the *sharp end* before was reporting on the German *blitzkrieg* through western Europe in 1940, but that had been done from the rear. Comfortable war reporting, with a car and an officer from the Propaganda section; interviews with generals, watching heavy artillery pounding away and ambulances bringing casualties back to the clearing stations. For that matter, it might be some of the same men shooting at him; he had followed the German Sixth Army through Belgium, and here he was meeting them again in Russia.

"Thanks," he said shakily to the NCO.

"Yo' was drawin' fire," the Draka decurion replied absently, crawling to a gap and cautiously glancing around, head down at knee-level, squinting against the young sun in the east.

Panting, the American put his back to the stones of the wall and watched the Draka. There were six: the other four members of the decurion's stick and a rocket-gun team of two. They lay motionless on the slope of rubble—motionless except for their eyes, flicking ceaselessly over the buildings before them. Mottled uniforms and helmet-covers blended into the mud-covered rock of the ruined building. He had picked this stick as typical, to do a few human-interest stories. It *was* typical, near enough: four men and three women, average age nineteen and three-quarters. Average height and weight five-eleven and 175 pounds for the males, five-six and 140 for the females. A redhead, two blonds, the rest varying shades of brown.

That much he could have gotten from a handbook. He had spent much of the winter getting to know A Century: the standard thing, get to know them as people, do articles on their background and families and so forth to build reader identification through "human interest," then show them fighting. Not easy, since Draka were xenophobes by habit, and detested the United States and all its works in particular by hereditary tradition. It had helped that Eric and he got along well—the Centurion was a popular officer. Trying his best to keep up did more.

Although my best wasn't very good, he admitted ruefully to himself, even though he was in the best condition he could remember. It was all a matter of priorities; the wealth and leisure to produce these soldiers had been wrung out of whole continents. He focused on one trooper . . .

Cindy, his mind prompted him. *Cindy McAlistair.* Although nobody called her anything but Tee-Hee.

Fox-colored hair, green eyes, a narrow, sharp-featured face—Scots-Irish, via the Carolina piedmont. Her grandfather had been a Confederate refugee in 1866, had escaped from Charleston in one of the last Draka blockade-runners, those lean craft that had smuggled in so many repeating rifles and steam warcars. He had established a plantation in the rich lands north of Luanda, just being opened by railways and steam-coaches for coffee and cotton.

His granddaughter rested easily, one knee crooked

and a hand beneath her; it might have looked awkward, if Dreiser had not seen her do six hundred one-hand pushups in barracks once, on a bet. Sweat streaked the black war paint on her face, dark except for a slight gleam of teeth. The Holbars rested beside her, the assault-sling over her neck; her hand held the pistol-grip, resting amid a scatter of empty aluminum cartridge cases and pieces of belt-link.

The dimpled bone hilt of a throwing-knife showed behind her neck, from a sheath sewn into the field jacket, and she was wearing warsaps—fingerless leather gloves with black-metal insets over knuckles and palm-edge—secured by straps up the forearms. For the rest, standard gear: lace-up boots with composition soles; thick tough cotton pants and jacket, with leather patches at knee and elbow and plenty of pockets; helmet with cloth cover; a harness of laced panels around the waist that reached nearly to the ribs, and supported padded loops over the shoulders. A half-dozen grenades, blast and fragmentation. Canteen, with messkit, entrenching tool, three conical drum magazines of ammunition, field-dressing, ration bars, folding toolkit for maintenance, and a few oddments. Always including spare tampons: *"If yo' don't have 'em, sure as fate yo' gonna need 'em, then things get plain disgustin'."*

The whole oufit had the savage, stripped-down practicality he had come to associate with the Draka. This was an inhumanly functional civilization, not militarist in the sense of strutting, bemedaled generals and parades, but with a skilled appreciation of the business of conquest, honed by generations of experience and coldly unsentimental analysis.

The decurion completed his survey and withdrew his head with slow care; rapid movement attracted the eye.

"Snipah," he said. "Bill-boy, Tee-hee, McThing—"
The three troopers looked up. "Yo' see him?"

Cindy giggled, the sound that had given her the
nickname. "Cross t' street, over that-there first
buildin', row a' windows?"

"*Ya*. We're gonna winkel him. You three, light out
soon's we lay down fire. *Jo!*" The rocket gunner
raised his head. "Center window, can do?"

The man eased his eye to the scope sight and
scanned. There was a laneway, then a cleared field of
sorts, scrap-built hutments for odds and ends, blocks
of stone and rubble. Then square-built stone houses,
on the rubble-pile; the second row of houses stood
atop those but set back, leaving a terrace of rooftop.
Distance about two hundred meters, and the win-
dows were slits . . .

"No problem hittin' roundabouts, can't say's I'll
get it *in*. Hey, dec, maybe more of 'em?"

"Na," the NCO snapped. "Would've opened up on
us 'fore we got to this-here wall. Just one, movin' from
window t' window. Wants us to get close. Jenny,
ready with t' SAW. *Now!*"

The rocket gun went off, *whump*-sssssst-*crash*. The
decurion and the trooper with the light machine gun
came to their knees, slapped the bipods of their
weapons onto the low parapet of the stone wall, and
began working automatic fire along the line of slit
windows.

And the three troopers *moved*. Lying with his
back to the wall, Dreiser had a perfect view; they
bounced forward, not bothering to come to their
feet, flinging themselves up with a flexing of arm and
legs, hurdled the wall without pausing, hit the other
side with legs pumping and bodies almost horizontal,
moving like broken-field runners. Dreiser twisted to
follow them, blinking back surprise. No matter how
often it was demonstrated, it was always a shock to

realize how *strong* these people were, how fast and flexible and coordinated. It was not the ox-muscled bull massiveness of the Janissaries he'd seen, but leopard strength. *Twenty years*, he reminded himself. Twenty years of scientific diet and a carefully graduated exercise program; they had been running assault courses since before puberty.

And—he had been holding his hands over his ears against the grinding rattle of automatic-weapons fire. The rocket gun fired again; the whole frontage along the row of windows was shedding sparks and dust and stone fragments.

He must have tripped, was the American's first thought. So quickly, in a single instant that slipped by before his attention could focus, the center Draka was down.

Dreiser could see him stop, as if his headlong dash had run into a stone wall; he could even see the exit wound, red and ragged-edged in his back. Two more shots struck him, and the trooper fell bonelessly, twitched once and lay still.

No dramatic spinning around, he thought dazedly. *Just . . . dead.*

Beside him, the machine gunner grunted as if struck in the stomach; the American remembered she had been the fallen trooper's lover. Her hand went out to grip the bipod and her legs tensed to charge, until the decurion's voice cracked out.

"None of that-there shit, he *dead*." He nodded grimly at her white-mouthed obedience, then added: "Cease fire. Tee-Hee 'n McThing there by now."

Dreiser jerked his head back up; the other two Draka had vanished. The sudden silence rang impossibly loud in his ears, along with the beat of blood; there was a distant chatter of fire from elsewhere in the village. It had been so *quick*—alive one second, dead the next. And it was only the second time in his

life he had seen violent death; the first had been . . .
yes, 1934, the rioting outside the Chamber of Depu-
ties in Paris, when the *Camelots du Roi* had tried to
storm the government buildings. A bystander had
been hit in the head by a police bullet and fallen
dead at his feet, and he had looked down and thought
that could have been me. Less random here, but the
same sense of *inconsequentialness*. You never really
imagined death could happen to you; something like
this made you realize it could, not in some comfort-
ably distant future, but right *now*, right *here*, at any
moment. That no amount of skill or precaution could
prevent it . . .

Beside him, the decurion was muttering. "If that-
there snipah knows his business, he outa there by
now. Maybe not; maybe he just sharp-eyed and don't
scare easy. Then he stay, try fo' anothah . . ."

Seconds crawled. Dreiser mopped at the sweat
soaking into his mustache, and started to relax; it was
less than an hour since the attack began, and already
he felt bone-weary. Fumes of cordite and rocket
propellant clawed at the lining of his nose and throat.
Adrenaline exhaustion, he thought. Draka claimed
to be able to control it, with breathing exercises and
meditation and such-like; it had all sounded too Yoga-
like, too much a product of the warrior-mystic syn-
drome for his taste. *Maybe I should have—*

There was a grenade blast; dust puffed out of
the narrow windows of the house from which the
sniper had fired. Almost instantly two blasts of
assault-rifle fire stuttered within; the Draka tensed.
A trapdoor flipped open on the roof and one of
the troopers vaulted out, doing a quick four-way
scan-and-cover. Then she crawled to the edge and
called:

"Got the snipah! What about Bill-boy?"

The decurion cupped a hand around his mouth,

rising to one knee. "Bill-boy is expended," he shouted. "Hold and cover."

Expended. Dreiser's mind translated automatically: dead. More precisely, killed in action; if you died by accident or sickness you *skipped*.

Jenny, the machine gunner, rolled over the wall and crouched, covering the roofs behind them. The other Draka rose and scrambled forward, moving at a fast trot, well spread out; at the body two of them stooped, grabbed the straps of the dead man's harness and half-carried, half-dragged him to the shelter of the wall. Dreiser noted with half-queasy fascination how the body moved, head and limbs and torso still following the pathways of muscle and sinew with a disgusting naturalness. The back of his uniform glistened dark and wet; when they turned him over and removed the helmet, Dreiser noted for the first time how loss of blood and the relaxation of sudden death seemed to take off years of age. Alive, he had seemed an adult, a man—a hard and dangerous man at that, a killer. Dead, there was only a sudden vast surprise in the drying eyes; his head rolled into his shoulder, as a child nuzzles into the pillow.

The others of the stick were stripping his weapons and ammunition with quick efficiency. Jenny paused to close his eyes and mouth and kiss his lips, then touched her fingers to his blood and drew a line between her brows with an abrupt, savage gesture.

This was not a good man, Dreiser thought. And he had been fighting for a bad cause; not the worst, but the Domination was horror enough in its own right. Yet someone had carried him nine months below her heart; others had spent years diapering him, telling him bedtime stories, teaching him the alphabet . . . He remembered an evening two months ago in Mosul; they had just come in from a field problem, out of the cold mud and the rain and back to the barracks. There had been an impromptu party—coffee and brandy and astonishingly fine singing. Dreiser had sat with his back in a corner, nursing a hot cup and his blisters and staying out of the way, forgotten and fascinated.

This one, the one they called Bill-boy, had started a dance—a folk dance of sorts. It looked vaguely Afro-Celtic to Dreiser, done with a bush-knife in each hand, two-foot chopping blades, heavy and razor sharp. He had danced naked to the waist, the steel glittering in the harsh, bare-bulb lights; the others had formed a circle around him, clapping and cheering while the fiddler scraped his bow across the strings and another slapped palms on a zebra-hide drum held between his knees. The dancer had whirled, the edges cutting closer and closer to his body; had started to improvise to the applause, a series of pirouettes and handsprings, backflips and cartwheels, laughing as sweat spun off his glistening skin in jewelled drops. Laughing with pleasure in strength and skill and . . . well, it was a Draka way of looking at it, but yes, beauty.

How am I supposed to make "human interest" out of this? ran through him. How the *fuck* am I supposed to do that? How am I supposed to make this real to the newspaper readers in their bungalows? Should I? If there was some way of showing them war directly, unfiltered, right in their living rooms, they'd *never* support a war. And it *is* necessary. They *must* support the war, or afterwards we'll be left alone on a planet run by Nazis or the Domination, and nothing to fight them with . . .

Shaking his head wearily, he followed the Draka into the building.

The sniper lay beside his weapon, a clumsy-looking, long-barreled automatic rifle with a scope sight. He was still alive, which was astonishing; a burst had caught him across the lower pelvis, and the light, high-velocity bullets of the Holbars had tumbled on impact, chewing and ripping their way through bone and meat. By some miracle none of the major veins and arteries had been cut, although the German was lying in a slowly widening pool of red, trickling away between the loosely fitted floorboards. The bowel had not been cut either. The smells were the salt of blood, and a sickeningly familiar odor Dreiser recognized from his Iowa childhood, from hog-butchering time. His mouth flooded with gummy saliva, and the skin of his forehead went cold and tight.

The big room was dark, its back to the east and the morning sun. There were cots and crates, tumbled equipment; a fire was burning in one corner, adding a reddish-orange tinge to the trickles of light from the slit windows and the hole knocked by a rocket-gun shell. The SS sniper's face twitched, young and regular with close-cropped fair hair, much like the folk who had killed him—a comeliness unbearable next to the grey and pink hideousness of the wound. Forcing down his gorge the American correspondent knelt, turning his head aside to present his ear and catch the words that trickled out, and also to avoid the sight.

The Draka had paused for a moment around the body, except for the lookouts, and even so they were positioned to cover the entrances.

"What's he sayin'?" the decurion asked, idly curious. "That's not German."

Dreiser looked up, swallowing again. "It's Latin. He's praying."

The man snorted, pushed a toe under the sniper's rifle and flicked it upright. "Tokarev," he said, examining it. Louder: "Sa, yo' people, we gotta war t' fight. Police it up, don't leave anythin' fo' the ragheads, let's get goin'."

Dreiser surged to his feet and grabbed the Draka by the shoulder. A second later he stood nursing a

wrist, his hand slapped aside hard enough to numb
it. Fingers like steel clamps spread, inches from his
throat. He looked into a face like a mask, met eyes
filled with frustration-borne anger, and spoke.

"You can't just *leave* him like that—for the love of
Christ, he's a human being!" "He was a soldier,
too!"

The paratrooper spat on the dying German. "There's
only two types of 'human being' in the world,
shithead—Draka an' serfs—so shut the fuck *up*. Bill-
boy was a friend of mine. *I'm* in command, and *I* say
leave the Fritz fo' the fuckin' *ragheads*."

"*Ya*," the machine gunner, Jenny, said. She kicked
the fallen German in the thigh. The nerves must
have been severed, for there was only a dull wet
sound and the gasping rasp of the Paternoster.

"Hey, dec, he's raht." The American looked around,
blinking in amazement. It was the redhead, McAlistair.
She snapped the selector on her assault rifle to single
shot and continued. "So he's not of the Race; not a
dawg, neithah. Hell, if'n his granpap had emigrated,
maybe-so he'd be raht heah with us'n. Won't take a
second. Pa always did say yo' should finish off game
yo' wounded."

"No."

"Ah, c'mon, dec, don't be such a fuckin' hardass—"

"I said *no*, McAlistair: better a hardass than a
candyass. Now *haul* it."

The fox-faced trooper's easy grin turned to a snarl
as she stepped closer, slapped aside the NCO's point-
ing finger, curled her own black-gloved hand into a
fingers-and-thumb gesture beneath his chin. The
American was not surprised; rank in the Citizen force
was a purely functional matter. There was no mys-
tique to it, unless won by personal example; a com-
mander was someone who directed the business of
fighting or unit movement, not a social superior.
This was an army where officers ate from the same

field kitchens as the troops, where KP and guard duty were settled by votes or flipping a coin. *Wouldn't work with Americans*, he reflected. *Too individualistic*. But Draka soaked up the concept of teamwork from infancy . . .

"Look, Dhalgren, yo' lettin' a field promotion go t' yo' *head*. This isn't the fuckin' *Janissaries*, my man. All that rank badge on yo' sleeve means is yo' gets t' call the shots in *combat*. This *isn't* combat, unless we waste mo' time on it, and that cheap stripe don't mean *shit* t' me. Got it?"

Silence stretched for an instant. The decurion's eyes slitted, flicked down to the SS man, back to his subordinate. The tip of his tongue came out to touch his upper lip.

"All raaht," he said in an even, conversational tone. "You wants t' expend him so bad, do it. Expend him." His hand caught the sling of her Holbars for a moment as she began to turn. "Didn't say yo' could *shoot* him. That'd be wastin' ammunition and it would just purely break my *heart*."

"*Fuck* yo', Dhalgren!" the trooper said with an unwilling smile. That was neatly within the letter of regulations.

"Any time, Tee-Hee; any time."

"Not until we run outta goats," she muttered, going to one knee and gripping the German's hair. The other hand was clenched into a fist behind her ear; she exhaled in a sharp *huff!* of breath and brought it down with a snapping whipcrack motion, putting the flexing twist of hip and back behind it. The metal inset of the warsap thudded into his temple; the German jerked once and went still. She rose, opening and closing her hand.

"Hope that gets yo' hard, dec," she said with ironic graciousness, walking to the rear exit and beginning her scan. It always paid to be careful when you were on point.

"Cock like a rock, Tee-Hee; that bettah 'n the girl-and-pony show at the Legion who'house," the decurion said with a grin. That turned colder as his eyes passed over Dreiser. "Welcome t' the real world, Yank. All raaht, Draka, ready . . . *move.*"

CHAPTER NINE

Holbars T-6 Assault Rifle, Model 1936

Caliber:	*5mm (5x45mm, aluminum case)*
Operating System:	*gas, selective fire (optional 3-round burst)*
Weight:	*9.7 lbs., loaded*
Length, overall:	*42 inches, stock extended*
	30 inches, stock folded
Feed device:	*75 round drum (disintegrating link, factory-packed)*
Sights:	*x4, optical (plus post & aperture emergency fallback)*
Muzzle velocity:	*3300 f.p.s.*
Cyclic rate:	*approximately 650 r.p.m. (variable by adjusting gas port)*
Notes:	*Folding bipod; barrel and all parts exposed to gas-wash are chrome-plated. Drum is ridged glass-reinforced plastic with transparent rear face.*
Design history:	*The Small Arms Study Project (1926 –28, Alexandria Institute) determined that the T-5 semiautomatic rifle used*

143

in the Great War "overkilled" at the usual battle ranges, and that a small-calibre, selective-fire alternative was preferable. Chief Engineer Sven Holbars and his design team produced the prototype T-6 in 1932; field trials followed and series production commenced in 1935 at the Alexandria, Archona, Alma Ata, and Constantinople Armories. Re-equipment of the last reserve, Janissary and Security Directorate/ Police units was completed in 1940. A squad automatic-weapon version with heavy quick-change barrel and larger magazine was produced concurrently.

Weapons of the Eurasian War by Colonel Carlos Fueterrez, U.S. Army (ret.)

Defense Institute Press, Mexico City

VILLAGE ONE, OSSETIAN MILITARY HIGHWAY APRIL 14, 1942: 0615 HOURS

The impromptu war council met by an undamaged section of the town hall's outer wall; the cobbles there were a welcome contrast to the mud, dung, and scattered rocks of the main square. It was a mild spring day, sunny, the sky clear save for a scattering of high, wispy cloud; the air was a silky benediction on the skin. Clear weather was doubly welcome: it promised to dry the soil which heavy movement was churning into a glutinous mass the color and consistency of porridge, and it gave the troopers a ringside view of the events above, now that there was a moment to spare. Contrails covered the sky in a huge arc from east to west, stark against the pale blue all along the northern front of the Caucasus; it was only when you counted the tiny moving dots that the numbers struck home.

"Christ," the field-promoted Senior Decurion of the late Lisa Telford's tetrarchy said, swiveling his binoculars along the front. "There must be hundreds of them. Thousands . . . That's the biggest air battle in history, right over our heads." He recognized the shapes from familiarization lectures: Draka Falcons and twin-engine Eagles, Fritz Bf 109's and Focke-Wulf 190's—even a few lumbering Bf 110's, wheeling and diving and firing. As they watched, one dot shed a long trail of black that ended in an orange globe; they heard the *boom*, saw a parachute blossom.

"So much for 'uncontested air superiority,'" said Marie Kaine dryly as she shaded her eyes with a palm. A Messerschmidt dove, rolled, and drove down the valley overhead with two Draka Eagles on its tail, jinking and weaving, trying to use its superior agility to shake the heavier, faster interceptors. The Eagles were staying well-spaced, and the inevitable happened—the German fighter strayed into the fire-cone of one while avoiding the other. A brief hammering of the Eagle's nose-battery of 25mm cannon sent it in burning tatters to explode on the mountainside; the Eagle victory-rolled, and both turned to climb back to the melee above. The air was full of the whining snarl of turbocharged engines, and spent brass from the guns glittered and tinkled as it fell to the rocky slopes.

The officers of Century A were considerably less spruce than they had been that morning: the black streak-paint had run with sweat; their mottled uniforms were smeared with the liquid grey clay of the village streets; most had superficial wounds at least.

So much for the glory of war, Eric thought wryly. Once the nations had sent out their champions dressed in finery of scarlet and feathers and polished brass.

Now slaughter had been industrialized, and all the uniforms were the color of mud.

A stretcher party was bearing the last of the Draka hurt into the building. Eric had made the rounds inside—a commander's obligation, and one he did not relish. In action, you could ignore the wounded, the pain and sudden ugly wrecking of bodies, but not in an aid station. There was a medical section, with all the latest field gear—plasma and antibiotics and morphine; most of the wounded still conscious were making pathetic attempts at cheerfulness. One trooper who had lost an eye told him she was applying for a job with the Navy as soon as a patch was fitted, "to fit in with the decor, and they'll assign me a parrot." And they all wanted to hear the words, that they had done well, that their parents and lovers could know their honor was safe.

Children, Eric thought, shaking his head slightly as he finished his charcoal sketch map of the village on a section of plastered stone. *I'm surrounded by homicidal children who believe in fairy stories, even with their legs ripped off and their faces ground to sausage meat.*

The commanders lounged, resting, smoking, gnawing on soya-meal crackers or raisins from their iron rations, swigging down tepid water from their canteens. There was little sound—an occasional grunt of pain from the aid station within, shouts and boot-tramp from the victors, the eternal background of the mountain winds. The town's civilians had gone to ground.

The Circassian patriarch stood to one side, McWhirter near him, leaning back with his shoulders and one foot against the building, casually stropping his bush knife on a pocket hone. The native glanced about at pale-eyed deadliness and seemed to shrink a little into himself; they were predator and prey.

"Nice of the Air Corps to provide the show," Eric began. "But business calls. As I see it—"

Sofie tapped his shoulder.

"Yes?"

"Report, Centurion; vehicles coming down the road from the pass. Ours . . . sort of."

The convoy hove into sight on the switchback above the town, the diesel growl of its engines loud in the hush after battle, a pair of light armored cars first, their turrets traversing to keep the roadside verges covered with their twin machine guns, pennants snapping from their aerials. Behind them came a dozen steam trucks in Wehrmacht colors. The machines themselves were a fantastic motley—German, Soviet, French, even a lone Bedford that must have been captured from the English at Dunkirk or slipped in through Murmansk before the Russian collapse; two were pulling field guns of unfamiliar make. Bringing up the rear were a trio of bakkies—cross-country vehicles with six small balloon wheels, mounting a bristle of automatic cannon and recoilless rifles. All were travelling at danger speed, slewing around the steep curves in spatters of mud and dust.

"Quick work," Eric commented, as the vehicles roared down the final slope, where the military road cut through the huddle of stone buildings. "I wonder who—"

The daunting hoot of a fox-hunter's horn echoed from the lead warcar, and an ironic cheer went up from the paratroopers.

"Need I have asked," the Centurion sighed. "*Cohortarch* Dale Jackson Smythe Thompson III."

The warcars rolled into the square at 90 kph, spattering passers-by in a shower of mud, their variable-pressure tires gripping at the earth and cobbles. The lead car finished its circuit with a charge directly at Eric's position, slewed about in a perfect 180 degree turn, and came to rest in front of Century

A's commander. There were fresh bullet scars shiny against its dark-grey battlepaint, and a puckered exit-hole in the hexagonal turret just to the right of the machine gun. A jaunty figure in immaculately pressed fatigues pulled himself from the commander's seat and stepped down to the deck, standing with boots braced; a beaming smile showed as he pulled down the silk scarf that covered his face and pushed his dust goggles back onto the brim of his helmet. His left arm was bandaged from elbow to wrist; the right slapped a riding-crop against his leg as he glanced around the square.

Gaping, blackened holes marred the face of the mosque and the town hall. *Just as well for that piece of miniature Stalinist wedding cake*, he thought. *Pity about the mosque—pretty in a quaint sort of way*. There were bodies in Waffen-SS camouflage still lying scattered about the irregular open space, or hanging motionless from windows; the last thirty lay in a neat row, with their hands bound behind their backs. He glanced behind; the rest of the convoy was pulling up at a more sedate pace.

"Nice piece of driving, Lucy," he called down into the warcar. A giggle came in answer; there was a clatter as a grenade looped out of the driver's port to land on the riveted aluminum of the deck. He ignored it, but the sight brought the beginnings of a dive for cover from the onlookers, until a woman's voice followed it:

"Never notice the pin's still in, do they?"

The cohortarch laughed, jumped to the cobbles and strode over, snapping a salute before extending a hand—a rarity in the Draka military and even rarer in the field. "Matters well in hand, I see," he called. "And how are you, Eric, dear boy?"

Eric returned the salute, smiling at the older man: a slight figure, freckled and sandy-haired and snub-nosed. "Busy. How are things in the cavalry, Dale?"

"The cavalry's in tanks, and that's the problem—if I'd wanted to crawl about in a giant steel coffin, I would have joined the navy . . . and flying makes me squeamish, so I'm left here, trying to bring some tone to this vulgar brawl of yours."

He nodded to the assembled commanders. "Now, I suppose you'd like to know how the war's going. . ." He assumed a grave expression. "Well, according to the radio, the Americans claim that resistance is still going on in the hills of Hawaii three months after the Japanese landings, and promise that McArthur's troops in Panama will throw the invader back into the Pacific—"

"Dale, you're impossible!" Marie burst out, with a rare chuckle.

"No, just a Thompson . . . Actually, we had a bit of a surprise."

"We heared about the tanks," Eric said.

"That was the *least* of it. Have you ever heard of a Waffen-SS unit, '*Liebstandarte Adolf Hitler*?' Perhaps met a few of them?" He smiled beatifically at their nods. "Well, it seems that the good old Fritz were so anxious to get those field fortifications at the southern end of the pass finished that they moved our friends of the lightning bolts up to help the engineers and forced-labour brigades we were expecting. Still stringing wire and laying mines when we dropped in right on their heads. Not on their infantry, praise god—on their H.Q., signals, combat engineers, vehicle park, artillery . . .

"Luckily, not all of them were there; still a fair number down in Pyatogorsk, from what the prisoners say. And we had complete suprise, which was just as well, seeing as we lost about a fifth of our strength to their flak before we hit the ground."

There was a general wince; that was twice the total casualties of a month's fighting in Sicily.

"Yes, quite distressing. *In* any case, we were

marginally less astonished than they, so we managed to split them up and fight them out of the entrenchments; particularly as they were facing the other way. Killed about a third—a third of the fighting men, that is—ran a third out south to join their confreres. Unfortunately, the *last* third escaped up into the hills and woods; there just weren't enough of us left to contain them all. Ever since, they've been regrouping, harassing—one group shot us up on the way down. That's what my warcar cohort is doing, keeping the road open between our units. These ruddy bastards are tough, they just won't give *up*. Most of the legion is in the line above Kutaisi; we've already had probing attacks from the south, one in strength, and it looks as if they're building up for a major assault. Soon.

"The rest of us are in hedgehogs down the length of the pass; the Fritz within our lines don't have heavy weapons, but they are making life difficult for our communications, and a secure perimeter is out of the question. So, I'm afraid, are those two Centuries you were supposed to get."

There was a stony silence, as the leaders of A Century realized that they had just been condemned to death; then a sigh of acceptance. The warcar commander looked slightly abashed.

"'The first casualty of war is always the battle plan,'" Eric quoted. "How's the general offensive going?" He produced a flat silver flask, took a sip and handed it around.

"Extraordinary, really. We saw the barrage start, it lit the whole southern horizon, thousands of guns lined up hub to hub. The Air Corps caught their planes on the ground around Tiflis; since then the Tac-Air johnnies've been all over them like, pardon the expression, flies on a cowflop. Fighter-bombers, ground-attack, mediums; cannon, guns, rockets, napalm, cluster bombs, fuel air bombs, and for all I know, ginger-beer bottles. You can watch it all like a map. Extraordinary!

"Then the Janissaries hit them south of Tiflis and Batumi; they're already backpedalling, with us at their rear. The Janissaries are piling up bodies in waves, but keep coming."

They all nodded; not surprising, given their indoctrination . . . and the Security Directorate machinegun detachments at their backs.

"Well!" the cohortarch concluded cheerfully. "Now to the good news. That air strike on your friends down the road in Pyatigorsk came off splendidly, according to the reports; also, they seeded a good few butterfly mines between thence and this, to muddy the waters as it were. What's more, we captured just about everything in the Liebstandarte divisional stores intact, apart from their armor—hence the two antitank pieces. Russian originally, but quite good. And all the other stuff you requested; blessed if I know what that food and so forth is for, but . . ."

"Also, they're putting in a battery of our 107 howitzers just up the way a piece, so you should have artillery support soon, and some Fritz stuff—150's. I brought along the observer. As to ammunition, there's plenty of 5mm and 15mm, but I'm afraid we're running a bit short of 85 and 120—we've already had an attack in brigade strength with armored support. They're desperate, you know."

Aren't we all, Eric thought. The Draka high command never expended citizen lives without need. There were only thirty-six million free citizens in the Domination, after all, and five hundred million serfs. On occasion it was necessary, and this was obviously one of the occasions.

Eric turned to the trucks, absently slapping one fist into his palm as he watched the unloading. It went quickly, aided by the two laborers in the rear of each vehicle; they were of the same breed as the drivers handcuffed to the steering wheels—sullen, flat-faced men in the rags of yellow-brown uniforms.

"Ivans?" he asked.

"Oh, yes; we, hmmm, inherited them from the Fritz." A snort of laughter. "Perhaps, if we're to do this often, they and we could set up a common pool?"

Even then, there was a chuckle at the witticism. Eric's eyes were narrowed in thought. "Surprised you got them to drive that fast," he said.

"Oh, I made sure that they saw explosives being loaded," Dale said. He grinned wolfishly: his family might be from the Egyptian provinces, where a veneer of Anglicism was fashionable, but he was Draka to the core. "It probably occurred to them what could happen if we stayed under fire long. 'Where there's a whip, there's a way.'"

"And there's more ways of killing a cat than choking it to death with cream," Eric replied and turned, pointing to the combat engineer. "Marie, what do you think of this place as a defensive position?"

"With only A Century?" She paused. "Bad. These houses, they're fine against small arms, but not worth jack shit against blast—no structural strength." Another pause. "Against anybody with artillery, it's a deathtrap."

"My sentiments exactly. What about field fortifications?"

"Well, that's the answer, of course. But we just don't have the people to do much . . ."

He chopped a hand through the air, his voice growing staccato with excitement. "What if you had a thousand or so laborers?"

"Oh, completely different, then we could . . . you mean the natives? Doubt we could get much out of them in time to be worthwhile."

"Wait a second. And stick around, Dale. I need that devious brain of yours.

"All *right*." Eric turned from his officers. His finger stabbed at the Circassian. "Old one, how many are your people? Are they hungry?"

The native straightened, met grey eyes colder than the snows of Elbruz, and did not flinch. "We are two thousand, where once there were many. Lord, kill us if you must, but do not mock us!

"Hungry? We have been *hungry* since the infidel Georgian pig Stalin—" he spat "—took our land, our sheep, our cattle, for the *Kholkohz*, the collective; sent our bread and meat and fruit to feed cities we never saw." The dead voice of exhaustion swelled, took on passion. "Then the Germanski war began. He took our seed corn, and our young men—those that did not flee to the mountain. This they called desertion, the NKVD, the Chekists; they killed many, many. What is it to us if the infidels slay one another? Should we love the Russki, that in the days of the White Czar they did to us what the Germanski would do to them? Should we love the godless dog Stalin, who took from us even what the Czars left us—freedom to worship Allah?"

He shook a fist. "When the Germanski came, many thought we would be free at last; the soldiers of the grey coats gave us back our mosque, that the Chekists had made a place of abomination. I hoped that God had sent us better masters, at least. Then the Germanski of the lightning came and took power over us—" he drew the runic symbol of the SS, and spat again "—and where the Russki had beaten us with whips, they were a knout of steel. They are mad! They would kill and kill until they dwell *alone* in the earth!"

He crossed his arms. "We are not *hungry*, lord. We are starving; our children die. And now we have not enough to live until the harvest, even if we make soup of bark—not unless we eat each other. What is my life to me, if I will not live to see my grandson become a man? Kill us if you will; thus we may gain Paradise. We have already seen hell—it is home to us."

Eric smiled like a wolf, but when he spoke his voice was almost gentle. "Old man, I will not slay your people; I will feed them. Not from any love, but from my own need. Listen well. We and the Germanski will do battle here; we and they are the mill, and your people will be as the grain between us. Of this village, not one stone will stand upon another. Hear me. If all those of your people who can dig and lift will work for one day, the others and the children may leave, with as much food as they can carry.

"If they labor well, and if twenty young men who are hunters and know the paths and secret places of the wood stay to guide my soldiers, then by my father's name and my God, if I have the victory, I will leave enough food for all your people until the winter—also cloth, and tools."

Much good may they do you once the Security Directorate arrives, his mind added silently. Still, the offer was honest as far as it went. The Domination of the Draka demanded obedience; its serfs' religion was a matter of total indifference, and a dead body was useful only for fertilizer, for which guano was much cheaper.

The Circassian patriarch had not wept under threat of death; now he nodded and hid his face in a fold of the ragged kaftan.

"Plan," Eric snapped. The tetrarchy commanders and the visiting cohortarch had their notebooks ready. There was silence, except for the scrunch of the commander's soft-treaded boots on the gritty stone of the square.

"We have to hold this town to hold the road, but it's a deathtrap. Look at how *we* took it. Marie, I just secured you about 1,500 willing laborers; also some guides who know the way through that temperate-zone jungle out on the slopes. Over to you."

She stood, thoughtful, then looked at the crude map of the village, around at the houses. She picked up a piece of charcoal, walked to the wall and began to sketch.

"The houses're fine protection from small arms, as I said, but too vulnerable to blast. So. We *use* that."

She began drawing on a stucco wall. "Look, here at the north end, where the highway enters the town. A lane at right angles to it on both sides, then a row of houses butting wall to wall. We'll take the timber from the Fritz stores, some of it, whatever else we can find—corrugated iron would be perfect—and build a shelter right *through* on both sides, and knock out the connecting walls. Then we blow the houses down on both; knock firing ports out to command the highway. Those Fritz-Ivan 76.2 mm antitank, they can be manhandled—you can switch firing positions under cover, with four feet of rock for protection. Couple of the 15mm's in there, too."

The charcoal drew, in diagrams, a schematic of the village. Her voice raced, jumping, ideas coalescing into reality.

"Time, that's the factor. So, that antitank stuff first. With three thousand *very* willing pairs of hands, though . . . Listen. This whole village, it's underlain by arched-roof cellars. They don't connect, but there's damn-all between them but curtain walls. Break through, here, here, here; put up timber pillars—" her hands drew a vertical shaft through the air "—pop-up positions; we blow the houses around them, perfect camouflage, let the Fritz get past you and hit them from *behind*.

"Then, we can't let them flank us. Get that angle iron, and the wire; wire in like this—" she sketched a blunt V from the woods to the edge of town "—downslope of these two stone terraces, and trenches

just above them. Only two hundred meters to the
woods on the east, three hundred to the west. Mine
the ground in front, random pattern. State those
fields are in, a thousand badgers could dig for a week
and you couldn't tell.

"If the Patriarch Abraham here is going to have
hunters show us the forest tracks, we'll mine the
forest edge, then the paths—put a few machine gun
nests in there, channel things into killing fields—
cohortarch, I'm going to need more of the Broad-
sword directional mines, can you get them? Good.
Also more radio detonators, and any Fritz mines you
can scavenge.

"And I can rig impromptu from that Fritz ammu-
nition," she murmured, almost an aside to herself.
That would be tricky; she'd better handle it herself.

"We'll need a suprise for their armor. We've got
that clutch of plastic antitank mines, lovely stuff.
Very good, they can't be swept. Those for the road.
That blasting explosive, with the radiodetonators, by
the verge . . . and there, there, where the turnoff
points are. And we—"

"All right," Eric broke in with a grim smile. Marie
was brilliant in anything to do with construction; he
could see a glow of pure happiness spreading over
her face—the joy of an artist allowed to practice her
craft. The problem would be keeping her from trying
to put up the Great Wall of China.

"We need immediate antitank while this is going
up," he continued briskly. "Tom, you take two of the
120's." His hand indicated where the tips of the V
met the woods. "Emplace 'em there. Spider pits for
the crews, with overhead protection, close enough to
jump to. Marie, push the third down the road, down
past the bend—somewhere where it can get one
flank shot off where it'll do the most good, and the
crew can run like hell. We don't have enough 120
ammunition to use three barrels. Booby traps along

the trail, if you've got time. Better ask for volunteers. Take half the rocket-gun teams, start familiarizing them with the woods up both sides of the valley, for if—when—the Fritz break through. And I want minefields *behind* us as well, don't get trapped thinking linearly." He paused. "Booby traps, as well. Everywhere."

He turned to the comtech. "Sofie, we're going to need secure communications. If we ran the Fritz field telephone wire all over the place, underground too, stripped, would it carry radio?"

She frowned. "Ought . . . *Ya*, Centurion."

"Coordinate with Sparks in Marie's tetrarchy. And set up the stationary radio; I'm going to need a steady link to cohort and up. Run more lines out to the woods, tack it up. A cellar, somewhere as far from the square as possible—those buildings are going to draw a *lot* of fire." He paused. "Anything impossible?"

"All that demolition," the sapper Legate said. "Chancy. Very. Especially if we use nonstandard explosives. I can estimate, some of my NCO's . . ."

" 'It has to be done, it can be,' " he quoted with a shrug. "If we're going to be sacrificial lambs, at least we can break a few teeth. There'll be a lot of details; solve 'em if you can, ask me or Marie if you can't."

"Now," he said, turning to the cohortarch. "Dale?"

"It's all a little, well, *static*, isn't it?" The ex-cavalryman paused. "Besides your skulkers in the woods, I'd say you need a mobile reaction force to maneuver in the rear, once they're fixed against your fieldworks."

Eric nodded. "Good, but we don't have any reserve left for that . . ."

Dale examined his fingertips. "Well, old man, I could run a spot down the road, conceal my vehicles, then—"

Eric shook his head. "Nice of you to offer, Dale,

but you're needed back above. That's going to be a deathride, and . . . I've got an idea." He looked around the circle of faces. "Tell you later if it works out. No— Let's *do* it, people; let's *move*."

There was a moment of silence, of solemnity almost. Then the scene dissolved in action.

Eric turned to the old man. "Hadj, those prisoners the Germanski were holding behind the hall—they are not of your people?"

The Circassian came to himself, blew his nose in the sleeve of his khaftan and shook his head.

"They are Russki—partisans, godless youths of the *komsomol* from the great city of Pyatigorsk that the Czars built, when they took the hot springs of the Seven Hills from my people. Even so, we would not have betrayed them to the Germanski with the lightning, if they had not demanded food of us that we did not have. There are more of them westward in the hills; many more. The garrison came here to hunt them." He bowed. "Lord, may I go to tell my people what you require of them?"

Eric nodded absently, tugging at his lower lip, then smiled and turned for the alley leading past the town hall.

Sofie trotted at his side, a quizzical interest in her eyes; her tasks would not be needed immediately, and a matter puzzled her. Eric was moving with a bounce in his stride; his eyes seemed to glow, his skin to crackle with renewed vitality. She remembered him at the loading zone, quiet, reserved; in the fighting that morning, moving with the bleakly impersonal efficiency of a well-designed machine. Now . . . he looked like a man in love. Not with her, her head told her. But it was interesting to see how that affected him; definitely interesting.

"Centurion," she said. "Remember Palermo?"

"What part?"

"Afterward, when we stood down. That terrace? We were talking, and you told me you didn't like soldiering. Seems to me you like it well enough now, or I've never seen a man happy."

He rubbed the side of his nose. "I like . . . solving problems. Important ones, real ones; doing it quickly, getting people to do their best. And understanding what makes them tick, getting inside their heads. Knowing what they'll do if *I* do this or that . . . I've even thought of writing novels, because of that. After the war, of course." He stopped, with an uncharacteristic flush. Sofie was easy to talk to, but that was not an ambition he had told many. Hurriedly, he continued: "Marie's a crackerjack sapper. I had some of the same ideas, but not in nearly so much detail. And I couldn't organize so well to get them done."

"But you could organize *her*, and the ragheads, and whatever these 'russki partisans' are good for." She smiled at his raised brow. "Hell, Centurion, I may not talk their jabber, but I know the word when I hear it. I can see all that's part of war." She frowned. "And the fighting?" Draka were supposed to like to fight; more theory than fact. She didn't, much; if she wanted to have a fun-risk, she'd surf. Yet there was a certain addiction to it. You could see how the combat-junkies felt, and certainly the Draka produced more of them than most people, but on the whole, no thanks. This had been hairier than anything before, and she had an uneasy feeling it was going to get worse.

"We're of the Race: we have our obligations."

There was no answer to that, not unless she wished to give offense. For that matter, there were many who would have stood on rank already.

"Think we'll have time to get all this stuff ready?"

"I don't know, Sofie," he said simply. "I hope so. Before the real attack, anyway. We'll probably get a probe quite soon. With luck . . ."

Senior Decurion McWhirter cleared his throat. "Say, sir, what was it you used on the old raghead? Thought he was a tough old bastard, but he caved in real easy."

"I used the lowest, vilest means I could," Eric said softly. The NCO's eyes widened in surprise. "I gave him hope."

CHAPTER TEN

From the beginning, sheer size was a driving factor in the evolution of the Domination. The Dutch colony which Admiral Cochrane seized in 1779—essentially, the modern Western Cape Province—was larger than France. By 1783 the Crown Colony was the size of all Western Europe; during the 1790's slaving bases and settlements were driven up the "eastern reach" to Zanzibar and Aden, and 1800 saw the conquest of Egypt and Ceylon. Inland labor raiders, ranchers, planters and prospectors leapfrogged each other in quest of workers, grazing, water and minerals; the arid climate and the large size of the initial land grants combined to keep settlement thinly spread.

Communications—of troops, administrators, information, goods—were a problem that could only increase with time. The continental interior was almost completely lacking in useful waterways, and the plateau was everywhere fringed with mountains. Stark necessity made roads and harbors a priority, and engineering schools were founded to provide experts to direct the forced-labour gangs. Gold mining paid much of the costs, and the steam engines imported to pump out shafts and crush ore suggested a means around the weaknesses of animal transport. Richard Trevithick's experimental locomotives (1803) and steam cars (1806) encountered none of the resistance that vested interests produced in Europe; not only Draka prosperity, but survival itself depended on swift transport. A precedent was established for the research pro-

*jects which produced the first successful dirigible airships in
the 1880's . . .*

200 Years: A Social History of the Domination
by Alan E. Sorensson, Ph.D
Archona Press, 1983

VILLAGE ONE, OSSETIAN MILITARY HIGHWAY APRIL 14, 1942: 0700 HOURS

The partisans were being held in what looked to
be a stock pen—new barbed wire on ancient piled
stone. A walking-wounded Draka trooper stood guard;
the German formerly assigned to that duty was lying
on his back across the wall, his belly opened by a
drawing slash from a bush knife and the cavity buzz-
ing black with flies. The prisoners ignored him; even
with Eric's arrival, few looked up from their frenzied
attack on the loaves of stale black bread that had
been thrown to them. One vomited noisily, seized
another chunk and began to eat again. There were
thirty of them, and they stank worse than the rest of
the village. They were standing in their own excre-
ment, and half a dozen had wounds gone pus-rotten
with gas-gangrene.

They were Slavs, mostly: stockier than the Circassian
natives, flatter-faced and more often blond, in peas-
ant blouses or the remnants of Soviet uniform. Young
men, if you could look past the months of chronic
malnutrition, sickness, and overstrain. A few had
been tortured, and all bore the marks of rifle butts,
whips, rubber truncheons. Eric shook his head in
disgust; in the Domination, this display would
have been considered disgraceful even for convicts
on their way to the prison-mines of the Ituri jungles
or the saltworks of Kashgar, the last sink-holes for
incorrigibles. Anybody would torture for informa-
tion in war, of course, and the Security Directorate

was not notable for mercy toward rebels. Still, this was petty meanness. If they were dangerous, kill them; if not, put them to some use.

One thick-set prisoner straightened, brushed his hands down a torn and filth-spattered uniform tunic and came to the edge of the wire. His eyes flickered to the guard, noted how she came erect at the officer's approach.

"*Uvaha hchloptsi, to yeehchniy kommandyr,*" he cast back over his shoulder, and waited, looking the Draka steadily in the eye.

Eric considered him appraisingly and nodded. *This one,* he thought, *is a brave man. Pity, we'll probably have to kill him if the Fritz don't do us the favor.* Aloud: "Sprechen zie Deutsch? Parlez vous Francais? Circassian?"

A shake of the head; the Draka commander paused in thought, almost started in surprise to hear Sofie's voice.

"I speak Russian, Centurion," she said. He raised a brow; everybody had to do one foreign language, but that was not a common choice. "Not in school. My Pa, he with Henderson when the Fourth took Krasnovodsk, back in 1918. He brought back a Russki wench, Katie. She was my nursemaid, an' I learned it from her. Still talk it pretty good. He just said: '*Watch out, boys, that's the commander.*'"

Sofie turned to the captives and spoke, slowly at first and then with gathering assurance. The Russian frowned and waved his companions to silence, then replied. The ghost of a smile touched his face, despite the massive bruise that puffed the left side of his mouth.

Grinning, she switched back into English. "*Ya,* he understands. Says I've got an old-fashioned Moscow accent, like a *boyar,* a noble. Hey, Katie always said she was a Countess; maybe it was true." A shake of the head. "S'true she was never much good at housework, wouldn't do it. Screwing the Master was all right, looking after children was fine, but show her a mop and she'd sulk for days. Ma gave up on trying . . ."

Actually, the whole Nixon household had been fond of Ekaterina Ilyichmanova; with her moods and flightiness and disdain for detail, she had fitted in perfectly with the general atmosphere of cheerfully sloppy anarchy. Sophie's father had always considered her his best war souvenir and had treated her with casual indulgence; she was something of an extravagance for a man of his modest social standing, and her slender, great-eyed good looks were not at all his usual taste. Sophie and her brothers had gone to some trouble to find their nursemaid the Christian priest she wanted during her last illness, and had been surprised at how empty a space she left in the rambling house below Lion's Head.

Eric nodded thoughtfully. "Good thinking, Sofie. All right . . . ask him if there are more like him in the woods, and the villages down in the plains."

The Russian listened carefully to the translation, spoke a short sentence and spat at the Draka officer's feet. Eric waved back the guard's bayonet impatiently.

"Ahhh—" Sofie hesitated. "Ah, Centurion, he sort of asked why the fuck he should tell a *neimetsky* son-of-a-bitch anything, and invited you to take up where the fornicating Fritzes left off." She frowned. "I think he's got a pretty thick country-boy accent. Don't know what a *neimetsky* is, but it's not nohow complimentary. And he says it's our fault they're in this mess anyway."

Eric smiled thinly, hands linked behind his back, rising and falling thoughtfully on the balls of his feet. There was an element of truth in that; the *Stavka*, the Soviet high command, had never been able to throw all its reserves against the Germans with the standing menace of the Domination on thousands of kilometers of southern front. And the Draka had

taken two million square miles of central Asia in the
Great War, while Russia was helpless with revolu-
tion and civil strife; all the way north to the foothills
of the Urals, and east to Baikal.

Fairly perceptive, the Draka officer thought. *Espe-
cially for a peasant like this. He must have been a
Party member.* The flat Slav face stared back at him,
watchful but not at all afraid.

Can't be a fool, Eric's musing continued. *Not and
have survived the winter and spring. He's not nervous
with an automatic weapon pointed at him, either.* Or
at the bayonet, for that matter; the damn things were
usually still useful for crowd control, if nothing else.

"Stupid," he said meditatively.

"Sir?" Sofie asked.

"Oh, not him; the Fritz. Talking about a thousand-
year Reich, then acting as if it all had to be done
tomorrow . . ." His tone grew crisper. "Ask his name.
Ask him how he'd like to be released with all his
men—with all the food they can carry, a brand-new
Fritz rifle and a hundred rounds each."

Shocked, Sophie raised her eyebrows, shrugged
and spoke. This time the Russian laughed. "He says
he's called Ivan Desonovich Yuhnkov, and he'd pre-
fer MP40 submachine guns and grenades. While we're
at it, could we please give him some tanks and a
ticket to New York, and Hitler's head, and what sort
of fool do you think he is? Sorry, sir."

Eric reached out a hand for the microphone, spoke.
Minutes stretched; he waited without movement,
then extended a hand to Sofie. "Cigarette?" he asked.

Carefully expressionless, she lit a second from her
own and placed it between his lips. *Well, the iron
man is nervous, too,* she thought. Sometimes she got
the feeling that Eric could take calculated risks on
pure intellect, simply from analysis of what was nec-
essary. It was reassuring that he could need the
soothing effect of the nicotine.

The other partisans had finished the bread. They
crowded in behind their leader, silent, the hale sup-
porting the wounded. A mountain wind soughed,
louder than their breath and the slight sucking noises
of their rag-wrapped feet in the mud and filth of the
pen. The eyes in the stubbled faces . . . covertly,
Eric studied them. Some were those of brutalized
animals, the ones who had stopped thinking because
thought brought nothing that was good; now they
lived from one day . . . no, from one meal to the
next, or one night's sleep. He recognized that look; it
was common enough in the world his caste had built.
And he recognized the stare of the others—the men
who had fought on long after the death of hope
because there was really nothing else to do. *That* he
saw in the mirror, every morning.

A stick of troopers came up, shepherding a work-
ing party of Circassian villagers, and the American
war correspondent. The Circassians were carrying
rope-handled wooden crates between them; Drei-
ser's face had a stunned paleness. *Well, he's seen the
elephant*, Eric thought with a distant, impersonal sym-
pathy. There were worse things than combat, but
the American probably wasn't in a mood to be re-
minded of that right now. The crates were not large,
but the villagers bore them with grunts and care,
and they made a convincing *splat* in the wet earth.

"Bill," the Draka said. "What's your government's
policy on Russian refugees?"

Dreiser gathered himself with a visible effort, watch-
ing as Eric reached up over his left shoulder and
drew his bush knife. The metal was covered in a soft
matte-black finish, only the honed edge reflecting mir-
ror bright. He drove it under one of the boards of a
crate and pried the wood back with a screech of
nails.

"Refugees? Ah . . ." He forced his thoughts into
order. "Well, better, now that we're in the war." He

shrugged distaste. "Especially since there isn't any prospect of substantial numbers arriving." Relations with Timoshenko's Soviet rump junta in west Siberia were good, but with the Japanese holding Vladivostok and running rampant through the Pacific, the only contact was through the Domination. Which visibly regarded the Soviet remnant as a caretaker keeping things in order until the Germans were disposed of and the Draka arrived. Attempts to ship Lend-Lease supplies through had met with polite refusals.

A few wounded and children had been flown out, over the pole in long-range dirigibles, to be received in Alaska by Eleanor Roosevelt with much fanfare.

"Back before Pearl Harbor, they wouldn't even let a few thousand Jews in. Well, the isolationists were against it, and the Mexican states, they're influenced by the Catholic anti-Semites like Father Coughlan."

"Sa." Eric rose, with a German machine pistol and bandolier in his hands. "Those-there are Russian partisans there in the pen, Bill. The Fritz captured 'em, but hadn't gotten around to expending them. Take a look."

Eric heard the American suck in his breath in shock, as he stripped open the action of the Schmeisser. Not bad, he thought, as he inserted a 32-round magazine of 9mm into the well and freed the bolt to drive forward and chamber a bullet. Not as handy as the Draka equivalent; the magazine well was forward of the pistol grip instead of running up through it; it had a shorter barrel, so less range, and the bolt had to be behind the chamber rather than overhanging it. Still, a sound design and honestly made. He took a deep breath and tossed the weapon into the pen.

The partisan leader snatched it out of the air with the quick, snapping motion of a trout rising to a fly. The flat slapping of his hand on the pressed steel of the Schmeisser's receiver was louder than the rustling murmur among his men; much louder than the tensing among the Draka. Eric saw the Russian's eyes flicker past him; he could imagine what the man was seeing. The rifles would be swinging around, assault slings made that easy, with the gun carried at waist level and the grip ready to hand. The troopers would be shocked, and Draka responded to shock aggressively. Especially to the sight of an armed serf, the very *thought* of which was shocking. Technically the Russians were not serfs, of course, but the reflex was conditioned on a deeper level than consciousness.

You did *not* arm serfs. Even Janissaries carried weapons only on operations or training, under supervision, were issued ammunition only in combat zones or firing ranges. *Draka* carried arms; they were as much the badge of the Citizen caste as neck tattoos were for serfs: a symbolic dirk in a wrist sheath or a shoulder-holster pistol in the secure cities of the Police Zone; the planter's customary sidearm; or the automatic weapons and battle-shotguns that were still as necessary as boots in parts of the New Territories. A Citizen bore weapons as symbol of caste, as a sign that he or she was an arm of the State, with the right to instant and absolute obedience from all who were not and power of life and death to enforce it. There was no place on earth where free Draka were a majority: no province, no district, no city. They were born and lived and slept and died among serfs.

They lived because they were warriors, because of the accumulated deadly aura of generations of victory and merciless repression. Folk-memory nearly as deep as instinct saw a serf with a weapon in his hands and prompted: *kill*.

Training held their trigger fingers, but the Russian saw their faces. Sweat sheened his, and he kept the machine pistol's muzzle trained carefully at the ground.

And yet, the weight in his hands straightened his back and seemed to add inches to his height.

"*Khrpikj djavol*," he muttered, staring at Eric, then spoke with wonder.

"Ummm, he says yo' one crazy devil, Centurion," Sophie translated. "Maybe crazy enough to do what you promise." She gave him a hard glance, before continuing on her own: "Yo' might just consider it's other folks' life yo' riskin', too, *sir*. I mean, he might've been some sorta crazy amokker."

Startled, Eric ran a hand over the cropped yellow surface of his hair. "You know, I never thought of that . . . you're right." More briskly: "Tell him that I promise to kill a lot of Germans; and that he can kill even more, with my help. After that I promise *nothing*, absolutely nothing." He pointed to Dreiser, standing beside him. "This man is not a Draka, or a soldier: he is an American journalist. About what happens after this fight, talk to him."

"Hey, wait a minute, Eric—" Dreiser began.

Eric chopped down a hand. "Bill, it's your ass on the line, too. Even if the Fritz roll right over us, the Legion will probably be able to hold the next fallback position well enough; we'll delay them, and the maximum risk is from the south, from the Germans in the pocket there trying to break out to the north. But that won't do *us* any good. Besides . . . what am I supposed to promise them, a merry life digging phosphates in the Aozou mines in the Sahara, with Security flogging them on? Soldiers don't get sold as ordinary serfs, even: too dangerous."

"You want me to promise to get them out? How can I?" Dreiser's eyes flinched away from the Russians, from the painful hope in their faces.

"Say you'll use your influence. True enough, hey? Write them up; your stuff is going through Forces censorship, not Security. They don't give a shit about anything that doesn't compromise military secrecy."

Dreiser looked back into the pen and swallowed, remembering. He had been in Vienna during the *Anschluss*. Memories— *The woman had been Jewish, middleclass* In her forties, but well kept, in the rag of a good dress, her hands soft and manicured. The SS men had had her down scrubbing the sidewalk in front of the building they had taken over as temporary headquarters; they stood about laughing and prodding her with their rifle-butts as others strode in and out through the doors, with prisoners or files or armfuls of looted silverware and paintings from the Rothschild palace.

"Not clean enough, filthy Jewish sow-whore!" The SS man had been giggling-drunk, like his comrades. The woman's face was tear-streaked, a mask of uncomprehending bewilderment: the sort of bourgeois *hausfrau* you could see anywhere in Vienna, walking her children in the Zoo, at the Opera, fussing about the family on an excursion to the little inns of the *Viennerwald*; self-consciously cultured in the tradition of the Jewish middle class that had made Vienna a center of the arts. A life of comfort and neatness, spotless parlors and pastries arranged on silver trays. Now this . . .

"Sir . . ." she began tremulously, raising a hand that was bleeding around the nails.

"Silence! Scrub!" A thought seemed to strike him, and he slung his rifle. "Here's some scrubbing water, whore!" he said, with a shout of laughter, unbuttoning his trousers. The thick yellow stream of urine spattered on the stones before her face, steaming in the cold night air and smelling of staleness and beer. She had recoiled in horror; one of the men behind her planted a boot on her buttocks and shoved, sending her skidding flat into the pool of wetness. That had brought a roar of mirth; the others had crowded close, opening their trousers, too, drenching her as she lay sobbing and retching on the streaming pavement . . .

Dreiser had turned away. There had been nothing he could do, not under their guns. A few ordinary civilians had been watching, some laughing and applauding, others merely disgusted at the vulgarity. And some with the same expression as he. Shame, the taste of helplessness like vomit in the mouth.

They were pissing on the dignity of every human being on earth, Dreiser thought as his mind returned to the present. He shivered, despite the mild warmth of the mountain spring and the thick fabric of his uniform jacket, and looked at the partisans. The Domination might not have quite the nihilistic lunacy of the Nazis, but it was as remorseless as a machine. *I just might be able to bring it off,* he thought. Just maybe; the Draka were not going to make any substantial concessions to American public opinion, but they very well might allow a minor one of no particular importance. The military might; at least, they didn't have quite the same pathological reluctance to see a single human soul escape their clutches that the Security Directorate felt. And here . . . here, he could *do* something.

"I could talk it up in my articles; they're already doing quite well," he said thoughtfully. "Russians are quite popular now anyway, since Marxism is deader than a day-old fish." He looked up at Eric. "You have any pull?"

"Not on the political side; I'm under suspicion. Some on the military, and more—much more—if we win." He paused. "Won't be more than a few of them, anyway."

Dreiser frowned, puzzled. "I thought you said there'd be more than these, still at large."

"Oh, there are probably hundreds, from the precautions the Fritz were taking. I certainly hope so. There won't be many *left*." The Draka turned to Sofie. "Ahhh . . . let's see. Sue Knudsen and her brother. Their family has a plantation near Orenburg,

don't they?" That was in northwest Kazakhstan—steppe
country and the population mostly Slav. "They prob-
ably talk some Russian. Have one of them report
here so Bill will have a translator. Get the tetrarchy
commanders, hunt up anybody else who does. We're
going to need them. Make it snappy," he glanced up
at the sun, "because things are going to get interest-
ing soon."

The pair of Puma armored cars nosed cautiously
toward the tumbled ruins of the village in the pass,
turrets traversing with a low whine of hydraulics to
cover the verges. The roadway was ten meters wide
here, curving slightly southwest through steep-sided
fields. Those were small and hedged with rough
stone walls and scrub brush, isolated trees left stand-
ing for shade or fodder or because they housed spir-
its. Even the cleared zones were rich in cover—perfect
country for partisans with mines and Molotov cock-
tails. Beyond the village the road wound into the
high mountains, forest almost to the edge of the
pavement; the beginning of "ambush alley," danger-
ous partisan country even before the Draka attack.
The Puma was eight-wheeled, well-armored for its
size and heavily armed with a 20mm autocannon and
a machine gun, but the close country made the driv-
ers nervous.

Too many of their comrades had roasted alive in
burning armor for them to feel invincible.

Standartenfuhrer Hoth propped his elbows against
the sides of the turret hatch and brought up his field
glasses. Bright morning sunlight picked detail clear
and sharp, the clean mountain air like extra lenses to
enhance his vision. The command car had halted half
a thousand meters behind the two scout vehicles;
from here, the terrain rolled upslope to the village.
The military highway cut through it, and he could
catch glimpses of the mosque and town hall around

the central square, more glimpses than he remembered; a number of houses had been demolished, including the whole first row on the north side of town. There was an eerie stillness about the scene; there should have been locals moving in the fields and streets, smoke from cooking fires . . . and activity by the SS garrison. He focused on the patch of square visible to him. Bodies, blast-holes, firescorch . . . And there had been nothing on the radio since the single garbled screech at 0500. He glanced at his watch, a fine Swiss model he had taken from the wrist of a wounded British staff officer in Belgium. 0835: they had made good time from Pyatigorsk.

Raising a hand, he keyed the throat mike and spoke. "Schliemann, stay where you are and provide cover. Berger, the road looks clear through to the main square. Push in, take a quick look, then pull back. Continuous contact."

"Acknowledged, Standartenfuhrer," the Scharfuhrer in the lead car replied. The second vehicle halted; for a moment Hoth felt he could sense the tension in its turret, a trembling like a mastiff quivering on the leash.

Nonsense, he thought. *Engine vibration*. A humming through arms and shoulders, up from the commander's seat beneath his boots. The air was full of the comforting diesel stink of armor, metal and cordite and gun-oil; even through the muffling headset the grating throb of the Tatra 12-cylinder filled his head. The two cars ahead were buttoned tight; he could see the gravel spurting from the tires of the lead Puma, the quiver of the second's autocannon muzzle as the weapon quivered in response to the gunner's clench on the controls. Fiercely, he wished he was in the lead vehicle himself, up at the cutting edge of violence . . .

"Wait for it, wait for it," Eric breathed into the

microphone. He was perched on the lip of the shattered minaret; the trench periscope gave him a beautiful view of the SS officer in the command vehicle, enough to see the teeth showing in an unconscious snarl below his fieldglasses. Yes, it had to be the command vehicle from the miniature forest of antennae the turret sprouted. Details sprang at him: fresh paint in a dark-green mottle pattern, unscarred armor, tires still sharp-treaded . . . it must be fresh equipment, just out from Germany. His fingers turned the aiming wheels to track the other two cars, one in a covering position, another edging forward down the single clear lane into the village.

"Let him get into the square," he said. "Anyone opens fire without orders, I'll blast them a new asshole." The positions on the north edge were complete, the first priority, but there was no need to reveal them to deal with light armor like this, and much need to make the enemy commander underestimate the position. Silently, he thanked a God in which he had not believed since childhood for the ten minutes warning the advantage of height and the position northward beside the road had given. Enough to get the Century and the Circassians under cover; it helped that most of them had been in the cellars, of course.

He could hear the Fritz car now as it entered the village: whine of heavy tires on the gravel, the popping crunch as stones spurted out under the pressure of ten tonnes of armorplate. Below, in the square, the bodies waited—the thirty dead SS men gunned down in a neat line, and as many others hurriedly stuffed in the jackets of Draka casualties. *Got to let him get a look at it,* Eric thought. He wanted the German commander overestimating the Draka casualties; easy enough to make him think his comrades had taken a heavy blood-price. Not too good a look at those corpses, though—the rest of their uniform was still Fritz, and besides, they were all male. But the view from inside a closed-down turret was not that good.

"Centurion." Marie's voice. "That second car is only two hundred meters out. We could get him with a rocket gun, or even one of the 15mm's."

"After we blast the lead car," Eric said. His voice was tight with excitement; this was better even than catsticking, hunting lion on horseback with lances. And these were enemies you could really *enjoy* fighting. The Italians . . . that had been unpleasant. Far less dangerous, but how could you respect men who wouldn't fight even at the doorsteps of their own homes, for their families? It made you feel greasy, somehow. This . . . if it weren't for the danger to the Century, he would have preferred it; he had long ago come to peace with the knowledge that he would not survive this war. *At least I won't have to live through the aftermath of it, either,* ran through him with an undercurrent of sadness.

The lead car was in the square. "Position one! Five seconds . . . *Now!*"

Below, the trooper snuggled the rocket gun into his shoulder. This was a good position, clear to the back with a good ledge of rubble for the monopod in front of the forward pistol-grip. Fifteen kilos of steel and plastic was not an easy load to shoulder-fire; still, better than the tube-launchers the more compact recoilless hybrids had replaced. The armored car was clear in the optical sight; no need for much ranging at less than a hundred meters, just lay the crosshairs on the front fender. He squeezed the trigger, twisted and dove back into the safe darkness of the foxhole without bothering to stay and watch the results. He had seen too many armored vehicles blow up to risk his life for a tourist's-eye view.

The 84mm shell kicked free of the meter-long tube with a *whump-fuff* as the backblast stirred a cloud of

dust behind the gun. At eighty meters there was
barely time for the rocket motor to ignite before the
detonator probe struck armor. The shell was slow,
low-velocity; even the light steel sheathing of a Puma
would have absorbed its kinetic energy with ease.
But the explosive within was hollow-charge, a cone
with its widest part turned out and lined with cop-
per. Exploding, the shaped charge blew out a narrow
rod of superheated gas and vaporized metal at thou-
sands of meters per second; it struck the armorplate
before it with the impact of a red-hot poker on thin
cellophane. Angling up, the jet seared a coin-sized
hole through the plate, sending a shower of molten
steel into the fighting compartment. The driver had
barely enough time to notice the lance of fire that
seared off his body at the waist; fragments of a sec-
ond later, it struck the fuel and ammunition. Shat-
tered from within, the Puma's hull unfolded along
the seams of its welds; to watching eyes it seemed for
an instant like a flower in stop-motion film, blossoming
with petals of white-orange fire and grey metal. Then
the enormous *fumph* sound of the explosion struck, a
pressure on skin and eyeballs more than a noise, and
a *bang* echoing back from the buildings, an echo
from the sides of the mountains above. Steel clanged
off stone, pattering down from a sky where a fresh
column of oily black smoke reached for the thin
scatter of white cirrus above.

The twisted remains burned, thick fumes from the
spilling diesel oil. Eric nodded satisfaction. "One
15mm only on the second car!" he barked into the
microphone. "See the third off but don't kill him."

Standartenfuhrer Hoth had been listening to the
lead car's commentary in a state of almost-trance, his
mind filing every nuance of data while he poised for
instant action.

"... bodies everywhere, Draka and ours. No sign

of movement. More in the central square; heavy battle damage . . . Standartenfuhrer, there are thirty of our men here in front of the mosque, lined up and shot! This . . . this is a violation of the Geneva Convention!"

For a moment Hoth wondered if he was hearing some bizarre attempt at humour. Geneva Convention? In *Russia*? On the *Eastern Front*? But there was genuine indignation in the young NCO's voice; what were they *teaching* the replacements these days? Thunder rolled back from the mountains, as the all-too-familiar pillar of smoke and fire erupted from a corner of the square out of his sight.

Schliemann in the second car was a veteran, and so was the Standartenfuhrer's own crew. They reacted with identical speed, reversing from idle in less than a second with a stamp of clutches and crash of gears. The turrets walked back and forth along the line of rubble that had been the northern edge of the village, 20mm shells exploding in white flashes, machine gun rounds flicking off stone with sparks and sharp *ping* sounds that carried even through the crash of autocannon fire. Brass cascaded from the breeches into the turret as the hull filled with the nose-biting acridness of fresh cordite fumes. Speed built; Pumas were reconnaissance cars, designed to be driven rearward in just this sort of situation. And they had come for information, not to fight; the luckless Berger had been a sacrificial decoy duck to draw fire and reveal the enemy positions.

No accident that he had been sent forward, of course. Most of the casualties in any unit were newbies—mostly because of their own inexperience, partly because their comrades, when forced to choose, usually preferred that it was a new face which disappeared. It was nothing personal; you might like a recruit and detest someone you'd fought beside for a year. It was just a matter of who you wanted at your back when the blast and fragments flew.

Hoth kept his glasses up, flickering back and forth to spot the next burst. It came, machinegun fire directed at Schliemann's car. He kicked the gunner lightly on the shoulder: "Covering fire!" he barked.

There was a flash from the rubble, a cloud of dust from the tumbled stones above the machinegun's position. A brief rasping flare of rocket fire, and a shell took Schliemann's car low on the wheel well. The jet of the shaped charge seared across the bottom of the vehicle's hull, cut two axles and blew a wheel away to bounce and skitter across the road before it slammed itself into a tree hard enough to embed the steel rim. The cut axles collapsed and the heavy car pinwheeled, caught between momentum and the sudden drag as its bow dug into the packed stone of the road with a shower of sparks. Other sparks were flying as the 15mm hosed hull and turret with fire; even the incendiary tracer rounds were hard-tipped, and the car's armor was thin. Some rounds bounced from the sloped surfaces; others punched through, to flatten and ricochet inside the Puma's fighting compartment, slapping through flesh and equipment like so many whining lead-alloy bees.

The radio survived. Hoth could hear the shouting and clanging clearly, someone's voice shouting "*Gott-gottgott—*", and Schliemann cursing and hammering at the commander's hatch of the car. The impact had sprung the frames, probably, jamming the hatches shut. That often happened. He could see the first puff of smoke as fuel from the ruptured tanks ran into the compartment and caught fire; hear the frenzied screaming as the crew burned alive in their coffin of twisted metal. It went on as the Standarten-fuhrer's command car reversed out of sight of the village, into dead ground farther down the pass. Reaching down, he switched the radio off with a savage jerk and keyed in the intercom.

"Back to Pyatigorsk!" Schliemann had been a good

soldier, transferred from the Totenkopf units: a Party man from the street-fighting days, an *alte kampfer*. And his death had bought what they came for—some knowledge of what they faced. Of course, once they overran the Draka in the village there would be more positions farther up. It depended on how many from the division's motorized infantry brigades had been killed, and what sort of counterattack the units to the south were staging. A thought came to him, and his face smiled under its sheen of sweat; the gunner looked around at him, shivered, turned his gaze back to the sighting periscope as the car did a three-point turn and headed down the road.

I must take prisoners for intelligence about the Draka fallback positions, the SS officer thought. *I will enjoy that. I will enjoy that very much.*

Eric sighed and lowered his eyes from the trench periscope. That rocket gunner had been a little impulsive, but the result suited well enough. No way of concealing their presence from the Germans, but he could hope to make them underestimate the position. Whoever the man in that command car was, time was his enemy. The paratroopers only had to hold until the main Draka force broke through to win; the Fritz had to overrun them and all the rest of the legion, in time to pull their forces back and bring up replacements to block the pass. With only a little luck the German would try to take them on the run with whatever he could round up.

"Von Shrakenberg to all units: back to work, people. *Move!*" He handed the receiver back to Sofie and rolled over on his back; he would be needed to coordinate, to interpret when the Circassians and the Draka reached the limits of their mutually sketchy German. But not immediately; these were Citizen troops, after all, not Janissaries. They were expected to think, and to do their jobs without someone looking over their shoulders.

The mid-morning sky was blue, with a thickening scatter of clouds; they looked closer here in high mountain country than down in the plains about Mosul, where they had spent the winter.

"Hey, Centurion?" Sofie held out the lighted cigarette, and this time Eric accepted it. "More ideas?"

He shook his head. "Just thinking about home," he said. "And about a Greek philosopher."

"Come again?"

"Heraklitos. He said: 'No man steps twice into the same river.' The home I was remembering doesn't exist anymore, because the boy who lived there is dead, even if I wear his name and remember being him."

"Ah, well, my Dad always said: 'Home is where the heart is.' Of course, he was a section chief for the railways, so we moved around a lot."

Eric laughed and turned to look over his shoulder at the noncom. "Sofie, you're . . . a natural antidote to my tendency to gloom."

Sofie's eyes crinkled in an answering grin; she felt a soft lurch in the bottom of her stomach. Jauntily, she touched the barrel of her machine pistol to her helmet. "Hey, any time, Centurion."

The Centurion's gaze had returned to the village and the burning Puma. "While this war does exactly the opposite," he whispered.

The comtech frowned. "Hell, I'd rather be on the beach, surfin' and fooling around on a blanket, myself."

"That wasn't exactly what I was thinking of," he said softly. Unwise to speak, perhaps, but . . . *I'm damned if I'm going to start governing my actions by fear at this late date.* "If we lose, we'll be destroyed. If we win . . . what's going to happen, when we get to Europe?"

"The usual?"

Eric shook his head. "Sofie, how many serfs can read?"

She blinked. "Oh, a fair number—'bout one in five, I'd say. Why?"

"Which ratio worries the hell out of a lot of highly placed people. Most of the places we've taken over have been like this—" he nodded at the village "—peasants, primitives. If they're really fierce, like the Afghans, we have to kill a lot of them before the others submit. Usually, it's only necessary to wipe out a thin crust of chiefs or intelligentsia; the rest obey because they're used to obeying, because they're afraid, and because the changes are mostly for the better. Enough to eat, at least, and no more plagues. No prospect of anything better, but then, they never *did* have any prospect of anything better. Sofie, what are we going to *do* with the Europeans? We've never conquered a country where everybody can read, is used to thinking. Security—" He shook his head. "Security operates preventively. They're going to go berserk; it's going to be monumentally ugly. And I'm not even sure it will *work*."

The comtech puffed meditatively, trickled smoke from her nostrils. "Never did have much use for the Headhunters," she said. "Keep actin' as if they wished we all had neck numbers."

He nodded. "And it's not just that." His hands tightened on the Holbars. "Killing . . . it's natural enough; part of being human, I suppose. But too much of it does things. To us, that will hurt us in the long run." He sighed. "Well, at least I won't be there to see it."

"How so?" Sofie's voice was sharper.

Eric snorted weary laughter. "Well, what are the odds on a paratrooper surviving the whole war?"

"Hell," Sofie said, shocked. *This has to stop, and quick*, she thought. It was far too easy to die, even when you wanted to live. When you didn't . . .

Surprised, Eric turned: she was standing with her hands on her hips, lips compressed.

"Hell of a thing t'say, Centurion. *I* do my job, but I intends to die in bed."

"Sorry—" he began.

"Not finished. Now, that was interestin', what you had to say. Food for thought. You're *not* the only one who does that. Thinkin', I mean. So: you don't like what you see happenin'; what're you going to do about it?"

"What can I do—"

"How the fuck should I know? Sir. You're the one from the political family; I'm just a track-foreman's daughter. Not even sure I'd agree with anything you wanted to do, but it'd be a damn sight more comfortin' to have you callin' shots than some of the *kill-kill-kill-rape-what's-left* brigade. If it's your responsibility—an' who appointed you guardian of the human race?—then start thinkin' on what you can *do*, even if it isn't much. Can't do more than we can, hey? Waste an' shame to do less, though. Never figured you for a coward or a quitter or a member of the Church'a Self-Pity. Sir. And if the future of the State and the Race *isn't* your look-out, an' I can't no-how see how the fuck it should be, then acting as if 'tis is pretty goddam arrogant. Unless it's really somethig personal?

"Meanwhile," she said, pausing for breath, "this-here Century *is* your responsibility; we're your people and your blood."

Stunned, Eric stared at her, aware that his mouth was hanging slightly open. *I shouldn't underestimate people. I really shouldn't* . . . his mind began. Then, stung, he fell back on pride: "You could do better, Monitor Nixon?"

Sofie glanced away. "Oh, hell no, sir. Ah . . ."

He brushed past her, movements brisk. Their boots clattered on the stairs of the shattered mosque. Sofie stubbed out her butt and flicked it out a slit window, watching the arch of its falling with a vast content. There was a time to soothe, and a time for a medicinal boot in the butt. It was a beautiful day for a battle, and there was no better way of . . . getting close.

Who knows, she thought, watching the energy in his stride. *We might even both live through it, with him to supply the ideas, and me to keep his starry-eyed head from disappearin' completely up his own asshole.* Shrewdly, she guessed it had been too long since he'd had to listen to anyone. And it promised to be a nice long war, so none of them were going anywhere . . .

CHAPTER ELEVEN

Armored Fighting Vehicles: *Hond III—Draka*
Weight: *58 tons, loaded.*
Dimensions: *length 23ft., height 8ft. 2in., width 12ft. 6in.*
Armor: *30mm-125mm hull, 35mm-150mm turret/ mantlet. All surfaces sloped for ballistic protection; fabrication welded and cast.*
Armament: *1x120mm cannon, 1x15mm coaxial machine gun, 1x40mm coaxial grenade launcher, 1x15mm bow machine gun. 2x15mm antiaircraft twin-barrel machine gun on turret roof pintle mounting.*
Engine: *1,200 hp. Kurenwor free-piston turbocompound.*
Suspension: *Seven road wheels; torsion bar/hydraulic hybrid. Track width 650mm.*
Speed, range: *30 mph cross-country, 45 mph road. Range 300 miles on internal fuel; 600 with external drop tanks.*
Crew: *5: commander, loader, gunner, driver, and radio operator/bow gunner.*
Notes: *Specifications drafted by Strategic Planning Board, 1932–3, calling for a vehicle with twice the protection and firepower of the 26-ton, 75mm gun Hond II and at least equal mobility. Design team from War Directorate (Technical Section) and Diskarapur Technological Institute; prototype testing 1936–1937. Armor School, Kolwezara, 1938. Operational deployment 1939 –1941. Basic chassis used for standard Hoplite*

184

personnel carrier, recovery vehicles, 155mm, 175mm, and 200mm self-propelled guns, Cobra antiaircraft tank, Aardvark combat-engineer vehicle, numerous special-purpose uses. Assembled by Ferrous Metals Combine and Trevithick Autosteam Combine, at Archona, Diskarapur, Kolwezara and Karaganda. In production 1939 –1953: total output 68,000, not including variants.

Weapons of the Eurasian War
by Colonel Carlos Fueterrez, U.S. Army (ret.)
Defense Institute Press, Mexico City, 1955

VILLAGE ONE, OSSETIAN MILITARY HIGHWAY APRIL 14, 1942: 1400 HOURS

The village waited quietly; at least, its shell did, for a village is a human thing, even a village starving under the heel of a foreign conqueror. The heap of stone was no longer a place where peasants lived and grew food; it was a fortress, where strangers intricately trained and armed would kill each other, thousands of kilometers from their homes. The last of the Circassians had left for the forest, bent under their sacks of food; all except for the aged *hadji*, who remained in the cellar beneath the mosque, praying in the darkness over a Koran long since committed to memory. Half the houses had been demolished, and the remainder were carefully prepared traps; the cellars below were a spiderweb network that the Draka could use to shift their personnel under cover, or to bring down death on anyone who followed them into the booby-trapped tunnels. Two hundred soldiers had labored six hours beside the natives, sledgehammer and pick, shovel and blasting charge. The troops were working for their lives and the hope of victory.

The villagers had motivation at least as strong;
their numbers had dropped by half since the *Lieb-
standarte* moved in, and every shovelful was a mea-
sure of revenge. Two hours past noon, and the de-
fenses were ready. The paratroopers rested at their
weapons, taking the opportunity for food, water, sleep,
or a crap—veterans knew you never had time later.

Eric sat back against the thick rough timbers of the
passageway, unbending his fingers with an effort.
Beside him, Sofie swore softly and broke out a tube
of astringent wound-ointment. The Centurion looked
aside as she began smearing the viscous liquid on the
tattered blisters that covered his hands, ignoring the
sharp pain. It had a thin, acrid petroleum smell,
cutting through the dry rock dust and the heavy
scent of sweat from meat-fed bodies. They were at
the northernmost edge of the village, where the
military road entered the built-up area. Two long
heaps of rubble flanked it now, where there had
been rows of houses; rubble providing cover for two
long timber-framed bunkers. The Draka commander
was on the left, the western flank; grey eyes flicked
south and east, to the forest where the people of the
village had gone.

"I hope you can see it, Tyansha," he murmured
softly in her language. "And for once, there is mercy."

Five meters away an improvised crew sprawled
about their Soviet/German 76.2mm antitank gun,
ready to manhandle it to any of the four firing posi-
tions in the long bunker. A pile of shells was stacked
near it; a ladder poked out of the floor nearby, and
more ammunition waited below with strong arms to
pitch it up. The sleek, long-barreled solidity of the
gun was reassuring; so was the knowledge that its
twin was waiting in the other bunker, across the street.
One of the gunners was singing, an old, old tune with
the feel of Africa in it; Eric remembered it murmured
over his cradle, as smooth brown arms rocked:

"A shadow in the bright bazarre
  A glimpse of eyes where none should shine
A glimpse of eyes translucent gold
  And slitted against the sun . . ."

His palms were sticky; strips of skin pulled free as
he opened and closed them, absently. There was
very little to do, until the action started. A fixed
defensive position with secure flanks was the sim-
plest tactical problem a commander could have; the
only real decision-making was when and where to
commit reserves, and since he didn't have any, to
speak of . . .

". . . faster than a thought she flees
  And seeks the jungle's sheltering trees
But he is steady on the track
  And half a breath behind . . ."

Sofie was speaking; he swiveled his attention back.
"—cking soul of the White Christ, Centurion, you
trying to punish yourself or something? And don't
give me any of that leading-by-example crap!" The
tone was a hissed whisper, but there was genuine
anger in it.

He smiled at her, flexing the hands under the
bandage pads; she maintained the scowl for a mo-
ment, then grinned shyly back. *You are really get-
ting quite perceptive, Sofie,* he thought. *And you
glow when you're angry.*

"She tastes his scent upon the breeze,
  And looking past her shoulder sees
He treads upon her shadow—
  She fears the hunter's mind."

"The Fritz will take care of any punishment needed
for my sins," he said. "Good, I can fight with these."

A pause. "Thank you." She blushed. "I was just thinking about the war again, and didn't notice, actually."

"Oh," she replied, hunting for something to say in a mind gone blank. "You . . . think we're going to win?"

"Probably. Depends what you mean by win."

"In woman form, in leopard hide
  Fording, leaping, side to side
She doubles back upon her track
  And sees her efforts fail."

She frowned, reached up to free the package of cigarettes tucked into the camouflage cover of her helmet, tapped one free and snapped her Ronson lighter. "Ahh . . . well, the Archon said we were fighting for survival. I guess, we come out alive and we've won?"

Eric laughed with soft bitterness. "Not bad. Did you hear what our esteemed leader said, after we attacked the Italians and they complained that we'd promised not to? 'You were expecting truth from a politician? Christ, you'll be looking for charity from a banker, next.' One thing I always liked about her, she doesn't mealymouth." He let his head fall back against the timbers. "Actually, she's right . . . it all goes back to the serfs."

". . . her gold flanks heaving in distress,
  Half woman and half leopardess
To either side, nowhere to hide
  It's time to fight or die."

She looked at him blankly, retaining one of the bandaged hands; he made no objection. "The serfs?" she said.

"Yes . . . look, our ancestors were soldiers mostly,

right? They fought for the British, they lost, and the British very kindly gave them a big chunk of African wilderness . . . inhabited wilderness, which they then had to conquer. And they made serfs of the conquered —there were too many of them to exterminate the way the Yanks did to their aborigines, so—serfdom. Slavery, near as no matter, but prettied up a little to keep the abolitionists in England happy. Or less unhappy." He sighed. "Can you spare one of those cancer sticks?"

She lit another from hers. "What's that got to do with the war?" The song tugged at her attention.

"*A sight none will forget*
  Who once have seen them, near or far,
In sunlight or where shadows are
  As, side by side they hunt and hide
No one has caught them yet."

"I'm coming to that. Look, what do you think would happen if we eased up on the serfs?"

"Eased up?"

"Let them move off their masters' estates or factory compounds, gave them education, that sort of thing."

"Oh." Sofie's face cleared; that was simple. "They'd rise up and exterminate us." She thought. "Not all of them; some'd stick by us. Some house servants, straw bosses 'n foremen, Janissaries, technicians, that sort. They'd get their throats cut, too."

"Damn straight, they would. And there would go civilization, until outsiders moved in and ate the pieces. So, once we'd settled in, we were committed to the serf-and-plantation system, took it with us wherever we went. We had the wolf by the ears: hard to hang on, deadly to let go. Did you know there were mass escapes, in the early years? Rebellions, too." His eyes grew distant. "My great-great-grandfather put one down, in 1828. Impaled four thousand rebels through the sugar country, from Virconium to Shanapur. He had a painting made of it, still hanging in the hallway at home." Tyansha had refused to look at it; he had wondered why, at the time. "Well, one of the main reasons for all that was the border country with the wild tribes: a place to escape to, hope for overthrowing us. So we had to expand. Also, you run through a lot of territory when every one of a landholder's sons expects an estate."

The comtech leaned forward, interested despite herself. Not that it was much different from the history she had been taught, but the emphasis and shading was something else entirely.

"Then, by the 1870's, we'd grown all the way up to Egypt, no borders but the sea and the deserts, and we'd started to industrialize, so we had modern communications and weapons."

"Hmmmm," Sophie said. "Why didn't we stop there?"

He grunted laughter and dragged smoke down his throat. "Because we'd gotten just strong enough to terrify people. Not afraid enough to leave us alone, though. People with real power, in Europe. And we were different—so different that when they realized what was going on, they were hostile by reflex. Demanding reforms we couldn't make without committing suicide." Eric gestured with the cigarette, tracing red ember-glow through the gloom. "So, there were murmurs about boycotts; propaganda, too. And we couldn't keep the city serfs completely illiterate, not if they were going to operate a modern economy for us. That's when the Security Directorate was set up, and it's been getting more and more power every decade since. Which means power over Citizens, too."

Caught up in his words, he failed to notice the comtech's worried glance from side to side. Unheeding, he continued. "Well, the Great War was a god-send; we took on the weakest of the Central Powers, and grabbed off Persia and Russian central Asia and western China too. And the War shattered Europe, which gave us time to consolidate; then we were a Great Power in our own right."

He grinned like a wolf. "Stroke of genius, no? Only now, we had thousands of kilometers of land frontier, with a hostile great power! See, liberal democrat, Communist, even Fascist, any different social system is a deadly menace to us, if it's close. And they're all different. All close, too; with modern technology the world's getting to be a pretty small place. The boffins say that after the war, radios will be as small and cheap as teakettles were, before. Imagine every serf village out in West Bumfuck having a receiver; we can jam, but . . . So, on to the war. Another heaven-sent stroke of luck, although we were counting on something like that. Divide and rule, let others wear themselves out and the Domination steps in—our traditional strategy. If we win, we'll have the earth, the whole of North Asia, and most of Europe besides what we took last time."

"Think we can do it?" Sofie asked in a neutral tone.

"Oh, sure. The problem will be holding it. Remember that cartoon in the Alexandria *Gazette?*" She nodded. The chief opposition newspaper had shown a python with scales in the Draka colors that had just throttled a hippo. It lay, bleeding and bruised, muttering: "Sweet Christ, now do I have to *eat* the bloody thing?" "But that won't be enough."

"What will?"

"In the end . . . we'll have to conquer the earth. The Archon was right, you see? To survive, we've got to make sure nobody else does, except as serfs." Eric, who had long since come to an acceptance of what his people and nation were, ground the cigarette out with short, savage motions of his hand. "We're like a virus, really: we'll never be safe with uninfected tissue still able to manufacture antibodies against us."

Sofie folded the hand in hers. "You don't sound . . . too enthusiastic about it, Centurion."

"It could be worse. That's the analysis the Academy will give you, anyway; they just think it's a wonderful situation."

She hesitated, then decided on bluntness. "What are you doing in a fighting unit, then?" she asked quietly.

He looked up, his mouth quirking; even then, she noticed how a lock of butter-yellow hair fell over the tanned skin of his forehead. "I love my people. Not like, sometimes, but . . . That's enough to fight and die for, isn't it?" And very softly, "But is it enough to live for?"

Their eyes met. And the comset hissed, clicking with Eric's code. Efficiency settled over him like a mask as he reached for the receiver.

"Ah," said Eric, watching the German column winding up the road toward the village. "There you see the results of Fritz ingenuity." A glance at his wrist. "1610—good time."

"Oh?" Marie Kaine asked, not taking her eyes from the trench periscope. She had always had doubts about the cost-effectiveness of tanks. So delicate, under their thick hides, so complex and highly stressed and failure prone . . . Still, it was daunting to have them coming at you.

The Fritz convoy had been dipping in and out of sight with the twists of the road from the north: six tanks, two heavy assault guns, tracked infantry carriers in the rear. The optics brought them near, foreshortened images trembling as slight vibrations in the tube were translated to wavering over the kilometer of distance. She could see the long cannon of the tanks swinging, the heads of infantrymen through the open hatches of the APC's, imagine the creaking, groaning, clanging rattle that only armor makes. They were still over two thousand meters out when a brace of self-propelled antiaircraft guns peeled off to take up stations upslope of the road. The sun had baked what moisture remained out of the rocky surface, and the heavy tracks were raising dust plumes as they ground through the crushed-rock surface of the military highway.

Military highway, she snorted to herself. Of course, the Soviets hadn't had much wheeled traffic. Even so, for a strategic road, this was a disgrace.

"Mmm. You know the Wehrmacht-SS situation?" the Centurion continued.

Marie nodded wordlessly. Sofie spoke, without looking up from the circuit board she was working on. "Elite units, aren't they? Volunteers. Like us, or Boss' Brass Knucks?" That was the Archonal Guard Legion; their insignia was a mailed fist.

"Yes, but they're not part of the regular army; they're organs of the Nationalsozialistiche Deutsche Arbeiterpartei. And they're always fighting with the regulars over recruits and equipment. So their organization took over the Russian factories to get an independent supply base." He nodded to the squat combat machines grinding their way up the road. "Those are Ivan KV-1 heavy tanks, with a new turret and the Fritz 88mm/L56 gun; cursed good weapon, plenty of armor and reasonable mobility. Better than their standard-issue machines. Hmmm . . . the assault guns look like the same chassis, with a 150mm gun-howitzer mounted in the front glacis plate. The infantry carriers and flakpanzers are on SU-76 bodies; that was the Ivans' light self-propelled gun. Ingenious; they've actually made a good thing out of departmental in-fighting."

"Sounds as bad as the pissing matches the Army and Air Corps and Navy are always getting into at home," Marie Kaine said. She made a final note on her pad and called instructions to the gun crew; a round of AP ammunition slid into the breech with a chunk-chang of metallic authority. Range would be no problem; a dozen inconspicuous objects had been carefully measured, and the guns were sighted in. First-round fire would be as accurate as the weapons permitted; Marie was not impressed with the standard of the machining. A sound design, but crude: there was noticeable windage in the barrel, even with lead driving bands, and the exterior finish was primitive in the extreme.

Sofie handed the sheet of electronic components back to the artillery observer, a harassed-looking man with thinning sandy hair and a small clipped mustache. He slid it back into the open body of his radio, reinserted the six thumb-sized vacuum tubes, and touched the leads with a testing jack. "Ahhh," he said. "Good work; all green. Thanks, our spares had a little accident on the way down, hate to have to run a field-telephone line in."

He rose, dusting off his knees, and peered out a slit. "Hmmm, our Hond III's are better. Not much heavier, twice the speed, better sloping on the armor, a 120mm gun."

"Oh, yes," Eric said. "And all sorts of extras: gyro-stabilizers on the gun, shock absorbers on the torsion bars . . . Only one problem." He pointed an imaginary pistol at the SS panzers. "Our armor is a hundred kilometers away; those machines are here. Got the battery on line?"

"Yessir." He handed over the receiver; Sofie's set would have done as well, but it was more efficient to have a dedicated channel.

"Palm One to Fist, over."

"Roge-doge, Palm One. Our 105's 're set up, and

the captured Fritz 150's. Covering your position and about 4,000 meters out. Going to need a firefall soon?"

"That's negative, Fist; this looks like a probing attack. Later."

"All go, Palm One. But watch it: this is the only decent position in range, so they've got it map-referenced for sure, they don't need observation to key in. And if they've got self-propelled heavies, no way I can win a counter-battery shoot. They're immune to blast and fragments; we're not and we can't move, either. And you know what the odds are on hitting armored vehicles with indirect fire: about the same as flying to the moon by putting your head between your knees and spitting hard."

"Green, Fist; we'll only need you once. What about the Air Corps boys?" Artillery observers doubled as ground-control liaison for strike aircraft.

A sour chuckle. "Yo' should hear the commo channels; everybody from here to Tiflis is screaming that the bogeyman's out of the closet, and will Momma fly in and help, please. At least there aren't any of Hitler's pigeons around shitting on *us* . . . For that matter, I could have used air support an hour ago myself—couple hundred of those-there Fritz hold-outs tried to rush my perimeter."

Eric winced. That could cause hard trouble; it was a good thing they had not waited for darkness. "Over and out, Fist."

"Kill a few for us, Palm One."

"Range, one thousand meters," Marie said expressionlessly. Eric leaned a hand on the bunker ceiling and watched. Six heavy AFV's, twelve infantry carriers with eleven men each . . . not counting the flakpanzers, about two lochoi of armor and a century of panzergrenadiers. The enemy was doing about what he'd expected; about what Eric would have done with the same information—trying to bull through with whatever could be scraped up at short notice and moved under skies controlled by the opposition, in the hope that there was nothing much to stop him. And he'd know his opponents were paratroopers, hence lightly equipped. On the battlefields of Europe, that meant negligible antitank capacity; the armed forces of the Domination had a rather different definition of *light*.

"Seven hundred meters," Marie said. "They're probably going to deploy their infantry any time now, Centurion." The diesel growl of the German engines was clearly audible now: Eric gave a hand signal to Sofie, and she relayed the stand-ready command. The bunker was hushed now. Tension breathed thick; it was silent enough to hear the steel-squeal and diesel growl from the enemy armor over the windsough from the forest.

The first of the German tanks was making the final turn, a move that presented his flank; after that it would be a straight path into the village. Eric raised a hand, lips parted slightly, waiting for the first tank to pass by a white-painted stone at the six-hundred-meter mark. Time stretched, vision sharpened; this was like hunting, not the adrenaline rush of close combat. For a moment he could even feel a detached pity for his opponent.

"Now!"

CRACK! and the antitank gun cut loose, a stunning blast of noise in the confined space. The dimness of the bunker went black and rank with dust, and the barrel of the cannon slammed back almost to the far wall; the crew was leaping in with fresh ammunition even as the cradle's hydraulics returned to "rest," and the casing rang on the stones of the floor. Downslope to the north, the lead tank stopped dead as the tungsten-cored shot took it at the junction of turret and hull, smashing through the armor and fighting compartment, burying itself in the engine block. There was a second's pause before the explosion, a flash, and the ten-tonne mass of the turret blew free and into the air, flipping end over end into the sky, landing twenty meters from the burning hulk.

That blocked the road. The German armor wheeled to deploy into the fields; the assault gun in the rear had turned just enough to present its flank when the second antitank gun in the other bunker fired—one round that twisted it askew with a tread knocked loose, a second that struck the side armor with the brutal *chunggg* of high-velocity shot meeting steel. Assault guns are simply steel boxes, with a heavy cannon in a limited-traverse mount in the bow. From the front they are formidable; from the flanks, almost helpless. The hatches flew open, and the crew poured out to throw themselves down in the roadside ditches; one was dragging a man whose legs had contested passage with twenty kilograms of moving metal, and lost badly. The damaged vehicle burned sullenly, occasional explosions jarring the ground and sending tongues of flame through its hatches and around the gun that lay slanting toward the ground, its mantlet slammed free of the surrounding armor. Another pillar of black oil-smoke reached for the mild blue of the afternoon sky.

The bunker crew had time for a single cheer before the response came. All the armored vehicles had opened up with their secondary armament, but the machine-gun fire was little menace to dug-in positions. The second Fritz assault gun was a different matter, and its commander was cool enough to ignore the burning wreckage before and behind him. The two muzzle flashes had given away the position of the gun that killed his comrades, and the third shot howled off the thick frontal armor of his gun. Carefully he traversed, corrected for range, fired. The sound of the six-inch howitzer was thicker and somehow heavier than the high-velocity tank guns, but at this point-blank range there was no appreciable interval between firing and impact. And the shell carried over a hundred pounds of high explosive.

Eric felt the impact as a flexing in the ground, as if the fabric of the bunker had withdrawn and struck him like a huge palm. Dust smoked down from the ceiling, between the heavy timbers; he sneezed. There was another impact, then a thudding to their right: the second bunker was catching it.

"Marie! Get that gun to the end firing position!" The crew sprang into action, manhandling the heavy weapon back and turning it; it rumbled off down the curved length of the bunker toward the firing slit at the western end.

"Follow me!" He turned and scuttled toward the eastern end of the bunker; this was not going to be a healthy sector in a few seconds. As they ran he cupped the hand radio to his ear.

"Gun two, gun two, come in. Come in, goddammit!" Then to himself: "Shit!" Even with a 150mm shell, it would have taken a direct hit to disable the other antitank gun. *Luck plays no favorites*, he thought bleakly. Chances were the other gun was out, which meant he was naked of antitank on the eastern side of the road, except for the 120mm recoilless dug in on the edge of the forest, and he had been hoping not to have to use that just yet. Aloud, he continued.

"Tom, try to get someone through to gun two's position. Report, and see if the machine gun positions in B bunker are intact." A different code-click. "East wing recoilless, engage any armor your side of the road, but not until within two hundred meters of our front."

The acknowledgements came through as they dropped to a halt beside the machine gun team at the east end of the bunker. Eric rested a hand on their shoulders, leaning forward to peer through the irregular circle of the firing port.

"Yahhh!" he snarled. The bunker shook as another heavy shell impacted; bullets spalled chips of stone from the rubble outside. Light poured through the opening—a yellow beam through the dust motes that hung, suspended, in the column of brightness. The three tanks had fanned out into the fields, swinging to present their frontal armor to the village and accelerating forward, their guns barking at the long heaps of rubble on either side of the road. And . . . yes! One leaped as a white flash erupted under a tread, settled back with a shattered road wheel. Now the Draka machineguns were opening up, hosing over the stranded behemoth. They could not penetrate the armor; not even the antitank gun could without a side shot, not without great good luck. But they could shatter optics, rattle the crew . . .

He hammered a fist into the wall in glee; the other two were falling back, unwilling to chance a mine field without engineers or special vehicles to clear it. Accelerating in reverse, they circled the assault guns and climbed back onto the road, retreating until they were hull down in a patch of low ground. Still dangerous, those long 88mm guns had plenty of range, but the bluff of his scanty handful of antitank mines had worked.

The German infantry carriers had halted well back; their thin armor offered protection from small arms and shell fragments only. Now they were opening up with the twin machineguns each carried, and the Waffen-SS panzergrenadiers were spilling out of the opened ramp doors at the rear of each vehicle. Eric could see them marshalling, fanning out west of the road. They could see the waiting V-spread of wire and trench that threatened to funnel them into a killing ground as they advanced south; their officers' shouts pushed them toward the sheltering forest, where they could operate under cover and flank the strong frontal positions. Even a few snipers and machineguns upslope from the village could make field trenches untenable.

"Smart, Fritz; by the book," he murmured. The Draka infantry were opening up with their crew-served weapons; a few of the Germans were falling under the flail of the 15mm's, but that was over a thousand meters, extreme range, and the Germans were making skillful use of cover. Happily, he waited for them to reach the protection of the woods. They would do it on the run; even well-trained soldiers threw themselves into cover when under fire. The trees would beckon, and they had already been shaken by what had happened to their armor.

"Now," he whispered. Now it was up to those at the treeline.

"*Not yet,*" the Draka decurion murmured to himself. The Germans had been coming in across the fields well spread out, but they bunched as they approached the treeline, the underbrush was thinner here and they were unconsciously picking the easiest way in. In out of the punishing fire coming from the Draka positions, up the valley to their left. Bunching, speeding up, their attention divided.

The moment stretched. Above him a bird sounded a liquid *di-di-di*, announcing its nesting territory to the world. The Draka soldier waited behind the log, his eyes steady on flickers of movement through a shimmering haze of leaves, confident in the near-invisibility of camouflage uniform and motionlessness. His tongue ran over dry lips, tasting forest mold and green dust. Insects buzzed, burrowed, dug.

'*Course, they-all could spot those dumbshit Ivans*, he thought. The Russian partisans were with him, a tetrarchy's worth with captured Fritz weapons. Forget about that, concentrate . . .

Ya . . . Now! His thumb clamped on the safety-release of the detonator, and he rapped it sharply three times on the moss-grown trunk of the fallen beech before him. Ahead of him the thick band of undergrowth along the forest edge exploded, erupted into a chaos of flying dust, shedded leaves, wood chips. Louder than the explosion was a humming like a hundred thousand metal bees: Broadsword directional mines, curved plates lined with *plastique*, the concave inner face tight-packed with razor-edged steel flechettes like miniature arrows. Pointed toward an enemy, mounted at waist-height, they had the effect of titantic shotgun shells. The German infantry went down, scythed down, the first ranks shredded, sliced, spattered back into their comrades' faces.

They halted for an instant, too stunned even to seek cover. The loudest sound was the shrill screaming of the wounded—men lying thrashing with helmets, weapons, harness nailed to their bodies. The decurion rolled to his Holbars, over it, came up into firing position and began picking targets, hammering three-round bursts.

"Ya! Ya! Beautiful, fuckin' *beautiful!*" he shouted. The others of his stick opened up from positions in cover, and a volley of grenades followed.

Grunting in annoyance, the Draka NCO noticed one of the Russian partisans he had been assigned kneeling, staring slack-jawed at the chewed bodies in SS uniforms that lay in clumps along a hundred meters of the forest edge. He was shaking his head, mouth moving silently, the Schmeisser dangling limply from his hands.

"*Shoot*, yo' stupid donkeyfucka!" The Draka dodged over and planted his boot in the Russian's buttocks with a thump. "Useless sonofabitch, *shmert, shmert Fritz!*"

The partisan scarcely seemed to feel the blow. He grinned, showing the blackened jagged stumps of teeth knocked out by a rifle butt; through the rags on his back bruises showed yellow and green and black.

"Da, da," he mumbled, raising the machine-pistol. Holding it clamped tight to the hip and loosing off a burst, then another; short bursts, to keep the muzzle from rising too much. He came to his feet, disregarding the return fire that was beginning to whine overhead and drop clipped-off twigs on their heads. His bullets hosed out, across the back of a wounded SS grenadier who was hobbling away with a leg trailing, using his rifle for a crutch.

"*Da! Da!*" he shouted.

The decurion dropped away. The partisans had opened up all along the treeline, thirty of them thickening up his firepower quite nicely. The SS were rallying, crawling forward now; a MG34 machine-gun began firing in support, and an 88mm shell from one of the tanks smashed a giant hornbeam into a pillar of splinters and fire. Thick green-wood smoke began to drift past as the first Germans reached the woodland and crashed through the tangled resiliency of the bushes. They were still taking casualties, of course, and still under fire from the village on their left flank. The Draka paused to smack a fresh drum into his Holbars, whistling tunelessly between his teeth. In a moment they would fall back, into the thick woods; the partisans could cover that. Fall back to the *next* ambush position; the trees would channel pursuit nicely. He doubted the Germans would come farther than that, this time.

Beside him, the Russian was laughing.

Eric watched as the SS infantry halted, rallied, began to fight their way into the woods. The armored vehicles had swiveled their weapons to support them; only the assault gun kept the village under fire, the heavy shells going over their heads with a freight-train-at-night rush. And the flakpanzers, moving forward and risking their thin plating to hose their quadruple 20mm autocannon over the village,

short bursts that hit like horizontal explosive hail-
storms. The Draka in the bunker dove for the floor,
away from the firing slits. Not that there was much
chance of a hit even so; the antiaircraft weapons ate
ammo too rapidly to keep up the support fire long
enough to saturate an area, but there was no point in
risking life for a bystander's view. The action was out
of range of their personal weapons, anyway.

Eric continued his scan, forcing the mind's knowl-
edge of probabilities to overcome the hindbrain's
cringing. Some of the SS infantry carriers were revers-
ing, ready to re-embark their crews; the Fritz com-
mander must be a cool one, prepared to cut his losses.

The Centurion closed his eyes for a moment, strug-
gling to hold the battle whole in his mind without
focusing on its component parts. *Know how a man
fights and you know what he is and how he thinks*:
the words ran through him like an echo. Who . . .
Pa, of course; that was one of his favorite maxims.
How had the German commander reacted? Well,
ruthlessly, to begin with. He had sacrificed that warcar
to gain information. Not afraid of casualties, then.
Bold, ready to gamble; he'd tried to rush through
with no more than two companies, to push as far up
the pass as he could before the Draka solidified their
defense.

Eric opened slitted eyes, scratched at the itching
yellow stubble under his chin. *Damnation, I wish I
had more information*. Well, what soldier didn't?
And he wished he could have spent more time with
the partisan leader, pumped him for details, but it
was necessary to send him off to contact the others, if
anything valuable was to come of that. After showing
him enough dead Germans to put some spirit in him
and backbone back into his followers, not to mention
what Dreiser had done, that was good work. Escape
from the cauldron of death that Russia had become
was a fine lure, glittering enough to furnish enthusi-

asm, but so distant that it was not likely to make
them cautious.

But it would have been good to learn a little more
about this man Hoth in Pyatigorsk. Still . . . there
had been a bull-like quality to the attack. Plenty of
energy, reasonable skill, but not the unexpected, the
simple after-the-fact novelty that marked a really in-
spired touch. The *Liebstandarte* had always been a
mechanized unit, no doubt the SS commander knew
the value of mobility, but did he understand it was as
much an *attitude* as a technique? Or was he wedded
to his tanks and carriers, even when the terrain and
circumstances were wrong?

What was that speech of Pa's again? *Don't think in
terms of specific problems, think in terms of the task.*
A commander who was a tactician and nothing else
would look at the Draka position in the village and
think of how to crush it; one problem at a time. *I
would have tried something different,* he thought.
*Hmmmm, maybe waiting until dark, using the time to
bring up reserves, filtered infantry through the woods
in the dark and then attacked from both sides.* It was
impossible to bypass the village completely, it sat
here in the pass like a fishbone in a throat; but there
were ways to keep to the principle of attacking weak-
ness rather than strength . . .

Ways to manipulate the enemy, as well. Pa again:
*If you hurt him, an untrained man will focus on the
pain. In rage, if he's brave and a fighter; without
realizing that even so he's allowing you to direct his
attention, that your Will is master.* Eric had found
that true in personal combat; so few could just *accept*
a hurt, keep centered, prevent their mind's eye from
rushing to the sensory input of the threatened spot.
The way some chess players focused on this check
rather than the mate five moves into the future.
*Discipline, discipline in your soul; you aren't a man
until you can command yourself, body as well as*

mind. Without inner discipline a man is nothing more than a leopard that thinks, and you can rule him with a whip and a chair until he jumps through hoops.

He reached for the handphone of the radio, brushing aside an old resentment. *So you're a bastard, I'm not so stupid I can't see when you're right,* he thought at the absent form of Karl von Shrakenburg.

Three quick clicks, two slow: recognition signal for the mortars. Focus on the valley below: the German panzergrenadiers falling back from the edge of the woods, dragging their hurt, the SS armor opening up again on the bunker positions, trying to keep the gunners' heads down and cover the retreat. Bright muzzle flashes, the heavy *crack* of high-velocity shot. Flickering wink of automatic weapons, and the sound of the jacketed bullets on rock, like a thousand ball peen hammers ringing on a girder. Stone rang; raw new-cut timber shifted and creaked as the shells *whumped* against rock and dirt filtered down from above and into his collar. He sneezed, hawked, spat grit out of his mouth, blinking back to the brightness of the vision slit.

Wait for it, wait for it. Now: now they were clustered around their vehicles.

"Firefall," he said.

Thick rock hid the sound of the automortars firing, the *fumpfumpfump* as their recoil-operated mechanisms stripped shells out of the hoppers and into the stubby smooth-bore barrels. Eric raised the field glasses to his eyes; he could see a flinching as the veterans among the SS troopers dove for cover or their APC's, whichever was closest. Survivors, who knew what to expect. Rifles and machineguns pin infantrymen, force them to cover, but it is artillery that does the killing, from overhead, where even a foxhole is little help. And all foot soldiers detest mortars even more than other guns; mortar bombs drop out of the sky and spread fragments all around them rather than in the narrow cone of a gun shell. Much less chance to survive a near miss, and there is more explosive in a mortar's round than an artillery shell, which needs a thick steel wall to survive firing stresses.

CRASH. *CRASHCRASHCRASH* . . . Tiny stick figures running, falling, lifting into the air with flailing limbs. Lightning-wink flashes from the explosions, each with its puff of smoke. Imagination furnished the rest, and memory: raw pink of sliced bone glistening in opened flesh; screaming and the low whimpering that was worse; men in shock staring with unbelief at the wreck of selves that had been whole fractions of a second before; the whirring hum of jagged cast-iron casing fragments flying too fast to see and the cringing helplessness of being under attack with no means of striking back . . .

"Sofie," he said. She started, forcing her attention back from the distant vehicles.

"Ya, sir?"

"Can you break me into the Fritz command circuit?" The SS personnel carriers were buttoning up, the hale dragging wounded up the ramps and doors winching shut. Even thin armor would protect against blast and fragments. The tanks had raised their muzzles, dropping high-explosive rounds in the village on the chance of finding the mortar teams that were punishing their comrades. Brave, since it risked more fire from the antitank guns in the forward positions, but hopeless. More hopeless than the Germans suspected; there were only three of the automortars with the Draka, their rate of fire giving them the impact of a century of conventional weapons. At that, the shells were falling more slowly, one weapon at a time taking up the bombardment, to save ammunitiion and spare the other barrels from heat buildup.

Another of TechSec's marvels, another nightmare

for the supply officers, a detached portion of Eric's mind thought. Officially, Technical Section's motto was "Nothing But the Best"; to the gun-bunnies who had to hump the results of their research into battle, it was commonly held to be "Firepower at All Costs."

Sofie had unslung the backpack radio, opened an access panel, made adjustments. Draka field radios had a frequency-randomizer, to prevent eavesdropping. It was new, experimental, troublesome, but it saved time with codes and ciphers. The Fritz, now, still . . . She put fingers to one earphone and turned a dial, slowly.

"Got 'em," she said cheerfully, raising her voice over the racket of combat. "They don't seem happy, nohow."

Eric brought the handset to his ear, willing distractions to fade until there was only the gabble of static-blurred voices. His own German was good enough to recognize the Silesian accent in the tone that carried command.

"Congratulations," he said, in the language of his ancestors. There was a moment's silence on the other end; he could hear someone cursing a communications officer in the background, and the measured thudding of explosions heard through tank armor.

"Congratulations," he repeated, "on your losses. How many? Fifty? A hundred? I doubt if we lost six!" He laughed, false and full and rich; it was shocking to the watching Draka, coming from a face gone expressionless as an axe. A torrent of obscenities answered him. *A peasant, from the vocabulary,* Eric thought. *Pure barnyard.* And yes, he could be distracted, enraged. Probably the type with cold lasting angers: an obsessive. The German paused for breath, and Eric could imagine a hand reaching for the selector switch of his intercom. With merciless timing, the Draka spoke into the instant. "Any messages for your wives and sisters? We'll be seeing them before you do!

"Our circuit," he continued, and then: "Cease fire."

A pain in one hand startled him. He looked down, saw that the cigarette had burned down to his knuckle, dropped it and ground the butt into the dirt. Two-score men had died since the brief savage encounter began: their bodies lay in the fields, draped over bushes along the western edge of the forested hills, roasting and shriveling in the burning fighting vehicles down below on the road. All in the time it might have taken to smoke a cigarette, and most of them had died without even a glimpse of the hands that killed them.

He snorted. "Someday TecSec will find a way of incinerating the world while sitting in a bunker under a mountain," he muttered. "The apothesis of civilized warfare."

"Sir?" Sofie asked.

Eric shook himself. There was the work of the day to be done; besides, it had probably been no prettier in chain-mail.

"Right. Get me the medics, I want a report on what happened in Bunker B. Put . . . Svenson, wasn't it, down on the treeline? Put him on as soon as he reports in; that was well done, he deserves a pat for it."

"So do you, sir."

Startled, he glanced over at her as she finished rebuckling the straps of the radio and stood with a grunt. Teeth flashed in the gloom as she reached over and ceremoniously patted him on the back; looking about with embarrassment, he saw nods from the other troopers.

"Luck," he said dismissively. Combat was an either-or business: you took information always scanty and usually wrong, made a calculated guess, then stood ready to improvise. Sometimes it worked, and you looked like a hero; sometimes you slipped into the shit head-first. Nobody did it right every time, not against an opponent less half-hard than the Italians.

"Bullshit, *sir*," Sofie said. "When yo' stop worryin' and do it, it gets fuckin' *done*." She shrugged at his frown. "Hey, why give the Fritz a call in the middle of things?"

"Because I always fancied myself as a *picador*, Sofie," he said, turning to watch the Germans disappear down the valley, infantry carriers first, the tanks following, reversing from one hull-down position to the next so that they could cover each other. "Let's just hope the bull I goaded isn't too much for our cape."

CHAPTER TWELVE

DATE: *02/04/42*
FROM: *Strategos Cynthia Carstairs*
           Planning Staff, Supreme G.H.Q.
           Castle Tarleton, Archona
TO: *Chiliarch Denford de Fourneault*
           Harmost [military governor], North Italy
           Milan
RE: *Your request of 07/10/41.*

Denied.

Service to the State!

[handwritten postscript]

Look, Dennie, I know we're asking you to make bricks without straw, but there just aren't any more troops or administrators to send you. I can't even spare any reliable old-territories serf personnel; we've stripped the Police Zone to the danger point to support the offensive. Hell, we're running the place with grandmothers and schoolkids as it is; Security tells me there's another of those loony cults running through the factory compounds, claiming all the Draka are being spirited away by their master Satan.

You'll just have to make do with what you've got; we persuaded the Security people to scale back on their liquidation-and-deportation schedule, I thought you said that would help? We can let you have some of the aerosol nerve gas, if you'd rather.

Tech Section was pleased with those job-lots of equipment and skilled workers you've been sending: something about "heavy water," whatever that means. Maybe one of the bombardment rocket projects. Anyway, keep up the good work and don't wear yourself out on the Woppo wenches.

Love, Cynthia

P.S. No, you can't have a combat command, either. You're too valuable there.

DRAKA FORCES BASE KARS, PROVINCE OF ANATOLIA APRIL 14, 1942: 0600 HOURS

The barrage lit the sky to the east, brighter than the false dawn. Forty kilometers, and the guns were a continuous flicker all along the arch of the horizon, as of heat-lightning, the sound a distant rumbling that echoed off the mountains and down the broad open valleys.

Johanna von Shrakenberg stood to watch it from the flat roof of the two-story barracks. She had risen early, even though her lochos was on call today and so spared the usual four-kilometer run; slipped out from between Rahksan and the sleeping cat, and brought her morning coffee and cigarette up here. The cold was bitter under the paling stars, and she

was glad of the snug, insulated flight suit and gloves.
Steam rose from the thick china mug, warm and
rich, soothing in her mouth as she sipped.

The guns had been sounding since the start of
the offensive. She tried to imagine what it was
like under that shelling: earth and rock churning
across square kilometers, thousands of tons of steel
and explosive ripping across the sky . . . the artil-
lery of sixty legions, ten thousand guns, every-
thing from the monster 240's and 200's of the Army
Corps reserve to field guns and mortars and rocket
launchers.

"*Only the mad inhuman laughter of the guns,*" she
quoted softly. Beyond that was the Caucasus, and
the passes where the Airborne legions had landed in
the German rear. Her brother among them . . . she
shook her head. Worry was inevitable and pointless,
but Eric's grip on life was not as firm as she would
have liked. *The sort of man who needs something or
someone to live for,* she thought. *I wish he'd find
one, this business is dangerous enough when you're
trying.*

Dawn was breaking, rising out of the fire and the
thunder. Shadow chased darkness down the huge
scored slopes of the mountains, still streaked with
old drifts. Rock glowed, salmon-pink; she could see a
plume of snow trailing feather-pale from a white
peak. Below clusters of young trees marked the man-
ors the Draka had built, and fields of wheat showed a
tender, tentative green. A new landscape, scarcely
older than herself.

There had been much work done here in the last
generation, she thought; it took Draka to organize
and plan on such a scale. Terraces like broad steps
on the hillsides, walled with stones carted from the
fields; canals; orchards and vineyards pruned and
black and dusted with green uncoiling buds. All of it

somehow raw and new, against this bleakness made by four thousand years of peasant axes and hungry goats.

Well, only a matter of time, she mused. Already the Conservancy Directorate was drawing a mat of young forest across the upper slopes; in another hundred years these foothills would be as lush as nature permitted, and her grandchildren might come here to hunt tiger and mouflon.

The scene about her was also Draka work, but less sightly. Kars was strategic, a meeting of routes through the mountains of eastern Turkey, close to the prewar Russian border. The conquest back in 1916–1917 had been a matter of foot infantry and mule trains and supply drops by dirigibles. Castle Tarleton had enough problems guarding six thousand miles of northern frontier without transportation worries; even before the Great War was over a million laborers had been rounded up to push through railways and roads and airship yards.

So when the buildup for the German war began there was transport enough; just barely, with careful planning. The air base around her sprawled to the horizon on the south and west, and work teams were still gnawing at scrub and gravel. Others toiled around the clock to maintain the roads pounded by endless streams of motor-transport; the air was thick with rock dust and the oily smell of the low-grade distillate the steam trucks burned. Barracks, warehouses, workshops, and hangars sprawled, all built of asbestos-cement panels bolted to prefabricated steel frames: modular, efficient, and ugly. On a nearby slope the skeletal mantis shape of an electrodetector tower whirled tirelessly.

Johanna flicked the cigarette butt over the edge of the roof and drank the last lukewarm mouthful of coffee. "Like living in a bloody construction site," she muttered, turning to the stairwell.

The bulletin board in the ready room held nothing new: final briefing at 0750, wheels-up half an hour later, a routine kill-anything-that-moved sweep north of the mountains to make sure the Fritz air kept its head down. *Merarch* Anders was going over the maps one more time as she passed through, raising his head to nod at her, his face a patchwork of scars from twenty years of antiaircraft fire and half a dozen forced landings. She waved in response, straightening a little under the cool blue eyes. Anders was the "old man" in truth, forty-two, ancient for a fighter pilot. He had been a *bagbuster* in the Great War, flying one of the pursuit biplanes that ended the reign of the dirigibles. And even in middle age the fastest man she had ever sparred with.

The canteen was filling with her fellow Draka. The food was good; that was one of the advantages of the Air Corps. The ground forces had a motto: "join the Army and live like a serf," but a pilot could fly out to fight and return to clean beds, showers, and cooked food. This time she took only a roll and some fruit before heading out to the field; combat tension affected everybody a different way, and with her it tightened the gut and killed her appetite, also any capacity for small talk.

The planes of her lochos were having a final check-over in their sandbagged revetments, sloping pits along either side of an accessway that led out into the main runway for this section. Technicians were checking the systems, pumps chugged as the fuel tanks filled, armorers coaxed in belts of 25mm cannon shells for the five-barrel nose battery.

Her ground crew paused to smile and wave as Johanna settled herself on the edge of the revetment and sat cross-legged, watching. On excellent advice, her father's among others, she had gone out of her way to learn their names and take an interest in their conditions. They were serfs, except for the team commander; not Janissaries, unarmed auxiliaries owned by the War Directorate, but privileged and highly trained. Their work would be checked by the inspectors, of course, but there was a world of difference between the best and just-good-enough.

She sighed as she watched them work on her aircraft. Even earthbound, with the access panels open, the Eagle was a beautiful sight: as beautiful as a dolphin or a blooded horse, enough to make your breath catch when it swam in its natural element above the earth. It was a midwing monoplane, the slender fuselage just big enough for pilot, fuel, and the five cannon, slung between two huge H-form 24 cylinder Atlantis Peregrine turbocharged engines in sleek cowlings. Twice the power of a single-engine fighter and far less than twice the weight: not quite as agile in a dogfight, but better armored and more heavily armed, and *much* faster . . .

Like most pilots, she had personalized her machine: a Cupid's bow mouth below the nose, lined with shark's teeth, and a name in cursive script: "Lover's Bite." There were five swastikas stenciled below the bubble canopy, the marks of her victories.

Johanna's mouth quirked. Flying was . . . flying was like making love after a pipeful of the best rum-soaked Arusha Crown *ganja;* she had always had a talent for it, and the Eagle was a sweet ship. And somewhat to her surprise, she had turned out to be an excellent fighter pilot; she had the vision and the reflexes, and most important of all the nerve to close in, *very* close, right down to 100 meters, while the enemy wings filled the windscreen and your guns hammered bits of metal loose to bounce off the canopy . . .

And frankly, I could do without it, she thought. There were worse ways to spend the war: sweating in the lurching steel coffin of a personnel carrier, or clawing your hands into the dirt and praying under a mortar barrage—but dead was dead, and she had not the slightest desire to die. Nor to spin in trapped in a burning plane, or . . .

She shrugged off the thought. War was the heritage of her people and her caste; it was just that she would have preferred to be lucky. Peacetime duty for her military service, then, hmmm, yes, Capetown for her degree. Nothing fancy; a three-year in Liberal Arts and Estate Management and an aristocratic A- grade. And days spent lying naked on the beaches of the Peninsula, surfing, going to the *palaestra* to run and wrestle, throw the disk and javelin and practice the pankration. Wearing silk and skirts; concerts and theaters and picture galleries, love affairs and long talks and walking under the olives on starlit nights . . .

"Well, on to the work of the day," she murmured. Then: "Got her ticking over?"

One of the technicians looked up, grinning as the last of an ammunition belt ran across the leather pad on her shoulders and into the drums, the aluminum casings dull against the color-coded shells: red for tracer-incendiary, brown for explosive, blue for armor-piercing.

"She-un loaded fo' lion, Mistis," the serf said. Johanna's mind placed the dialect: Police Zone, but not the Old Territories—Katanga or Angola, perhaps . . . serf specialists were given a thorough but narrowly technical education, which did not include master-class speech patterns. "Giv't to tha Fritz, raaht up they ass," she continued.

"I intend to, Lukie-Beth," the Draka said, and considered lighting a cigarette. No, a bad example to break regulations around so much high-octane. Instead she threw the package to the crew chief, who tucked one behind his ear and handed the others around. He nodded a salute as she rose, touching the steel hook on the stump of his left wrist to his brow.

". . . and engage targets of opportunity on the ground," the briefing officer concluded.

Merarch Anders rose and walked to the edge of the dais. "All right, yo' glory hounds," he said. The harsh voice dampened the slight murmur that had swelled across the ranks of folding chairs.

Here begineth the lecture from the Holy Book of Air Operations, section V, paragraph ii, Johanna thought with resignation.

"A few reminders of the facts of life," the Merarch continued. "The Air Corps does not exist so yo' can dogfight and rack up kills. It exists to help the Forces win wars. Its most important function is reconnaissance; the second most important is ground support. We have a fighter arm to protect the scouting and ground-support units, and to shoot down any enemy aircraft who try to do the important stuff for the other side.

"Another fact of life: Eagles are *pursuit* craft. They are designed to shoot down *bombers*. The *Falcons* are supposed to shoot down fighters; that's why we have lochoi of the buggers flying cap-cover for us. Yo' will *not* engage enemy fighters except defensively, and then only if n yo' can't run, which should be easy, seeing as the Domination has gone to the trouble of giving yo' the fastest aircraft on earth. I see anyone glory-hunting—" his seamed face jutted forward, one half a pattern of scars, the other smooth "—I goin' to see that he *suffer*. Understood?"

"Sir, yes *sir!*" the lochos replied.

The cockpit smelled of rubber, oil, and old sweat. Johanna wiggled her shoulders in the straps and folded the seat back into the semi-reclining position that helped you take g-force without blacking out.

Her hand moved the stick, feet pumped the pedals; she glanced back over one shoulder to check the flaps and rudder, and the flipped-up visor of her bone-dome went *clack* against the metal rim of the seat. The synthetic of the face mask rested cool and clammy against her cheeks, and sounds came muted through the headphones of her helmet, even the start-up roar of engines. That faded again as she gave a thumbs-up to the ground crew and the bubble canopy slid down over her head.

Training sent hands and eyes in a final check over the instrument panel: gyrosight, fuel, oil pressure, RPM, pitch-control. Static buzz and click in her ears, sound-offs as each plane called go-condition, her own voice like a stranger's.

"Green board, von Shrakenberg," she said.

The override call of the control center came through: *"Lochos cleared, two and four, Merarch. Next ten minutes."*

Her fingers touched the throttles, and the *Lover's Bite* rolled out of the revetment and onto the holding strip. She moistened her lips in the cool, rubber-tasting air flowing from the mask, and touched the shoulder pocket of her flight suit that held Tom's picture. They had exchanged special photographs, cased in plastic with a lock of hair: two "Knights of the Air" going into battle with their lover's favor on their sleeve.

Policy let spouses or fiances serve in the same unit if they chose, but suddenly she was glad they had decided against it; he could spend the next few years in safe boredom, deterring the Japanese in China. There would be no war with Nippon, not now; the Domination would let the Americans pour out blood and treasure to break the island empire's strength, then leave the Yankees holding a few South Sea isles while the Draka snapped up Japan's rich Asian provinces.

She saw him, sharply: broad freckled face and hazel eyes cold with that ironic humor; wide thin-lipped mouth; stocky muscled body fitting so comfortably against hers . . . They had settled the future. A land grant in Italy, Tuscany by preference, Pa could probably swing that, and there were plenty of nice villas that could be renovated easily enough. Children, of course: four, that was enough to do one's duty by the Race. Breeding horses, dabbling in estate-bottled premium wine, snapping up a surplus light transport so they could fly over to Alexandria for big-city amusements now and then.

She smiled more widely and touched the pocket on the other shoulder. Rahksan had presented her with a favor, too: a silk handkerchief, with a lock of *her* hair and an inked pawprint from Omar, Johanna's cat—"*jist t' get us awl in theyah, Jo' darlin'.*" Johanna sighed: it was good to have that gentle and undemanding affection to hand, and Rahksan would make a good nursemaid, she was marvelous with children.

Oh, what a happy little Draka I shall be, she thought mordantly. *If I survive—so stop woolgathering, woman!*

The planes of the 211th Lochos taxied in file down the approach lane; an orange-uniformed flight launcher waited with signal paddles in hand to key them on to the take-off runway. Engine roar rose to a grating howl as the dozen Eagles boosted their craft from idle. Her turn came; she glanced across at her wingman, young de Grange, and gave a clenched-fist salute. He answered with exaggerated decisiveness.

Natural, she thought. A newbi—this was only his second combat mission. In air-to-air combat the minority of veterans did most of the killing, the novices most of the dying. Unfair, like life. The solution was to *win*; and as the old saying went, if you couldn't win, *cheat*.

She pressed the throttles forward, props biting the air at coarse pitch, then released the brakes. Acceleration pushed her back into the padding of the seat; the tailwheel came up; the controls went light as the *Lover's Bite* left the earth, with a tiny slip-sway as her hand firmed on the stick.

Formation came automatically, a tight box of pairs here in the crowded airspace over Kars. The airfields were laid out in circles, neat as a map beneath her as she gained altitude: rings of silver thousand-foot transport dirigibles; rows of six-engined Helot cargo planes, like boxes with great slab wings; rank after rank of Rhino ground-strike craft, shuttling back and forth at low altitude to the front. And the vehicle parks of the armored legions, huge blunt wedges stacked beside the roads, flat beetle shapes of the tanks and infantry carriers, flashes as their heavy self-propelled guns fired, tasked to support the Janissary units in contact with the the enemy.

The Eagles climbed, clawing at the thin air with whining turbochargers, through a layer of cirrus clouds into a high brightness under a sky that seemed ready to bleed lapis lazuli as the props sliced it. Four thousand meters altitude, and the front was invisible as they passed, only a ragged pattern of explosions pale in the bright sunlight, lines and clumps that must indicate Fritz strongpoints, fading to scatterings on road junctions behind the lines. Columns of smoke rose, black pillars fraying at their tops, brutal and emphatic in the cool pastels of the upper air. Ahead were the mountains, through the clouds and ringed by them, snow-peaked islands lapped by fleece-surf and patches of darkness where earth showed through.

Johanna waggled her craft and her wingman closed up with a guilty spurt of acceleration. The lochos had spread out into the loose pairs-of-pairs formation that was most effective for combat, and she began a constant all-around scan. That was the reason pilots wore silk scarves, to prevent chafing; not derring-do, but survival. The electrodetectors in the dirigible warning and control craft hovering south of the mountains were supposed to pick up enemy aircraft long before visual contact, but electrodetection was in its infancy. You could still get jumped . . .

Minutes stretched. She concentrated on her breathing, keying into the state of untense alertness that kept you alive. If you let your glands pump adrenaline into the bloodstream you could end up wringing wet and exhausted in minutes, even standing still. They reached cruising altitude at six thousand meters and crossed the mountain peaks; there was less cloud cover north of the Caucasus, a clear view of forested slopes rippling down to an endless steppe, bright-green squares of young grass and coal-black ploughland. And . . .

"Target," the Merarch's voice spoke in her ears. "Three o'clock; Stukas. Follow me."

Christ, he's got good eyes, she thought, tilting her craft to scan down and to the right. Black dots crawling north; they must be hedgehopping to avoid detection, moving up to support the Fritz units trying to clear the passes, or even hoping to cross the mountains. Smoothly, the lochos peeled off and began a power dive toward their prey.

Her hands moved on the controls, and the *Lover's Bite* banked, turned, fell. There was a moment of weightlessness while the world swung about her, then a giant soft hand lifting and pushing. Her own gloved palm rammed the throttles forward, and the engines answered with a banshee shriek. They were diving head-on toward the Germans, a three-thousand-meter swoop that closed at the combined speed of the two formations. Acceleration pushed her back into the padding of the seat; she could feel it stretching the tissues of her face, spreading lips into a death's-head grin beneath her face mask. The airplane began to buck and rattle, the stick quivering and then shuddering in her hand.

Mach limit, she thought, easing back slightly on the throttles until the hammer blows of air driven to solidity died down to a bearable thrumming. Air compression just under the speed of sound could break an aircraft apart or freeze the controls. They were closing fast now, altimeter unreeling in a blurr, the Germans turning from specks to shapes. Stuka dive-bombers, single-engined craft with the unmistakable "cranked" gull-wing and spatted undercarriage. Johanna's thumb flicked back the cover over the firing button on the head of her joystick, and the gyrosight automatically projected a circle on the windscreen ahead of her. *Dream target*, went through her gleefully. Only a single rear-mounted machine gun for defensive armament, slow, unhandy.

Less than a thousand meters, and the Germans spotted the Draka fighters stooping out of the sun and scattered, their formation breaking apart like beads of mercury on glass, diving to hug the ground even more closely. Johanna braced and pulled back on the stick, grey creeping in at the edges of sight as the g-force mounted. The black wings grew, filling the center ring of the gunsight, then overlapping the outer circle. Time slowed; her thumb came down on the firing button as the Stuka's fuselage touched the outer rim. The aircraft were closing at well over seven hundred kph; the burst was on target for barely four-tenths of a second. Beneath her the revolver-breeches of the cannon whirled, and two hundred shells hosed out as her thumb tapped the button; more than half of them struck.

The Stuka exploded in a globe of orange light, folded in half and tumbled to leave a burning smear on the ground a hundred meters below, all at once. The shock wave slapped the Draka Eagle upwards, even as Johanna pulled back on the stick, rolling up in an Immelman and trading speed for height.

"*Ngi dHa!*" she shouted, the old triumph cry her ancestors had borrowed from the tribes they overran: *I have eaten.* The sudden jolt of exultation ran belly-deep, raw and primitive.

"Warning." The voice cut through the static and chatter on the lochos circuit, cool and distant; from the control dirigible south of the mountains. "Hostiles approaching from northeast your position, altitude ten thousand meters. Speed indicates fighters; estimated intercept, two minutes." Johanna could feel the excitement wash out of her in a wave, replaced by a prickling coldness that tasted of copper and salt. She worked pedals and stick, snapped the *Lover's Bite* back level, scanned about. Most of the Stukas were splotches of black smoke and orange flame on the rumpled landscape below, the Eagles were scattered to the limits of visibility and beyond, and her wingman was nowhere to be seen.

"*Shit!*" That was Merarch Anders. She could imagine what was running through his mind; height and speed were interchangeable, and the Fritz had too much. Too much for the Draka to run for it.

"Anders, control. *Where are our Falcons?*"

"Sorry, Merarch: diverted on priority."

The lochos commander wasted no time on complaints. "Form on me, prepare for climb," he said. "One pass through them, then we turn and head south."

Johanna closed in, climbing, and keyed her microphone. "De Grange, close up. *De Grange!*"

"I've almost got him—"

"*Leave the fucking rabbit and close up!*"

"Yessir . . . ah . . . where are you?"

She could imagine his sudden frightened glance around a sky empty of motion. "Look for the *smoke plumes*, de Grange." She switched to lochos fre-

quency. "Merarch, my wingman's got himself out of
visual."

"He'll have to find his own way home. Radio
silence."

The lochos climbed steeply, clawing for altitude as
they drove northeast to meet the approaching Ger-
mans. A head-on passing engagement was quick, and
would leave the Draka above their opponents, able
to turn and head for home. *If we live,* Johanna thought,
moistening her lips as she flipped down the sun visor
of her helmet and squinted into the brightness ahead:
pale blue sky and white haze and the sun like a
blinding tic at the corner of her eye. The insides of
her gloves were wet, and she worked the fingers
limber around the molded grip of the joystick.

"One minute." The voice of the controller sounded,
olympian and distant; Johanna felt a moment's fierce
resentment that faded into the blank intensity of
concentration. Nothing . . . then a line of black dots.
Growing, details; single-engine fighters. Large cano-
pies set well back, long cylindrical noses. Focke-
Wulf 190's, the best the Germans had.

Oh, joy, she thought sardonically, picking her tar-
get. This would be a celestial game of chicken, with
whoever banked first vulnerable. The oncoming line
seemed to swell more swiftly, speed becoming visi-
ble as the range closed. Hands and feet moved on
pedals and stick, feedback making the Eagle an ex-
tension of her body. Like *another* body: she had
seen a barracuda once, spear-fishing along a reef off
Ceylon, on a summer's holiday with a schoolfriend;
hung entranced in the sapphire water, meeting an
eye black and empty and colder than the moon. A
living knife, honed by a million years of evolution.
Here she had that, the power and the *purity* of it . . .

The Focke-Wulf was closing. Closing. Toy-model
size, normal, huge, filling the windscreen the crazy
fucker's not turning *now.*

Her thumb clamped the firing button just as lights sparkled along the wingroot firing ports of the Focke-Wulf. Fist-blow of recoil, like a sudden headwind for a fractional second, and a multiple *punk-tingggg* as something high-velocity struck the Draka aircraft's armor. Then she was banking right as the German flipped left; they passed belly-to-belly and wings pointing to earth and sky, so close that they would have collided had the landing gear been down.

A quick glimpse into the overhead mirror showed the German going in. Not burning, but half his rudder was missing. Johanna flipped the Eagle back onto the level with a smile that turned to a snarl as a red temperature warning light began to flicker and buzz on the control panel. Her hand reached for the switches, but before she could complete the movement a flare of light caught at the corner of her right eye. A rending *bang* and she felt the *Lover's Bite* shake, pitched on her side and dove for the earth six thousand meters below in a long spiral, trailing smoke from the port engine nacelle; more than smoke, there were flames licking from ruptured fuel lines; a sudden barrage of piston heads and connectors hammered the side of the cockpit as the roar of a functioning engine abruptly changed to the brief shriek of high-tensile steel distorting under intolerable stress.

G-force worse than the pull-out from a power dive pushed Johanna into a corner of the seat, weighing on her chest like a great soft pillow. Will and training forced her hand through air that seemed to have hardened to treacle, feathering the damaged engine and shutting the fuel lines, opening the throttle on the other. *Stamp* on the pedal *left* stick . . . she could almost hear the voice of her instructor, feel the wind rattling the wires of the training biplane: *recruit, next time yo' needs three tries to pull out of a spin I'll put us'n into a hill myself to spare the Race the horror of yo' incompetent genes . . .*

So you were right, she thought. *You're still a son of a bitch*. The *Lover's Bite* came out of the spin, straight and level. Also horribly slow and sluggish, and she had to keep the stick over . . .

"Mayday." Her voice was a harsh blur in her own ears. "Mayday, engine out, altitude—" she blinked out the cockpit at muddy fields grown horribly close, unbelievably fast "—three thousand." A glance at the board. "B engine running, losing hydraulics slowly, fuel fast."

"Acknowledged." The Merarch's voice was steady, calming. "Run for it, we'll cover as long as we can." A pause. "And your stray duck de Grange is back."

"Acknowledged," she answered shortly. Mind and body were busy with the limping, shuddering aircraft. For a moment sheer irritation overrode all other feeling; the effortless power and response of the Eagle had become part of her life, and this limping parody was like a rebellion of her own muscles and nerves. Her eyes flicked to the gauges. Hydraulic pressure dropping steadily; that meant multiple ruptures somewhere. The controls were growing soft, mushy; she had to overcorrect and then correct again. A glance at the ruined engine: still burning, fuel must be getting through somehow, and the gauge was dropping as if both engines were running on maximum boost. And—

The Focke-Wulf dove from over her left shoulder. Reflex made her try to snap the Eagle aside, and the unbalanced thrust of the single engine sent the aircraft into the beginnings of another flat spin that carried her six hundred meters closer to the ground. Cannon shells hammered into the rear fuselage; then the *Lover's Bite* pitched forward in the shockwave of an explosion. Pieces of the German fighter pitched groundward, burning; another Draka Eagle swooped by, looped and throttled back to fly wing-to-wing, the pilot giving her a thumbs-up signal. He was as impersonal as a machine in bonedome, dark visor and face mask, but she could imagine the cocky grin on de Grange's freckled face.

"Thanks," she said. "Now get back upstairs."

"Hell—"

"That's an *order*, Galahad! If I want a knight-errant, I'll send to Hollywood." Reluctantly, he peeled off and climbed. She fought down a feeling of loneliness; an Eagle had the advantage in a diving attack on a Focke-Wulf, but in a low-and-slow dogfight the smaller turning radius of a single-engine fighter made it a dangerous opponent.

Until then emergency had kept her focused, consciousness narrowed down to the bright point of concentration. Now she drew a ragged breath and looked about. More smoke and fire trailed from the right engine, and she could smell somewhere the raw stink of high-octane fuel. That was bad, fuel didn't explode until it mixed with air . . . Ahead and high above shone the peaks of Caucasus; *very* high, she must be at no more than two thousand meters. A push at the stiff joystick and the plane responded, slowly, oh so slowly. Still losing pressure from the hydraulics; it was a choice between the controls freezing up, midair explosion, and the last of the fuel coughing through the injectors. As for clearing the mountains, even through one of the passes, as much chance of that as of flying to the moon by putting her head between her knees and spitting hard.

But I'm *me*, something gibbered in the back of her mind. I'm only twenty, I can't die, not *yet*. Images flashed through her mind: Tom, Eric, Rahksan, her mother's body laid out in the chapel, Oakenwald . . . her father giving her a switching when she was seven, for sticking one of the housemaids with a pin in a tantrum. *"You will use power with restraint and thrift, because your ancestors bought it with blood and pain. The price is high; remember that, when it comes your turn to pay."*

"Dying, hell," she said. "Damned if I'm going to do that until I'm fuckin' *dead*." Her hand reached to hammer at the release catch of the canopy. Jammed: she flipped up a cover on the control panel and flicked the switch beneath that should have fired the explosive bolts.

"No joy," she muttered, then looked down sharply. Fuel was seeping into the cockpit, wetting the soles of her boots. "*Shit!*" A touch keyed the microphone. "Merarch, she's a mess, no hope of getting her home."

"Bail out. We've seen those Fritzes off, we'll cover you."

"Can't. Cockpit cover's jammed, I think part of the engine hit it. I'll have to ride her in." There was a moment's silence filled with static buzz and click. "I'll see if I can shoot out the catch, then make it to our lines on foot. Got my 'passport,' anyway." That was the cyanide pill they all carried; Draka did not surrender and were not taken alive.

"Right . . . goodbye."

The other voices murmured a farewell; high above, she could see the silver shapes turning and making for the south. Johanna set her teeth and forced her eyes to the terrain ahead, easing back on the throttle. If the fuel lines were intact it would have been better to fly the *Lover's Bite* empty, less risk of fire, but by then the stuff would be sloshing around her feet. Easy . . . the plain was humping itself up into foothills, isolated swells rising out of the dead-flat squares of cultivation. All the arrangements had been made: updated letters to Tom and Eric and her father, a new home for her cat Omar, a friend who had promised to see Rahksan safely back to Oakenwald, and Pa would see her right. Patches of forest among the fields now, the blackened snags of a ruined village, a rutted road . . . Almighty Thor, it was going by fast; speed that had seemed a crawl in the upper air becoming a blurring rush as she dropped below a hundred meters.

Slow *down*. Throttle back again, flaps down, just above stalling speed. Floating . . . *up* over that damned windbreak, White Christ she's hardly responding at all . . . good, meadow, white-and-black cows scattering . . . floating, nose up and—

Slam, the belly hit, rending scream of duralumin ripping, pinwheeling, body flung forward in the harness, something struck her head . . .

Blackness.

CHAPTER THIRTEEN

"... so the Draka are not different from other peoples because they violate the Golden Rule, or Bentham's derivative idolatry of the 'greatest good of the greatest number.' Everyone does. We do not violate them, we reject them.

Others have conquered and ruled; we alone conquer for conquest's sake, and dominate for no other purpose than Domination itself; the name we half-consciously chose for our State is no accident. We, and we alone, have spoken aloud the great secret: that the root function of all human society is the production and reproduction of power—and that power is the ability to compel others to do your will, against theirs. It is end, not means. The purpose of Power is Power.

The Draka will conquer the world for two reasons: because we must, and because we can. Yet of the two forces, the second is the greater: we do this because we choose to do it. By the sovereign Will and force of arms the Draka will rule the earth, and in so doing remake themselves. We shall conquer; we shall beat the nations into dust and reforge them in our self-wrought image: the Final Society, a new humanity without weakness or mercy, hard and pure. Our descendants will walk the hillsides of that future, innocent beneath the stars, with no more between them and their naked will than a wolf has. Then there will be Gods in the earth."

Meditations: Colder than the Moon
by Evira Naldorssen
Archona Press, 1930

CASTLE TARLETON, ARCHONA
APRIL 15, 1942: 1200 HOURS

Arch-Strategos Karl von Shrakenberg leaned his palms on the railing and stared down at the projac map of Operations Command. Steel shutters rose noiselessly behind him, covering the glass wall and darkening the room, to increase the contrast of the glass surface that filled the pit beneath them. That white glow underlit the faces of the ten *Archstrategoi* spaced around the map, pale ovals hanging suspended, the flat black of their uniforms fading into the darkness beyond, the more so as few of them wore even the campaign ribbons to which they were entitled. Scattered brightwork glowed in soft gold stars against that background: here a thumb ring, there the three gold earrings that were the sole affectation of the *Dominarch*, the Chief of the Supreme General Staff.

Ghosts, jeered a mordant shadow at the back of Karl's mind. *Hovering over a world we cannot touch directly.* Below them the unit counters moved, Draka forces crowding against the shrinking German bridgeheads south of the Caucasus, pushing them back toward the blocking positions of the airborne Legions at their rear.

Ghosts and dreams, he thought. *We stand here and think we command the world; we're lords of symbol, masters of numbers, abstractions.* So antiseptic, so cool, so rational . . . and completely out of their hands, unless disaster struck. Twenty years they had planned and trained; worked and argued and sweated; moved millions of lives across the game board of the world. *Or does the world dream us? Are we the wolf-thought-inescapable that puts a face on their fear?*

Karl looked around at the faces: his contemporaries, colleagues—his friends, if shared thoughts and work and belief were what made friendship. Quiet well-kept men in their middle years, the sort who were moderate in their vices, popular with their grandchildren, whose spare time was spent strolling in the park or at rock-meditation. When they killed it was with nod or signature, and a detachment so complete it was as empty of cruelty as of pity.

For a moment he blinked: a fragment of song went through his mind, a popular thing, how did it . . . *frightened of this thing that I've become* . . .

And yet we were young men once. Karl looked across at John Erikssen, the Dominarch. His head was turned, talking to his aide, young Carstairs. *Ha. I must be nodding to my end—she's forty and I think of her as "young."* John and he had been junior officers together in the Great War. He remembered . . .

The shell hole. Outside Smyrna: winter, glistening grey mud under grey sky, stinking with month-old bits of corpse. Cold mud closing about him, flowing rancid into his gasping mouth, the huge weight of the Turk on his chest. The curved dagger coming down, straining millimeter by millimeter closer to his face as his grip on the other man's wrist weakened, and he would lie there forever among the scraps of bone and rusty barbed wire . . . There had been a sound like the *thock* of a polo mallet hitting a wooden ball, and the Turk had gone rigid; another crunch, softer, and his eyes had widened and rolled and Karl rose, pushing the corpse aside. John had stood looking at the shattered buttplate of his rifle, murmuring, "Hard head. *Hard* head."

Now, that was real, the elder von Shrakenberg mused. The hands remembered, the *skin* did, as they did the silky feel of his firstborn's hair when he lifted him from the midwife's arms. John had stood godfather, to a son Karl named for him.

But the cobra of ambition had bitten them both deeply, even then. That was back when there was still juice in it, the wine of power, every victory a new birth and every promotion a victory. He had commanded a *merarchy* of warcars later in the Great War, Mesopotamia and Persia. Clumsy things by modern standards; riveted plates and spoked wheels and steam-powered, as only civilian vehicles and transport were today. Sleek and deadly efficient in their time . . .

Power exercised through others, men and machines as the extensions of his Will; the competition of excellence, showing his skill. Scouting for the Archonal Guard legion, vanguard of Tull's V Army as it snapped at the heels of the retreating enemy. They had caught the Ottoman column by surprise on a plain of blinding-white alkali, swinging around through *erg* and dry wadi-beds. For a quarter-hour while the rest of the unit came up they had watched the enemy pass beneath them, dark men in ragged earth-brown uniforms. Ambulance carts piled with the wounded; soldiers dropping to lie with cracked and bleeding lips; the endless weary shuffle of the broken regiments, and the stink of death.

The gatlings had fired until the turrets were ovens, the floors of the warcars covered in spent brass that glittered and shifted underfoot, the crews choking on cordite and scorched metal. That was when he had burnt his hand, reaching down to the gunner who sat slack-faced, hands still gripping the triggers as the pneumatics hissed and drove the empty barrels through their whirring circle. He had not felt the pain, not then, his mind's eye seeing over and over again the ranks dropping in the storm of tracer, tumbled, layered in drifts that moaned and stirred; afterward silence, the sough of wind, bitter dust, and steam. There had been nothing for John's truck-born infantry to do but collect ears and bayonet the wounded.

The stink, the stink . . . they had gotten very thoroughly drunk that night, with the main body there to relieve the vanguard. Drunk and howling bad poetry and staggering off to vomit in the shadows. A step further, and another.

He had transferred to the Air Corps, valuable experience for one slated for Staff. The last great dirigible raid on Constantinople: Karl von Shrakenberg had been on the bridge of the *Loki* in the third wave, coming in at five thousand meters over the Golden Horn to release her biplane fighters while the bombardment ships passed below. The airship was three hundred meters long, a huge fragile thing of braced alloy sheeting; it had trembled in the volcanic updrafts from the tracks of fire across the city spread out below them like a map, burning from horizon to horizon, the beginnings of the world's first *firestorm*. Traceries of flame over the hills, bending like the heads of desert flowers after spring rain. Streets and rivers of fire, casting ruddy blurs on the underside of soot-black cloud; heat that made the whole huge fabric of the airship creak and pop above him as it expanded. Diesel oil and burning and the acrid smell of men whose bodies sweated out the fear their minds suppressed.

He had been calm, he remembered; yet ready to weep, or to laugh. Almost lightheaded, exalted: a godlike feeling; he was a sky god, a war god. Searchlights like white sabers, cannon fire as bright magenta bursts against the darkening sky where no stars shone, muzzle flashes from the antiairship batteries of the Austrian battlewagons at anchor below. The great dome of the Hagia Sophia shining, then crumbling, Justinian's Church of Holy Wisdom falling into the fire. He had watched with a horror that flowed and mingled with delight at the beauty of that single image, the apotheosis of a thousand years. The ancient words had come of their own volition:

"Who rends the fortified cities
  As the rushing passage of time
Rends cheap cloth . . ."

Other voices—*"Prepare for drop—superheat off—
stand by to valve gas!" "Dorsal turret three, fighters
two o'clock."* A new shuddering hammer as the chin-
turret pom-pom cut loose. *"Where're the escorts—
that's Wotan, she's hit."*

The ship ahead of them had staggered in the sky, a
long smooth metal-clad teardrop speckled with the
flickers of her defensive armament. Then the second
salvo of five-inch shells had struck, punched through
cloth-thin metal, into the gas cells. Hull plating blew
out along the lines of the seams; four huge jets of
flame vomited from the main valves along the upper
surface, and then enough air mixed with the escap-
ing hydrogen to ignite; or it might have been the
bombload, or both. For a moment there was no night,
only a white light that seared through eyelids and up-
flung hand. The *Loki* had been slammed upright on
her tail, pitched forward; he could recall the captain
screaming orders, the helmsmen cursing and praying
as they wrestled with the man-high rudder wheels . . .

One moment a god, the next a cripple, the general
thought, shaking himself back to the present. Men
told him he had been the only bridge officer to
survive the shellburst that struck in the next instant;
that he had stood and conned the crippled airship
with one hand holding a pressure bandage to his
mangled thigh. He had never been able to recall it;
the next conscious memory had been of the hospital
in Crete, two heads bending over his leg. A serf
nurse, careful brown hands soaking and clipping to
remove the field-dressing. And the doctor, Mary,
looking up with that quick birdlike tilt of the head
when his stirring told her he was awake. Fever-blur,
and the hand on his forehead.

"*You'll live, soldier*," she had said. She had smiled, and it wiped the exhaustion from her eyes. "*And walk, that's all I promise*."

And that too was power, Karl von Shrakenberg thought, looking around at his fellow-commanders. *Strange that I never minded being helpless with her*.

He flexed his hands on the smooth wood. He must be getting old, if the past seemed more real than the present. Time to retire, perhaps; he was just sixty, old for active service in the Domination's forces, even at headquarters.

"Well." Karl was almost startled to hear the Chief of Staff speak in a normal voice, overriding the quiet buzz and click of equipment and sough of ventilators. He nodded at the map. "Seems to be going as well as can be expected."

The German fronts were receding, marked by lines like the tide-wrack of an ocean in retreat from the shore. *And Eric behind to stop an armed tide with his flesh*, Karl thought. *I wish there were gods that I could pray for you, my son. But there is only what we have in ourselves; no father in the sky to pick you up and heal your hurts. I knew, Eric, I knew that someday you would have nothing but yourself; we ask the impossible of ourselves and must demand it of our children*. Harshness was necessary, sometimes, but . . . *Live, my son. Conquer and live*.

The Dominarch turned to his aide. "Appraisal."

That woman frowned meditatively. "Second Legion can't hold until we break through. Their bridgehead is contiguous but shrinking from both ends . . ." A pause. "Basic reason things're goin' so well with First Legion over on the Ossetian Highway is the situation on the north. Century A of 2nd Cohort is savin' it; they're guardin' the back door."

Erikssen nodded. "Accurate, chiliarch. That's your boy, Karl, isn't it?" The elder von Shrakenberg nodded. "*Damned* good job."

Karl felt a sudden, unfamiliar sensation: a filling of the throat, a hot pressure behind the eyelids. *Tears*, he realized with wonder, even as training forced relaxation on the muscles of neck and throat, covered the swallow with a cough. And remembered Eric as a child, struggling with grim competence through tasks he detested, before he escaped back to those damned books and dreams . . .

"Thank you, sir," he muttered. *Tears. Why tears?*

The Chief of the General Staff looked down at the map again. "*Damned* good," he murmured. "Better to get both passes, but we have to have one or the other, or this option is off. There's always an attack out of Bulgaria, or an amphibious landing in the Crimea, or even a straight push west around the top of the Caspian, but none of them are anything like as favorable . . ."

The *strategoi* nodded in unconscious agreement. It would not be enough to push the Germans back into Europe; to win the war within acceptable parameters of time and losses they had to bring the bulk of the Nazi armies to battle on the frontiers, close to the Draka bases and far from their sources of supply in Central Europe. The sensible thing for the Germans to do would be to withdraw west of the Pirpet marshes, but Hitler might not let them. The Draka *strategoi* had a lively professional respect for their opposite numbers, and a professional's contempt for the sort of gifted amateur who led the Nazis.

"And not just good, unconventional," the Dominarch said. "Daring . . . where's that report?" He reached around, and one of the aides handed him the file. "Your boy didn't just freeze and wait for the sledgehammer, which too many do in a defensive position. Interesting use of indigenous assets, too—those Circassians and Russki partisans. That shows a creative mind." A narrow-eyed smile. "That American

has Centurion von Shrakenberg travellin' all around
Robin Hood's barn for tricks . . ." A hand waved.
"Lights, please." The shutters sank with a low hum,
and they blinked in the glare of noon.

"With respect, Dominarch . . ." Silence fell, as
the beginnings of movement rippled out. An officer
of the Security Directorate had spoken; the sleeve of
his dark-green uniform bore the cobra badge of the
Intervention Squads, the anti-guerilla specialists who
worked most closely with the military. "Ah've read
the report as well. *Unsound* use of indigenous assets,
in our . . . mah opinion. Partisans, scum; savin' ef-
fort now at the price of more later. The internal
enemy is always the one to be feared, eh?"

Karl leaned his weight on one elbow, looking al-
most imperceptibly down the beaked von Shrakenberg
nose. *An overseer's sense of priorities*, he thought.
Aloud:

"Most will die. This American seems anxious to
remove the survivors; if that is inadvisable, we can
liquidate them at leisure."

"Strategos von Shrakenberg, mah Directorate's func-
tion is to ensure the security of the State, which
cannot be done simply by killing men. We have to
kill *hope*, which is considerably moah difficult.
Particularly when sentimental tolerance fo' rebel-
dog Yankee—"

The Dominarch broke in sharply. "That is enough,
gentlemen!" Institutional rivalry between the two
organizations which bore arms for the State was
an old story; there was a social element, as well.
The old landholder families of scholar-gentry pro-
duced more than their share of the upper officer corps,
mostly because their tradition inclined them to seek
such careers. While Security favored the new bureau-
cratic elites that industrialization had produced . . .

"Von Shrakenberg, kindly remember that we are
all here to further the destiny of the Race. We are

not a numerous people, and *nobody* loves us; we are all Draka—all brothers, all sisters. *Including* our comrades from the Security Directorate; we all have our areas of specialization."

Karl nodded stiffly.

The Dominarch turned to the liaison officer from the secret police. "And Strategos Beauregard, will *you* kindly remember that conquest is a necessary precondition for pacification. Consider that we began as a band of refugees with nothing but a rifle each and the holes in our shoes; less than two centuries, and we *own* a quarter of the human race and the habitable globe. Because we never wavered in our aim; because we were flexible; because we were *patient*. As for the Yankee—" he paused for a grim smile "—as long as they serve our purposes, we'll let his reports through. Right now we need the Americans; let this Dreiser's adventure stories keep them enthralled. Their turn will come, or their children's will; then you can move to the source of the infection. Work and satisfaction enough for us all, then . . . along with the rape and pillage!"

There was an obligatory chuckle at the Chief of Staff's witticism. Erikssen's eyes flicked to Karl's for a moment of silent understanding. *And if those reports make your son something of a hero in the Domination as well, no harm there either, eh, old friend?*

The Dominarch glanced at his watch. "And now, gentlemen, ladies: just to convince ourselves that we're not *really* as useful as udders on a bull, shall we proceed to the meeting on the Far Eastern situation? Ten minutes, please."

The corridor gave on to an arcaded passageway, five meters broad, a floor of glossy brown tile clacked beneath boots, under arches of pale granite. Along the inner wall were plinths bearing war trophies:

spears, muskets, lances, Spandau machineguns. The
other openings overlooked a terraced slope that fell
away to a creek lined with silverleaf trees. Karl von
Shrakenberg stood for a long moment and leaned his
weight on his cane. Taking in a deep breath that was
heady with flowers and wet cypress, releasing it, he
could feel the tension of mind relaxing as he stretched
himself to *see*. Satori, the condition of *just-being*.
For a moment he accepted what his eyes gave him,
without selection or attention, simply *seeing* without
letting his consciousness speak to itself. The moment
ended.

*The eye that does not seek to see itself, the sword
that does not seek to cut itself*, he quoted to himself.
And then: *What jackdaws we are*. The Draka would
destroy Japan some day, he supposed; they saw noth-
ing odd in taking what was useful from the thoughts
of her Zen warrior-mystics. *The Scandinavian side of
our ancestry coming out*, he thought. *A smorgasbord
of philosophies*. Although consistency was a debatable
virtue; look what that ice-bitch Naldorssen had done
by brooding on Nietzche, perched in that crazy aerie
in the High Atlas.

Stop evading, he told himself, turning to the Intel-
ligence officer.

"Well, Sannie?"

Cohortarch Sannie van Reenan held up a narrow
sheaf of papers. "A friend of a friend, straight from
the developer . . . They did the usual search-and-
sweep around the last known position, and they found
the plane, or what was left of it." She paused to
moisten her lips. "It came in even, in a meadow:
landed, skidded, and burned." The scored eagle face
of the strategos did not alter, but his fingers clutched
on the mahogany ferrule of his cane. "Odd thing,
Karl . . . there was a Fritz vehicle about twenty
meters from the wreckage, a kubelwagon, *and it was
burned, too*. At about the same time, as far as it's

possible to tell. Very odd; so they're sticking to *Missing in Action*, not *Missing and Presumed Dead.*"

He laughed, a light bitter sound. "Which is perhaps better for her, and no relief to me at all. How selfish we humans can be in our loves." It was not discreditable, strictly speaking, for him to inquire about his daughter's fate; it *would* be, if he made too much of it when his duties to the Race were supposedly filling all time and attention.

The sun was bright, this late-fall morning, and the air cool without chill; sheltered, and lower than the plateau to the south, Archona rarely saw frost before May, and snow only once or twice in a generation. The terraces were brilliant with late flowers, roses and hibiscus in soft carpets of reddish gold, white and bright scarlet. Stairways zigzagged down to the lawns along the river bank, lined with cypress trees like candles of dark green fire. Water glittered and flashed from the creek as it tumbled over polished brown stone; the long narrow leaves of the trees flickered brighter still, the dove-grey of the upper side alternating with the almost metallic silver sheen of the under.

"Johanna . . ." he began softly. "Johanna always loved gardens. I remember . . . it was '25; she was about three. We were on holiday in Virconium, for the races, we went to Adelaird's, on the Bluff, for lunch. They've got an enclosed garden there, orchids. Johanna got away from her nurse, we found her there walking down a row going: *pilly flower . . . pilly flower*, snapping them off and pushing them into her hair and dress and . . ." He shrugged, nodding toward the terraces.

"Gardens, horses, poetry, airplanes . . . she was better than I at enjoying things; she told me once it was because I thought about what I thought about them too much. Forty years I've tried for *satori*, and she just fell into it."

You're a complicated man by nature, Pa, she had
said, that last parting when she left for her squadron.
*You tangle up the simplest things, like Eric, which is
why you two always fight; issues be damned. I'm not
one who feels driven to rebel against the nature of
what is, so we're different enough to get along.* She
had seemed so cool and adult, a stranger. Then she
had seized him in a sudden fierce hug, right there in
the transit station; he had blinked in embarrassment
before returning the embrace with one awkward arm.
I love you, Daddy, whispered into his ear. Then a
salute; he had returned it.

"I love you too, daughter." That as she was turn-
ing; a quick surprised wheel back and a delighted
grin.

"I may be an old fool, Johanna, but not so old I
can't learn by my mistakes when a snip of a girl
points them out to me." He touched a knuckle to her
chin. "You'll do your duty, girl, I know." He frowned
for unfamiliar words. "Sometimes I think . . . re-
member that you have a duty to live, too. Because
we need you; the earth might grow weary of the
Race and cast us off, if we didn't have the odd one
like you."

She had walked up the boarding ramp in a crowd
of her comrades, smiling.

*And if she had wisdom, surely she inherited it
from her mother.* He mused, returning to the pres-
ent. *Eric . . . did I show my daughters more love
because my heart didn't seek to make them live my
life again for me?*

He jerked his chin toward the brown-clad serfs in
the gardens below, weeding and watering and pruning.

"D'you know where they come from, Sannie?" he
asked more briskly.

She raised a brow. "Probably born here, Karl.
Why?"

"Just a thought on the nature of freedom, and

power. I'm one of the . . . oh, fifty or so most power-
ful men in the Domination; therefore one of the
freest on earth, by theory. And they are property,
powerless; but I'm not free to spend my life in the
place I was born, or cultivate my garden, or see my
children grow around me."

She snorted. "Jean-Jacques Rousseau has been dead
for a long time, my friend; also, other people's lives
always look simpler from the outside, because you
can't see the complexities. Would you change places?"

"Of course not," he said with a harsh laugh. "Even
retirement will probably drive me mad; and she may
not be dead, at all. She's strong, and cunning, and
she wants to live very much . . ."

He forced impassiveness. It was not often he could
be simply a private person; that was another sacrifice
you made for the Race. "Speaking of death, for our
four ears: I suspect that headhunter in green would
like to do at least one von Shrakenberg an injury,
and the General Staff through him."

Sannie van Reenan nodded decisively. Keeping
track of Skull House's activities was one of the Intel-
ligence Section's responsibilities, after all. "They *don't*
like that son of yours, at all. Still less now that he's
achieving some degree of success, and by . . . unor-
thodox means. The headhunters never forget, forgive,
or give up on a suspicion; well, it's their job, after
all."

The master of Oakenwald tapped his cane on the
flags. "Sannie, it might be better if that man Drei-
ser's articles found a slightly wider audience. In *The
Warrior* for instance." That was one of the Army
newspapers, the one most popular with enlisted per-
sonnel and the junior officer corps. "Unorthodox,
again. Things that happen to people in the public
view provoke questions, and are thus . . . less likely
to happen."

The woman nodded happily. "And Security's going

to be over-influential as it is, after the war. Plenty of work to do in Europe; we'll be working on pacification and getting ready to take the Yanks, which is a two-generation job, at least. Better to give them a gentle reminder that there are *some* things they'd be well advised to leave alone."

Karl looked at his watch. "And more ways of killing a cat than choking it to death with cream. Now, let's get on to that meeting. Carstairs keeps underestimating the difficulties of China, in my opinion . . ."

"You've assigned a competent operative?"

"Of course, sir." *How has this fussbudget gotten this high?* the Security Directorate Chiliarch thought, behind a face of polite agreement. *Of course, he's getting old.*

"No action on young von Shrakenberg until *after* we break through to the pass. Then, the situation will be usefully fluid for . . . long enough."

The car hissed quietly through the near-empty streets. The secret-police general looked out on their bright comeliness with longing; a nursemaid sat on a bench, holding aloft a tow-haired baby who giggled and kicked. Her uniform was trim and neat, shining against the basalt stone like her teeth against the healthy brown glow of her skin.

Tired, he thought, pulling down the shade and relaxing into the rich leather-and-cologne smell of the seats. *Tired of planning and worrying, tired of boneheaded aristocrats who think a world-state can be run like a paternalist's plantation*. He glanced aside, into the cool, intelligent eyes of his assistant. They met his for an instant before dropping with casual unconcern to the opened attaché case on his lap. *Tired of your hungry eyes and your endless waiting, my protégé. But not dead yet*.

"The son's the one to watch. The old man will die in the course of nature, soon enough; the General

Staff aren't the only ones who know how to wait, after all. The daughter's missing in action; besides, she's apolitical. Smart, but no ambition."

"Neither has Eric von Shrakenberg, in practical terms."

"Ah," the older man said softly. "Tim, you should look up from those dossiers sometimes; things aren't so cut and dried as you might think. Human beings are not consistent; nor predictable, until they're dead." *And you will never believe that and so will always fall just short of your ambitions, and never know why.* "Black, romantic Byronic despair is a pose of youth. And war is a great realist, a great teacher." A sigh. "Well, the Fritz may take care of it for us." He tapped the partition that separated them from the driver. "Back to Skull House; autumn is depressing, outdoors."

CHAPTER FOURTEEN

"... the Ottoman collapse in 1917 gave the Draka their long-awaited Turkish spoils; the Thousand-Dirigible Raid on Constantinople and the occupation of Thrace and cis-Danubian Bulgaria rounded off the new acquisitions. Neutral Persia had been overrun in 1916, ostensibly to help supply the Czar's forces. This much had been expected; what was not was the Russian collapse following the Brusilov offensive and the Bolshevik coup. Britain was totally committed to the Western Front, and could no longer do more than scold; dazzling opportunities presented themselves. The Domination had more than eight million troops under arms, and alone of the major Powers had suffered bearable casualties—most of those Janissary serf soldiers driven into the machine guns and the wire. The only serious dispute in Castle Tarleton was between those who wished to drive north into the Ukraine and the 'Easterners.' A Ukrainian offensive would have involved a major confrontation with the German army, which the Draka had carefully avoided. Instead, it was decided to launch the great push to the northeast: the initial objectives were Tashkent, Samarkand and Alma-Ata, and operations would continue until strong resistance was met.

None was, and in the end the offensive petered out only when the logistical strain became unbearable, in western China and the headwaters of the Yangtze. Six million square miles, near two hundred million souls; only sober second thoughts prevented a drive to the Pacific. The spearpoint legions were *being supplied by dirigible, every round of ammunition and gallon of fuel brought six thousand miles from railheads them-selves ten thousand miles from the industrial cities of central Africa. By 1920, it had become clear that the Domination was committed to a generation of overstrain if the New Territories were to be held, pacified, and settled. From this much flowed: the break with Britain, the enhanced role of the Security Directorate, the decision to extend compulsory military service for Citizen women, the clashes with Japan along the Mongo-lian border in 1938–1939. . . . by 1940 twenty years of effort were bearing fruit. Road and rail links spanned the whole area from Sofia to Mongolia; scores of new cities had been built, the oil resources of Arabia and Kashgar tapped, new planta-tions established by the hundred thousand. Most of all, from a strategic liability, the new serf populations had become a source of docile labor and reliable recruits . . .*

200 Years: A Social History of the Domination
by Alan E. Sorensson, Ph.D.
Archona Press, 1983

VILLAGE ONE, OSSETIAN MILITARY HIGHWAY APRIL 15, 1942: 0230 HOURS

"Sir." A hand on his shoulder. "Sir."

"Mmmmph." Eric blinked awake from a dream where cherry blossoms fell into dark-red hair and sat up, probing for grains of sleep-sand until the warning twinge of his palms forbade; grimacing at the taste in his mouth. He glanced at his watch: 0230, five hours' sleep and better than he could expect. The command section was sleeping in the cellar-cum-bunker he had selected as the H.Q.: a cube four meters on a side, damp and chilly, but marginally less likely to be overburdened with insect life.

The floor was rock because the earth did not reach this deep, five meters beneath the sloping surface. The walls and arched ceiling were cut-stone blocks, larger and older and better-laid than the stones of the houses above, even though the upper rows were visibly different from the lower. This village was *old*, the upper sections had probably been replaced scores of times, after fire or sack or the sheer wasting of the centuries. The cold air smelled of rock, earth, the root-vegetables that had been stored here over the years, and already of unwashed soldier. One wall had a rough doorway knocked through it, with a blanket slung across; a dim blue light spread from the battery lamp someone had spiked to one wall.

Shadows and blue light . . . equipment covered much of the floor: radios, a field telephone with twisted bundles of color-coded wires snaking along the floor and looping from nail to nail along lines driven between the stone blocks. The rest was carpeted in groundsheets and sleeping rolls, now that they had had time to recover their marching packs and bring the last of the supplies down from the gliders, with scavenged Fritz blankets for extra padding. Someone had improvised a rack along one wall to hang rifles and personal gear, strings of grenades, spare ammunition, a folding map table. Somebody else had one of the solid-fuel field stoves going in a corner, adding its chemical and hot-metal odor to the bunker, along with a smell of brewing coffee.

"Thanks," Eric muttered as hands pushed a mug into his hands: Neal, the command section rocket-gunner, a dark-haired, round-faced woman from . . . where was it? Taledar Hill, one of those little cow-and-cotton towns up in the Northmark.

"Patrol's in," she said. He remembered she had a habit of brevity, for which Eric was thankful; waking quickly was an acquired and detested skill for him. He sipped; it was hot, at least. Actually not bad, as coffee; a lot closer to the real thing than ration-issue wine.

McWhirter was awake, over in his corner, back to the wall, head bent in concentration over tiny

slivers of paper that his fingers creased and folded
into the shapes of birds and animals and men . . .
not the hobby he would have predicted. A muttering
at his feet. Sofie lay curled beneath the planks that
supported the static set, headphones clenched in one
sleeping hand and head cradled on her backpack,
machine pistol hanging by its strap from one corner
of the table. A foot protruded, its nails painted
shocking-pink; he grinned, remembering the disrep-
utable and battered stuffed rabbit he had glimpsed at
the bottom of her rucksack. She slept restlessly, with
small squirming motions; for a moment her nose
twitched and she rubbed her cheek into the fabric.

Now, I wonder . . . he thought. *Have I been avoid-
ing Citizen women because I don't think I'm going to
live or is that an excuse not to give any more hos-
tages to fortune?*

He shook his head and turned back to Neal. "So,
what's it like out there—"

A gloved hand swept the blanket-door aside, let-
ting in a draft of colder air from cellars not warmed
by body heat as the command bunker had been. The
figure behind was stocky, made more so by the drip-
ping rain poncho and hood; her Holbars was slung
muzzle-down, and it clicked against the stone as she
leaned her weight on one hand and threw back the
hood. She had a square face, tanned and short-nosed,
pale blue eyes and irregular teeth in a full smiling
mouth, sandy-blond hair plastered wetly to her
forehead.

"Sir, it's just such a fuckin' *joy* out there, what
with bein' dark laak a coal mine, about 6 degrees C,
an' the gods pissin' down our necks an' branches
a'slappin' us in the face, we just naturally cannot
contain our urge to roll nekkid in th' flowers, laak-so
it was Saturday night at the Xanadu in Shahnapur.
Sir."

She reached behind her and pulled a native forward by his elbow; the Circassian was young, and unlike most of the villagers his sopping rags were what remained of native garb rather than a European-style outfit. One of the hunters they had been promised . . . painfully thin, huge dark eyes hollowed in a face that quivered and chattered its teeth with the cold. Then the eyes bulged at the sight of Sofie Nixon sitting up naked to the waist and lighting a cigarette.

"An' this-here's one of yo' tame ragheads. Says laak he's heard somethin'."

Eric yawned, stretched, snapped his fingers to attract the man's attention. "You saw the greycoats?" To Neal, in English: "I think monitor Huff could use a cup, too, trooper."

The Circassian swallowed and bowed awkwardly. "Not saw, lord, but heard. Down below, where the trail crosses the third hill, before the hollow: many of the—" a Slavic-sounding word Eric did not recognize. Tyansha had been the child of Circassians settled in Turkey, descendants of refugees from Russian conquest, chieftains and their followers. The tongue she had taught him was more formal and archaic than the Russian-influenced peasant dialect spoken here.

Eric made a guess. "Steam wagons—carts that go of themselves?"

The Circassian nodded eagerly.

"Yes, lord. Many, many, but not of the ones with the belts of metal that go around and around."

Treads, Eric's mind prompted. "They stopped?"

A quick nod. "Yes, and then the engines became quiet, but there was much talking in the tongue of the *Germanski*. Perhaps three hundreds, perhaps more." A sniff. "*Germanski* are always talking, very loud, also they make much noise moving in the woods."

"Do they, now," Eric mused. Then: "McWhirter." The NCO looked up, his hand slowly closing to crush the delicate figure of a flying crane. "My compliments to Einar, and 2nd tetrarchy ready on the double. *La jou commence*."

Sofie had risen, yawning, and was stamping her feet into her boots to the muttered complaints of nearby sleepers.

"No need to go out in the wet," Eric said. "I'm just taking the 2nd. Einar's sparks can handle it."

"Nah, no problem," she replied, with a shrug and a slight sideways jerk of the head. "Wallis c'n handle this end, we'll need somebody listenin' . . ." She prodded a recumbent figure with a toe. "Hey, skinny, arse to the saddle, ready to paddle."

There was a slight, rueful smile on her face as she turned away to check her weapons and strap an extra waterproof cover on the portable set. *And someone has to look after you, hey?*

Einar Labushange's tetrarchy had drawn the ready-reaction straw that night; most of them had been sleeping with their boots on, in a cellar with a ladder to the surface. Several rolled out of their blankets as he ducked into the cellar, assault rifles ready even before full consciousness. The tetrarchy commander smiled without humor; there were merits to sleeping with your rifle, but he hoped nobody was doing it with the safety off and the selector on full-auto.

"On your feet, gun-bunnies!" The rest woke with a minimum of grumbling, shrugging into their equipment, handing around cups from the coffee urn one of them had prepared and using it to wash down caffeine pills and the inevitable ration bars and *choko*, sweet chocolate with nuts for quick high energy. Being a paratrooper was less comfortable than being in a line unit. Most Citizen Force units had attached serf auxiliaries who handled maintenance and support tasks; the air-assault troops had to do for themselves in the field, but nobody grudged taking their turn. A half-second slowness from lowered blood sugar could kill you, and a body needed care to perform at full stretch.

"Right, shitcan the 15," Einar said, and the team with the heavy machinegun gratefully let it drop back onto the tripod they had been preparing to disassemble. The soldiers were shadows in the dim gleam of a looted kerosene lamp; the light of the flame was soft, blurring through dusty air full of the muffled metallic clicks and snaps of gear being readied. "Just one of the rocket guns; other team, hump in the mortar. Oh, and this-here is goin' to be close-in work, just us and some satchelmen from Marie's bunch; black up." The soldiers broke out their sticks of greasepaint.

He turned as Eric ducked through the hole in the wall. With him were five of the combat engineers, the Circassian, his signaler and the two sticks of rifle infantry from the H.Q. tetrarchy. The dripping form of Monitor Huff followed, moving over to rejoin her lochos.

"Also, it rainin'," he added, breaking out his slicker and turning it out to the dark-mottled interior: better camouflage at night than the dirt-and-vegetation side. There was a chorus of groans.

Eric threw up a hand and grinned. "Nice to know y'all happy to see me," he said dryly. "Gather round." McWhirter stepped through the ragged "door" and spoke.

"Go with Cohort. Got a good mapref—good enough for a blind shoot."

The Centurion nodded without turning, crouching and spreading a map on the floor. The helmeted heads leaned around, some sitting or kneeling so that the others could see; there were thirty-three troopers in a Draka tetrarchy at full strength, and 2nd tetrarchy had only had three dead and five too hurt to fight. Eric pulled the L-shaped flashlight from his webbing belt, and the fighting knife from his boot to

use as a pointer. "Right. Our trusty native guide—"
He pointed back over his shoulder with the knife,
glanced back and saw the man shivering, then switched
briefly to Circassian: *"There is coffee and food in the
corner; take it, I need you walking."*

"Our trusty native guide informs me that he heard
vehicles. And Fritz voices." The knife moved. *"Here."*
See, this valley we're in is shaped like a V down to
here. Then it turns right, to the east, and opens out
into rolling hill country. Foothills." The point stabbed
down. "Right *here*, right where the valley and road
turn east, is a *big* hill, more like a small mountain,
with low saddles on either side. The road goes east,
then loops back west through this valley—and it
passes only two klicks north of the big hill, the loop's
like a U on its side with the open end pointing west,
so. And *that*—" his knife pointed at the large hill
"—is where Ali Baba here heard the Fritz trucks."

"Another attack up the valley?"

Eric shook his head. "On a narrow road, over
uncleared minefields, in the dark? Besides, they were
transport, not fighting vehicles, stoppin' and disem-
barking troops." The blade moved again, tracing a
path around the shoulder of the hill, then south up
the west side of the valley to the mountainside where
the paratroops had landed. *"That's* the way they're
going to come, and on foot. The natives say this side
of the valley is easier: lower slope, more trails, some
of which the Fritz will know since they've been here
six months. Then they'll either try to take us from
the rear, or wait until their armor arrives tomorrow
morning."

"How many, sir?"

Eric shrugged. "No telling; all they can scrape up,
if their commander is as smart as I think. There was
a regimental *kampfgruppe*, about four cohorts' equiv-
alent, down in Pyatigorsk. The Air Corps reported
hitting 'em hard—"

"Probably meanin' they pissed on 'em from a great height," someone muttered. Eric frowned at the interruption.

"—and they've been hit since, besides which we've been dropping butterfly mines. Probably lost more vehicles than men." He shrugged. "Anything up to a cohort of infantry, call it four hundred rifles and supporting weapons. It's—" he looked at his watch "—0245, they jumped off at about 0200, they're 'turtles' so, moving on unfamiliar trails in the dark, they're less than a klick into the forrest by now. Woods and scrub all the way . . ."

He looked up, face grim. "They're counting on us not knowing the lie of the land. We have guides who *do*, better than the Fritz. That's worse than Congo jungle out there; so we go straight down the road, then deke left into the woods and onto the trails. We'll split up into sections and sticks, lie up, hit, run, hit them again, then it's 'mind in gear, arse to rear.'"

"Sir?" That was one of the troopers at the back, a gangling, freckled young man with his hands looped up to dangle casually over the light machine gun lying across his neck and shoulders. "Ah . . . this means, yo' saying, that we're goin' out on account these Fritz?" Eric nodded, and the soldier grinned beatifically.

"Brothers an' Sisters of the Race!" he cried in mock ecstasy. "These are *great times*. Do yo' realize what this means?" He paused for effect. "For once— just like we always dreamed in Basic—just this one time in our young nearly-maggot-recruit lives, bros, we gets a chance to *kill* the sumbitch donkeyfuckahs that're roustin' us out of bed in the middle of the fuckin' night!"

The voices of the tetrarchy lifted, something halfway between laughter and a baying cheer. Eric waved his followers to silence, fighting to keep down his own smile; fighting a sudden unexpected prickling in the eyes as well. These were no unblooded amateurs; they knew the sort of blindfolded butchery he was leading them into, and trusted that it was necessary, trusted him to get as many out as could be . . . and god *damn* but nobody could say the Draka were cowards, whatever their other vices!

Behind him, Senior Decurion McWhirter stroked the ceramic honing stick one last time down the edge of his Jamieson semi-bowie and then slid it back into the hilt-down quick-draw sheath on his left shoulder. He remembered cheers like that . . . long ago. So long ago, with his friends. Where were his friends? Where . . . He jerked his mind from the train of thought; he was good at turning his mind away from things. Sometimes it squirmed in his grasp, like a throat or a woman, and he had to squeeze tighter. Someday he would squeeze too tight and kill it, and then . . . think about something else. The centurion was talking.

Eric jerked his thumb southwards. "Look, no speeches, I'm not going to quote that woo-woo Naldorssen at you. The rest of the Legion and our Eagle are up there across the pass, holding off ten times their number; there is a *world* of hurt coming down there, people. We've gotten off lucky because most of the *Liebstandarte* are south of the mountains, and Century A's given them a bloody nose cheap twice, because we caught them on the hop— well, what're the Airborne for? Tomorrow they'll hit us with everything and keep coming; think how we'd do it if it was our friends trapped behind this pass, eh? These aren't Draka, but they aren't gutless woppos or brainless Abduls, either. They're trying to flank us tonight; if it works we're sausage meat and the rest of our Legion gets it from behind. Hurt them, people; hurt them *bad*, it's our last chance before the crunch. Then come back walking. Bare is back without brother to guard it."

He nodded to Einar. "Now let's *do* it, let's *go*."

The tetrarchy commander hesitated a moment on the pole ladder. "Yo' realize, sir, it's not really needful to have the Century commander along. Or, ah, maybe we could make it a two-tetrarchy operation?"

Eric smiled and signed him onward. "Yo're from Windhaven, eh, Einar?" The other man nodded, seized by a sudden fierce nostalgia for the bleak desert country south of Angola: silver-colored grass, hot wind off sandstone pinnacles, dawn turned rose-red . . .

The Centurion continued: "You've trained in forest; I *grew up* in wet mountains covered with trees. Never sacrifice an edge . . . We're taking one tetrarchy because if we lose it, the village can still hold out long enough to make a difference. Two, and there wouldn't be enough of us-here left to slow them even an hour come dawn, an' it's hours that'll count. This is a delayin' operation, after all. Now, let's go."

Unnoticed in his corner, the Circassian had started and paused for a second in the process of stuffing the undreamed-of luxury of chocolate into his mouth. Stopped and shivered at the sound of the cheer, swallowing dryly. That reminded him, and he swigged down half a mugful of scalding-hot coffee before taking another bite of the bar. These *Drakanski* were fierce ones, that was certain. Good; then they could protect what they had taken. You expected masters to be fierce, to take the land and the girls and swing the knout on any who opposed them, but it was not often that a *hokotl*, a peasant, had the opportunity to eat like a Party man.

Urra Drakanski, he thought, stuffing bars of chocolate into the pockets of the fine rainproof cape he had been given, and hefting the almost-new *Germanski* rifle. Powerful masters for all that their women were shameless, masters who would feed a useful servant well: better than the Russki, who had been bad in the White Czar's time and worse under the Bolsheviki, who beat and starved you and made you listen to their godless and senseless speeches as well. The *Germanski* . . . He grinned as he followed the new lords of Circassia up the rough ladder, conscious of the rifle and the sharp two-edged khinjal strapped to his thigh. It would be a *pleasure* to meet the Germanski again.

The cold rain beat steadily on the windscreen of the Opel three-ton truck, drumming on the roof and the canvas cover of the troop compartment behind. Standartenfuhrer Felix Hoth braced himself in the swaying cab and folded the map; the shielded light was too dim for good vision anyway. For a moment he could imagine himself back in the kitchen of his father's farm in Silesia: on leave last month, with his younger sister sitting in his lap and the neighbors gathered around, eating *Mutti*'s strudel at the table by the fire while sleet hissed against the windows. His bride-to-be playing with one of her blonde braids as he described the rich estates in the Kuban Valley that would be granted after the war. *Vati* had leaned back in the big chair with his pipe, beaming with pride at his officer son, he who had been a lowly *feldwebel* through the Great War . . .

I could never tell them anything, he thought. How could you talk to civilians about Russia? Reichsfuhrer Himmler was right: those who bore the burden of cleansing the Aryan race's future *lebensraum* bore a heavy burden, one that their families at home could not hope to understand.

Enough. I defend them now. If Germany was defeated, his family would be serf plantation hands. Or—he had been in Paris in 1940, doing some of the roistering expected of a soldier on leave. One of the *Maisons Tolerees* had had a collection of Draka pornography; it was a minor export of the Domination, which had no morals censorship to speak of. He felt his mind forming images, placing his fiancee Ingeborg's face on the bodies of the serf girls in the glossy pictures; of his sister Rosa naked on an auction-block in Rhakotis or Shahnapur, weeping and trying to cover herself with her hands. Or splayed open under a huge Negro Janissary, black buttocks pumping in rhythm to her screams . . .

He opened the window and the lever broke under his hand; cold wet wind slapped his face with an icewater hand that lashed his mind back to alertness. The convoy was travelling barely faster than a man could run, with the vehicles' headlights blacked out except for a narrow strip along the bottom. Thirty trucks, four hundred *panzergrenadiers*, half his infantry, but he had left the tracked carriers behind. Too noisy for this work, and besides that they ate petrol. The supply situation was serious and getting worse: Draka aircraft were ranging as far north as the Kuban, meeting weakening resistance from a Luftwaffe whose fighters had to work from bases outside their enemy's operational range. The oil fields at Maikop were still burning, and the Domination's armor had taken Baku in the first rush . . .

It can still come right. Despite his losses so far, shocking as they were; if he could get this force up on the flank, they could carry the village in one rush at first light. It would be a difficult march in the dark, but his men were fresh, and as for the Draka . . . they had no mechanical transport, no way to get down from the village in time even if they knew of the attack, which was unlikely in this night of black rain. He turned his head to look behind. There was little noise: the low whirring of fans ramming air into the steam engines' flashtube boilers, the slow *shuusss* of hard-tired wheels through the muddy surface of the road; all were drowned in the drumming of rain on the trees and wet fields. Not very much to see, either, no moon and dense overcast.

I can't even see the ground, he thought. *Good.* Not that it was at all likely the Draka would have any sentries here; it was ten kilometers to Village One, in a straight line. It was tangled ground, mostly heavily wooded, and the invaders were strangers here, while the Liebstandarte had been stationed in the area since the collapse of Soviet resistance in Caucasia back in November of '41.

The armor and self-propelled artillery would be moving up later, now that they had paths cleared through those damnable air-sown plastic mines. Everybody would be with them, down to the clerks and bottle-washers, everybody who could carry a rifle, with only the communications personnel and walking wounded left in Pyatigorsk. Everything would be in place by dawn.

"It should be . . ." he muttered, risking a quick flick of his light. "Yes, that's it." A ruined building— the Ivans had put up a stand there last year. Nothing much, no heavy weapons; they had simply driven a tank through the thin walls. A suitable clearing; and the trail over the mountain's shoulder started here. He twisted to thrust his arm past the tilt-covered cab of the truck and blinked the light three times.

The paratroop boots hit the pavement with a steady *ruck-ruck-ruck* as 2nd Tetrarchy ran through the steady downpour of rain. It was flat black, clouds and falling water cutting off any ambient light—dark enough that a hand was barely a whitish blur held before the eyes, invisible at arm's length. Equipment rustled and clinked as the Draka moved in their steady tireless lope, rain capes flapped; Eric heard someone stumble, then recover with a curse:

"Shitfire, it dark as Loki's asshole!"

"Shut the fuck up," an NCO hissed.

The tetrarchy was running down the road in a
column four abreast, spaced so that each trooper
could guide himself by the comrades on either side,
with the outside rank holding to the verge of the
crushed-rock surface. There was a knockdown hand-
cart at the rear, with extra ammunition and their two
native guides, who had collapsed after the first three
kilometers; they were hunters who had lived hard,
but their bodies were weakened by bad food and
they had never had the careful training in breathing-
discipline and economical movement that the Citizen
class of the Domination received. It was hard work
running in the dark; moving blind made the muscles
tense in subconscious anticipation, waiting to run
into something. The ponchos kept out the worst of
the rain, but their legs were slick with thin mud cast
up from the rutted surface of the road, and bodies
sweated under the waterproof fabric until webbing
and uniforms clung and chafed; they were carrying
twenty kilos of equipment each, as well. Nothing
unbearable, since cross-country running in packs had
been a daily routine from childhood and the para-
troops were picked troops unusually fit even for Draka.

"Lord . . . lord . . ." one of the Circassians wheezed.
Eric whistled softly and the tetrarchy halted with only
one or two thumps and muffled *oofs* proclaiming col-
lision. The native rolled off the cart, coughed, retched,
then wormed through to the Draka commander.

The Centurion crouched and a circle of troopers
gathered, their cloaked forms making a downward-
pointing light invisible. The sound of his soldiers'
breathing was all around him, and the honest smell
of their sweat; they had covered the ten klicks of
road faster than horse cavalry could have, in a cold
and damp that drained strength and heart—after a
day with a paradrop, street combat, hours of the
hardest sort of labor digging in, then another battle
and barely four hours' sleep. Now there would be

more ground to travel, narrow trails through unfamiliar bush, with close-quarter fighting at the end of it . . . only Draka could have done it at all, and even they would be at less than their best. Well, this was war, not a field problem in training. The enemy had been rousted out of bed, too, but they had spent the trip from their base in dry comfort in their trucks; not fair, but that was war, too.

He rested on one knee, breath deep but slow, half regretful that the run was over. You could switch off your mind, running; do nothing but concentrate on muscle and lung and the next step . . .

"Here," the panting local said. "Trail—" he coughed rackingly. "Trail here."

White Christ and Heimdal alone know how he can tell, Eric thought. *Years of poaching and smuggling, no doubt.* He shone the light on his watch, estimated speed and distance, and fitted them over a map in his mind. Yes, this would be where the road turned east.

"Einar. Straight west, split up and cover the trails. If they're moving troops in any number they'll probably use all three. Everybody: do *not* get lost in the dark, but if you do, head *upslope* and wait for light if the Fritz are between you and the road. Otherwise, back to the road and burn boot up to the village."

The lanky tetrarch shrugged, a troll shape in the darkness. "No wrinkles, we'll kill 'em by the shitload and send them back screamin' fo' their mommas." To his troops: "Lochoi A an' B with me, and the mortar. Huff, yo' take C an' the rocket gun. Hughes, run D up to that little trail on th' ridge. *Go.*"

The troopers sorted themselves into sections and moved off the road, the Circassians in the lead, an occasional watery gleam of light from a flashlight: nobody could be expected to walk over scrub and rock-strewn fields in *this*. Rain hid them quickly, and the woods would begin soon after that. *Dense* woods, with thick undergrowth.

Eric waited by the side of the road as the columns filed past, not speaking, simply standing present while they passed, dim bulks in the chill darkness; a few raised a hand to slap palms as they went by, or touched his shoulder. He replied in kind, with the odd word of the sort they would understand and appreciate, the terse cool slang of their trade and generation: *"Stay loose, snake." "Stay healthy for the next war."*

The gods would weep, he thought. If they didn't laugh. The only time they could be themselves among themselves, show their human faces to each other, was when they were engaged in slaughter. The Army, especially a combat unit up at the sharp end, was the only place a Draka could experience a society without serf or master; where rank was a functional thing devoted to a common purpose; where cooperation based on trust replaced coercion and fear. *And how we shine, then,* he thought. Why couldn't that courage and unselfish devotion be put to some *use,* instead of being set to digging them deeper into the trap history and their ancestors had landed them in?

At the last, he turned to the command tetrarchy and the satchelmen from the combat engineers.

"Follow me," he said.

Felix Hoth watched the last of his grenadiers vanish into the blackness. This close to the trees the rain was louder, a hissing surf-roar of white noise on a million million leaves, static that covered every sound. The trails would be tunnels through the living mass of vegetation, cramped and awkward—like the tunnels under Moscow. *Blackness like cloth on his eyeballs, crawling on knees and elbows through the filthy water, a rope trailing from his waist and a pistol on a lanyard around his neck* . . . He jerked his mind back from the image, consciously forcing his breath to slow from its panting, forcing down the overwhelming longing for a drink that accompanied the dreams. Daydreams, sometimes, the mind returning to them as the tongue would obsessively probe a ragged tooth, until it was swollen and sore. But Moscow, that was more than six months gone, and the men who had fought him were dead. He would kill the dreams, as he had killed *them*—shot, suffocated, gassed, or burned in the sewers and subways of the Russian capital. *This* battle would be fought in the open, as God had meant men to fight.

And this time he would win. The troops he had sent into the woods were heavily burdened, but they were young and fit; they would be in place on the slopes overlooking Village One by dawn, plentifully equipped with mortars and automatic weapons, and the best of his snipes with scope-sighted rifles. The Draka in the village would be pinned down, there were simply not *enough* of them to hold a longer perimeter. The other pass, the Georgian Military Highway, was nearly clear. He had had radio contact with the units over the mountains, they were pressing the Draka paratroops back through the burning ruins of Kutasi; they were taking monstrous casualties, but inflicting hurts, too, on an enemy cut off from reinforcement. The Janissaries were at their rear, but once in the narrow approaches over the mountains, they could hold the Draka forever. Perhaps negotiate a peace; the Domination was known to be cold-bloodedly realistic about cutting its losses.

The trucks had laagered in the clearing, engines silent. The air smelled overwhelmingly of wet earth, a yeasty odor that overrode burnt fuel and metal. Only the drivers remained, mostly huddled in their cabs, a platoon of infantry beneath the vehicles for guards, and the radio-operator. The bulk of the regiment would be here in a few hours; pause here to regroup and refuel, then deploy for action. Wehrmacht units were following, hampered by the hammering the road and rail nets were taking, but force-marching nonetheless. He would roll over Village One, and they would stop the Draka serpent.

"We must," he muttered.

"Sir?" That was his regimental chief of staff, Schmidt.

"We must win," Hoth replied. "If we don't, our cities will burn, and our books. A hundred years from now, German will be a tongue for slaves; only scholars will read it—Draka scholars."

"I wonder . . ."

"What?" The SS commander turned his light so that the other's face was visible; the wavering grey light through the wet glass of the torch made it ghastly, but the black circles under the eyes were genuine. There had been little sleep for Schmidt these past twenty hours: too much work, and far too much thought.

"Wonder about Poles having this conversation in 1939, or Russians last year," Schmidt said, exhaustion bringing out the slurred Alsatian vowels. "They had to hold, everything depended on it. But they didn't hold."

"They were our racial inferiors! The Draka are Aryans like us; that is why they are a threat! The Leader himself has said so."

Schmidt looked at him with an odd smile. "The Draka aristocrats are Nordic, yes, Herr Standartenfuhrer. But they are a thin layer; most of the Domination's people are Africans or Asians. Most even of their soldiers and bureaucrats, at the everyday level: blacks, mulattoes, Eastern Jews, Arab Semites, Turks, Chinese, a real *schwarm*. Would that not be an irony? We National Socialists set out to cleanse Europe of *juden* and slavs and gypsies, and it ends with the home of the white race being ruled and mongrelized by chinks and kikes and Congo savages—" He laughed, an unpleasant, reedy sound.

"Silence!" Hoth snapped. The other man drew himself up, his eyes losing their glaze. "Schmidt, you have been a comrade in arms, and are under great stress; I will therefore forget this . . . defeatist obscenity. Once! Once more, and I will myself report you to the Security Service!"

Schmidt swallowed and rubbed his hands across his face, turning away. Hoth forced himself back to calm; he would need a clear head.

And after all the man's from Alsace—he's an intellectual, and a Catholic, he thought excusingly. A good fighting soldier, but the long spell of antipartisan work had shaken him, the unpleasant demands of translating Party theory into practice. Combat would bring him back to himself.

He swung back into the radio truck and laced the panel to the outside, clicking on the light. This was going to be tricky; it was all a matter of time.

This is going to be tricky timing, Eric thought as they reached the edge of the clearing. Even trickier than threading their way through the nighted bush; they had followed the Circassian blindly, had dodged aside barely in time and lain motionless in a thicket of witch hazel as a long file of Germans went past. One of them had slipped and staggered; Eric had felt more than seen the boot come down within centimeters of his outstretched hand. He heard a muttered *scheisse* as the SS-man paused to resettle his clanking load of mortar-tripod, then nothing but the rain and fading boots sucking free of wet leaf mold. He felt his face throb at the memory of it, like a warm wind; the rich sweet smell of the crushed brush was still with him. Extreme fear was like pain: it fixed memory forever, made the moment instantly accessible to total recall . . .

The native hunter crept up beside him and put his mouth to the Draka's ear; even then, Eric wrinkled his nose slightly at the stink of rotten teeth and bad digestion.

"Here, lord." His pointing arm brushed the side of Eric's helmet, and he spoke in a breathy whisper. Probably not needful, the rain covered and muffled sound, but no sense in taking chances. "The road is no more than five hundred meters that way. Shall I go first?"

"No," Eric said, unfastening the clasp of his rain cloak and sliding it to the ground. "You stay here, we'll need you to guide us back. In a hurry! Be ready."

And besides, it isn't your fight. Except that the Draka would let his people live and eat, if they obeyed. He brought the Holbars forward and jacked the slide, easing it through the forward-and-back motion that chambered the first round rather than letting the spring drive it home with the usual loud *chunk.* Safety or no safety, he was not going to walk through unfamiliar woods in the dark with one up the spout . . . Soft *clack-clicks* told of others doing likewise.

His mouth was dry. *How absurd,* he thought. His uniform was heavy with water, mud and leaves plastered on his chest and belly, and his *mouth* was dry.

A brief glimpse of yellow light from downslope to the north. Sofie slapped his ankle; he reached back to touch acknowledgement, and their hands met, touched and clasped. Her hand was small but firm. She gave his hand a brief squeeze that he found himself returning, smiling in the dark.

"Stay tight, Sofie," he whispered.

"You too, Eri—sir," she answered.

"Eric's fine, Sofie," he answered. "This isn't the British army." Slightly louder, coming to his feet: "Ready."

He crouched, eyes probing blindly at the darkness. Still too dark to *see,* but he could sense the absence of the forest canopy above; it was like walking out of a room. And the rain was individual drops, not the dense spattering that came through the leaf cover. Ripping and fumbling sounds, the satchelmen getting out their charges. *Why am I here?* he thought. *I'm a commander, doing goddam pointman's work. I could be back in the bunker, having a coffee and watching Sofie paint her toenails.* His lips shaped a whistle, and the Draka started forward at a crouching walk. Their feet skimmed the earth, knees bent, ankles loose, using the soles of their feet to detect terrain irregularities.

Nobody's indispensable, another part of his mind answered. His belly tightened, and his testicles tried to draw themselves up in a futile gesture of protection against the hammering fire some layer of his mind expected. *Marie can handle a fixed-front action as well as you can. And you've been expecting to die in battle for a long time now.*

But he didn't want to, the White Christ be his witness.

Eric's step faltered; he recovered, with an expression of stunned amazement that the darkness thankfully covered. He grunted, as if a fist had driven into his belly.

I don't, I truly don't, he thought with wonder. Then, with savage intensity: *There are hundreds within a kilometer who don't want to either.* He was acutely conscious of Sofie following to his right. *You still can, and everyone with you. Careful!*

CHAPTER FIFTEEN

". . . never regretted my articles. I was not among those who sentimentalized our arrangement with the Draka, or imagined that it was a true alliance of mutual interest and shared values like that with Britain or the new Indian government. History is something that tends to be re-edited in the light of current needs, particularly when politicians and their journalistic flacks are involved; to understand what was done, we must make an effort of the mind to recapture what was felt at the time. Otherwise, we lend ourselves to witch-burnings like the late, unlamented Senator from Wisconsin's hunt for 'Drak-symps' in high places.

What is most difficult to remember is that in the 30's, even the early 40's, nobody was afraid of the Draka. Our bipolar world, divided between the Alliance and the Domination, was a nightmare that only a few radicals could imagine, just as the balance of terror under the shadow of Oppenheimer's sun-bomb and Clarke's suborbital missile was an idea a few scientifiction writers played with. Perhaps our own racial prejudices were at fault. In the nineteenth century abolitionists and humanitarians complained, but who was willing to spend blood and treasure to save Africa from the Domination? It was only negroes falling under the yoke, after all. In the Great War it was only Asians, 'wogs' (or only Bulgarians and Slavs, on the fringes); if most of the public in North America or Western Europe thought of it at all, they assumed the Domination was no more than a harsher form of colonial imperialism. That the Draka would bring the rule of plantation and compound, impaling stake and sjambok to the European heartlands of Western civilization, was unthinkable.

Perhaps there is something to the fashionable liberal idea that the Domination is Afro-Asia's revenge on the West for five centuries of pillage and exploitation. Certainly, the results of the Eurasian War are a fitting punishment for our sins of omission and commission: allowing the Domination to expand in the Great War, the appeasement of Nazi, Soviet, and Japanese aggression that followed, the isolationism and wishful thinking that left us with no choice but that between bad and worse. Yet, given the choices left to us, what other course was open? Japan attacked us directly, and as for the Third Reich—the Domination aspires to rule the world, not destroy it, and they are patient. The Nazi leadership was not. "If we perish, we shall take a world with us; a world in flames." Hitler's words, and they were meant. The fall of Europe was apocalyptic enough; had the National Socialist dream not ended in the ruins of Munich, his scientists might have given him the means to make his dreams literal truth. Liberty is not peace, but constant struggle. Each generation must fight the enemy that history deals it."

Empires of the Night: A '40's Journal
by William A. Dreiser
MacMillan, New York, 1956

VILLAGE ONE, OSSETIAN MILITARY HIGHWAY APRIL 15, 1942: 0350 HOURS

Trooper Patton wiped the sap from her bush knife and sheathed it over her shoulder; carefully, with both hands. It was *far* too sharp to fling about in the dark. Then she knelt to run her fingers over the product of her ingenuity: a straight sapling, hastily trimmed to a murderous point at both ends.

One point was rammed into the packed earth of the trail; the middle of the stake was supported by the crutch of a Y-shaped branch cut to just the right length. The other end slanted up . . . Patton stood against it, measuring the height. Just at her navel, coming up the trail from the north. The briefing paper *did* say that the Fritz SS had a minimum height requirement, so it should hit . . .

The Draka woman was grinning to herself as she slid back four meters to her firing position to the left of the trail, behind the trunk of a huge fallen beech; laughing, even, an almost soundless quiver. One that Trooper Huff beside her knew well. Lips approached her ear, with crawling noises and a smell of wet uniform.

"What's so fuckin' amusin', swarthy one?" asked Monitor Huff, commander of C lochos, the squad.

Patton was dark for a Draka, short and muscular, olive-skinned and flat-faced; their people had a Franco-Mediterranean strain that cropped out occasionally among the more common north-European types. Huff could imagine the disturbing glint of malicious amusement in the black eyes as she heard the slightly reedy voice describe the trap.

"Belly or balls, Huffie, belly or balls. Noise'll give us a firin' point, eh?"

"Yo're sick. Ah love it." Their lips brushed, and Huff rolled back to her firing position. *Gonna die, might as well die laughin'*, she thought.

Down the trail, something clanked.

"Clip the stickers," Tetrarchy Commander Einar Labushange said as he crawled past the last of his fire teams. This was the largest trail; half the tetrarchy was with him to cover it, where a ridge crossed the path and forced it to turn left and west below the granite sill. Less cover, of course, but that had its advantages. He touched the bleeding lip he had split

running into a branch, tasting salt. "And be careful, if'n I'm goin' to die a hero's death, I don't want to do it with a Draka bayonet up my ass."

He slid his own free and fixed it, unfolding the bipod of his Holbars, worrying. The little slope gave protection, but it also gave room for the Fritz to spread out. And withdrawing would be a cast-iron bitch, down the reverse slope at his back and over the stream and up a near-vertical face two meters high. At least they could all rest for a moment, and there was was no danger of anybody dropping off, not with this miserable cold pizzle running down their—

The sound of a boot. A hobnailed boot, grating on stone. The heavy breathing of many men walking upslope under burdens. *Close, I can hear them over the rain. Very close.* He pulled a grenade out of his belt and laid it on the rock beside him, lifting his hips and reaching down to move a sharp-edged stone. He rose on one elbow to point the muzzle of the assault rifle downslope and drew a breath.

Eric could smell the trucks now, lubricants and rubber and burnt distillate, overpowering churned mud and wet vegetation. They must be keeping the boilers fired; he could hear the peculiar hollow drumming of rain on tight-stretched canvas, echoing in the troop compartments it sheltered. Only a few lights, carefully dimmed against aircraft; that was needless in an overcast murk like tonight's, but habit ruled. To his dark-adapted eyes it was almost bright, and he turned his eyes away to keep the pupils dilated. There was an exercise to do that by force of will. Dangerous in a firefight, though; bright flashes could scorch the retina if you were overriding the natural reflex. He counted the trucks by silhouette.

There must be at least some covering force. Adrenaline buzzed in his veins, flogging the sandy feel of weariness out of his brain; he would have to be careful, this was the state of jumping-alert wiredness that led to errors. Some of the trucks would mount automatic weapons, antiaircraft, but they could be trained on ground targets. Eight assault rifles, including his, and the demolitions experts from Marie's tetrarchy; they were going to be grossly outnumbered. Mud sucked at the soles of his boots and packed into the broad treads, making the footing greasy and silence impossible.

Thank god for the rain. Darkness to cover movement, rain to drown out the sounds. That made it impossible for him to coordinate the attack, once launched; well, Draka were supposed to use initiative.

"*Halten zie!*" A German voice sounded from out of the darkness, only a few meters ahead now: more nervous than afraid, only barely audible over the drumming rain. He forced himself to walk forward, each footfall an eternity.

"Ach, it's just me, Hermann," he replied in the same language. "We got lost. Where's the *Herr Hauptman?*" And knew his own mistake, even before the spear of electric light stabbed out from the truck's cab. *Hauptman* was German for "Captain." At least in their Regular army, of which the Liebstandarte was no part.

The SS don't use the German Army rank system! The night lit with tracer fire, explosions, weird prisms of chemical light refracted into momentary rainbows through the prism of the falling rain. The Germans were shooting wild into a darkness blacker to them than their opponents.

He flung himself down and fired, tracer flicking out even before his body struck the ground. Grenades went off somewhere, a sharp *brak-brak* sound; a fuel truck went up with a huge woosh and orange flash in the corner of his eye. A bullet went over his head with the unpleasantly familiar CRACK of a high-velocity round; the Holbars hammered itself into his shoulder as he walked it down the length of the truck, using the muzzle flash to aim. Stroboscopic vision. Lightflash, blinkblinkblinkblink.

Blink. The driver tumbling down from the open door, rifle falling from his hands. Blink. Metal dimpling and tearing under the ratcheting slugs. Blink. A machine gunner above the cab trying to swing his weapon toward him, jerking and falling as the light slugs from the Holbars struck and tumbled and chewed. Ping-*ting*, ricochet off something solid. Blink. Shots down the canvas tilt, sparks and flashes, antennae clustering on its roof . . .

"Almighty Thor, it's the command truck!" Eric whooped, and ran for the entrance at the rear. His hand was reaching for a grenade as he rounded the rear of the truck, skidding lightly in the torn-up wet earth. The canvas flap was opening at the rear. The Draka tossed the blast grenade in and dove to one side without breaking stride, hit the ground in a forward roll that left him low to the earth in the instant the detonation came, turned and drove back for the truck while it still echoed. You had to get in *fast*, that had been an offensive grenade, blast only, a hard lump of explosive with no fragmentation sleeve. Fast, while anybody alive in there was still stunned . . .

Standartenfuhrer Hoth had been listening on the shortwave set in the back of the radio truck, to the broadcasts from over the mountains. It was all there was to do; as useful as Schmidt's poring over the maps, there by the back of the vehicle. Reception was spotty, and he kept getting fragments. Fragments of the battle south of the passes, in German or the strange slurred Draka dialect of English; his own command of that tongue was spotty and based on the British standard. Evaluations, cool orders, fire-correction data from artillery observation officers, desperate appeals for help . . . There were four German divisions in the pocket at the south end of the Ossetian Military Highway—the Liebstandarte, split by the Draka paratroops and driving to clear the road from both ends, with three Wehrmacht units trying to hold the perimeter to the south. Trying and failing.

Time, time, he thought. The faint light of dials and meters turned his hands green; the body of the truck was an echoing cavern as the canvas above them drummed under the rain.

"Are you getting anything?" he said to the operator.

The man shook his head, one palm pressed to an earphone and the fingers of the other hand teasing a control. "Nothing new, Standartenführer. Good reception from Pyatigorsk and Grozny, a mishmash from over the mountains—too much altitude and electrical activity tonight. And things skipping the ionosphere from everywhere: a couple of Yank destroyers off Iceland hunting a U-boat, the Imperial Brazilian news service . . ."

The first explosion stunned them into a moment of stillness. Then Schmidt was leaping to his feet, spilling maps and documents. Hoth snatched for his helmet. Firing, the unmistakable sound of Draka automatic rifles, more explosions; only a few seconds, and already orange flame-light was showing through the canvas. The truck rocked, then shook as bullets struck it, a shuddering vibration that racked downward from the unseen cab ahead of them. Slugs tearing through the rank of electronic equipment, toppling boxes, bright sparking flashes and the lightning smell of ozone. The radio operator flew backwards across the truck bed with a line of red splotches across his chest, to slump with the headphones half pulled off and an expression of surprise on his face.

Hoth was turning when the grenade flew through the back of the truck, between the unlaced panels of the covering. It bounced back from the operator's body, landed at Schmidt's feet. There was just light and time enough to recognize the type, machined from a hard plastic explosive. It was safe at thirty feet, but more than enough to kill or cripple them all in the close quarters of the truck. He had enough time to feel a flash of anger: he *could* not die now, there was too much to do. It was futile, but he could feel his body tensing to hurl himself forward and kick the bomb out into the dark, feel the flush of berserker rage at the thought of another disaster.

Eyes locked on the explosive, he was never sure whether Schmidt had thrown himself forward or slipped; only aware of the blocky form plunging down and then being thrown up in a red spray. That barrier of flesh was enough to absorb the blast, although the noise was still enough to set his ears buzzing. The SS commander was a fast heavy man, with a combat veteran's reflexes: in a night firefight, you had to get *out* this was a deathtrap. There was a motive stronger than survival driving him forward, as well.

The past day had seen his life and his cause go from triumph to the verge of final disaster. *He* had seen his men cut down without an opportunity to strike back while he blundered like a bull tangled in the matador's cape. Out there was something he could kill. A thin trickle of saliva ran from one corner of his mouth as he lunged for the beckoning square of darkness.

A step brought Eric back to the rear of the truck. He had just time to wonder why the explosion had sounded so muffled when a German stepped over the body of the comrade who had thrown himself on the Draka grenade and kicked Eric in the face, hard.

The Draka's rifle had been in the way. That saved him from a broken jaw; it did not prevent him from

being flung back, stunned. The ground rose up and
struck him; arms and legs moved sluggishly, like the
fronds of a sea anemone on a coral reef; the strap of
his Holbars was wound around his neck.

Self-accusation was bitter. Overconfidence. He had
just time enough to think *stupid, stupid* when a
huge weight dropped on his back. The darkness lit
with fire.

Down. Reflex drove Sofie forward as motion flicked
at the corner of her eye, letting the Centurion run
on ahead. She landed crouched on toes and left
hand, muscle springing back against the weight of
body and radio. Shins thudded against her ribs, and
the German went over with a yell; she flung out the
machine pistol one-handed and fired, using muzzle
flash to aim and recoil to walk the burst through the
mud and across the prone Fritz's back, hammering
cratering impacts as the soft-nosed slugs mushroomed
into his back and blew exit wounds the size of fists in
his chest. Eric had stopped ahead of her, walking a
line of assault-rifle fire down the truck. Explosions;
there was light now, enough to seem painful after
the long march through the forest. Eric—

Ignore him, *have* to. She twisted and pivoted, flick-
ing herself onto knees and toes, facing back into the
vehicle park, its running shouting silhouettes. Her
thumb snapped the selector to single-shot and she
brought the curved steel buttplate to her shoulder,
resting the wooden forestock on her left palm; there
was enough light to use the optical sight now, and
the submachine gun was deadly accurate under fifty
meters. The round sight-picture filled her vision,
divided by the translucent plastic finger of the inter-
nal pointer, with its illuminated tip. Concentrate: it
was just school, just a night-firing exercise, pop-up
targets, outline recognition. A jacket with medals,
lay the pointer on his chest and stroke the trigger

and *crack*. The recoil was a surprise, it always was when the shot felt just right. The Fritz flipped back out of her sight; she did not need to let her eyes follow. More following him, this truck must mean something; quickly, they could see the muzzle flashes if not her. Crack. Crack. Crack. The last one spun, twisted, only winged; she slapped two more rounds into him before he hit the ground.

A bullet snapped through the space her stomach would have been in if she had been standing; she felt the passage suck at her helmet. Aimed fire, if she hit the dirt he might still get her, or the centurion in the back. Scan . . . a helmet moving, behind one of the bodies. Difficult . . . Her breath went out, held; her eyes were wide, forcing a vision that saw everything and nothing. The Fritz working the bolt of his Mauser. Blood from a bitten cheek. The pointer of her scope sinking with the precision of a turret-lathe, just below the brim of the coal-scuttle helmet. Her finger taking up the infinitesimal slack of the machine pistol's trigger. They fired together; the helmet flipped up into the ruddy-lit darkness with a *kting* sound that she heard over the rifle bullet buzzing past. A cratered ruin, the SS rifleman's head slipped down behind the comrade he had been using as a firing rest.

Sofie blinked the afterimage of the Mauser's flash out of her eyes, switching to full-auto and spraying the pile of dead, you never knew. Knee and heel and toe pushed her back upright as her hands slapped a fresh magazine into her weapon, hand finding hand in the dark. Unnoticed, her lips were fixed in a snarl as she loped around the truck Eric had been attacking; her eyes were huge and dark in a face gone rigid as carved bone. He could not be far ahead. She would find him; his back needed guarding. She would.

Plop.

The Fritz flare arched up from behind a boulder.
Harsh silver light lit the trees, leeching color and
depth, making them seem like flat stage sets in an
outdoor theater, turning the falling rain to a streak-
ing argent dazzle. The Draka section hugged the
earth and prayed for darkness, but the flare tangled
its parachute in the upper branches and hung, sput-
tering. Einar Labushange laid his head on his hands;
the light outlined what was left of the Draka firing
line on the ridge with unmerciful clarity. He was
safer than most, because when his head dropped, the
dead SS trooper in front of him hid him from the
front. He could feel the body jerking with pseudo-life
as bullets struck it, hear the wet sounds they made.
Rounds were lashing the whole ridge; the firepower
of the Fritz infantry was diffuse, not as many auto-
matic weapons per soldier, but their sheer numbers
made it huge now that they were deployed.

Not as many as there had been when the Draka
had caught them filing along below. Forgetting, he
tried to shift himself with an elbow: froze, and sank
back with a sound that only utter will prevented
from being a whimper. Briefly, some far-off profes-
sional corner of his mind wondered if he had been
justified in using an illuminating round, that fifteen-
minute eternity ago. Yes, on the whole. The Fritz
had been in marching order; he did not need to raise
his head to see them piled along the trail, fifty or
sixty at least. More hung on the undergrowth behind
it, shot in the back as they waded through vine and
thicket as dense as barbed wire. *Clumsy*, he thought,
conscious even through the rain of the cold sweat of
pain on his body, the slow warm leakage from his
belly. Open-country soldiers, Draka would have gone
through like eels or used their bush knives.

Stones and chips *tinked* into the air; a shower
of cut twigs and branches fell on the soldiers of the
Domination, pattering through the rain. They crouched

below the improvised parapet; occasionally a marksman would pop up for a quick burst at the muzzle flashes, roll along to another position, snap-shoot again at the answering fire that raked their original shooting stand.

"Fuckahs never learn!" he heard one call out gleefully. There was no attempt at a firing line; the survivors of the two *lochoi* would rise to fire when the next charge came in. Overhead, a shell from 2nd Tetrarchy's 60mm mortar whined. Only one, they were running short. Short of everything; and the Fritz still had more men. Despite the dozens shattered along the trail, the scores more lying in windrows up the slope they had tried to storm, and thank the One-Eyed that the bush was too thick to let them around the flanks easily . . .

Einar did not move. As long as his body stayed very still, the knee that had been shattered by the sniper's bullet did not make him faint. He could feel the blood runneling down his face from the spot where he had bitten through his lip the last time the leg had jerked. It would be the bayonet wound in the stomach that killed him, though.

He struggled not to laugh: it was very bad when he did that. A flare had gone off just as the last Fritz charge crested the ridge, too late for either of them to alter lunges that had the weight of a flung body behind them. Just time enough to see each other's faces with identical expressions of surprise and horror; then, his bayonet had rammed into the German's throat, just as the long blade on the end of the Mauser punched through his uniform tunic right above the belt buckle. It had been cold, very cold; he could *feel* it, feel the skin parting and the muscle and crisp things inside that popped with something like a sound heard through his own bones. Then it had pulled free as the Fritz collapsed, and he had watched it come out of him and had thought *how odd, I've been killed* as he started to fall. That was very funny, when you thought about it. Unlikely enough to be killed with a bayonet; astronomical chance for a Draka to lose an engagement with cold steel. Of course, he had been very tired . . .

Light-headed and a little sleepy, as he was now. He must not laugh. The stomach wound was death, but slowly; just a deep stab wound, worked a little wider when the blade came out. Not the liver or a kidney or the major arteries, or he'd be dead by now. The muscles clamped down, letting the blood pool and pressure inside rather than rush out and bring unconsciousness as the brain starved. But there were things in his gut hanging by strained threads.

It was very bad when he laughed.

And he was *very* sleepy; the sound of the firing was dimming, no louder than the rain drumming on his helmet . . .

He rocked his ruined leg, using the still-responsive muscle above the tourniquet. The scream was probably unheard in the confusion of battle; he was very alert, apart from the singing in his ears, when the second decurion crawled up beside him, the teen-aged face white and desperate in the dying light of the flare.

"Sir. Pederssen and de Klerk are expended, the mortar's outa rounds, they're working around the flanks, an' we can't stop the next rush what'm I supposed to *do*!" The NCO reached out for his shoulder, then drew his hand back as Einar slapped at it.

"Get the fuck out. No! Don't try to move me; I can feel things . . . ready to tear inside. I'd bleed out in thirty seconds. Go on, burn boot, *go* man, *go*."

The sounds died away behind him; the buzzing whine in his ears was getting louder. Nobody could say they hadn't accomplished the mission: the Fritz must have lost a third or better of their strength, they would never push on farther into this wet black-

ness with another ambush like this waiting for them.
A hundred dead, at least . . . Somehow, it did not
seem as important now, but it was all that was left.

The flare light was dimming, or maybe that was
his eyes. Maybe he was seeing things, the bush
downslope stirring. Clarity returned for a moment,
although he felt very weak, everything was a mon-
strous effort. No choice but to see it through now
. . . *Oh, White Christ, to see the desert again* . . . It
would be the end of the rains, now. A late shower,
and the veld would be covered in wildflowers, red
and magenta and purple; you could ride through them
and the scent rose around you like all the gardens in
the world, blowing from the horizon. *No choice,
never any choice until it's too late, because you don't
know what dying is, you just think you do* . . .

Einar Labushange raised his head to the sights of
his rifle as the SS rose to charge.

"Ah. Ah. Ahhhhhaaaaa—"

It was amazing, Trooper Patton thought. The Ger-
man impaled on the stake still had the strength to
moan. Even to scream, occasionally, and to speak,
now and then. Muzzle flashes had let her see him,
straddling as if the pointed wood his own weight had
punched into his crotch was a third leg. Every now
and then he tried to move; it was usually then that
he screamed. The bodies behind him along the trail
were still; she had put in enough precautionary bursts,
the trail was covered with them, and a big clump
back down the trail about twenty meters. That was
where the rocket-gun shell had hit them from be-
hind, nicely bunched up and focused on the fire
probing out of the night before them.

"Amazing," she muttered. Her voice sounded dis-
tant and tinny in ears that felt hot and flushed with
blast; she wished the cold rain would run into them.
Amazing that nothing had hit him. There was a pile

of spent brass and bits of cartridge belt by her left
elbow, some still noticeably hot despite the drizzle,
and two empty drums; the barrel of her rifle had
stopped sizzling. She thought that there was about
half of the third and last ammunition canister left,
seven or eight bursts if she was lucky and light on
the trigger. Cordite fumes warred with wet earth,
gun oil and a fecal stink from the German, who had
voided his bowels as he hung on the wood. Uneasily,
she strained her battered ears. She and Huff had
been reverse-point; the plan was that they would
block the trail, the Fritz would pull back to spread
out, and then the rest of the lochos would hit them,
having let them pass the first time to tempt them to
bunch. It had worked fine, only there was no more
firing from farther north. Glimpses had been enough
to estimate at least a tetrarchy's-worth of dead Fritz;
the other six troopers of their lochos couldn't have
killed all the rest, so . . .

"Huffie."

"Ya?"

"Yo' thinkin' what I—"

They had both risen to hands and knees, when
Patton stopped. "Wait," she said, reaching out a
hand. "Give me a hand, will yo'?" She felt in the
darkness, grabbed a webbing strap and pulled the
other soldier toward the trail. Outstretched, her hand
touched something warm and yielding; there was a
long, sobbing scream that died away to whimpers.

"What the *fuck* yo' doin'?"

"Lay him out, lay him out!" Patton exclaimed fe-
verishly. And yes, there was a tinge of light. *Couldn't*
be sunlight, the whole action was barely ten minutes
old. Something was burning, quite close, close enough
for reflected light to bounce in via the leaves. "Easy
now, don' kill him. Right, now give me yo' grenades."

There was a chuckle from the dim shape opposite
her. The German was crying now, with sharp intakes

of breath as they moved him, propped the stake up to keep the angle of entry constant, placed the primed grenades under his prone body, wedging them securely. The flesh beneath their fingers quivered with a constant thrumming, as if from the cold. Huff paused as they rose, dusting her hands.

"Hey, wait. He still conscious; he might call a warnin'."

Patton looked nervously back up the trail. If the Germans had spread out through the bush to advance in line, rather than down the trail . . . but there was no time to lose. It depended on how many of them were left, how close their morale was to breaking. "Right," she grunted, reaching down and drawing the knife from her boot. The Fritz's mouth was already open as he panted shallowly; a wet fumbling, a quick stab at the base of the tongue, and the SS trooper was forever beyond understandable speech.

The cries behind them were thick and gobbling as the pair cautiously jog-trotted down the trail.

"Fuckah *bit* me," Patton gasped as they stopped at a sharp dip. There was running water at her feet; she rinsed her hands, then cupped them to bring it to her lips. Pure and sweet, tasting of nothing more than rocks and earth, it slid soothingly down a sore and harshened throat.

"Never no mind; this's where we supposed to meet the others." Again, they exchanged worried glances at each other without needing to actually see. The ambush force was supposed to pull out before they did; that was the only explanation for the silence. Or one of only two possible explanations . . .

To the south there was a multiple crash, as of grenades, then screams, and shouts in German.

"*Shit*," said Huff. There had been seven of them in the lochoi assigned to this trail . . . "Like the boss-man said, mind in gear—"

"—Ass to rear. Let's *go*."

*   *   *

Silently, the two Draka ran through the exploding
chaos of the vehicle park. Eric had tasked the
satchelmen in general terms: to destroy the SS trucks,
especially fuel or munitions carriers, or block the
road, or both, whichever was possible. Most of the
satchelmen had run among the trucks with a charge
in each hand, thumbs on the time fuses, ready to
switch the cap up. *Get* near a truck, *throw* the
charge, *dive* out of the way . . .

Trooper McAlistair shoulder-rolled back to elbows
and knees, bipod unfolded, covering the demolition
expert's back. *Blind-sided chaos*, she thought. Feet
ran past on the other side of an intact truck; she
snap-shot a three-round burst and was rewarded with
a scream. That had not been the only set of feet;
without rising she scuttled forward, moving in a leop-
ard crawl nearly as fast as her walking pace, under
the truck and over the sprattling form of the Fritz,
who was clutching at a leg sawn off at mid-shin. She
rolled again, sighting, wishing she was on full-auto as
she saw the group rounding the truck. Six. Her
finger worked on the trigger, brap-brap-brap, tracer
snapping green into their backs; one had a machine
gun, a MG42. He twisted, hand clamping in dying
reflex and sending a cone of light upwards into the
grey-black night as the belt of ammunition looped
around his shoulders fed through the weapon, then
jammed as it tightened around his throat, dropping
him backwards into the mud. The overheated barrel
hissed as it made contact with the wet soil, like a
horseshoe when the farrier plunges it from the forge
into the waiting bucket.

The satchelman had not been idle on the other
side of the truck. The target had been especially
tempting, an articulated tank-transporter with a spe-
cialized vehicle aboard; that was a tank with a motor-
ized drum-and-chain flail attached, meant for clearing

mine fields before an attack. The charge of plastique flashed, a pancake of white light beneath the transporter's front bogie. All four wheels flew into the night, flipping up, spinning like coins flicked off a thumb. The fuel tank ruptured, spreading the oil in a fine mist as the atomizer on a scent bottle does to perfume. Liquid, the heavy fuel was barely flammable at all without the forced-draft ventilation of a boiler. Divided finely enough, so that all particles are exposed to the oxygen, anything made of carbon is explosive: coal dust, even flour.

The cloud of fuel oil went off with the force of a 155mm shell, and the truck and its cargo disintegrated in an orange globe of fire and fragments that set half a dozen of its neighbors on fire themselves. The *crang* blasted all other sound out of existence for a second, and echoed back from hills and forest. Most of the truck's body was converted into shrapnel; by sheer bad luck a section of axle four feet long speared through the satchelman as a javelin might have, pinning him to the body of another vehicle like a shrike's prey stuck on a thorn. Limbs beat a tattoo on the cab, alive for several seconds after the spine had been severed; there was plenty of light now, more than enough for the Liebstandarte trooper to see the bulge-eyed clown face that hung at his window, spraying bright lung-blood from mouth and nose beneath burning hair. Since the same jagged spear of metal had sliced the thin sheeting of the door like cloth and crunched through the bones of his pelvis, he paid very little attention.

Tee-Hee McAlistair flattened herself; the ground rose up and slapped her back again as the pressure-wave of the detonation passed. For an instant, there was nothing but lights and a struggle to breathe. Above her the canvas tilt of the Opel truck swayed toward her, then jounced back onto its wheels as the blast proved not quite enough to topple it past the ballast-weight of its cargo. Vaguely, she was conscious of blood running from ears and nose, of a thick buzzing in her skull that was not part of the ratcheting confusion of the night battle. That had been a *much* bigger bang than it was supposed to be. Doggedly, she levered herself back to her feet, ignoring the blurred edges of her sight. The buzzing gave way to a shrilling, as needles seemed to pierce slowly inwards through each ear. The satchelman—

"Shitfire, talk about baaaad luck," she muttered in awe, staring for an instant across the hood of the truck at the figure clenched around the impaling steel driven into the door. That drooped slightly, and the corpse slid inch by inch down the length of it, until it seemed to be kneeling with slumped head in a pool that shone redly in the light of the fires. Behind, the transporter was a large puddle of fire surrounded by smaller blazes, with the flail tank standing in the middle, sending dribblets of flame up through the vision slits in the armor. As she watched, a segment of track peeled away to fall with a thump, beating a momentary path through the thick orange carpet of burning oil.

A burst crackled out of nowhere her dazzled eyes could see, ripping the thin sheet metal of the truck's hood in a line of runnels that ended just before they reached her.

"Gotta get out of the plane a'fire," she said to herself. It was strange, she could hear the words inside her head but not with her ears . . . Turning, she put her foot on the fender of the truck and jumped onto the hood, then the cab roof, a left-handed vault onto the fabric cover of the hoops that stretched over the body of the truck. That was much more difficult than it should have been, and she lay panting and fighting down nausea for an instant before looking around.

"Whoo, awesome." The whole cluster of Fritz vehicles was burning; there was a fuzziness to her vision, but only the outermost line near the road was not on fire. There was plenty of light now, refracted through the streaked-crystal lines of the rain; muzzle-flashes and tracers spat a horizontal counterpoint to the vertical tulip shapes of explosions and burning vehicles, all soundless as the needles of pain went farther into her head. It occurred to her that the Fritz must be shooting each other up—there were more of them and the Draka had gotten right into the position. That would have made her want to giggle, if her ears had not hurt so much; and there seemed to be something wrong with her head, it was thick and slow. She should *not* be watching this like a fireworks show. She should . . .

One of the trucks pulled out of the line and began to turn back onto the road; its driver executed a flawless three-point and twisted bumping past the guttering ruin of the first to be destroyed; other explosions sounded behind him, nearly as loud. The actions of hands and boots on wheel and throttle were automatic; all the driver could see was the fire, spreading toward him: fire and tracers probing out of the unknowable dark.

Tee-Hee reacted at a level deeper than consciousness as the truck went by. Kneeling, she raked the body of it with a long burst before leaping for the canvas tilt. The reaction almost killed her; it calculated possibilities on a level of performance no longer possible after blast-induced concussion slowed her. Her jump almost failed to reach the moving truck, and it was almost chance that she did not slide off to land in the deadly fire-raked earth below. She sprawled on the fabric for an instant, letting the wet roughness scratch at her cheek. But her education had included exhaustion-drill—training patterns learned while she was deliberately pushed to the verge of blackout, designed to keep her functioning as long as it was physically possible at all. Crawling, she slithered to the roof of the driver's cab and swung down, feet reaching for the running board and left hand for the mirror brace to hold her on the lurching, swaying lip of slick metal.

That seemed to clear her head a little. Enough to see the driver's head turning at last from his fixed concentration on the road and escape; to see the knowledge of death in his widening eyes as she raised the assault rifle one-handed and fired a burst through the door of the cab. His lips shaped a single word: "nein."

The recoil hammered her back, bending her body into an arch and nearly tearing loose the left-hand grip. Then she tossed the weapon through the window and tore the door open, reaching in and heaving the dying German out; pulling herself into the cab with the same motion, hands clamping on the wheel. She took a shaky breath, wrenched it around to avoid a wreck in her path.

"Freya, what's that stink?" the Draka soldier muttered, even as she fumbled with the unfamiliar controls. It was still so hard to think; out to the road, then shoot out the wheels. Grenade down the fuel pipe. Block the road, back to the woods, where was the throttle . . . Not totally unfamiliar; after all, the autosteamer had been *invented* in the Domination, the design must be derived . . . there!

Shit, she thought, slewing the truck across the narrow road. There was a steep dropoff on the other side, this should slow them a little once she popped a charge to make the hulk immovable. *Literally. I'm sitting in what the Fritz let out. White Christ have mercy, I'll never live it down!*

At that moment, the SS trooper fired his Kar-98 through the back of the cab. It was not aimed; there

was no window, and it was the German's last action
before blood loss slumped him back onto the bullet-
chewed floorboards. Chance directed it better than
any skill; the heavy bullet slapped the Draka be-
tween the shoulder blades; she pitched forward against
the wheel, bounced back against the back rest, then
forward again.

But I won, was her last astonished thought. *I can't
die, I won.*

Eric felt the German's impact like a flash of white
fire across his lower back and pelvis. Then there *was*
white fire, dazzling even though his head was turned
away: explosion. Eric's bruised face was driven deeper
into the rocky earth; his tongue tasted earth and the
tenderness of grass. Fists pounded him, heavy knobby
fists with thick shoulders behind them, driven with-
out science but with huge strength into back and
shoulders, ringing his head like a clapper inside the
metal bell of helmet that protected neck and skull.
His conscious mind was a white haze, disconnected
sense-impressions flooding in: the breathy grunts of
the man on his back as each blow slammed down;
the bellows action of his own ribs, flexing and spring-
ing back between knuckles and ground; shouts and
shots and some other, metallic noise.

Training made him turn. That was a mistake; there
was no strength in his arms; the movements that
should have speared bladed fingertips into the oth-
er's throat and rammed knuckles under his short ribs
turned into feeble pawings that merely slowed and
tangled the German's roundhouse swings.

Bad luck, he thought, rolling his head to take the
impact on his skull rather than the more vulnerable
face; he could hear knuckles pop as they broke. Fists
landed on his jaw and cheek, jarring the white lights
back before his eyes; he could feel the skin split over
one cheekbone, but there was no more pain, only a

cold prickling over his whole skin, as if he were
trying to slough it as a snake does. One hand still
fumbled at the SS officer's waist; it fell on the butt of
a pistol; he made a supreme effort of concentration,
drew it, pressed it to the other's tunic and pulled the
trigger.

Nothing. Safety on, or perhaps his hand was just
too weak. He could see the Fritz's face in the ruddy
glow of burning petrol and lubricants and rubber:
black smudged, bestial, wet running down the chin.
The great peasant hands clamped on his throat. The
light began to fade.

Felix Hoth was kneeling in the mud behind his
radio truck, and yet was not. In his mind the SS man
was back in a cellar beneath the Lubyanka, stran-
gling a NKVD holdout he had stalked through the
labyrinth and found in a hidden room with a half-
eaten German corpse. He did not even turn the first
time Sofie rang the steel folding butt of her machine
pistol off the back of his head; she could not fire, you
do not aim an automatic weapon in the direction of
someone you want to live.

Hoth *did* start to move when she kicked him up
between the legs where he straddled the Centurion's
body, very hard. That was too late; she planted her-
self and hacked downward with both hands on the
weapon's forestock, as if she were pounding grain
with a mortar and pestle. There was a hollow *thock*
sound, and a shock that jarred her sturdy body right
down to the bones in her lower back; the strip steel
of the submachine gun's stock deformed slightly un-
der the impact. If the butt had not had a rubber pad,
the German's brains would have spattered; as it was,
he slumped boneless across the Draka's body. With
cold economy she booted the body off her command-
er's and raised her weapon to fire.

It was empty, the bolt back and the chamber

gaping. Not worth the time to reload. The comtech kneeled by Eric's side, her hands moving across his body in an examination quick, expert, fearful. Blood, bruises, no open wounds, no obvious fractures poking bone-splinters through flesh . . . So hard to tell in the difficult light, no *time* . . . She reached forward to push back an eyelid and check for concussion. Eric's hand came up and caught her wrist, and the grey eyes opened, red and visibly bloodshot even in the uncertain, flickering light. The sound of firing was dying down.

"Stim," he said hoarsely.

"Sir—Eric—" she began.

"*Stim*, that's an *order*." His head fell back, and he muttered incoherently.

She hesitated, her hands snapping open the case at her belt and taking out the disposable hypodermic. It was filled with a compound of benzedrine and amphetamines, the last reserve against extremity even for a fit man in good condition; for use when a last half hour of energy could mean the difference. Eric was enormously fit, but *not* in good condition, not after that battering; there might be concussion, internal hemorrhage, *anything*.

The sound echoed around the bend of the road below: steel-squeal on metal and rock, treads. Armored vehicles, many of them; she would have heard them before but for the racket of combat and the muffling rain. Their headlights were already touching the tops of the trees below. She looked down. Eric was lying still, only the quick, labored pumping of his chest marking life; his eyes blinked into the rain that dimpled the mud around him and washed the blood in thin runnels from his nose and mouth.

"Oh *shit*!" Sofie blurted, and leaned forward to inject the drug into his neck. There, half dosage, Wotan pop her *eyes* if she'd give him any more.

*   *   *

The effect of the drug was almost instantaneous. The mists at the corners of his eyes receded, and he *hurt*. That was why pain-overload could send you into unconsciousness, the messages got redundant . . . He hurt a *lot*. Then the pain receded; it was still there, but somehow did not matter very much. Now he felt good, very good in fact; full of energy, as if he could bounce to his feet and sweep Sofie up in his arms and *run* all the way back to the village.

He fought down the euphoria and contented himself with coming to his feet, slowly, leaning an arm across Sofie's shoulders. The world swayed about him, then cleared to preternatural clarity. The dying flames of the burning trucks were living sculptures of orange and yellow, dancing fire maidens with black soot-hair and the hissing voices of rain on hot metal. The trees about him were a sea that rippled and shimmered, green-orange; the roasting-pork smell of burning bodies clawed at his empty stomach. Eric swallowed bile and blinked, absently thrusting the German pistol in his hand through a loop in the webbing.

"Back—" he began hoarsely, hawked, spat out phlegm mixed with blood. "Back to the woods, *now*."

McWhirter stepped up, and two of the satchelmen. The Senior Decurion was wiping the blade of his Jamieson on one thigh as he dropped an ear into the bag strapped to his leg. The lunatic clarity of the drug showed Eric a face younger than he recalled, smoother, without the knots of tension that the older man's face usually wore. McWhirter's expression was much like the relaxed, contented look that comes just after orgasm, and his mouth was wet with something that shone black in the firelight.

The Centurion dismissed the brief crawling of skin between his shoulder blades as they turned and ran for the woods. It was much easier than the trip out, there was plenty of light now; enough to pinpoint them easily for a single burst of automatic fire. The feeling of lightness did not last much beyond the first strides. After that each bootfall drove a spike of pain up the line of his spine and into his skull, like a dull brass knife ramming into his head over the left eye; breathing pushed his bruised ribs into efforts that made the darkness swim before his eyes. There was gunfire from ahead and upslope, muffled through the trees, and *there* a flare popping above the leaf canopy. He concentrated on blocking off the pain, forcing it into the sides of his mind. *Relax* the muscles . . . pain did not make you weak, it was just the body's way of forcing you to slow down and recover. Training could suppress it, make the organism function at potential . . .

If this is wanting to be alive, I'm not so sure I want to want it, he thought. *Haven't been this afraid in years.* They crashed through the screen of undergrowth and threw themselves down. The others were joining him, the survivors; more than half. The shock of falling brought another white explosion behind his eyes. Ignore it, reach for the handset. Sofie thrust it into his palm, and he was suddenly conscious of the wetness again, the rain falling in a silvery dazzle through the air lit by the burning Fritz vehicles. Beyond the clearing, beyond the ruined buildings by the road, the SS armor rumbled and clanked, metal sounding under the diesel growl, so different from the smooth silence of steam.

He clicked the handset. The first tank waddled around the buildings, accelerating as it came into the light. Then it braked, as the infantry riding on it leaped down to deploy; the hatches were open, and Eric could see the black silhouette of the commander as he stood in the turret, staring about in disbelief at the clearing. Wrecked trucks littered it, burning or abandoned; one was driving slowly in a circle with the driver's arm swaying limply out the window.

Bodies were scattered about—dozens of them: piles of two or three, there a huddle around a wrecked machine gun, there a squad caught by a burst as they ran through darkness to a meeting with death. Wounded lay moaning, or staggered clutching at their hurts; somewhere a man's voice was screaming in pulsing bursts as long as breaths. Thirty, fifty at least, Eric estimated as he spoke.

"Palm One to Fist, do y'read."

"Acknowledged, Palm One." The calm tones of the battery-commander were a shocking contrast to Eric's hoarseness. "Hope yo've got a target worth gettin' up this early for."

"*Firefall.*" Eric's voice sounded thin and reedy to his own ears. "Fire mission Tloshohene, *firefall*, do it *now.*"

He lowered the handset, barked: "Neal!" to the troopers who had remained with the guide in the scrub at the edge of the woods.

The rocket gunner and her loader had been waiting with hunter's patience in a thicket near the trail, belly-down in the sodden leaf mold, with only their eyes showing between helmets and face paint. With smooth economy the dark-haired woman brought the projector up over the rock sill in front of her, resting the forward monopod on the stone. She fired; the backblast stripped wet leaves from the pistachio bushes and scattered them over her comrades. The vomiting-cat scream of the sustainer rocket drew a pencil of fire back to their position, and then the shell struck, high on the turret, just as it began to swing the long 88mm gun toward the woods. The bright flash left a light spot on Eric's retina, lingering as he turned away; the tank did not explode, but it froze in place. Almost at once bullets began hammering the wet earth below them, *smack* into mud, crack-*whinnng* off stone. The rocket gun gave its deep *whap* once more, and there was a sound overhead.

The Draka soldiers flinched. The Circassian guide glanced aside at them, then up at the deep whining rumble overhead, a note that lowered in pitch as it sank toward them. Then he bolted forward in terror as the first shellburst came, seeming to be almost on their heels. Eric hunched his head lower beneath the weight of the steel helmet; no real use in that, but it was psychological necessity. The Draka guns up the valley were firing over their heads at the Fritz: firing blind on the map coordinates he had supplied, at extreme range, using captured guns and ammunition of questionable standard. Only too possible that they would undershoot. Airburst in the branches overhead, shrapnel and wood fragments whirring through the night like circular saws . . .

The first shells burst out of sight, farther down the road and past the ruined buidlings, visible only as a *wink-wink-wink-wink* of light, before the noise and overpressure slapped at their faces. The last two of the six landed in the clearing, bright flashes and inverted fans of water and mud and rock, bodies and pieces of wrecked truck. He rose, controlling the dizziness.

"On target, on target, *fire for effect*," he shouted, and tossed the handset back to Sofie. "Burn boot, up the trail, *move*."

It was growing darker as they ran from the clearing, away from the steady metronomic *whamwham-wham* of shells falling among the Fritz column, as the fires burnt out and distance cut them off. A branch slapped him in the face; there was a prickling numbness on his skin that seemed to muffle it. The firefights up ahead were building; no fear of the SS shooting blind into the dark, with their comrades engaged up there. Although they might pursue on foot . . . no, probably not. Not at once, not with that slaughterhouse confusion back by the road, and shells pounding into it. Best leave them a calling card, for later.

"Stop," he gasped. Something *oofed* into him, and he grabbed at brush to keep himself upright. "Mine it," he continued.

Behind him, one of the satchelmen pulled a last burden out of her pack. Unfolding the tripod beneath the Broadsword mine, she adjusted it to point back the way they had come, downslope, northwards. Then she unclipped a length of fine wire, looped one end through the detonator hook on the side and stepped forward. One step, two . . . around a handy branch, across the trail, tie it off . . .

"Good, can't see it mahself. Now, careful, careful," she muttered to herself as she stepped over the wire that now ran at shin height across the pathway and bent to brush her fingers on the unseen slickness of the mine's casing. The arming switch should be . . . *there*. She twisted it.

"Armed," she said. Now it was deadly, and very sensitive. Not enough for the pattering raindrops to set it off, she had left a little slack, but a brushing foot would detonate it for sure. The trail was lightless enough to register as black to her eyes, with only the lighter patches of hands and equipment catching enough of the reflected glow to hover as suggestions of sight. Still, she was sure she could detect a flinch at the words; mines were another of those things that most soldiers detested with a weary, hopeless hatred; you couldn't do anything much about them, except wait for them to kill you.

The sapper grinned in the dark. People who were nervous around explosives did not volunteer for her line of work; besides that, her training had included working on live munitions blindfolded. And Eddie had not made it back; Eddie had been a good friend of hers. *Hope they-all come up the trail at a run*, she thought vindictively, kissing a finger and touching it to the Broadsword.

Eric stood with his face turned upward to the rain while the mine was set, letting the coolness run over his face and trickle between his lips with tastes of wood and greenness and sweat from his own skin; he had been moving too fast for chill to set in. The scent of the forest was overwhelming in contrast to the fecal-explosive-fire smells of the brief battle—resin and sap and the odd musky-spicy scents of weeds and herbs. *Alive,* he thought. Gunfire to the south, around the slope of the mountain and through the trees, confusing direction. A last salvo of shells dragged their rumble through the invisible sky. Sofie was beside him, an arm around his waist in support that was no less real for being mostly psychological.

"Burn boot, people," he said quietly, just loud enough to be heard over the rain. "Let's go home."

They were nearly back to the village before he collapsed.

CHAPTER SIXTEEN

" ... had spent the 1920's and 30's preparing for a war, but not necessarily the war that actually happened. The Soviet Union consolidated itself and began to industrialize far more rapidly than the Strategic Planning Board had anticipated, and the Draka conquests in western China enabled Japan to quickly overrun and occupy the seaboard provinces. With their vast manpower and mineral resources, the last constraints on the development of Imperial Japan's industrial-military potential were removed. And with the Domination entrenched in Thrace and Bulgaria, we now had a border with the Balkans—a chaotic power vacuum after the breakup of the Austro-Hungarian Empire, but a natural field of German expansion once the Reich had recovered from the Great War and thrown off the paper shackles of the Versailles Treaty. For most of the first post-War decade these threats remained only potentials, but the specter of a war on three fronts increasingly haunted the planners in Castle Tarleton. All that they could do was press ahead with preparations for the inevitable conflict; it was obvious that it would be a continental war of mass armies and airfleets.

A combination of skill and sheer good fortune avoided that nightmare. The border clashes with Japan in the late 1930's *revealed that while determined and very tenacious, her ground forces had fallen behind the times. Japan's primary attention would now be turned south and east, to the islands and archipelagoes of southeast Asia and the Pacific. Hitler's daring gamble against the Soviets succeeded, destroying an enemy which might have been a deadly threat if their efficiency had matched their sheer numbers and weight of metal, but it left National Socialist Germany critically overextended. The strategic opportunity this presented was too dazzling to be missed—a chance to destroy the only remaining Power in northern Eurasia, push the borders of the Domination to the North Atlantic, advance by a generation the great plan to fulfill the destiny of the Race. A possible dream, as well. Only the Domination had had the resources and determination needed to rearm in depth as well as breadth; the United States had the capacity, but chose to expend her industrial energies on washing machines and private autosteamers rather than turret-castings and artillery barrel forges. The power was there, if only it could be applied . . .*

Fire And Blood: The Eurasian War
V. I: The Gathering Thunder, 1930–1941
by Strategos Robert A. Jackson (ret.),
New Territories Press, Vienna, 1965

OSSETIAN MILITARY HIGHWAY, VILLAGE ONE APRIL 15, 1942: 0510 HOURS

William Dreiser clicked off the tape recorder and patted the pebbled waterproof leather of the casing affectionately. It was the latest thing—only the size of a large suitcase, and much more rugged than the clumsy magnetic-wire models it had replaced—from Williams-Burroughs Electronics in Toronto. The Draka had been amazed at it; it was one field in which the United States was incontestably ahead. And it had been an effective piece: the ambush patrol setting out into the dark and the rain, faces grim and impassive; the others waiting, sleeping or at their posts, a

stolid few playing endless games of solitaire. Then
the eruption of noise in the dark, confusing, bewil-
dering, giving almost no hint of direction. Imagina-
tion had had to fill in then, picturing the confused
fighting in absolute darkness. Finally the survivors
straggling in, hale and walking-wounded and others
carried over their comrades' shoulders . . .

He looked up. The command cellar was the warmest
place in the warren of basements, and several of the
survivors had gathered, to strip and sit huddled in
blankets while their uniforms and boots steamed be-
side the field stove. Some were bandaged, and oth-
ers were rubbing each other down with an oil that
had a sharp scent of pine and bitter herbs. The dim
blue-lit air was heavy with it, and the smells of damp
wool, blood, bandages, and fear-sweat under the brew-
ing coffee. Eric was sitting in one corner, an unno-
ticed cigarette burning between his fingers and the
blanket let fall to his waist, careless of the chill. The
medic snapped off the pencil light he had been using
to peer into the Centurion's eyes and nodded.

"Cuts, abrasions an' bruises," he said. "Ribs . . .
better tape 'em. Mighta' been a concussion, but pretty
mild. More damage from that Freya-damned stim.
They shouldn't oughta issue it." He reached into the
canvass-and-wire compartments of his carryall. "Get
somethin' to eat, get some sleep, take two of these-
here placebo's an' call me in the mornin'."

Eric's answering smile was perfunctory. He raised
his arms obediently, bringing his torso into the light.
Sofie knelt by his side and began slapping on lengths
of the broad adhesive from the roll the medic had
left. Dreiser sucked in his breath; he had been with
the Draka long enough to ignore her casual nudity,
even long enough that her body no longer seemed
stocky and overmuscled, or her arms too thick and
rippling-taut. But the sight of the officer's chest and

back was shocking. His face was bad enough, bruises turning dark and lumpy, eyes dark circles where thin flesh had been beaten back against the bone and veins ruptured, dried blood streaking from ears and mouth and turning his mustache a dark-brown clump below a swollen nose blocked with clots. Still, you could see as bad in a Cook County stationhouse any Saturday night, and he had as a cub reporter on the police beat.

The massive bruising around his body was something else again: the whole surface of the tapered wedge was discolored from its normal matte tan to yellow-grey, from the broad shoulders where the deltoids rose in sharp curves to his neck, down to where the scutes of the stomach curved below the ribs. Dreiser had wrestled the young Draka a time or two, enough to know that his muscle was knitted over the ribs like a layer of thick india rubber armor beneath the skin. What it had taken to raise those welts . . . *Christ, he's not going to be so good-looking if this happens a few more times*, the American thought. And I'm *damn* glad I'm not in this business. Even then, he felt his mind making a mental note; this would be an effective tailpiece to his story. "Wounded, but still thoroughly in command of the situation, Centurion von Shrakenberg . . ."

Sofie finished the taping, a sheath like a Roman's loricated cuirass running from beneath his armpits to the level of the floating ribs. Eric swung his arms experimentally, then bent. He stopped suddenly, lips thinning back over his teeth, then completed the motion; then he coughed and spat carefully into a cloth.

"No blood," he muttered to himself. "Didn't think doc was wrong, really, but—" He turned his head to give Sofie a rueful smile, stroking one hand down the curve of her back. "Hey, thanks anyway, Sofie."

She blushed down to her breasts; looked down and noticed the goosebumps and stiffened nipples with a slight embarrassment, coughed herself, and drew on a fresh uniform tunic. "*Ya*, no problem," she said. "Ymir-cursed cold in here . . ." She turned to pick up a bowl and dampen a cloth. "*Ag, cis*, Centurio— Eric, we need y' walkin', come dawn."

He sighed and closed his eyes as she began to clean the almost-dried blood from his face, pushing back damp strands of his hair from his forehead. The cigarette dangled from one puffed lip.

"Better at walkin' than thinking, from the looks of tonight's fuckup," he said bitterly.

"Bullshit." Heads turned; that had been McWhirter, from the place where he sat with the neatly laid-out parts of an assault rifle on a blanket before his knees; he had more than the usual reluctance to let a rifle go without cleaning after being fired. He raised a bolt carrier to the light, pursed his lips and wiped off excess oil. "With respect, sir. From a crapped out bull, at that."

Eric's eyes opened, frosty and pale-grey against the darkening flesh that surrounded them. The NCO grinned; he was stripped to shorts as well, displaying a body roped and knotted and ridged with muscle that was still hard, even if the skin had lost youth's resilience. His body was heavier than the officer's, thicker at the waist, matted with greying yellow hair where the younger man's was smooth, and covered with a pattern of scars, everything from bullet wounds and shrapnel to what looked like the beginning of a sentence in Pushtu script, written with a red-hot knife.

"Yes, Senior Decurion?" Eric said softly.

"Yes, Centurion." The huge hands moved the rifle parts, without needing eyes to guide them. "Look, *sir*. I've been in the Regular Line since, hell, '09.

Seen a lot of officers; can't do what they do—the good ones—Mrs. WcWhirter didn't raise her kids for that, but Ah can run a firefight pretty good, and *pick* officers. Some of the bad ones—" he smiled, an unpleasant expression "—they didn't live past their second engagement, you know? Catchin' that Fritz move up the valley was smooth, real smooth. *Had* to do somethin' about it, too. Can't see anything else we could've done. Sir."

He slapped the bolt carrier back into the receiver of the Holbars, drew it back and let the spring drive it forward. The sound of the *snick* had a heavy, metallic authority. "An' we did do something. We blew their transport, knocked out say two-three more tanks, killed, oh, maybe two hundred. They turned back; next attack's goin' to come straight up our gunsights. For which we lost maybe fifteen effectives. So please, cut the bullshit, get some rest and let's concentrate on the next trick."

"My *trick* lost us half of 2nd Tetrarchy," Eric said.

The NCO sighed, using the rifle to lever himself erect and sweeping up the rest of his gear with his other hand. "With somewhat *less* respect, sir, y'may have noticed there's a *war* goin' on, and it's mah experience that in wars people tend to get killed. Difference is, is it *gettin' the job done or not?* That's what matters."

"*All* that matters," he added with flat sincerity from the doorway. " 'Course, we may all die tomorrow." Another shrug, before he let the curtain drop behind him. "Who gives a flyin' fuck, anyhow?"

Eric blinked and started to purse his lips, stopping with a wince. Sofie dropped the cloth in the bowl and set it aside, staring after the Senior Decurion with a surprised look as she gathered a nest of blanket and bedroll around herself and reached out a hand to check the radio.

"He's got something right, for once," she muttered. Everything green, ready . . . She shivered at the memory of the palm on her shoulder. *Can it. Later. Maybe.*

"Well, *Ah* give a flyin' fuck," said a muffled voice from the center of the room. It was Trooper Huff, lying face-down on the blankets while her friend kneaded pine oil into the muscles of her shoulders and back. The fair skin gleamed and rippled as she arched her back with a sigh of pleasure.

"Centurion? Now, all *Ah* want is to get back—*little lower, there, sweetlin'*—get back to Rabat province an' the plantation, spend the rest of mah life raisin' horses an' babies. Old Ironbutt the deathfuckah is *still* right. If those Fritz'd gotten on our flank tomorrow they'd have had our ass for *grass,* Centurion." She sighed again, looking up. "Yo're turn." The dark-haired soldier handed her the bottle and lay down, and Huff rose to her knees and began to oil her palms. Then she paused. "Oh, one last thing. Didn't notice you askin' anyone to do anythin' yo' wouldn't do yoself."

Eric's face stayed expressionless for a moment, and then he shook his head, squeezing his eyelids closed and chuckling ruefully. "Outvoted," he said, suddenly yawning enormously. He grinned down at Sofie, eyes crinkled. "I'm not going to indulge in this-here dangerous sport of plannin' things to do once the war is over," he said in a tone lighter than most she had heard from him. "Bad luck to price the unborn calf. But did you have anything planned for yo're next leave, Sofie?"

"Hell, no, Eric *sir!*" she said with quiet happiness, grinning back.

"Dinner at Aladdin's?" he said. That was a restaurant built into the side of Mount Meru, in Kenia province. The view of the snowpeak of Kilimanjaro rising over the Serengeti was famous, as were the game dishes.

"Consider it a date, Centurion," she said, snuggling herself into the blankets and closing her eyes. Tomorrow was going to be a busy day.

Eric looked across at Dreiser. "That's private, Bill, but we could all three get together for some deep-sea fishing off Mombasa afterwards. Owe you something for those articles, anyway; they're going to be . . . useful, I think. Better than the trip you had with that writer friend of yours—what was his name, Hemingway?"

Dreiser laughed softly. "Acquaintance; Ernest dosen't have friends, just drinking buddies and sycophants. I'll bet you don't get drunk and try to shoot the seagulls off the back of the boat . . . and you seem to be in a good mood tonight, my friend."

"Because I've got things to do, Bill, things to do. And with that, goodnight." He stubbed out the cigarette, swilled down the last of the lukewarm coffee. *And probably about twenty hours of life to do them with*, he thought. Pushing the sudden chill in his gut away: *White Christ and Wotan one-eye, what's different about that? The odds haven't changed since yesterday.* But his wants had, he forced himself to admit with bleak honesty, and his vision of his duty—an expanded one, which required his presence, if it could be arranged.

There was one good thing about the whole situation. Whatever happened, he no longer had to face death with an attitude indistinguishable from Senior Decurion McWhirter's. *That* he had *never* felt comfortable with.

Dreiser waited while the room grew still; half an hour and there were no others awake, save himself and the cadaverous brown-bearded man who had the radio watch. The cold seemed deeper, and he pulled another blanket about himself as he laid down the notebook at last. They were not notes for his articles; those could be left to the tape, flown out with the STOL transports that took out the wounded, given to the world by the great military broadcast stations in Anatolia. These were his private journals, part of the series he had been keeping since his first assignment to Berlin in 1934.

If I'm going to be a fly on the wall of history, something ought to come of it, he thought. Something truer than even the best journalism could be. Get the raw information down now; raw feeling, as well. Safe in silence, where the busy censors of a world at war could not touch it. Safe on paper, fixed, where the gentle invisible editor of memory could not tint and bend with subconscious hindsight.

Later he would write that book: a book that would have the truth of his own observations in it, what he could research as well, written in some quiet lonely place where there would be nothing between him and his thoughts. A truth that would last. Add up the little truths, and the big ones could follow. This action tonight, for example. A Draka tetrarchy had given a force twenty times its size a bloody nose, turned back a major attack by the enemy's elite troops and inflicted demoralizing casualties. And it still *felt* like defeat, at least to a civilian observer. Maybe every battle was a defeat for all involved; some just got more badly beaten than others. Soldiers always lost, whichever set of generals won.

Ambition, he mused, looking across the room at the battered face of the Draka officer. *Strange forms it takes*. What was Eric's? Not to be freed from a world of impossible choices, not any longer. And not simply to climb the ladder of the power machine and breed children to do the same in their turn—not if Dreiser knew anything of Eric's truth.

Do we ever? The truth is, we may be enemies. But for now, we *are* friends.

It was late, and he was tired. What was that Draka poet's line? "Darkness *is* a friend of mine . . . Sometimes I have to beat it back, or it would overwhelm me . . ." And sometimes it was well to welcome it. He closed his eyes.

CHAPTER SEVENTEEN

Citizens were never more than 15 percent of the total population, usually rather less; many of the serfs at any given time were foreign-born, newly incorporated by conquest. Careful organization kept them disorganized and split into isolated groups on plantations, mines, and factory compounds. Well-trained police and military forces were always poised to move, along the superb roads, railways, air-transport lines for which the Domination was famous; informer networks spread through the subject populations like mold through a loaf of bread. Yet guns and fortresses, barbed wire and spies, floggings and electroshock and impalements by themselves were never enough; repression and terror alone could not be the answer. Especially outside the cities, serfs were always a huge majority, always possessed the preponderance of immediate physical force. Each master could not have troops at his back, and orders must be obeyed even without a free supervisor to enforce them.

Human social organizations exist because human beings believe they exist; for the Draka to be safe, it was essential that the forces of belief and myth be enlisted on their side. Knowledge that a successful uprising meant annihilation provided the incentive for a monolithic group solidarity among

*the master class; the necessary arrogant self-confidence was
the product of power itself—power of life and death over
other human beings, from birth, by hereditary right. A Citizen
knew that he or she was superior, a different order of being.
And it was necessary that at least a majority of the serfs
agree, at least to the extent of believing that resistance and
death were one. Partly this was a purely rational matter, a
knowledge that the* lex talonis *would take a hundred serf lives
for a Draka killed or injured. But on a deeper level it was
essential to make myth reality, as had earlier systems such as
the Spartan agoge; the endless training that pushed each
Citizen child to the limit of his or her potential had a function
beyond that of producing a better soldier or administrator.
With training that emphasized self-reliance, the ability to act
alone under stress, as much as pure deadliness; by adulthood,
the individual Citizen was superior, visibly. That this superior-
ity was the product of training rather than some divine* mana
*was irrelevant; that the serfs themselves provided the wealth
and leisure to make it possible did not matter . . .*

200 Years: A Social History of the Domination
by Alan E. Sorensson, Ph.D.
Archona Press, 1983

NORTH CAUCASUS, NEAR PYATIGORSK
APRIL 14, 1942: 0800 HOURS

Johanna blinked. *I'm alive*, she thought. *Fuckin' odd,
that.*

There was not much pain, no more than after a fall
from a horse or surfboard, apart from a fierce ache in
her neck. But there was no desire to move anything,
and she was *hot*.

She blinked again, and now things came into focus
behind the blue tint of her face shield. The wreck of
the *Lover's Bite* was pitched forward, down thirty
degrees at the nose over some declivity in the
ploughed field. She was hanging limp in the safety
harness, only her buttocks and thighs in contact with
the seat. Her view showed a strip of canopy with

blue sky beyond it, the instrument panel, the joystick flopping loosely between her knees. And her feet, resting in a pool of fuel that was up to her ankles where they rested on the forward bulkhead by the control pedals. The stink of the fuel was overwhelming; she coughed weakly, and felt the beginnings of the savage headache you got from breathing too much of the stuff.

Flames licked at the corner of her vision. She swiveled an eye, to see the port wing fully involved, roaring white and orange flames trailing dirty black smoke backward as a steady south wind whipped at it. The engine was a red-metal glow in the center of it, and . . . yes, the plane was slightly canted down to that direction, that was *lucky*, the fuel would be draining into the flames and not away from it.

Feeling returned; fear. She was sitting *in* a firebomb, in a pool of high-octane, surrounded by an explosive fuel-air mixture. Probably no more than seconds before it went.

Got to get *out*, she thought muzzily. Her left hand fumbled at a panel whose heat she could feel even through her gloves, looped through the carrying strap of the survival package. Her right was at her shoulder, pawing at the release-catch of her harness. *Good*, she thought. It opened, and her body fell, head slamming into the instrument panel.

Consciousness returned with a *slam* against her ear and a draft of incredible coolness. A hand reached down and lifted the helmet from her head.

Voices speaking, as she was lifted from the cockpit; in German, blurred by a fire that roared more loudly as the canopy slid back. She felt disconnected, hearing and thought functioning but slipping away when she tried to focus, as if her mind were a screw with the thread stripped.

"The pilot's alive . . . Mary Mother, it's a girl!" A

young man, very young. Bavarian, from the sound of his voice; a thorough knowledge of German was a family tradition among the von Shrakenbergs.

Girl, hell, Johanna thought muzzily. She was new enough to adulthood to be touchy about it. *Two years since I passed eighteen.*

"*Quick, get her out, this thing's ready to blow.*" An older voice, darker somehow, tired. Plattdeutsch accent, she noted: no *pf* or *ss* sounds.

"*I can't—her hand's tangled in something. A box.*"

"*Bring it, there may be documents.*" That would be her survival package, rations and map, machine-pistol and ammunition.

The cold air brought her back to full awareness, but she let herself fall limp, with eyes closed. The younger man braced a boot on either side of the cockpit, put his hands beneath her armpits, and lifted. She was an awkward burden, and the man on the ground grunted in surprise as his comrade handed her down and he took the weight across his shoulder. She was slim but solid, and muscle is denser than fat. He gave a toss to settle her more comfortably, and she could feel the strength in his back and the arm around her waist, smell the old sweat and cologne scent. Her stomach heaved, and she controlled it with an effort that brought beads of sweat to her forehead. *He might suspect I was conscious if I puked down his back.* She had her "passport" pill, but you could always die.

The German carried her some distance, perhaps two hundred meters; she could see his jackboots through slitted lids, tracking through the field, leaving prints in the sticky brown-black clay. Camouflage jacket, that meant SS. The hobnails went *rutch* on an occasional stone, *slutch* as they pulled free of the earth; the soldier was breathing easily as he laid her down on the muddy ground beside the wheels of some sort of vehicle. Not roughly, but without any particular gentleness; then his boots vanished, and she could hear them climbing into the . . . it must be a field car of some sort; her head had rolled toward it, and she could see the running board dip and sway under the man's weight.

The other soldier hurried up, panting, his rifle in one hand and the sheet-metal box of her survival kit in the other. Johanna could feel him lean the weapon against the vehicle and begin to speak. Then there was a crashing bang, followed by a huge muffled thump and a wave of heat. Light flashed against the side of the scout car, and heat like lying too close to the fireplace, and a piece of flaming wreckage sliced into the dirt in front of the wheels.

"Just made it," the man in the car said. Johanna let her eyes flutter open, wishing they had taken the trouble to find a dry spot; she could feel the thin mud soaking through her flight suit, and the wind was chill when it gusted away from the pyre of her aircraft. Sadness ran through her for a moment. It had been a beautiful ship . . .

It was a tool, and tools can be replaced, she chided herself. The young soldier was kneeling and leaning over her, face still a little pale as he turned back from the blaze to his left. That might have been him . . . Nineteen, she thought. Round freckled face, dark-hazel eyes and brown hair, still a trace of puppy fat. A concerned frown as he raised her head in one hand and brought a canteen to her lips. She groaned realistically and rolled her head before accepting the drink; the water was tepid and stale from the metal container, and tasted wonderful.

That let her see his companion. *Another dish of kebab entirely*, she thought with a slight chill. Stocky and flat-featured, cropped ash-blond hair over a tanned square face, in his mid-twenties but looking older. He was standing in the bed of the car, a little open-topped amphibian with balloon wheels, a *kubelwagen*, keeping an easy all-corners watch. The campaign ribbons he was wearing on the faded and much-laundered field tunic told a good deal; the way he moved and held the Schmeisser across his chest rather more. Most of all the eyes, as he glanced incuriously her way: flat, empty, dispassionate. Familiar, veteran's eyes, the thousand-meter stare, she had been seeing it now and again all her life and it always meant someone to watch out for. People to whom killing and dying were neither very important any more . . .

"Ach," the young SS trooper was saying, "she's just a young maiden—"

Not since I was fifteen, or thirteen if you count girls, she thought, wincing in half-pretended pain and taking inventory. Good, everything moving. She accepted another sip of the water.

"—and of fine Nordic stock, just look at her, even if they've cut that beautiful blond hair so short. And look," he indicated the name tag sewn over her left breast, " '*Johanna von Shrakenberg,*' " a German name. What a shame, to be fighting our own stock; and a crime, to expose a potential Aryan mother to danger like this." He clucked his tongue, tsk-tsking.

Why, you son of a bitch, Johanna thought indignantly as the fingers of her right hand curled inconspicuously to check the hard lump at her wrist. Ignore the one holding her . . . the other SS trooper was keeping up his scan of the countryside around them, eyes scanning from far to near, then moving on to a new sector. They flicked down to her for an incurious second, then back to look for danger.

"Don't like von-types," he grunted.

Johanna groaned again, and let her eyes come into focus, reaching a hand up to the young Bavarian's shoulder as if to steady herself. He patted it clumsily, and put away the canteen.

Are these people total idiots? she wondered. The

way they were acting . . . Almighty Thor, they hadn't
even searched her . . .

She smiled at the young soldier, and he blushed
and grinned in return.

"Do you speak German?" he asked. "Chocolaten?"
He began to fumble a package of Swiss bonbons from
his breast pocket. Johanna took a deep breath, pushed
pain and fear and battering out to the fringes of her
mind.

"Perfectly," she whispered in the same language.
"And no, thanks." He leaned close to hear, her left
hand slid the final centimeter to his throat. Thumb
and fingers clamped down on the carotid arteries;
the soldier made a single hoarse sound as what felt
like slender steel rods drove in on either side of his
larynx. She jerked forward savagely and he followed
in reflex, falling over her on his elbows; otherwise
half his throat would have been torn free. Johanna
ignored the ugly, queasy popping and rending sensa-
tions beneath her fingers; her hands were strong, but
surely not strong enough to punch through the neck
muscles. She *hoped* not.

Her right hand flicked. The knife came free of the
forearm sheath and slapped into her hand in a single
practiced movement, smooth metal over leather
rubbed with graphite. Just barely into her palm, her
fingers almost dropping the leather-wrapped hilt. She
was still groggy; the loss of speed and coordination
was frightening.

Damn worse than I thought! went through her as
she turned the point in, poised, thrust. The knife
was more delicate than the issue-model Jamieson
tucked into her boot, hand-made by Ildaren of Mar-
rakesh, a slender-edged spike of steel fifteen centi-
meters long. It slid through the tunic without
resistance, through the skin, slanting up under the
breastbone and through the diaphragm with a crisp
sensation like punching through a drumhead. Up

into the heart, razoring it in half, then quarters as she wrenched the weapon back and forth in the wound. The youngster's face was less than the breadth of a hand from hers, close enough for her to smell the mints on his breath. His eyes and mouth jerked open, shut, open again in perfect circles, like a gaffed fish; she could see the pupils dilating. No sound, even though the tongue worked in the pink cavern of his mouth. Her free hand slipped from his throat to his chest to hold the twitching, juddering body off hers as she wrestled with the knife.

For a moment the fierce internal spasm of the German's muscles clamped the blade tight, but it was narrow and supernally sharp. The steel slid free. With it came a warm rushing tide that flowed over her breasts and stomach, and the seawater smell of blood. The man's eyes rolled up and glazed as the dropping pressure in his veins starved the brain into unconsciousness. Johanna's knife hand moved, flipping the blade and taking a new hold on the point, three fingers and a thumb. Her arm moved it under the sheltering corpse above her, her face tracking like a gun turret for the next target.

The other SS *panzergrenadier* was intent on his surroundings. You did not survive a year on the Eastern Front by being careless, and there were too many clumps of forest within rifle-range. Not that a partisan needed trees; they crept through grass or scrub like lice in the seams of a uniform worn too long, almost impossible to exterminate. Alertness was second nature; he could check for movement and breaks in the pattern while thinking of other things. Women, *schnapps,* how home leave was a waste of time, the front was home now . . . He looked down at his partner's body, bent over the prisoner's, giving one last shiver and then going limp. The Draka slut's eyes were on his over Lothair's shoulder, fixed and glaring, lips ruched back from her teeth. He frowned. *That* was not like Lothair; little bastard thought he was Siegfried . . .

He opened his mouth, began to speak. The body was tossed aside, there was a glint of steel . . .

"Lothair, what're you screwing arou—"
Johanna knew the throw had gone wrong even as she wrenched the dead German's body aside, using it for leverage as her right arm snapped across and up. The hilt had been touching her left ear; the motion ended with her arm extended toward the standing SS man. Even caught by surprise he was too *fast*, crouching, turning, the muzzle of his submachinegun coming up in a smooth controlled arc as his words turned into a formless shout of rage. The Draka could see his finger tightening on the trigger as the knife turned, room for four rotations in the five meters between them.

I never trained with a wet knife and gloves! something within her wailed. The position's wrong, the sun's behind him, my head hurts, it isn't *fair*. Flick-rolling, ignoring the jagged pain that ripped up between her shoulders at the sudden motion, curling her feet beneath her, a no-hold leap with arm outstretched and fingers curled back to strike with the heel of the hand. Impossible. Too *slow*.

The knife had been aimed at his throat; an eye-shot was impossibly risky in the circumstances, the ribs armored the heart, a stab wound in the gut took too long to kill a gunman whose weapon could rip you open. Her own error and the German's speed placed it just below his pelvis, in the meaty part of the upper thigh near his groin. He twisted; the startled yell of pain and the first *peckapeckapecka* of the Schmeisser were simultaneous. The aim was thrown off: craters in the mud, chopping into the other SS-man's body in dimples of red and tattered cloth, an impact on her foot that flung her sprawling from the beginnings of her leap. And saved her life; the shots whipcracked the air over her head as her shoulder thudded into the man's stomach. Pink-*ting* as rounds punctured the thin metal of the vehicle's hood and struck something solid beneath.

"Frikken hond!" the German screamed, in rage fueled by pain. His wounded leg slammed the dashboard and buckled, and he pitched on his back, bracing his elbows wide to prevent himself from falling into the narrow well in front of the seats. The knob of the gearshift struck him in the lower back, and for a moment his body dissolved in a liquid flash that seemed to spread through every nerve, a web extending to his finger tips.

Johanna bounced as her torso struck the trooper and the kubelwagon's door, resilient flesh and metal absorbing her momentum and throwing her back, tuck-rolling as she fell, curling forward to cast her weight against the fall. A quarter of a forward roll and it was a crouch, facing the kubelwagon again and two meters away. No sign of the SS man; he could be out, she could have time to stop and pick up a weapon and finish him. Or the Schmeisser might be rising, about to clear the side of the vehicle and kill her. Training deeper and faster than thought made her decision, and the long muscles of her thighs uncoiled like living springs.

Half a second. That was a long time in personal combat. Her body was parallel to the ground for an instant, and her hands slapped down on the top of the scout car's door. She pivoted, legs together swinging wide and high over the windscreen—movements etched into her nerves by ten thousand hours of practice in gymnasium and salle d'armes. Legs *bend*, a quick hard push off her hands, and she was rotating in midair. There was a moment when she seemed to hang suspended, combat-adrenaline slowing the in-

stant to a breathless pause, like the endless second at
the top of an Immelman or the crest of a roller
coaster. She came down on the SS-man knees-first as
he struggled up on one elbow, eyes wide with shocked
surprise.

The breath went out of the soldier with an explo-
sive *whuff!* as one knee rammed home into the pit of
his stomach. Her other came down painfully on the
receiver of the Schmeisser, slid; then she was on
him, the weapon trapped between their bodies, one
of his arms immobilized by the strap. They grappled,
snarling, the Draka gouging for the nerve clusters;
she could feel the man's muscles coiling and bunch-
ing, forcing him upward from the awkward slump
into the gap between seat and dashboard. Johanna
arched herself against the panel behind her and pushed
him back; one hand fell on the hilt of the knife in his
thigh, and she jerked it free. A harsh gasp broke the
struggling rasp of his breath, and he bucked in a
convulsive twist that left them lying face to face on
their sides across the seats. The SS-man's palm slapped
onto her wrist as the point of her knife drove for his
face.

His *right* hand, the arm stretched across his body;
the outer arm was still trapped at the elbow by the
sling of his machine pistol. Useless, he kept the left
fist flailing at her hip and ribs in short punishing arcs
but the seatback protected her vulnerable spine and
kidneys. Johanna's right arm was free, and she had
solid bracing to push against; the German had lever-
age against him, and his grip on her wrist was re-
versed, weak, the thumb carrying the whole weight
of her arm and body. The knife hung trembling
above and between them, a long spike, motionless
save for the quiver of locked muscle, slow red drops
spilling down on the German's face. Johanna's was
close enough to catch the spatter, close enough to
smell the garlic and stale beer on his breath and the

harsh musk of male sweat. To see the eyes widen in surprise as the blade jerked forward a fraction, and hear the quiver in his breath as he halted it again.

Never wrestle with a man: the instructors had told her that often enough. They simply had stronger arms. It didn't make much difference in block-and-strike fighting—if a blow landed on the right place just hard enough that was all you needed, and if you missed it didn't matter how hard you punched the air.

She jerked a breath in, clenched down and forced it out with the muscles of the gut, where strength comes from. Felt it flow into her arms, felt her face fill with blood and saw traceries of vein across her eyes. How many hours at school, swinging the practice bar and the weights, squeezing the hand-spring? Waking stiff and sore despite the saunas and massage, rolling out of bed for the morning set of chinups . . .

Her heart beat in her ears. Her left hand forced its way between their bodies; no chance of getting it free for a strike or eye-claw, but . . . Johanna's thumb forced its way into the sweat-wet warmth of the German's armpit. Into the nerve cluster where the arm meets the shoulder, just above the beginning of the bicep. Pushed.

Her enemy made a sound, something halfway between a yelp and a snarl. The grip on her wrist was weakening, slipping, the German's arm bending back, faster as the angle changed and cast the whole strain on his forearm. Johanna wrapped one leg around the man's and heaved, twisting him onto his back and rising to throw her weight behind the knife. It crept into her sight; first the point, and then the crusted blade itself. Then their hands, his bare and dusted with freckles and sun-bleached hairs like gold wires, her fingers slim and night-black in the thin kidskin gloves; and the pommel of the knife, steel showing through the rawhide binding. She willed force into

knife-hand and thumb; the German's eyes widened
as the steel touched his throat and he began to buck
and twist, frantic; screamed once as all the strength
left his arm and the knife punched down.

It had the suddenness of pushing at a stuck door
and then having it open all at once; the point went
through with no more effort than pushing a lump of
meat onto a skewer around the fire at a braai-party.
Her weight came down on the hilt and the blade
sliced through the thick neck, like the upper blade of
a pair of scissors; she collapsed forward into a bright
spray of arterial blood, breathed it in with her first
sobbing inhalation and threw herself back, sitting on
her heels astride the still-quivering body and cough-
ing, retching up and spitting out a mouthful of thin
bile. And wiping at the blood: blood on her hands, in
her eyes, in her hair, running down in sticky sheets
over her face and neck and under her flight suit to
join the cooling, tacky-thick mass from the younger
German. Blood in her mouth, tasting of iodine and
iron and salt; she spat repeatedly as she forced her
breathing to go slow and deep, suppressing the in-
stinctive but inefficient panting.

There was a sharp hiss, as the bullet-punctured
flashcoil of the kubelwagen's boiler released its steam
and joined the stink of overheated metal to the fecal
odor of death. With floodgate abruptness feeling re-
turned, overwhelming the combat concentration. Fear
first, cold on the skin, and a tight prickling up from the
pubis. She looked down at the dead German; he had
been so *strong*, quick too. She could never have
taken two Draka like this, but this one had had
potential, far too much.

His head lolled, opening the great flap of muscle
and skin, blood still welling. How much blood there
was, and tubes and glands showing . . . she glanced
away. Physical sensation next: the ache in her head,
a dozen minor scratches and bruises where her body

had been hammered against projecting metal. They had gone unnoticed in the brief savage fight, but now the abrasions stung with salt sweat and blood, and the bruises ached with a to-the-bone sick feeling, the feeling that meant they would turn a spectacular green and yellow in a day or two. And one knee was throbbing every time she moved it, where it had come down on the machine pistol when she landed on the Fritz.

Johanna looked down over one shoulder at her foot. *No pain there*, she thought dazedly. Or at least none of the pain that a real wound would cause, just another ache. One heel of her boot had been torn off, left dangling by a shred of composition rubber. "Never bet on the horses again, woman, you've used it all up," she muttered to herself.

A shout brought her head up, and she clutched at the wheel against a wave of dizziness. A line of figures was trotting toward her from the copse of forest to the east, twenty of them. They were still five hundred meters away, but they looked too ragged to be Fritz, and German troops would have come up in a vehicle, anyway. Russians, then; the situation reports had mentioned partisan activity. They might be hostile, or not. The German yoke had lain heavy here, and she had two very dead Fritz for credentials. On the other hand . . . as the saying went, nobody loved the Draka. Russians least of all, after the bite the Domination had taken out of the lands east of the Caspian back in the Great War; and there had been a generation of border clashes since. A Russian young enough to be in the field now had probably been brought up on anti-Draka propaganda and atrocity stories, at least half of which were true.

A heavy, weary annoyance seized her for a moment. "Mother Freya," she said to herself, scrubbing a forearm over her lips again. "I really don't want to be here." Not so much the fear or discomfort, they were bearable, but she definitely did not want to be here in this cold and foreign place, covered in blood and sitting on a corpse. "I want to be *home*." Rahksan giving her a massage and a rubdown with Leopard Balm liniament and a cuddle, twelve hours' sleep, waking up clean and safe in her own bed with her cat on the pillow, with no dangers and nobody telling her what to do . . . " 'Nothing's free, and only the cheaper things can be bought with money'; you never said a truer word, Daddy."

She stood, feeling the raw breeze as her breathing slowed. One hand clenched on the other. Time enough to move when the shaking stopped.

The partisans came up in a wary half-circle as Johanna finished strapping on the gear from her kit, murmuring and pointing as they reconstructed the brief fight. None of them was pointing a weapon at her: she recognized "Drakansky" among the liquid slavic syllables, and wary sidelong glances. That was reasonable enough; she must look a sight, with drying blood matted in her hair and smeared about her mouth. From the way some of them leaned into the kubelwagon and then glanced back at her, fingering their necks, she imagined they were speculating that she had torn out the second SS trooper's throat with her teeth; it was obvious enough that neither of the Germans had been shot. There was awe in the glances, too, at the woman who had climbed out of a burning plane and killed two armed soldiers of the SS elite with her hands . . .

She ignored them with studied nonchalance as she slipped a magazine into the pistol grip of the machine pistol, clipped the bandolier to her belt and tossed back two pills from one of the bottles; aspirin, for the pounding ache between her eyes and the stiff neck and shoulders. Limping as little as her bruised foot and the missing heel would allow, she walked

over to the corpse of the young Fritz on the ground.
There were already flies, crawling into the gaping
wound in his stomach and across dry eyeballs frozen
in a look of eternal surprise. The heavy smell of
excrement brought the bile to the back of her throat
as she flipped his rifle up with a toe and tossed it to a
startled Russian.

*They never mention the smell of shit in the old
stories*, she thought, fighting down the vomit. *Maybe
they had tighter assholes in the days of the sagas*.
Johanna did not consider herself more squeamish
than the average Draka, but there was nothing pleas-
ing about looking at the ruin that had once been a
person. Once, with an adolescent's fascination for
horrors, she had gone to the public execution ground
in Hyancitha, the market town nearest Oakenwald,
to see a serf broken on the wheel and impaled for
striking an overseer. Once had been enough.

Enough. She had an audience, and upchucking
with buck fever was *not* the way to impress them.
Not that this was the first time she had killed, but
aerial combat was a gentlman's form of killing. You
didn't have to see the results of it, they fell out of the
sky in a convenient and sanitary fashion and you
went home . . . Gritting her teeth, she forced herself
to reach out, grasp the ear, make a quick slash. Her
blade was still sharp enough to cut gristle with two
drawing strokes . . . The grenade in the German's
boot went into hers, and she walked grimly over to
the scout car and repeated the docking process; a
little frightfulness was always good for a first impres-
sion, or at least so the textbooks said. Cleaning and
sheathing the knife, she looked back once; for an
outlander, that Fritz had not been bad at all. It was
going to be an expensive war if there were more like
him.

The partisans had come a little closer; their weap-
ons held ready but not immediately threatening; there

were about twenty of them, incredibly filthy, ragged, armed with a motley collection of Russian and Fritz weaponry, with a lean starved ferocity about them. None of them seemed to have blanched at the ear collection; from the look of it, affection for the Fritz in general and the SS in particular was running low in this part of Russia. They stank, with a smell of unwashed filth and the sour odor of men who have not had a good meal in a very long time. She walked toward them, and suddenly it was all she could do not to laugh and skip.

Alive, suddenly bubbled up within her. She felt a giddy rush of sensation, the blood cooling and drying on her chest, mild spring air, bright morning sunlight and the sweet vanilla-green scent of flowering oaks from the copse at the top of the hill ahead of her. Feelings pushing at her control: tears, affection, incredibly a sudden rush of sexual arousal. *Freya, what a time to feel horny*, she giggled to herself, and then it faded out into a vast well-being. Fighting down the smile that threatened, she walked through the partisan line. Their leader seemed to be a thin man with no front teeth and a long scar where one eye should be; he had been waiting for her to stop and speak, and her steady pace threw him off his mental center, as if he had reached the bottom of a stairwell one tread too soon.

PD, she thought. Psychological dominance, keep 'em off balance. It might not work, but on the other hand . . . *Every moment of my life from now on is a bonus*. She waited until the partisans had walked after her toward the woods for a good ten meters, until she could sense their leader about to reach out and touch her sleeve. Then she turned, pulled the grenade from her boot, yanked the tab and tossed it up in the air, caught it as the Russians dived flat with a chorus of yells and threw it back toward the Fritz scout car.

Perfect. The throw felt right, a smooth heavy arc that her mind drew to the target. Suddenly, she could do no wrong: the stick grenade pinwheeled through the air and dropped neatly into the kubel-wagen's front seat. She stayed casually erect, hands on hips, tapping a foot to time the fuse. One . . . two . . . three . . .

Whump! Stamped-steel panels blew out of the German car, and the doors sprang open and stayed that way, sprung on their hinges. The body was flung out of the front seat to land a few yards away; flames began to pool and lick beneath it as the fuel tank ruptured. Johanna glanced from it to the shattered, burning framework of the *Lover's Bite*. Turn about's fair play, she thought, and looked to the figure at her feet. The partisan leader had been holding his tattered fur cap down around his ears with both hands. Unclenching hands and eyes, he looked up at her with the beginnings of anger. The fragments of casing could have been lethal, if the grenade had not fallen into something that absorbed them.

"Sprechen sie Deutsch?" she asked calmly, narrow blonde head tilted to one side, an eyebrow elegantly arched.

"Crazy devil woman!" he began in an understandable pidgin of that language, then continued more slowly. "Ja, ein weig." *Yes, a little.* Strange things were happening, the partisan thought, since the Draka had attacked the *neimetsky.* Ivan escaping certain death over in the village on the highway, calling them all together . . . Caution was always wise, and at least there was an opportunity to shovel his intimidating whatever-she-was onto somebody *else's* plate. "My name Dmitri Mikhaelovitch Belov."

"Good," Johanna answered, with cool friendliness. "Then take me," she tapped a foot lightly against his shoulder for emphasis, "to your leader."

* * *

It took them most of a day to reach the guerilla rendezvous. Hard marching, through increasingly rugged hills, always south toward the snowpeaks of the Caucasus. Forest closed in until they were always under cover, diving for thickets when aircraft snarled by overhead; Johanna watched a dogfight far above with a sudden thick longing that was more than fear and aching feet and the strain of keeping up a show of tireless strength for her escort-captors. Tiny silver shapes, wheeling in the sad blue light of early evening. *That* was where she belonged . . .

Or with Tom on the sheepskins in front of a crackling fire, she added to herself as they waded through a stream whose iciness spoke of a source in melting glaciers. Thick woods now, huge moss-grown beeches and oaks, a carpet of leaves and spring wildflowers and occasional meadows where the scent grew dizzying. Simple enough to ignore the blisters in boots never designed for walking; her well-fed fitness made the march easy enough. Surprising that these scarecrows could set a pace that pushed her even a little, even still feeling the mild concussion from the crash. But then, anyone who had stayed alive and under arms in Russia for the last year or so was going to be a real survivor type.

A break in the bird-chorus warned them to go to earth just after cautiously crossing a rutted "road," and they laid up in the undergrowth while a column of German half-tracks and armored cars thundered by. There was little chance of discovery, with the speed the Germans were making; also, they seemed to be primarily worried about the sky above them, had probably chosen this trail precisely because it had branches meeting above it.

After that the partisans seemed to relax, an almost subliminal feeling. Their weapons still stayed at the ready, and nobody spoke; the fieldcraft was not up to Draka standards, but far from bad.

Probably the noisy-ones all died this last year, she thought. Dmitri tapped her on the shoulder, indicating a cleft in the hill up which they toiled.

"Fritz never come this far," he whispered. "This place."

A sharp hail brought them to a halt, and suspicious figures appeared out of the woods around them. The partisans who had found her engaged the others in a lengthy question-and-answer session; this group seemed marginally less ragged and better armed, and it included several women as tough-looking as any of the men. Johanna could puzzle through a simple Russian sentence, if it was written in Roman script; this rapid conversation left her with no more than the odd word—"Drakansky," "Fritz", "Aeroplane." Pretending boredom, she split the cellophane cover on a package of cigarettes, tapped one out, lit it with her American Ronson.

That brought attention—a circle of faces, bearded and desperate; she handed the package to Dmitri. He seemed to be expanding on the subject of the strange Draka, rather like a man who had brought home some dangerous exotic and called his friends around to see the basilisk, the more so as she sensed him a stranger here. Even the ear-cropping devil woman who tore out Fritz throats was not as interesting as tobacco, though; hands mobbed him, clawing. Dmitri shouted, and then used the butt of the rifle to restore order and hand the cigarettes out in halfs and quarters.

"No smoke for long," he said, puffing happily as they walked toward the steep path up the cliff. "For Fritz only, eh? Always vodka while potatoes is, but no *rhakoria*. Dasvedanya!"

The hollow inside was crowded despite covering several thousand square meters, and Johanna guessed that this was a gathering of several bands, more than its usual population. Bluffs and dense forest surrounded it and the scattering of lean-tos, tents and brush shelters. Cooking fires were few and carefully smokeless, but otherwise the scene was a cross between the military and the domestic; there were even a few silent children, if no toddlers. Murmurs ran among them, and a steady stream began moving toward the party walking through the entrance. Johanna's eyes moved in on a face whose slight smile remained fixed, noting the dug-in machineguns farther upslope, slit trenches and the absence of stench that told of good latrine discipline, several mortars and stacked ammunition, a knocked-down heliograph set . . .

And one solid log-and-stone hut, the door opening to show a bearlike figure with dramatic crossed cartridge belts across a bulging stomach, belt full of daggers, baggy trousers and black astrakhan-wool cap . . . Dmitri snapped a salute, then continued his animated speech to the gathering crowd, full of hand gestures, swooping like planes, teeth worrying an imaginary neck.

Well, if it isn't Boris the Cossack, Terror of the Steppe, Johanna thought, glancing aside at the hulking figure by the hut. With a slight chill; there was no foolishness in the narrow black eyes. A figure in a patched but recognizable Soviet uniform followed the huge man: pale intelligent face and long thin hands. Green tabs on the collar. *NKVD*, she thought. Oh, joy.

The big man rumbled a question; his face was round and puffy, but strong with thick red lips. Dmitri answered, then seemed to be arguing; there were murmurs from the crowd around them, until the big man turned on them and roared. That quieted most; when the man with the green tabs spoke, it grew silent enough for Johanna to hear breathing, and the whistling sough of wind through the leaves.

Dmitri turned to her unhappily. "This," he said, indicating the man with the bandoliers, "Sergeant Sergei." Another rumble from the hulk. "Pardons, *Comrade Colonel* Sergei Andropovitch Kozin." A frightened glance. "With . . . helpings-man? Ah, *aide*, Comrade Blensikov. Comrade Colonel is being our *leader*—" he used the literal German term, *fuhrer*, with a slight emphasis "—while our commander, Ivan Yuhnkov, was prisoner of SS. Commander Ivan—" using the Russian word *kommandyr* "—is becoming here again in charge soon now, has called all First Partisan Brigade to meet him here."

Johanna pursed her lips, feeling sweat trickle down her flanks from her armpits. Her back crawled with the consciousness of so many about her: wild serfs, strange ones, not domesticated, and armed . . . And these two were not going to be rhinoed that easily. She forced her perceptions into action, to see them as individuals, reading the clues of hands and face and stance. *The tool that speaks can also think*, she reminded herself. *You're supposed to be more intelligent—outthink them!*

It was not comforting. The big one was an animal, and the bug-under-the-rock type a fanatic. From the signs, a smart fanatic. But . . . this was like running down a steep hill. If you kept running, you *might* fall on your ass; if you tried to stop, you *certainly* would.

"Tell them," she said in neutral tones, "that I will speak to this Commander Ivan, when he comes."

Dmitri translated, his ravaged face becoming even unhappier. "They . . . they saying you talking to them, now, in *khutzba*, in hut." He held out his hand. "Gun?"

Too many of them out here, she thought with tight-held control. Brushing him aside, she followed the NKVD officer into the hut, blinking at the contrast between the bright sunlight through the leaves outside and the gloom of the interior. That deepened

as the other man filled the door, swung it to behind
him with a heavy thud. He did not bother to shoot
home the bar.

The interior of the hut smelled rank, like an ani-
mal's den, but with an undertone of clean wood.
Johanna breathed deep and slow, needing the oxy-
gen and the *prahnu*-trained calmness that the rhyth-
mic flexing of her diaphragm produced. It would all
depend on . . .

The thin man seized her, hands on her *upper*
arms, thumbs digging into her shoulder blades, trying
to make her arch her chest out. She let the muscles
go limp under his grip, the shoulders slump. There
was no fear now. *Ju*, went through her. *Go-with*. The
big man stepped close, very fast for someone his
size; he must be twice her weight easily, and there
was plenty of muscle there. A hand clamped pain-
fully on her breast, kneading and twisting; another
behind her head, pulling her mouth up to meet his.
The smell of him filled her nostrils, strong, like a
mule that has been ploughing in the sun. The two
men crowded her between them; they must be ex-
pecting her to try to kick shins like a child.

Is *everybody* outside the Domination a complete
idiot about immobilizing an enemy? she thought in
momentary wonderment. Her arms could not move
forward or back to strike . . . and did not need to.
Instead her elbows punched *out*, away from her sides.
The NKVD officer found his grip slipping; instinct-
ively raising his own stance, he found himself push-
ing down on her shoulders rather than gripping her
upper arms. The Draka's own hands shot down to
clasp the fabric of the Cossack trousers; she let her
knees go limp, and pulled herself downward with a
motion that drew on the strength of back and stom-
ach as much as arms. The thin Russian found the
rubbery muscle and slick fabric vanishing from his

hands, bent to follow them. His forehead met his comrade's descending kiss with a *thock* of bone on teeth that brought a roar of pain from the giant.

Johanna found herself squatting, her knees between the big Russian's straddled legs, her face level with the long swelling of his erection. There were several means of disabling a large, strong man from that position; she chose the most obvious. Her hand dropped to the ground, clenched into a fist, punched directly up with a twist of hip and shoulder, flexing of legs, *hunnnh* of expelled breath that put weight and impact behind it. The Russian would probably have been able to block a knee to the groin while she was standing; against this, there was no possibility of defense. The first two knuckles of her fist sank into his scrotum, with a snapping twist at the moment of impact that flattened the testicles against the unyielding anvil of his pubic bone. He did not scream; the pain was far too intense for that. His reflex bending was powerful enough to send his comrade crashing into the bunk at the rear of the cabin, and he staggered away clutching his groin and struggling to breath through a throat locked in spasm.

Johanna flowed erect, turning. The NKVD man turned out to be a fool, after all: he staggered to his feet and threw a punch at her head, rather than going for his gun. She relaxed one knee, swaying out of the fist's path; her right palm slapped onto his wrist, drawing him farther along . . . *pivot* on the heel, *straddle* stance . . . *throw* the weight into it . . . her left elbow drove into his side just below the armpit, with the force of his own momentum behind it. Her left arm went tingling numb, but she heard something snap audibly, felt bone give under her blow. She kept control of the Russian's arm, bent, twisted, heaved. His body left the ground, began a turn, ran into the door three-quarters of the way

through it. Something else snapped, and he went
limp to the split-log floor.

One down, the Draka thought, turning again. The
machine pistol was out of immediate reach on her
back . . . and the giant was coming at her again.

She blinked, backing, almost frozen with surprise.
He was moving with one hand pressed to his groin,
as if he could squeeze out the pain, but the other
held a knife, a khidjal, held it as if he knew how to
use it. His face worked; he spat out a broken tooth,
grinning with a blood-wet mouth in an expression
that was nothing *like* a smile. The knifepoint made
small circles in the air.

Johanna snapped out her own, hilt low, point an-
gled up. Left hand bladed, palm down, shuffling
back in a flat-footed crouch. This was *not* good, the
Russian had a full ten centimeters' advantage of reach
and there was no room to maneuver, the whole
Loki-cursed hut was only four meters on a side, and
the knife was *not* a weapon to duel with. It was fine
for surprise, good for an ambush in the dark, but in a
straight-on knife fight the one who ended up in the
hospital was the winner.

What do I do now? she thought. Then: *Kill or die,
what else?*

The Cossack straightened a little and came in. The
blade moved up, feinting a thrust to the belly, and
his left hand reached, going for a hold. Stupidity
again, still trying to subdue her. She spun, slashing,
and the blade sliced up the outside of the other's arm
from wrist to elbow. Cloth parted under as the edge
touched meat, cutting a long, shallow gash. The giant
roared and attacked, thrusting and slashing in deadly
earnest this time.

Some far-off portion of her mind wished for a
heavier blade; the narrow steel strip she carried in
her wrist-sheath was a holdout weapon, without the

weight for a good cut. There are few places on a human body where a stab is quickly disabling, and none of them is very vulnerable at arm's length to an alert opponent. To kill quickly in a knife fight you must slash, cut every exposed surface to ribbons and rely on blood-loss to knock the other out.

That seemed unlikely. A long blade and longer arm were reaching for her life, and she backed, parrying steel-on-steel, the most difficult of all defenses, drawing out the exchange until an opening let her side-slip past the Russian and back into the center of the room. The effort had been brutal; she stood and breathed in deep careful motions, eyes never leaving her opponent's. He waited for an instant, face gone blankly calculating, even the pain in his crotch forgotten. The three-second passage had let them feel each other out; Johanna knew that she was more skilled with the knife, and faster—just enough to compensate for the cramped quarters and her enemy's longer reach and heavier knife—and she would have less margin for error. Desperation surged; could she reach the gun before . . .

Her back was to the door as it opened, forcing the limp body of the NKVD man aside. Light speared in, taking the huge Russian in the eyes, and he squinted, peering. Then his face changed, first to a fresh rage, then sudden fear. Johanna almost had him then, and his recovery cost him a cut across the face. Johanna bored in, knocked his knife wrist aside with a bladed palm, skipped her left foot forward and flick-kicked. The toe of her boot landed solidly under one kneecap, and there was a tearing *pop* as cartilage gave way; she spun back out of reach as he bellowed and tried to grapple. The Russian stayed on his feet, but his face was grey and all the weight on one leg. Now to finish it: she came in low and smooth and fast, and—

—one foot skidded out from underneath her in a patch of blood. The floor slammed into her back, hard enough to knock the breath out of her. She saw lights before her eyes, and knew the knife would come down before she could recover.

"*Shto,*" a cool voice from behind her said. "*Ruki verch, Sergei.*" Then purling Russian syllables, meaningless. A woman's voice, with crowd-mutter behind her. And a very meaningful metallic click—the safety of a pistol being flicked off. The man before her kept his involuntary crouch, and pain-sweat dripped into his thin black beard; he licked blood off his lips as he dropped the knife and put his open hands above his shoulders, speaking in a wheedling tone. The woman's voice cut him off sharply, a sneer in it.

Johanna rolled out of the line of fire and came erect. She stood, slipping the knife back into its sheath as she took a careful step to the side, slowly, hands well out and empty. Turned slowly also, in a position where she could see her opponent as well as the door. She was not going to turn her back on that sort of strength—not until she knew what the score was.

At first the woman in the doorway was nothing but a silhouette, surrounded by sun-dazzle and haze. Then her pupils adjusted, her body lost the quivering knowledge of steel about to slice into vulnerable flesh. *Tall*, was her first thought; about the Draka's own height. Long straight hair the color of birchwood, gathered in a knot at the side of her head. Open coat, fine soft-tanned sheepskin edged with embroidery and astrakhan, reaching almost to the floor. Pressed-silk blouse, tailored pleated trousers tucked incongruously into muddy German boots a size too large and stuffed with straw. *Young*, was her next impression. Not much more than the Draka's own age. Pale oval face, high-cheeked in the Slav manner, but not flat. High forehead, eyes like clover-honey, straight nose, full red lips drawn back slightly from even white teeth. Broad shoulders emphasized by the coat; full high breasts above a narrow waist; hips tapering to long dancer's legs . . .

With a Walther P-38 in one elegantly gloved hand, pointed unwaveringly at the other Russian's face.

Interesting, Johanna mused. *That is a seven-hundred-auric item, if I ever saw one.* A thought crossed her mind: if they both came through this alive, it would be almost a charitable act to acquire . . .

The pistol swiveled around to her. Johanna considered the black eye of it, followed up the line of the arm to meet the amber gaze. *Then again, no. Definitely not. This is not someone to whom I can imagine saying "lie down and play pony for me."* Pity. *Lovely mouth, really.*

"Valentina Fedorova Budennin," the woman said. "Once of the Linguistic Institute, now of the partisan command, and just out of Pyatigorsk. At your service, although you seem to need less rescuing than Dmitri led me to expect." Astonishingly, she spoke in English, almost without accent except for a crisp British treatment of the vowels. "Air Corps, I see. You may have paid me a very pleasant visit yesterday, then." She smiled, an expression which did not reach her eyes.

"Pilot Officer Johanna von Shrakenberg," the Draka said, keeping the surprise out of her voice. "Believe me, the effort was appreciated. Although," she frowned, "this is the *second* time today I've survived because somebody assumed I was a harmless idiot. Not complainin' about the results, but it's damned odd."

"Ah." The smile grew wider, but remained something of the lips only. "That would be because you are a woman. I have been relying on men underesti-

mating me because of that for some time; the more
fools, they." The Russian woman called over her
shoulder. "Ivan!" and a sentence in her own lan-
guage. A stocky Russian walked in with a Fritz ma-
chine pistol over his shoulder and . . . a *Draka* field
dressing on one side of his face, nobody else used
that tint of blue gauze.

To Johanna: "This will seem odd, but I think I
have a man here who knows your brother. We should
talk." Her gaze went back to Sergei, backed against
the wall, eyes flickering in animal wariness. "After
we dispose of some business." The pistol turned back
and slammed, deafening in the enclosed space. A
black dot appeared between the big Russian's eyes,
turning to a glistening red. The impact of his falling
shook the floor.

It was much later before Ivan and Valentina could
talk alone, low-voiced before the fireplace of the hut,
ignoring the bodies at their feet.

"Impressive," Ivan said, nodding to the door. Jo-
hanna had gone for a tactful walk, while they consid-
ered her advice.

"The Draka did not get where they are by acci-
dent," Valentina said, seating herself and crossing
one leg elegantly over another. "Which leaves the
matter of your decision. There are two alternatives:
to attack Pyatigorsk while the Germans are occupied,
or to strike at the rear of the SS column attempting
to clear the pass."

"What do *you* think we should do, Valentina
Fedorova?" Ivan asked, feeling with his tongue for
the loose tooth. Truly, it was a little better, and the
gums had stopped bleeding. Amazing things, these
vitamin pills.

The woman shrugged. "Whatever helps that Draka
officer you spoke to; it is our best chance. Finding

his sister here," she shrugged. "Well, the truly impossible thing would be a world in which the unlikely never happened."

"Best chance for us, but what of the Revolution? The Party? Russia?"

She turned her head and spat, lofting the gobbet across the room to land on the dead NKVD agent.

"The Revolution and the Party are as dead as that dog. Stalin killed them, but the corpse-lover kept his mother aboveground until Hitler came with a shovel. Do not delude yourself, Ivan Desonovitch, the way that one did."

The partisan commander looked down, fiddling with the strap of his Schmeisser; it was more comfortable than meeting the woman's eyes. "And our people?"

Valentina sighed, rubbing two fingers over her forehead. "The *narod*, the Russian people . . . we survived Genghis Khan and the Tatar yoke; we endured the czars, the boyars . . . we can outlive the Draka, too." She smiled coldly. "My grandmother was a serf; a nobleman in St. Petersburg pledged her for a gambling debt, and bought her back for two carriage horses."

"We could fight them!" He laid an encouraging hand on her shoulder, then snatched it back with a muttered apology as she froze in distaste.

Valentina shook her head. "We fought the Nazis, my friend, because they would not only have enslaved us, they would have killed three-quarters of us first whether we fought or not. I did not lie on my back for that mad dog Hoth for six months without learning something of them! If the Draka win, and we try to fight on here, at first there would be partisans, yes." She paused to kick the dead Sergei and spit again, in his face. "Then only bandits like this dead Cossack pig, preying on their own people because it was easier. In the end, hunted animals, eating roots and each other in the woods until the Draka killed the last one; and our peasants would be glad, if it gave them a chance to work and eat and rear their children without the thatch being burnt above their heads."

She turned on him, and he shrank slightly from the intensity of her. "No, Ivan Desonovitch, we shall retreat because that is the way to work and fight for our people; retreat to the Americans, who will fight the Draka someday, because they must. If there is a hope that our people may be free, that is it." She laughed, chillingly. "Free. For the first time. Everything possible must happen in the end, no?"

CHAPTER EIGHTEEN

"In the end, I was left with nothing but fading memories and the stereotypes of popular culture to build the father in my head. Yet, however tempting, the strutting uniforms and sinister drawls of Hollywood's Draka never seemed enough; cutout shapes against a background of sun-bomb missiles and jets and nuclear submarines prowling the Atlantic. All my life I had been conscious of the layers of consciousness itself: there was the me I had shown to my schoolmates, the me my adoptive parents knew, the surfaces and masks I showed to friends and lovers, the fragments of self that became the characters of my work. There was even a me kept for New York editors, almost as deep as the one I saved for my agent. None of them was the me to whom I spoke in darkness, the secret self that said 'I am I.' Yet all of these, roles, masks, fragments, were me to the people who saw them; all of me. And I was those masks while I wore them; they were ... partial things, but not lies. The single thing that has always stood in my memory as the bridge between childhood and maturity, the gap between myself-as-I-am and the young alien whose memories I bear, was the realization that this was as true for others as myself.

That was the beginning of all my art and my deepest contact with my father. There was a time when I collected his photograph obsessively: newspaper clippings, from the back-jackets of his books, plastered over the walls of my Manhattan loft. Yet it was a line from one of his works that made him real to me, as the images could not: 'A man's mind is a forest at night.' Was he the man who had owned and used my mother, and discarded me as an inconvenience? Or the father who loved her, and me enough to risk life and reputation to give me freedom? Both, and neither; we cannot know each other, or ourselves; there is no knowing, only an endless self-discovery, 'often as painful as collisions in the dark, truths rough as bark and sharp as thorns. Knowledge is a journey; when it ends, we die.'"

> *Daughter to Darkness: A Life*
> by Anna von Shrakenberg
> Houghton & Stewart, New York, 1964

VILLAGE ONE, OSSETIAN MILITARY HIGHWAY APRIL 17, 1942: 1300 HOURS

CRASH. CRASH. CRASH. CRASH—
The shells were falling at three-second intervals. The bunker vibrated with every impact, stone and timber groaning as they readjusted under the stress, ears popping in the momentary overpressure. Dust filtered down in clouds that coated mouth and nose and lungs with a dryness that itched; the blue light of the lamp was lost in the clouds, a vague blur to eyes that streamed water, involuntary tears. The wounded satchelman in the corner was breathing slowly, irregularly, each painful effort bubbling and wheezing through the sucking wound in his chest. Eric sneezed, hawked, spat, wiped his eyes on his sleeve and looked about. There were nearly twenty crowded into the room besides the wounded, mostly squatting and leaning on their weapons; one or two praying, more with their eyes shut and wincing as the hammerblows struck the rubble above. More waited, locked in themselves or holding hands.

Sofie knelt by the communications table, fingers working on the field telephone. "Sir, can't raise bunker four, it's not dead, just no answer."

Eric sneezed again. "Wallis! Take a stick and check it out. If Fritz is in, blow the connector passage."

Five troopers rose and pulled their kerchiefs over mouth and nose, filing over to the door. They moved more slowly than they had earlier. *Exhaustion*, Eric thought. Not surprising; the shelling had started well before first light. An attack at dawn, three more since then, each more desperate than the last. Combat was more exhausting than breaking rock with a sledgehammer; the danger-hormones of the fight-flight reflex drained the reserves down to the cellular level.

And when you got tired, you got slow, you made mistakes. The cellars had saved them, let them move through the village under cover and attack where they chose. But there was only so much you could do against numbers and weight of metal; they were killing ten for one, but there was always a Fritz number eleven. The casualties had been a steady drain, and so had the expenditure of fungibles, ammunition, explosives, rocket-gun shells. That last time, the Fritz had come down the holes after them, hand-to-hand in the dark, rifle butt and bayonet, bush knife and boots and teeth . . . if there had been a few more of the SS infantry, it would have been all over. The Draka garrison of Village One was running out, out of blood and time and hope.

"Lock and load," Wallis said, and there was a multiple rattle as bolts were drawn back and released. They vanished, heads dipping below the ragged stone lintel, like a sacrificial procession in some ancient rite.

Eric reached for his canteen, trying to think over the noise that hammered like a huge slow heart. The dark closed in; they were listening to that heartbeat from the belly of the beast. The war had become very small, very personal.

Gods and demons, aren't the bastards ever going to run out of ammunition? It was heavy stuff falling —150's and 170's, long-range self-propelled guns. As beyond any countermeasure as weapons mounted on the moon would have been, turning the village above into a kicked-over mound of rubble, raising and tossing and pulverizing the stone. Splinters of steel, splinters of granite, fire and blast; nothing made of flesh could live in it. Just keeping lookouts up there under shelter was costing him, a steady trickle of casualties he could not replace.

There was a stir. Something different, in the private hell they had all come to believe was timeless. It took a moment for the absence to make itself felt; the lungshot sapper had stopped breathing with a final long sigh. After a moment Trooper Patton released her friend's hand and crawled over, to shut the man's eyes and gently remove the canvas sack of explosives that had been propping up his head and shoulders.

Let something happen, he prayed. *Anything.*

"Third Tetrarchy reporting—"

He snatched at the handset, jamming a thumb into his left ear to drown out the noise. Third Tetrarchy was holding the trenchline west of the village, or was supposed to be; the connection had been broken an hour ago. There was as much at the other end, but . . .

". . . hold, can't hold; we're being overrun, pulling back to the woods. Stopped the infantry but the tanks are through, no antitank left, they're into the village as well—" The line went dead again.

White Christ have mercy, they're sending the armor in alone through their own shellfire, rammed into him. Brutally dangerous, but it might work, the odds against a round actually *hitting* a tank were still vanishingly small . . .

"Up and at 'em!" he barked, his finger stabbing out twice. *"You* two stay, Sofie put it on the wire, all bunkers, everybody *move."* The Fritz could saturate the village, then bring in sappers to pump the bunkers full of jellied gasoline, or lay charges heavy enough to bury them . . .

He went through the doorway with an elbow crooked over his mouth to take the worst of the dust; coughed, and felt the ribs stab pain. He was panting, and the breath didn't seem to be doing any *good,* as if the inside of his lungs had gone hot and stretched and tight, unable to suck the oxygen out of the air. The cellars were dim-dark, full of sharp edges and projections looming up to bruise and cut and snag. Full of running soldiers and the sound of composition-soled boots on gritty stone under the monstrous anger of the guns, sound that shivered in teeth and bone, echoed in the cavity of the lungs. As the survivors of Century A dashed for the remaining pop-up holes, Eric flung himself at the rough timbers of the ladder, running up into the narrow darkness one-handed, the other holding his Holbars by the sling, until . . .

"Fuck it!" he screamed, voice raw with dust and frustration. There was a section of wooden-board wall toppled over the carefully concealed entrance, and something heavier on that. He let the assault rifle fall to hang by its strap, turned, braced his back against the obstruction and his face against the stones of the wall. Took a deep breath, relaxed, drew into himself. Pushed, pushed until lights flared red behind his closed lids, pushed against the stone and his hatred of the place that held him entrapped.

"God *damn!"* There was a long yielding slither, and a crunch of breaking oak boards.

Then he was blinking in the light that poured through the hole, coughing again, breathing by willpower against the greater pain in his chest. Rubble had shifted, and the way was clear into what was left of the ground floor of the house. Still a roof overhead, that was good, and the row across the street was almost intact. Flash-*crash* and he dropped his face into the broken stone, waiting for the last of the shrapnel to ping-ting into harmlessness, then leopard-crawled into the interior of the building. Out here the shellbursts sounded harder, the edges of the sound unblurred. Impact bounced at him, lifting his body and dropping it again on hard-edged ruins. Above him the long timbers that upheld the second story creaked and shifted, their unsupported outer ends sagging further, rock and less identifiable objects hitting and bouncing around him with a patter and *snak-snak*.

Sunlight was blinding even with the overcast, after the perpetual night of the cellars. He glanced at his watch as the other six followed him and flowed over the uneven rock to the remnant of the roadside wall; there was enough of it to make a decent firing-parapet if nothing killed them from above. 1330 hours. Early afternoon; unbelievable. A flicker of movement from the second-story rooftop opposite; good, the others were in place. Elbows and knees to the low heap of the wall; and—

—the shelling of the long-range heavies stopped. Tank guns still sounded, and the direct-fire assault weapons, the two the Fritz had left. But that was nothing, now; silence rang in his ears, muffled, like cotton wool soaked in warm olive oil. Now he could catch the background: shattered bits of wall and fires burning, mostly, a great pillar of soot-black coming from the next street over. That was where the P-12 had crashed, when the Air Corps came in to give them support against the first wave. The Fritz had 88's and twin-30mm flakpanzers high up the shoulders of the valley; the cloud cover was at five hundred meters, low level attack was suicide. They had

come in anyway, with rockets and napalm; one had
lost control right above the village, and the explosion
had done as much damage as the Fritz shelling.
Another fire in the street outside: an SS personnel
carrier, simple thing, not much more than a thin
steel box on treads; the 15mm slugs from the heavy
machine gun had gone through it the long way. It
was still burning, in the middle of a round puddle of
sooty-orange flame from the ruptured fuel tanks. Prob-
ably rendered fat from the crew, too; the screaming
had stopped long ago, but he was glad that the dust
was cutting off most of the smell. Grit crunched
between his teeth and he spat again, black phlegm.

"Too soon," he muttered, as he came up beside
Sofie and spread the bipod of his Holbars. From
here you could *just* see down a little of the long
curve of the street: parts still blocked by houses on
either side, others merely a lower patch in a sea of
stone lumps, bits of broken timber, bodies, wrecked
vehicles. "Too soon to stop the shelling. Why?"

"Herr Standartenfuhrer, I just cannot raise them!"
The radioman in the command tank winced in
anticipation, but the SS commander's face remained
set. Voices were crackling in, demanding to know
why the artillery support had ceased. One minute,
magenta flashes and cedar-shaped blossoms of dust
white and black, walls collapsing, thunder echoing
back from the walls of the valley, fire. Now, *nothing*.

How should I know? his mind complained, as hands
levered him back into a sitting position in the turret
and he turned to look north and west. Futile, the
guns were behind the ridge and two kilometers away,
but instinct did not work on the scale of modern
warfare. He switched circuits.

"Weidner. Take two carriers, get back there and
find out what the problem is with those guns!" He

paused, considering. "Radioman, get me Pyatigorsk; perhaps *they* have a through connection."

Waiting, he turned to consider the remnants of the Circassian town. That was all that was left, the flanking trenches had been pounded out of existence. Shell-holes pocked the uneven surface of the fields, the shattered stumps that had been the orchards around it. Even now that the buildings were mostly battered down he could not see much past the first mounds of broken stone blocks, but columns of smoke pocked it; the sharp rattle of automatic fire, grenade-blasts, glimpses of moving vehicles. There were more of those south, up the valley—tanks and carriers moving past the ruins and onto the Ossetian Military Highway once more. Slowly, cautiously; the Draka had taught them that, and the special mine-clearing tanks were burning wreckage in the fields below the village.

Unwillingly, his eyes shifted down. More pillars of smoke from wrecks, far too many. Here a twisted mass after an ammunition explosion in a pierced hull; there a turret flipped forty meters from its tank, still gleaming wetly even though the rain had stopped hours ago. Another that had shed its track and turned helplessly in a circle as the length of flexible metal unreeled behind it; the crew lay where the machine-guns had caught them bailing out. Fuel and scorched metal, burnt flesh and explosive, wet dung-smell from the fields. More bodies lying in the glistening chewed-up grey mud, in straggling lines, in bits where the mines had gone off, singly and in clumps where they had been shot off the tanks they rode toward the buildings . . . His infantry had suffered even more than the tanks; many were still slow and exhausted from last night's ambush-fiasco in the woods. He flushed, hammering a hand into the side of the hatch.

"Lieber Herr *Gott*, how am I going to explain

this?" Professional reflex ran a tally in his head. A hundred tanks and assault guns yesterday at dawn; barely twenty now, and that was including the damaged ones that were still mobile. The infantry? Four hundred down, dead or with incapacitating wounds, many more still on their feet and carrying weapons who should be in hospital beds. He rammed the side of his hand into the solid steel again. *The transport, you had that shot out from under you last night, don't forget that.* All his painfully accumulated motor transport, most of his fuel supply, all of the specialized engineering and mine-clearing equipment except for the two machines burning before his eyes. Two mornings ago he had had a regimental combat group, a third of the strength of the best Panzer division Greater Germany could field. Two days of combat had destroyed it, and for what?

To overrun one single, reinforced company of light infantry, who even yet held out. "They will stand me up against a wall, and they will be right," he muttered, putting a hand to his bandaged head. He did not clearly remember how he had come to be lying unconscious in the mud, but whatever had hit him had come within a fraction of cracking his skull. Or might have indeed; the medic had not wanted to qualify him for duty, but there was no time for weakness. A benzedrine tablet had brought back alertness enough.

"What sort of trolls am I fighting? Why are they so hard to kill?" he continued, in the same inaudible murmur that barely moved his lips; the SS commander was unconscious of making any sound at all. Then in a sudden snarl: "Shoot!"

Crack and the 88mm gun of his tank cut loose. The long flash dazzled him for an instant, backblast drying the sweat on his face with an instant of chill-heat. He could feel the massive armored weight of the vehicle rock on its treads beneath him with the recoil, an almost sexual shuddering. Spray and bits of road surface flew up, droplets hissing on the muzzle-brake of the long probing gun. The tank was like a steel womb, warm and comforting, nothing like the dark clamminess of earth and stone. A glance skyward; the low cover was holding, a gift of Providence. With luck—

"Standartenfuhrer, H.Q. in Pyatigorsk."

"Ja." The voice of the regimental medical officer, with his heavy Dutch accent, sounded tinny in his ears, like someone from Hanover with a head cold. H.Q. had been completely stripped; he was senior officer, but Felix Hoth did not like it, or the Hollander. It was policy to accept kindred Nordics in the SS, but . . .

"Yes? Any report from the battery?"

"No, Standartenfuhrer."

That was suspicious; Oosterman always said "Sir" unless something had gone wrong. Unless he had done something wrong. Had the pig been into the medicinal drugs again? One more offense and it wouldn't be demotion, he would have him *shot*, and never mind that his sister was married to the head of the Dutch Nazi party. "What is it, man? Spit it out!"

"Your . . . the *osthilfe* volunteer Valentina, she is missing."

"*What!*" he screamed. Then his voice dropped to a flat tone that was far more menacing. "You are wasting time on a command circuit with news about subhuman Slavic whores?" You decadent cosmopolite pimp masquerading as a National Socialist, his mind added. It was time to *do* something about Oosterman, even if he did have protection.

"Standartenfuhrer, she left an antipersonnel mine in your quarters rigged to the door, four men were killed!"

He stopped himself just in time from barking "impossible." Even Oosterman would not dare to lie to him so, over an open circuit. "Continue," he said weakly.

"There was a written message."

"But . . . she cannot even *speak* decent German," the SS commander said in bewilderment. This—no, there was no time. "Condense it."

"It . . . Herr Standartenfuhrer, it lists our order of battle for the last six months, and, ah, is signed 'Comrade Lieutenant Valentina Fedorova Budennin, *Politruk* and Military Intelligence Officer, First Caucasian Partisan Brigade.' " There was gloating under the fear in the Dutchman's voice; Hoth the incorruptible would have some trouble explaining *this*.

The gunner of Hoth's tank had been peppering the village with machine-gun fire from the co-axial MG38, on general principle. Even over that ratcheting chatter, gunner and loader both heard the sound their commander made. They exchanged glances, and the loader crossed himself by unconscious reflex. Usually the gunner did not let that pass, being a firm neopagan and believer in Hoerbiger's ice-moon theory, the *Welteislehre*. This time he simply licked his lips in silence and turned back to the episcope, scanning for a target. The antitank weapons in the village frightened him, but he could shoot back at *them*.

"Forward, all reserve units, into the village, *kill* them." Hoth's voice rasped over the command circuit, with a catch and break halfway through the sentence.

"Sir." That was the squadron-commander. "Herr Standartenfuhrer, we have lost more than two-thirds of our strength, the enemy is neutralized and time is of the essence; why don't we just pass through the cleared lanes, and leave a blocking force to contain enemy survivors until the Army infantry comes up?"

"*That is an order!*"

A hesitation. "Jawohl. Zum befehl."

Hoth switched to the intercom. "Forward. Schnell!"

With a grunting diesel roar, the command tank threaded
its way around the huge crater in the road and the
circle of overturned fighting vehicles; the driver geared
down and began the long climb to the burning town.

Johanna flattened as the Fritz artillery fired, then
raised her head again. The noise was overwhelming,
as much a blow against the ears as a sound, echoing
from the hills and the blank wall of the forested
mountain behind her. The guns were spread out
along the narrow winding road: a two-lane country
track, barely good enough for an internal plantation
way in the Domination. The surface was broken,
beginning to disintegrate into mud—mud like the
soupy mass she was lying in, that coated her from
head to foot after the long night march through the
rain. It was nearly thirty hours since she had slept.
There had been nothing to eat but a heavy bread full
of husks; she belched, adding to the medley of stale
tastes in her mouth. The branches above were still
dripping, adding their load of wet misery to the grey
color of the day, and the pain in her neck had never
left her since the crash . . .

In the infantry after all, she thought disgustedly.
Knights of the Sky, bullshit.

A five-gun battery was firing from the little clear-
ing ahead of her, amid the hulks of burnt-out trucks
and a wrecked tank and old-looking roofless farm
buildings. The road fell away on the other side, but
there were more guns there, from the sound of it.
The guns themselves were simple field weapons,
long-barreled 170mm's mounted in open-topped boxes
atop modified Soviet tanks, nothing like the custom-
built models with enclosed turrets and 360-degree
traverse her own people used. But they were pump-
ing out death effectively enough, the recoil digging
the spades at the rear of the guns deeper into the
muck, crews dashing between the supply tractors

and the breeches, staggering back in pairs bearing
shell and charges in steel-rod carrying frames. The
men were stripped to the waist, sweating even in a
damp raw chill that let her see their breath as white
puffs around their heads. She shivered, and swal-
lowed again, her throat hot and scratchy.

"A cold," she muttered to herself. "Happiness,
happiness." They were close, close enough to see
liquid earth splash from the running feet of the near-
est crew . . .

The partisan, Ivan, crawled in beside her and put
his mouth to her companion's ear. He whispered:
unnecessarily, between the firing and the engines
they could have shouted without much risk of being
overheard, and the SS were fiercely concentrating on
their tasks. Valentina translated in a normal tone:
"Where are their infantry? That is most of the
Liebstandarte's Divisional artillery regiment, there
should be at least two companies for perimeter
defense."

How should I know? I'm a fighter pilot, Johanna
answered in her head. Aloud: "Up the valley,
attacking."

"If they've done that, Pyatigorsk should be wide
open." Valentina translated the remark, then an-
swered it herself before continuing to the Draka: "I
said again, there is no use in blowing up fuel depots
there if the Fritz come back victorious."

Ivan sighed, raised the flare-pistol he had bor-
rowed from her. Johanna tensed, bringing a leg be-
neath her and raising the machine pistol.

Eric, if you only knew, she thought. There was
none of the fear-exhilaration of aerial combat. *Just
plain fear,* went through her. She belched again, felt
her stomach rumble, tightened her rectum instinct-
ively. *Oh no, not that.* Eyes were on her: the Rus-
sians', her father's . . .

The flare went *pop,* pale against the massive muzzle flashes of the cannon. Three hundred partisans rose and threw themselves forward. *Urra! Urra!* Her feet pushed her upright and after them, gaining, in among the wet green-grey hulks, breathing their burnt-oil and propellant stink. Crewmen and gunners turned, snatching for personal weapons and pintle-mounted machineguns. Finger clenching, bucking weight in her hands, pingpingping across armorplate, a German falling with red splotches across his hair-matted chest, a silver crucifix winking.

Something struck the weapon in her hand. *Hard*: she spun, feet going out from under her on the slippery rock-strewn mud. A tread came up to meet her face, dun-colored mud on massive linked grey steel flecked with rust. Impact, earth, hands on her collar. Warmth, and a fading . . .

"Here they come," Eric said. Engine rumble and steel-squeal from around the curve. He sucked the last drops from the canteen and tossed it behind him. The tanks were visible now. A *line* of them, turrets traversed alternately to left and right; even as he watched, the first one fired into the base of a building and the walls collapsed, straight down with an earthquake rumble. The tank came on through the cloud of debris, its machineguns winking from turret and ball-mount in the glacis plate of the bow. Rounds went *crack* overhead, tracer drawing lines through the air where he would have been if he had stood. Then the second tank in line fired into the ruin on the opposite side of the road, and the others. They were going to repeat that, all the way to the central square. Then back out again, until nothing moved; then they would squat on the ruins, while foot soldiers searched for the entrances. After that, it would be like pouring insecticide down a broken ant heap . . .

"Neal!" he called. "That last round, make it count!"

Eight tanks, probably with infantry following up behind. Eight was nearly half of what the Fritz had left; unfortunately, Century A had run out of antitank just slightly before the enemy ran out of tanks.

"Yep."

It might have been marksman's instinct that brought the heavyset rocket gunner to her knees for a better aiming point, or a coldly calculated risk. A mistake, in either case; a machinegun bullet punched her back just as her finger stroked the trigger. The rocket lanced into the already holed personnel carrier five meters before the moving tank, slewing it around and actually clearing the road for the advancing SS armor.

"We'll never stop them now." Eric did not know who had made that statement, but there was no reason to doubt it; heading back into the bunker would be simply a slower form of death. Neal's heels drummed on the clinking rubble for an instant, then were still. The beams overhead had begun to burn, set alight by a stray incendiary round. Long and slim, the barrel of the lead tank's 88 was swinging around to bear on them.

"They'll never stop them," Trooper Huff said. There was nobody else alive on the rooftop across the laneway from Eric's position to hear her. She looked down at Meier's slumped body; if the burst had come up through the floorboards a few centimeters farther right, it would have struck her instead. As it was— She forced herself to look down at the wound in her thigh; there were bone splinters in the pulped red-and-purple wound, and the blood was runneling down past her clenched hands. Shock was keeping out the worst of the pain, but that would come. If the blood loss did not kill her first; she estimated that at no more than two minutes, with unconsciousness in less.

The centurion was across the way, with five others. And Patton.

"Heavy," she muttered, fumbling at the dead trooper's body. She had had an improvised antitank weapon with her, a bundle of unscrewed grenade heads strapped around an intact stick-grenade with a bungie-cord. *Suicide system*, she thought: that was the nickname for it. "Scarcely applies nahw, do it?"

The journey to the edge of the roof was endless, her wet fingers fumbling with the tab of the grenade. She imagined, that she could hear it sizzling, once she pulled the button. *Up, use it like a crutch, gotta see t' place dang thing . . .*

The second tank had an alert pair of eyes head-and-shoulders out of the hatch, with the pintle-mounted MG38 ready to swing; that was one reason for the in-echelon formation. There is a natural tendency to fire too high when aiming up; still, the first round of the burst took Huff just above the nose, and left with her helmet and much of the top of her skull. The bundle of grenades dropped at her feet, harmless except to corpse and roof; the body twisted off the edge, turned once and landed broken-backed across the hull of the wrecked personnel carrier below. Blood and pink-grey brain dripped into the burning oil, hissing.

"They shot Huff! The dirty bastards shot Huff!" Patton's voice cracked. Then she was moving, fast and very smooth, scooping up the satchel charge, arming it, hurdling the low wall into the street and across it while bullets flicked sparks around her feet. Less a dash than a long leap, screaming, a forward roll *through* the puddle of flame that surrounded the wreck. Still screaming as she vaulted with her uniform and hair burning onto the deck, three steps down it with the plating booming, over the body, diving into the air head-first toward the SS panzer. A shrieking torch that the green tracer slapped out of the air to fall beneath the treads. The satchel charge detonated.

Tank designers crowd their heaviest plating onto the areas that are likely to need it: the mantlet that holds the gun, the glacis plate at the bow, the frontal arc of the turret. Not much is left for the rear deck . . . or the bottom of the hull. The satchel charge held twenty pounds of plastique, confined between the forty-four ton weight of the tank and the unyielding ground. Thin plating buckled as the globe of hot gas expanded; there was no *time* for it to go elsewhere. Pieces of it bounced through the fighting compartment, slicing, supersonic. Fire touched the wrenched-open cases of 88mm ammunition on the floor of the panzer, still nearly a combat load.

The first explosion bounced the tank onto its side and threw it across the road, a huge armored plug across the laneway. The second opened the hole in its belly into a splayed-out puncture wound, like a tin can left too long in the fire. Yet the hull barely moved; recoil balanced recoil as the turret and its basket blew out the other side of the vehicle, flying twenty meters down the laneway and demolishing a wall with its ten-ton weight. Surprise froze the Draka for a moment. Eric recovered first.

"Back down, back down, quick, go go *go*," he shouted, slapping shoulders and legs as they went by him, back toward the narrow opening at the rear of the room. Already, figures in camouflage uniforms were trying to edge past the blockage of the wrecked tank, and he snapped a burst at them. They fell; hurt or taking cover was impossible to say even at ten meters' distance as thick metallic-smelling smoke drifted across his eyes. The pain of the Holbars hammering against his raw shoulder brought him back to himself, and he slithered feet-first to the opening. Hands caught and assisted him; they half-fell into the welcome gloom, scrambling back beyond a dog-leg that kept them safe from a grenade tossed down their bolthole.

"Back to the radio room, this is it, it's over, we've got to tell Legion H.Q. and then get out. Split up and carry the word, south end and bug out to the woods, *move*, people." They paused for a single instant, dim gleams of teeth in faces negro-black with soot and dirt. "Good work," he added quietly, before spinning and diving through the next ragged gap. "Fuckin' good."

Dreiser felt very lost in the dark tunnel. Everybody else had seemed to know what to do, even when the order went out to scatter; he clutched the precious tapes through the fabric of his jacket and lurched into a bank of stone jags. For a moment pain blinded him in the echoing dark, then hands gripped him and jerked him aside through an L-angle where one cellar joined another through an improvised passage. A palm clapped over his mouth, hard and calloused.

"Shuddup," hissed into his ear, as he was passed through another set of hands and parked against a wall. The American struggled to control his breathing, feeling his heart lurching between his ribs; that might have been a bullet or a dagger. Fighting a feeling of humiliation as well: he was *tired* of being handled like a rag doll. The blackness was absolute, silence broken by dripping water and the distant explosions. Then hobnails rutching on stone, and closer a long, faint *schnnnng* sound, a bush knife being drawn from its sheath. Dreiser found himself holding his breath without concious decision.

A light clicked on: only a handlight, but blinding to dark-accustomed eyes. It shone directly into the faces of the two Germans who had turned the corner. They had been keeping close to the right-hand wall, facing forward; the Draka were on the left, across the two-meter width and parallel to their opponents. Nearest to Dreiser was the woman with the bush knife, reaching as the light came on. Her left hand jerked the SS trooper forward by the blouse while the right thrust the two-foot blade forward, tilted up. Dreiser could see the German's face spasm, hear the wet slicing and grating sound as she twisted the broad machete blade and withdrew it in a wrenching, motion. The next Draka was a man, tall enough to stoop slightly under the seven-foot roof. He merely slammed a fist forward as the German turned toward him; it connected with the SS man's face, and the Draka was wearing warsaps. Bone crunched under the metal-reinforced glove, and the German's helmet rang as his head bounced backward and rebounded off stone.

The third Draka had been kneeling nearest the L-junction. He dropped the light as his comrades struck, swept up his assault rifle, and fired. Dreiser blinked in puzzlement. The curve was sharp, there was no direct line of fire at the room beyond, and the paratrooper was firing *up*. Then the American followed the line of tracer up to the groined vault of the ceiling: continuous fire, long, ten-second bursts, the roar of the shots in the enclosed space of the cellar almost hiding the whining ping of the ricochets. His mind drew a picture of the narrow stone reach beyond the exit, bullets sawing back and forth . . . There were screams from around the corner now, and the sound of bodies falling, and blind crashing retreat. The morale of the SS men was growing shaky.

And no wonder, Dreiser thought, wiping an arm across his face. The slightest misjudgment or ill luck and those metal wasps could have come bouncing back into this section of tunnel; that risk was why the fighting below was mostly cold steel or cautious grenades. The Draka gunman was shaking the empty drum out of his Holbars, snapping in a fresh one with a contented grin but leaving the bolt back to allow the chamber to cool. Darkness returned as he snapped out the light. There was a moaning, then the sound of a boot stamping on a throat, as unbearable as fingernails on slate.

"C'mon, Yank," one of them said. "We'll drop yo' at the aid station. Clear path from there to the south end. Lessn' yo' meets cousin Fritz, a'course."

My morale would be shot, too, the correspondent's musing continued as he coughed raw cordite fumes out of his throat and stumbled along with the retreating troopers. The Draka were nearly as deadly as they thought they were, and they never gave up; hunting them down here would be like going blindfolded and armed only with a spear into a maze full of tigers.

Tigers with the minds of men.

"Nobody in here but the wounded!" Dreiser shouted, in German. The cellar beneath the mosque was the aid station; his post the only place a noncombatant could do any good. The darkness was thick with muffled noise, or the louder shouts of the delirious, but he had heard the SS men talking in the next chamber. And "grenade" was hard to miss. "We surrender!"

A cautious hand and head came through, flicked on a torch, speared Dreiser where he stood plastered against a wall, zigzagged briefly across the rows of bandaged figures.

"*Ja*," the German barked over his shoulder, and another figure with a Schmeisser followed. Perhaps it was the dim glow, but the American thought he could see the strain of fighting in this warren on their faces, death waiting in cramped blackness like the inside of a closet. They straightened, relaxing.

"Hande hoche!" one said to the American, tucking the grenade back into his belt.

"I am an American war correspondent," Dreiser began. The burst of automatic fire caught him almost as much by surprise as it did the two SS troopers it smashed back against the stone.

The flashlight fell, bounced, did not break as it came to rest on the stomach of a staring red-headed corpse, lighting the expression of shocked amazement on her freckled face. The glow diffused quickly in the dusty air, but Dreiser could see a head that was a ball of bandage with a slit for the eyes, and the muzzle of the Holbars poking through the blankets that had concealed it. The head eased back down to its pack-pillow, and the assault rifle dropped out of sight again.

"Keep . . ." a halt, and a grunt. "Keep 'em comin', Yank."

"No answer," Sofie said. She and Eric were alone now in what had been the command bunker, except for the corpse of the sapper in one corner. It *felt* abandoned, colder somehow, darker despite the constant blue glow and the flicker of lights from the radio at which the comtech labored. A burst of assault-rifle fire echoed on the stone, bringing their heads up.

"Scan the cohort and tetrarchy frequencies, then," he said, laying down his Holbars to load the bandoliers with extra drums. "Quick."

Her fingers turned the dials; static, German voices, then snatches:

"Sir, sir, come in, *please*." A young voice, tight-held. "Sir, the centurion went out half an hour ago and didn't come back, I can hear them talking in Fritz outside the door, what'm I supposed to—" Shots, static.

"Fall back to the green line an' regroup, fall back—"

This is Palm One, Palm One, I've got Fritz armor coming at me from north'n south both, I'm spikin' mah guns and pullin' out, over." A decisive click.

Sofie abandoned the radio, tearing off the headset and throwing it at the communications gear, turning to him with a snarl.

"That's *it?*" she said, her voice shrill. "That's *it?* It was all fo' *nothin'?*"

"It's never for nothin', Sofie," he said gently. "We fight for each other; the job is what we do together." Sharply: "Now *move*, soldier!"

"*Shit!*" The obstacle was soft, and might once have lived. Eric tripped, and his hand came down into something yielding and wet. "Light, Sofie." They had to risk that; information was worth a brief stop. A click, and he was blinking down into the turned-up face of the old Circassian, the *Hadj*. Something had sliced halfway through his skull, something curved that pulled out raggedly and spilled the brain that had seen Mecca and spent fifty years in a losing fight to protect his people. The Draka recognized the signs: a sharpened entrenching-tool swung like an axe, not popular among the Domination's forces, who preferred the ancestral bush knife. He hoped it was not one of his who had killed the old man, in a moment of fear or frustration. Grunting, he knelt up and turned to look at Sofie.

And froze. The shovel gleamed beyond her head, held like a spear in a two-handed grip, point down and ready to chop into her back. *No firing angle* went through him, as he watched the reflected light glint on the honed edges. But the weapon was trembling, and it had not fallen. Sofie saw the fear in his eyes, checked her turning motion before it began at his lips' silent command. He could see her face glisten, but the hand with the torch did not shake, or even move.

Slowly, slowly, Eric came to his feet. *No aggressive movement*, he thought, with a sudden huge calm. He could not afford to fail, and therefore he would not. Not now, or ever. Up, half-crouch, erect. There was a German behind her, standing rigid as a statue save for the trembling of the hands clenched on the haft of the spade. The underlit face quivered as well, lumps of muscle jerking under the skin, tears pouring down through dirt and soot, cutting clear tracks down from the wide-held eyes, a swath of bandage covering the back of his head. White all around the iris, pupils enormous, staring through time and space. It was eerie to hear words coming from that face; it was as if a statue had spoken, or a beast.

"You . . . killed them," he said. "You. You."

Standartenfuhrer, Eric thought, reading the tabs. Meeting the eyes was more of a strain than he would have believed possible; like peering inside one of the locked, red-glowing tombs of Dante's hell. The Draka spoke very softly, in the other's language, as much to himself as to his enemy.

"Yes. *We* killed them, all of them, both of us." The other's face seemed to change, and the uplifted spade wavered. Eric extended his left hand to Sofie; hers joined, the palm warm and dry against the wet chill of his. She turned, facing the German.

"Inge—Ingeborg?" he asked. It was a different voice, a boy's. "What are you doing here? This is Moscow—this is no place for you." The shovel came down to the stone with a light *clink*, and something went out of the man. Eric and Sofie took a step backward, and another; there was nothing to prevent the centurion from using the Holbars hanging at waist level in its assault-sling. Nothing physical, at least. The SS man faded out of their circle of light.

"I am not afraid," he said, in a conversational tone. "Not afraid of the dark, Ingeborg. Not any more. Not any more."

The panzer rumbled toward them as they turned the corner at the south end of the village; the steel helmets of infantry riders showed behind its massive turret. There was no escape, not even back to the tunnels.

Sofie cursed and scrabbled for her weapon, feeling even more naked now that the familiar weight of the backpack radio was gone. Eric controlled his impulse to dive for cover; what point, now?

So tired, he thought, raising the Holbars. One of the soldiers stood, black face dull grey in the overcast afternoon light.

"*Black* face?" Eric said, as the man shed his German helmet and stood, waving a rifle that was twin to the one in the Draka's arms. A vast white grin split his face as he leaped to earth. The rest of his *lochos* followed, spreading out and deploying past the two Draka toward the ruins and the sound of the guns.

The turret of the tank popped open, and another man stiff-armed himself out of the hatch. A Draka, thin, sandy-haired, with twin gold earrings and the falconer's-glove shoulderflash worn by Citizen officers commanding the Domination's serf soldiers.

"Hey, point thayt-there somewheres else," he called. "This here a *ruse*, my man. A plot, a wile, a *stratagem* y'know." There were more vehicles behind the tank with its Liebstandarte markings, light eight-wheeled personnel carriers, *Peltast*-class.

"The Janissaries," Sofie said, in a voice thick with tears. "Oh, how I love the sight of their jungleboy faces." A warm presence at his side, and an arm about his waist. "And you, Eric."

"Me too, Sofie, me too," he said. The Holbars fell to earth with a clatter. "And, oh, gods, I want to sleep."

Shapes were coming down the road to the south, low broad tanks whose armor was all smooth acute slopes. A huge wedge-shaped turret pivoted, the long 120mm gun drooping until he could almost see

the grooves spiraling up it; he could make out the
unit blazon on the side of the turret, an armored
gauntlet crushing a terrestrial globe in its fist: the
Archonal Guard. A flash, the crack of the cannon a
moment later. Clatter as the split halves of the light-
metal sabot that had enfolded the APDS round fell to
earth five meters beyond the muzzle; from down
range a fractional second later the heavy chunnnk! of
a tungsten-carbide penetrator slapping into armor.

We won, Eric thought, more conscious of the warm
strong shoulders in the circle of his arm. It might be
years, this was a big war, but nothing could stop
them now. Victory.

Victory had the taste of tears.

There were fifty members of Century A left, when
the medics had taken the last of the seriously wounded;
enough casualties were coming in from the direction
of Pyatigorsk that walking-wounded would be left
until there was spare transport to evacuate them all
to the rear. The Ossetian Military Highway was bear-
ing a highway's load, an unending stream of Hond
III tanks and Hoplite APC's, ammunition carriers and
field ambulances and harried traffic coordinators. The
peculiar burbling throb of turbocompound engines
filled the air, and bulldozers were already working,
piling rubble from the ruins of the village to be used
for road repair when time permitted.

The noise was deafening, even inside the shat-
tered remnants of the mosque, where walls still rose
on three sides. Especially when the multiple rocket
launchers of the Archonal Guard Legion cut loose
from their positions in the fields just to the south,
ripple-firing on their tracked carriages, painting the
clouds above with streaks of violet fire like a silk
curtain across the sky. The explosions of their 200mm
warheads on the Fritz positions eight kilometers to
the north echoed back, grumbling, from mountains

shrouded in cloud like a surf of fire, glittering like
sun on tropical spray, each shell paced with a score
of submunitions, bomblets. Behind them came the
deeper bark of the self-propelled 155mm gun-howitzers.

"I—" Eric began, looking around the circle of
faces. There was no one there but his own people;
they had taken the medical help and the rations and
nobody had cared to intrude further. Or to object to
Dreiser's presence.

"I—" he rubbed a hand over his face, rasping on
the stubble, feeling an obscure shame at the grins
that answered him. "Oh, shit, people, congratula-
tions. We made it." A cheer, that he shouted down.
"Shut up, I got the most of us killed!"

"Bullshit again, sir. That was the Fritz, near as I
recall," said McWhirter, a splinted leg stretched out
before him, leaning on his crutch. "You saw the job
got done." More laughter, and he shook his head,
turning away and wiping at his eyes.

"I'm turning into a fuckin' sentimentalist, Bill," he
said. The American shut his notebook with a snap
and stood.

"Not likely, Eric," he said, and extended his hand.
"And my thanks, too. For what will be the story of a
lifetime if I'm lucky!" More seriously: "It's time I
went home, I think. I have things to do; but I won't
forget, even if we have to be enemies someday."

"We may," said Eric quietly, gripping his hand.
"But I won't forget either. If only because this is the
place where I learned I have things to do, as well."
He glanced over at Sofie, smoking a cigarrette and
leaning against the scrap of wall. She met his eye,
winked, blew a kiss. "Other reasons as well, but that
mainly."

"Things to do?" Dreiser said, carefully controlling
eagerness. He had more than a reporter's curiosity,
he admitted to himself. Eric's face was different; not
softer but . . . more animated, somehow.

"I'm going to write those books we talked about, Bill. Got a more def'nite idea of them now. Also . . ." he drew on his own cigarette ". . . I've about decided to go into politics, after the war."

"Good!" Dreiser clapped him on the shoulder. "With someone like you in charge, there could be some much-needed *changes* in this Domination of yours."

Eric stared at him for a moment, then burst into laughter, fisting him lightly on the shoulder. "Don't look so astonished, my friend; I was just reflecting on how . . . how *American* that was. How American yo 're, under that reporter's cynicism you put on."

Slightly nettled, the correspondent raised a brow.

"How much of a believer in 'Progress'," Eric amplified, his face growing more serious. "An individualist, a meliorist, an optimist, a moralist; someone who doesn't really believe that History can happen to them . . ." Another flight of rockets went overhead, cutting off all conversation for the ninety seconds the salvo took to launch. Eric von Shrakenberg propped a foot on the tumbled stone of the mosque and leaned on his knee, watching the armored fist of the Domination punching northward; the turrets of the tanks turning with a blind, mechanical eagerness, infantry standing in the open hatches of their carriers. The noise sank back to bearable levels.

"Which shows me how much of a Draka *I* am. A believer in the ultimate importance of what you Will; that what life is about is the achievement of honor through the fulfillment of duty." He smiled again, affection rather than amusement, the expression turned slightly sinister by the yellowing green of his bruises. "I always loved my people, Bill; enough to die for them. Now, well, I've found more to *like* about them. Enough to work and live for them, if I can.

"Bill—" his hand tightened on his knee, "*nothing* is inevitable. The Draka have always been a hard people; we're a nation of masters, oppressors, if you will. But it's a human evil, limited by what human beings can do. I've tried to look into our future, Bill; I've seen . . . possibilities that even *Security's* headhunters would puke at, if they had the imagination. Read Naldorssen again someday, only imagine a science that could make her ravings something close to reality." He made a grimace of distaste. "It doesn't *have* to be that way."

Dreisér frowned. "Like I said, Eric: changes."

"Oh, Bill." The Draka crushed his cigarette out underfoot. " 'To desire the end is to desire the means: if you are not prepared to do what is necessary to achieve it, you never wanted it at all.' *That's* a Draka philosophy I believe in. To have any chance at prominence at all, I'll have to gain my people's respect in the way they understand. Doin' . . . questionable things." His face went hard, and a hand chopped out over the village, to a fragment of wall that stood forlornly upright. "*This*! It isn't enough to be willing to die for my people, I have to be willing to *kill* for them. It's what they know an' respect.

"And changes? At best, with a lifetime's effort, if I'm *very* smart an' *very* lucky, I can hope to . . . lay the beginnings of the foundations for others to build on. Delusions of omnipotence is one national vice I haven't fallen prey to. For a beginning, for the Draka to change they'd have to stop bein' afraid, which means all their external enemies are defeated. Then maybe they could face the internal one with something besides a *sjambok*. I know—" more softly "—I know it can be done on an individual scale. Then, perhaps in a hundred or a thousand years—"

Reliable operative, the Security Directorate Chiliarch thought. *Yo' want reliable, do it yourself.*

He was surprised at how . . . alarming the offensive was, at close range. Especially now that they were passing the forward artillery parks; even inside the scout car's armor, the noise was defening. Still, it all ought to be over soon. Then back to Archona, back to the center of things. With a kudu on his dossier that the ultimate masters would note.

The old fool's past it, he thought with satisfaction, then cursed as the car lurched. They were driving well off the shoulder of the road, away from the priority traffic pouring down from the heights of Caucasus.

Did he really expect I'd let him have the credit for this?

Eric looked up as the three ragged figures limped into the ruined mosque. *Ivan the partisan, by almighty Thor!* he thought, looking around for Dreiser. The American was deep in his notebooks; time enough to roust him out later. It would be tricky to get the Russian survivors out, but not impossible; he had heard the awe in the voices of the relieving troops, and the legend would grow. Such myths were useful to the Domination. *And to me, in this case.*

There were two others with the Russian—women, one in muddied finery that could not disguise an almost startling loveliness, the other in the wreck of an Air Corps flight suit, cut away for the bandages that covered right arm and leg and that side of her face. She was tall, hair yellow-blonde, visible eye grey . . .

Sofie let out a squawk as his grip on her hand grew crushing; then he was running as if his fatigue had vanished, nimble over the uncertain ground.

"Johanna!" he shouted. At the last moment he checked his embrace, careful of her wounds; hers was one-armed, tentative. Held close her body felt somehow more fragile, the familiar odor of her sweat mixed with a sharp medicinal smell.

"How bad is it?" he asked, holding her at arm's length.

"Goddam wonderful, I'm *alive*," she said, reaching out to grasp him by the torn lapels of his tunic. "An' so are you." She pushed her hands gently against his chest. "I'm glad, my brother." More briskly: "They told me I'd probably keep the eye, know in a year or two, fly a desk until then. Who's this glarin' at me?"

Sofie saluted. "Monitor Tech-Two Nixon . . ." She peered more closely at the other Draka's name tag. "Oh, yo're his *sister*. Hell, I'm Sofie." She grinned, and rattled off a sentence in Russian to the two partisans.

Eric opened his mouth to speak, closed it again slowly as he looked over their shoulders. Two vehicles were bouncing through the uneven surface where the entrance of the mosque had been: not large, simple flattened wedges of steel plate with four soft pillow-tires, but green painted, with the Security Directorate's badge on their flanks. They halted, and metal pinged and cooled. The rear doors opened, and three figures disembarked. The drivers' heads showed through the hatches: serfs, carefully disinterested. The others . . . two Intervention Squad troopers, and an officer. Not any type of field man; the uniform was far too neat, the boots polished, ceremonial whip at his belt and an attaché case in one hand.

Political Section, Police Zone Division, Eric thought. *A Chiliarch, they're doing me proud.*

The others looked around. "Headhunters," Sofie said.

"Shit," Johanna added. "Metaphorically an' descriptively."

"Well, well, well," McWhirter said. The survivors of Century A had closed in a semicircle about the secret police vehicles. "Aren't you people a *lot* closer to the sharp end a' things than yo' like?"

"Right." That was Marie Kaine. "Of course, so far back from the front, the brain tends to be ninety percent asshole, anyway; maybe they got lost."

Eric raised a hand, a quiet gesture that stilled the muttering. "Let me guess—" he began.

"No need for guessing here, von Shrakenberg," the secret policeman said. "We've been watching; we always are. Ah am requirin' you to accompany me for investigations under Section IV of the Internal Security Act of 1907, which provides for detention by administrative procedure, for—"

" '—actions or thoughts deemed prejudicial to the security of the State'—yes, Chiliarch, I'm familiar with it." *Nearly having been its victim once before.* "I also recall legislation statin' that members of the Citizen Force on active service in a war zone may only be arrested by the military police, for arraignment or trial before a duly constituted court-martial."

The Chiliarch was a thin man, with a redhead's complexion despite his dark hair and pencil mustache. "Don't try to play the lawyer with me, von Shrakenberg! Yo'd be well advised to take a cooperative attitude—*well* advised. Now, come along; this isn't an arrest, merely a detention for investigation. Yes, and the American too. And—" his eyes noticed Valentina Budennin, and his mouth smiled "—yes, this Russian too. I'll interrogate at our field headquarters in Kars. We'll round up the rest of these 'partisans' in due course."

Eric was silent for a long moment. The sounds in the background seemed to recede, dying down into a murmur no louder than the blood in his ears. *Well,* he thought.

"Y'know, Chiliarch," he said conversationally. "I think yo'd be surprised at the direction those subversive thoughts of mine have been taking. I *learned* something here."

The police agent snorted. "What, pray tell?" They might have to restrain him after all.

Eric indicated the ring of soldiers. "That these are my people. Killers? Yes. But they have courage, and honor, and love and loyalty to each other. Those are real virtues, and on that something can be built, something can grow."

He drew the Walther P-38 that was still thrust into the waistband of his battle harness.

The two Security troopers had come expecting an arrest, not combat. Yet they were Draka, too; their rifles came up with smooth speed to cover Eric. Policemen's reflex, that let them ignore the two-score paratroopers within arm's reach, and a fatal mistake. One managed to get a burst off, cracking the air over the security Chiliarch's head. There was a moment of scuffling, a meaty *thud*, a wet *schunk* sound; the secret policeman wheeled to see the Security troopers going down, and the bayonets flashing again and again. Two of Century A's survivors were staggering away, one clutching white-faced at a broken arm, the other squeezing at a stab wound in his thigh; the Century's own medics were moving forward.

"The drivers, too," Eric called coolly. "No noise." He averted his eyes slightly as the two serfs were dragged from their hatches and their throats slit. They submitted in stunned silence, one jerking and bleating as the steel went home.

"Where was I?" Eric continued to the secret policeman. "Sayin' that the 'convenient accident' in a moment of confusion can work both ways? Pity about yo're party runnin' into those Fritz holdouts. Or extending my analysis. Ah, yes. From *them* something can be built, in time. What you are is a disease, and the only thing yo'll ever produce is rot."

The Security agent turned back again; his face was even paler now, about the lips, but his voice was steady.

"I *know* you, it's all in the dossier! You don't have the guts—"

Eric shot him, low through the stomach. He dropped, unbelieving eyes fixed on the red leak between his fingers, legs limp from a shattered spine. The centurion felt Sofie's arm go about his waist. His left arm looped over her shoulders.

"Thanks, Sofie," he said, and looked up at the rest of them. "Thanks, all of you."

"Hell," Marie Kaine said. "It's a long way to the Atlantic Coast and the end of the war, Eric. We all want yo' in charge till then."

Suffering eyes turned up to him, over a gaping mouth that soon would scream.

Make an end, do it clean, he thought. "And there's one thing you should never have forgotten," he said to the man who had come to arrest him. "Whatever *else* I may be, I'm still a von Shrakenberg." The pistol barked.

TIMELINE OF THE DOMINATION

[Places are listed under their Draka-timeline names. Their equivalent in our history is given in parenthesis on first mention. Thus Virconium (Durban, South Africa); Shahnapur (Maputo, Mozambique); etc. Events prior to 1783 with an outcome different from that in our history are marked, thus*.]

1776 — Outbreak of American Revolution. Major Patrick Ferguson invents early breechloading rifle.

1779 — France, Spain, Netherlands* declare war on Great Britain.

1779 — British fleet under Admiral Lord Cochrane lands occupying force in Capetown.*

1780 — Colonel Ferguson's loyalists victorious in battle of King's Mountain.* Several Loyalist units, including Tarleton's Legion and the newly formed Ferguson's Legion, re-equipped with Ferguson breechloaders.* Savage partisan warfare throughout Southern colonies.

1781 — General Cornwallis besieged at Yorktown in Virginia, surrenders to American rebels and their French allies.

1782 –   British naval victories in Caribbean, occupation of Haiti and Trinidad.*

1783 –   Second Peace of Paris. American independence recognized; British Florida and her conquests in Caribbean are exchanged for possession of Dutch Cape Colony.*

1783 –   Loyalty Acts passed by British Parliament: the Cape is renamed the Crown Colony of Drakia, and all colonials who fought or otherwise suffered for their loyalty to the Crown are offered transport and land grants; so are the Hessian and other German mercenaries in British service at the time. Legislative Assembly meets in Capetown. General Patrick Ferguson is first Governor-General.

1780–83 – First Loyalist refugees arrive in Capetown. Conquest of Southern Africa begun; border pushed to Tugela River.

1783–86 – 95,000 Loyalists and their families (not including some 10,000 slaves) arrive; 10,000 Hessians soon follow, with relatives and families arriving in a steady trickle from Germany. At this time the Dutch-Afrikaner population is less than 9,000, and is soon assimilated through intermarriage.

1784 –   Founding of Virconium (Durban, South Africa), and Venta Belgarum (East London, South Africa). General Banastare Tarleton becomes first Commander-in-Chief.

1783–84 – Volcanic eruptions devastate Iceland. 25,000 Icelanders offered asylum in Drakia, arriving 1783–86.

1784 –   Diamonds discoverd in northern interior.
            Founding of Archona (Pretoria, South Africa).

1785 –   Gold discovered on Whiteridge (Whitwater-
            strand) and in eastern Archona Province
            (Transvaal). First steam engines imported.
            Output reaches 1,000,000 ounces by 1786.

1786 –   Drakian Legislative Assembly passes Inden-
            tured Labor and Master and Servant Acts,
            establishing system of debt-peonage for con-
            quered nonwhite population. This rapidly
            becomes indistinguishable from chattel slav-
            ery, which is also practiced.

1786–90 – Rapid growth of economy and population.
            Export trades in diamonds, gold, copper,
            sugar, wool, salt, hides, ivory, etc., estab-
            lished. Drakian ships active in Atlantic and
            Indian Ocean slave trades. Zanzibar seized
            in 1789; Aden, 1791. Free population reaches
            175,000; slave/serf 2,000,000. Transportation
            Directorate established to build road net-
            work to mines and settlements of far interior.

1788 –   Colonel Freiherr Augustus von Shrakenberg
            retires, receives 20,000 acre land grant un-
            der Maluti Mountains, South Interior prov-
            ince (Lesotho). Marries Alexandra Hugeson,
            of a New Jersey loyalist family.

1790–92 – Universities of Cape Town, Virconium, and
            Archona founded. Anglican bishoprics es-
            tablished in Cape Town and Virconium.

1792 –   Conquest of Northmark (Rhodesia/Zimbabwe);
            settlement and development proceed. Gold
            output exceeds 2,000,000 ounces annually.

1793 –   *First coal mine in northern Natalia. Out-
            break of French Revoulutionary/Napoleonic
            wars.*

1790–96 –   *Period of rapid growth continues, with seri-
            ous slave/serf revolts in 1792, 1794 and
            1795–97. Slave Code of 1797 grants all free-
            men power of life and death over "slaves and
            other bondservants." Militia Act of 1792 es-
            tablishes peacetime conscription and reserve
            service to age 60. Women's Militia Auxiliary
            founded as volunteer group. First Janissary
            Legion recruited from slaves bought in West
            Africa.*

1795 –   *African Mining and Metals Combine founded.
            Granted monopoly of large-scale mining,
            leases smaller deposits to discoverers. School
            of Mines founded in Archona.*

1796 –   *Richard Trevithick arrives in Virconium from
            Cornwall, appointed Inspector-General of
            Steam Engines by Mining Combine.*

1799 –   *Founding of Diskarapur (Newcastle, South
            Africa) and Shahnapur (Maputo, Mozam-
            bique). Trade with India produces fad for
            Persian/Moghul artwork.*

1794–97 –   *French population of Santo Domingo/Haiti
            flees before slave revolt. 11,000 arrive in
            Drakia. Royalists from European France
            follow.*

1800 –   *Free population reaches 350,000. First iron-
            works, machine shops, shipbuilding yards
            started as Revolutionary/Napoleonic wars
            render imports uncertain. Cotton becomes*

important crop. Large-scale public works in roads, harbors, irrigation.

1800–02 – Conquest of Egypt (occupied by French) and Ceylon, a possession of Dutch Republic allied with France. French colonies in West Africa seized.

1803 –   Revolt in Egypt suppressed; 300,000 rebels deported to Sinai work camps to begin construction of Suez Canal.

1803 –   High-pressure steam engine perfected by Richard Trevithick. Construction of Archona-Virconium railway line begins in 1805.

1804 –   First steam "drags" (trucks) and steamships.

1807 –   Ottoman Empire declares war on Britain due to Drakian refusal to evacuate Egypt. Drakian forces seize Cyprus, Crete, Tunisia. Suez Canal completed.

1812 –   Americans overrun and annex British North America.

1815–16 – Peace of Vienna confirms Africa as British/ Drakian preserve. Portuguese colonies of Angola and Mozambique purchased. British veterans and Napoleonic refugees immigrate. Madagascar conquered.

1820 –   Cache of papyrus manuscripts found in Western Desert by Drakian Camel Corps patrol. Virtually all lost works of Classical literature and philosophy recovered (e.g., Sappho, Euripides, Aristotle, etc.). Classical revival affects Drakian culture. Foundation of Alex-

andria; growth of Combines. Petroleum first used as motor fuel, 1831.

1820–40 – *Rapid growth of export agriculture and manufacturing/transport. Abolitionist groups in England and northern U.S. begin cultural/political campaign against Drakia for alleged "depravity" and other violations of Victorian middle-class norms. This produces defiant anti-bourgeois sentiment in Drakia. Thomas Carlyle emigrates to Drakia.*

1800–40 – *"Drakia" becomes elided to "Draka" in popular usage. Free population reaches 1,000,000. Conquest of North Africa requires mobilization of over 150,000 men for most of period 1825–1850. Increased employment of citizen women produces legal reforms, franchise agitation.*

1848–49 – *Mexican-American War. "Young America" faction forces annexation of all of Mexico over objections of President Polk.*

1850 – *First transcontinental railway (Shahnapur-Luanda). Katanga copper discovered. Mombasa-Nile line built. Conquest of Sudan and Senegal. Brass-cartridge repeating rifle adopted by Draka forces. R.J. Gatling settles in Diskarapur, develops world's first practical machinegun.*

1854–57 – *Draka expeditionary forces assist British in Crimean War and Indian Mutiny. Dominion of Draka Act, 1858, grants "responsible government" to Draka (practical sovereignty in effect). Hall process patented by Ferrous Metals Combine, enables steel to be pro-*

duced as cheaply as wrought iron. Rival
Bessemer method quickly eclipsed.

1854 –   Cuba, Philippines, Hawaii, Haiti, and Santo
Domingo annexed by United States. Japan
opened to Western trade. "Empire of Cen-
tral America" established by Southern ad-
venturers under command of William Walker;
extends from Guatemala to Panamanian ter-
ritories seized from Columbia.

1860–1866 American Civil War begins as President
Douglas bombards Savannah. Dominion of
Draka provides massive clandestine aid—
repeating rifles, gatling guns, steam warships,
steam-powered warcars—to Confederacy.
Union casualties exceed 700,000, including
large numbers of Mexican conscripts. Mexi-
can territories achieve statehood. Douglas
assassinated in 1865 by Confederate fanatic;
Vice-President Lincoln inaugurated.

1866–70 – Louis Pasteur, at Shahnapur Institute of
Tropical Medicine, establishes mosquito vec-
tor of malaria. World total of private auto-
steamers reaches 100,000, 75 percent of them
in Dominion of Draka. Panama Canal under
construction. Taiping Dynasty established in
China, failure of effort to modernize. Bis-
marck unites Germany. Antiseptic surgery,
anesthetics.

1865–68 – 150,000 Confederate refugees settle in Do-
minion of Drakia. Central American Empire
annexed by United States. Freidrich Nietzsche
immigrates to Domination.

1872 –   Steam turbine perfected by Alexandrian Tech-
nological Institute. First rigid dirigibles.

*Archona and Alexandria become first cities
to establish telephone networks. Uruguay and
Paraguay annexed by Empire of Brazil. Co-
lumbia, Venezuela, and Ecuador establish Re-
public of Grand Columbia. Australasian
Federation unites Australia, New Zealand.
Electric lighting.*

1879–82 – *Anglo-Russian war, fought largely in Bul-
garia and Afghanistan. Dominion of Draka
rescues British from defeat; Odessa destroyed
by Draka dirigible raid; worldwide condem-
nation of 50,000 civilian casualties. Draka
introduce land mines, submarines, poison
gas. Austro-German alliance with Ottoman
Empire, construction of Berlin-Baghdad rail-
way. Uprisings in Congo Basin result in large-
scale deportations and unrest.*

1882 – *First transAtlantic flight by Draka dirigible,
from Apollonaris (Dakar, Senegal) to Recife,
Brazil. Women's Auxiliary Corps made per-
manent part of Draka forces (in noncomba-
tant roles). Free population of Dominion
reaches 10,000,000. Bondservant Identifica-
tion and Control Act requires fingerprinting
and neck-tattooing of all serfs. Security Di-
rectorate founded as successor to General
Constabulary. Karl von Shrakenberg born.*

1883 – *Revolt of serfs in textile mills of Alexandria
(Alexandria, Egypt) suppressed; 150,000 dead.
Cape Town–Alexandria railway completed.*

1890 – *Nomenclature Amendment Act makes popu-
lar term "serf" for debt-peons official.*

1891 – *Libyan and Algerian oil fields discovered.
Submachine gun developed by Technical Sec-
tion of Draka armed forces.*

1892–96 – *Regular airship lines established in several continents. Diesel engines come into general use for dirigible and other special uses. Autostreamer output in U.S. surpasses Dominion of Draka's for first time.*

1897 – *Diskarapur Institute team achieves heavier-than-air flight with steam-turbine aircraft. An internal-combustion model flies in France a year later.*

1898 – *Hawaii, Cuba, and Philippines become states of U.S. Guatemala and other Central American territories follow. William Jennings Bryan President.*

1899 – *Military reform in England produces general election. Chinese-Japanese war; Japan annexes Formosa, Hainan, Korea, several ports. Thermionic valve invented. Radio braodcasts.*

1900 – *Japanese-British naval alliance. Anglo-German naval/dirigible armaments race begins. Germany, Austria, and Turkey sign Triple Alliance. France and Russia form Double Entente. Britain begins staff talks with France. Motion pictures with sound become common in U.S., shortly later, elsewhere.*

1905 – *Russo-Japanese war, catastrophic Russian defeat; first instance of battleships sunk by aerial bombardment. Japan annexes Manchuria, establishes quasi-protectorate over weak Taiping government of China; attempts at occupation bog down. Revolution in Russia produces limited constitutional monarchy, administrative chaos. Experimentation with internal combustion engine for ground transport, esp. for military purposes. Wars in Balkans, etc. Women declared liable for peacetime conscription for noncombatant and second-line tasks in Domination. Steam turbine used for railways.*

1914 – *Dominion of Draka has free population of 28,000,000; serfs, 210,000,000. Total population of U.S. reaches 140,000,000. GNP of both nearly identical, but with great differences in distribution, etc.*

1914–19 – *Great War between Triple Alliance and Entente powers (joined by U.S. in 1917, under President Theodore Roosevelt). Draka defeat Austrian and Turkish forces, occupy Middle East, Thrace, Bulgaria. Widespread use of dirigible bombers, firestorms and poison-gas bombardments. Biplane pursuit fighters developed as defense. Civilian casualties in the 500,000–3,000,000 range in all major combatants except the Draka and U.S. Revolution in Russia followed by Draka seizure of Central Asia, much of western China. Turbocompound engine developed; antibiotics, self-loading rifles, portable machine guns. Tank introduced on stalemated Western Front by both sides in 1916. John von Shrakenberg born.*

1918 – *Eric von Shrakenberg born. Draka Women's Auxiliary Corps abolished; women integrated into military. More noncombat and near-combat tasks opened to female personnel.*

1919 – *Unconditional surrender of Germany. Peace of Versailles. Draka refuse mediation of Powers, annex all conquests, enter period of economic and diplomatic isolation; last ties with Britian cut off, "Domination" becomes offi-*

cial title. U.S. also enters isolationist phase.
Defeat of attempt at Prohibition in U.S. Mar-
ijuana becomes major social problem, Mexi-
can gangsters prominent in many cities. "Jazz
Age."

1920–22 – Second Russian Civil War between rivals to
succeed Lenin. Stalin victorious. "Hermit
Kingdom" established, forced-draft industri-
alization.

1921 –   Mussolini takes power in Italy, seizes Dal-
matian coast and Montenegro. Japanese de-
throne last Taiping emperor and annex all of
China not overrun by Draka.

1925 –   Domination invades and annexes Afghani-
stan. Prolonged resistance results in death
of 65 percent of population; wars of pacifi-
cation in other areas of New Territories.
Gradual abolition of remaining restrictions
on female personnel in Draka armed forces,
with complete unification in 1933. Fuel cell
developed as power source; experimental use
in submarines. Hormonal contraceptives. Ad-
vances in quantum theory.

1930 –   Stock market crisis leads to mild but chronic
recession outside Domination. First chain
reaction observed. Closed-circuit television.
Eva and Asa von Shrakenberg born. Death
of Mary von Shrakenberg.

1932 –   Hitler elected with majority in Germany.
F.D. Roosevelt elected President in U.S.; de-
clares "New Deal" for lower classes, Hispan-
ics, etc. Limited recovery.

1936–37 – Civil war in Spain; defeat of Nationalists
by 1937. Soviet Republic of Spain estab-

lished. Germany takes Austria. French and British abandon Czechoslovakia; Sudeten War follows. Clashes on Draka-Japanese and Draka-Soviet borders. Experiments with electrodetection (radar) in several countries. Domination begins long-term project to harness nuclear energy. Albert Einstein, Enrico Fermi move to U.S.

1939 – *France and Britain guarantee Poland. Eurasian War begins. Nazi-Japanese alliance. Transistor invented in Toronto, State of Ontario. First commerical tape recorder.*

1940 – *Fall of France. Battle of Britain ends in stalemate; Nazi submarines effectively close Atlantic. Japanese aggression in Southeast Asia produces severe tension with U.S., Australasian Federation.*

1941 – *Domination attacks Italy with tacit consent of Germany. Germany attacks and defeats Soviet Union. Moscow falls October 1; Germans reach Urals and Caucasus by first snow. Imperial Japan attacks U.S. on December 3rd, occupies eastern Siberia, destroys entire American Pacific Fleet in Pearl Harbor. Hawaii, Philippines overrun, West Coast raided, landings made in Panama. U.S. declares war on Japan and Germany.*

1942 – *January - March: Hawaii overrun by Japanese; widespread atrocities. Philippines conquered; Japanese begin roundup of 900,000 'North Americans' (U.S. citizens from the mainland states); West Coast raided, Acapulco bombarded by battleships lead by Yamato, landings made in Panama.*

*April: Draka airborne legions sieze passes
over Caucasus mountains.*

*German Sixth Army surrenders. Battle of
the Kuban; massive armoured engagements.
Leapfrogging pincer movements combined
with offensive from northwest Kazahkstan
shatter German Army Group South. Draka
amphibious forces land in Crimea. In Sep-
tember, another front is opened in Balkans,
with Draka attack out of the Domination's
Bulgarian province. By October, all of the
Ukraine is in Draka hands, and the Ger-
mans are forced to withdraw their Army
Group Center to the eastern frontiers of
Poland.*

*November: Belgrade falls to Arch-Strategos
Edgar Tull's 4th Army. Arch-Strategos Estelle
Finbogasson's 7th Army reaches Hungarian
frontier. Draka airborne forces sieze Tri-
este, reach Adriatic. Ten divisions of Ger-
man troops cut off in Serbia; many escape to
mountains, join partisan forces of Mihailovic.*

*December: Dec. 15, Hitler dies—officially of
heart attack, actually poisoned by agents of
Admiral Canaris, head of German Military
Intelligence. Coalition government of mili-
tary, Nazi party, SS and anti-nazi conserva-
tives takes power, with Herman Goering as
Chancellor. ("Fuhrer" is declared a unique
position which only the inspired Adolf Hitler
could bear.) New regime promises increased
autonomy for west Europeans (although per-
secution of Jews continues as* quid pro quo
*for unreconstructed Nazi elements) and calls
on all Europeans to rally to Germany for
defense against the Draka, sends peace feel-*

ers to U.S. and Britain. Domination secretly threatens to ally with Japan if Western powers make a separate peace with Germany. America and U.K. remain technically at war with Third Reich. Indian National Congress takes power in India, declares independence and neutrality.

Widespread support from France, Belgium, Scandinavia for new German government. Soviet Republic of Spain remains neutral.

1942–43 – Both sides in European war pause; the Draka have outrun their logistic train and are frantically building up supplies and repairing road-rail links in the territories behind their lines. Germany has lost 2,500,000, dead and prisoner, plus most of the heavy equipment stationed in the East and much productive capacity. Scores of new French, Belgian, Dutch, Danish, Norwegian, Swedish and Swiss divisions are raised. Minor ground action and intensive air action along front lines.

Technological developements 1940–1943: millimetric wave radar. Reaction-jet fighters in Domination, Germany, U.K., U.S. Helicopters deployed for observation, casualty evacuation by Draka, U.S., Germany. Draka test prototype tiltrotor VTOL transport, VTOL jet with plenum-chamber boost. Fuelcell powered submarines by Germany, U.S. All-transistor programable digital computer (U.S., 1943); first nuclear power reactors, plutonium (Domination 1941, U.S. 1942). Long-range liquid fuel rockets, Germany. Television-guided glide bombs, radar-guided cruise missiles (U.S. Both crude, but useable.)

1943 — U.S. jet fighters and glide bombs inflict severe defeat on Japanese navy in Battle of the Sea of Cortez, defeat attempt to land in Baja California. Japanese evicted from Panama Canal Zone. South American powers sign first Treaty of Rio with U.S., declare war on Axis and co-ordinate economic, diplomatic policy. U.S. submarine fleet begins destruction of Japanese merchant marine on huge scale. U.S., Brazilian, Australasian forces totalling 2,000,000 defeat Japanese in New Guinea (a highly-developed area in Domination's timeline) and begin offensive into Indonesia. U.S. surface navy reappears in Pacific, together with British forces. Tension and skirmishes but no full-scale warfare between Domination and Japanese Empire on land frontiers in Asia. Vast economic mobilization in Western hemisphere, armament production of U.S.-U.K.-S.American-Australasian Alliance For Democracy outpaces Domination and Third Reich combined.

April-September: German counter-offensive is allowed to penetrate central Rumania, then cut off by Draka. Draka attack on 1,000-mile front, intially mostly with Janissary forces. Armoured breakthrough into central Poland followed by attack to Baltic; German forces in East Prussia cut off. Some rocket-research project personnel (e.g. von Braun) and much equipment evacuated to Bordeaux, France. Others siezed by Draka, turned over to Technical Section. Bohemia, Hungary overrun; Janissaries enter outskirts of Budapest on June 1, Vienna on September 10. Both sides now using nerve-gas, jet and rocket-propelled fighters, long-distance rockets.

*September-December: main Draka offensive
begins across north Poland. Vistula and Oder
lines forced, Silesia overrun. Heavy casual-
ties on both sides; offensive into Bavaria
bogs down in difficult mountain country.
Fortress Berlin encircled November 25; War-
saw falls November 29th. German and other
European forces manage to contain Draka
offensive along upper Danube, Elbe. Out-
skirts of Hamburg under Draka artillery fire
by year's end; slow, grinding offensive con-
tinues. "Pan-European" emergency govern-
ment under Edouard Daladier meets in
Brussels, de Gaulle returns to continent, fur-
ther purge of National Socialist elements from
new pan-European military (now less than
1/2 German). Soviet Spain joins pan-Europe.
Nazi concentration camps in East are liber-
ated by Draka, who make adroit use of their
propaganda value to keep U.S. hostile to
Europeans.*

*Alliance (basically Anglo-U.S.) aircraft car-
riers meet, defeat Japanese navy's main strike
force west of Hawaii. Reconquest of Hawaii
begins; well-armed Japanese garrison resists
fanatically. Alliance forces also advancing in
eastern Indonesia, again with heavy losses.
Japanese begin to strip forces on Asian main-
land to meet Alliance threat. U.S. subma-
rines sink more than 40% of Japanese cargo
tonnage, begin economic strangulation of Jap-
anese heartland as food, raw materials and
petroleum cut off.*

1944 –   *Taos Project detonates first fission bomb (plu-
tonium, shaped-charge implosion type, 40
kilotonnes) on February 1st, in New Mexico.
First Draka test (uranium bomb, two sub-*

*critical masses) March 4, in central Sahara.
Both countries begin work on series produc-
tion, fusion weapons.*

*April: Draka jet bombers deliver five-weapon
nuclear strike against Ruhr valley, Brussels.
Conventional offensive smashes through to
Rhine; amphibious landings in southern Spain
are contained in narrow beachheads. Last
resistance in Berlin eliminated. Emergency
pan-European fission project unsuccessful, due
to uranium and heavy-water shortages. Mass
flight of refugees from western Germany to
France, Belgium. Famine in Central Europe.
Covert Anglo-American aid to Europeans.*

*Two nuclear-armed cruise missiles fired from
Alliance submarines against main Japanese
fleet in lagoon of Truk island, central Pa-
cific. One malfunctions; the other destroys
three of the seven remaining Japanese fleet
carriers and much else besides. Alliance of-
fensives continue across Pacific and north
from Indonesia.*

*May-July: Draka cross Rhine in three places;
2nd Airborne legion destroyed in attempted
siezure of Strasbourg. Widespread casual-
ties from fallout, little understood by either
side. Demoralization among remaining Eu-
ropean forces.*

*August-October: Paris falls. Mass exodus of
European refugees across Channel to En-
gland, also from Denmark (now cut off),
Norway—totalling 5,000,000 before Draka
forces reach Atlantic. France occupied; Eu-
ropean forces fall back to Pyrenees.*

December: Tokyo destroyed by cruise missile from Alliance submarine; Imperial family and most high government officials killed, casualties exceed 150,000. New government of fanatical younger officers takes power, vows revenge. Widespread starvation in Japan as imports cut off; 80% of merchant tonnage sunk. Most remaining naval units destroyed in Battle of Philippines. Japanese control now limited to Siberia, eastern China, Korea and the home islands.

1946 –   *January-March: Sweden surrenders, Norway, Netherlands occupied by Draka; Finland and Switzerland isolated for future attention. Pyrenees forced after blitz with remaining stockpile (12) of fission weapons wipes out major concentrations of Euro-Spanish forces, communication centers etc. Spain overrun. Massive shift of Draka forces to Far East begins by rail and airship. Europe from the Urals to the Atlantic, from North Cape to Gibraltar, is under Draka occupation—also devastated and starving. The Draka forces are thinly stretched, concentrating on the main cities and lines of communication. Hundreds of thousands of refugees, armed fragments of European armies and followers of dozens of political and nationalistic movements are drifting, regrouping and beginning active resistance, only momentarily cowed by the psychological impact of nuclear weapons.*

Alliance forces occupy Taiwan and Hainan. Widespread revolt in areas of China occupied by Japanese; Peking largely destroyed in reprisals. Kyushu invaded, occupied at cost of 250,000 Alliance dead. Osaka destroyed by Alliance fission bomb.

*June: Draka launch Far Eastern offensive
with 4,000,000 troops, from the Amur river
in the north to Wuhan in the south. The
Japanese forces are cut into pockets and iso-
lated as the Domination's heavy armour,
mechanized infantry and airmobile forces (in-
cluding several helicopter-born chiliarchies)
sweep through to the Pacific, overrunning all
of China and Korea. The "pockets" of Japan-
ese later prove expensive to mop up, in one
case requiring a nuclear weapon. Archon
Palme declares annexation of all territories
occupied during the course of the war. South-
ern border of Domination now rests on Pa-
cific, from there across northern Vietnam,
Burma, India and south to Indian Ocean.
All the rest of continental Eurasia is "under
the yoke."*

*July: Japanese surrender unconditionally to
Alliance when faced with the prospect of a
Draka invasion and further nuclear bom-
bardment.*

EURASIAN WAR ENDS.
"COVERT STRUGGLE" BETWEEN ALLIANCE AND
DOMINATION BEGINS.

*2nd Treaty of Rio continues Alliance For
Democracy on permanent basis. Grand Coun-
cil of U.S., U.K., Brazil to set policy. As-
sembly of member states includes all S.
America, Southeast Asian Federation (Indo-
china, Thailand, Malaysia, Indonesia), India
(includes our Pakistan and Burma), Austral-
asian Federation. Free trade, joint military
forces, joint currency, local autonomy.*

1945 – *Strategos Eric von Shrakenberg married to Sofie Nixon, Nova Cartago (Bizerte, Tunisia). Civil ceremony, Johanna and Karl von Shrakenberg witnesses.*

1946 – *Senior Decurion McWhirter killed by terrorist time-bomb while on antipartisan duty near Bratislava, Carpathian Province. Italy declared open for settlement; Johanna von Shrakenberg married to Centurion Thomas Ingolfsson at Claestum Plantation, their Tuscan estate. Eric and Sofie von Shrakenberg witnesses; Karl von Shrakenberg, Dominarch John Teesdale also present.*

1946–50's– *Guerilla and terrorist warfare in newly occupied portions of Domination. Deportations, executions, etc. All schools in Europe closed, printed material confiscated. Death penalty for unauthorized education, possession of radio receiver. Partial demobilization of Draka armed forces; conversion to airmobile light-infantry units widespread, Janissaries kept at strength and new units recruited from Europe, Asia. Plantations set up in more secure zones of new territories, compound-factory system extended. Massive economic reconstruction, "megaprojects": damming of Mediterranean Sea at Gibraltar, redirection of Arctic rivers to Central Asia, etc.*

Reconstruction in Japan, self-government and membership of Alliance by 1952. Broadcast television, first widespread use of computers in process industry, large-scale data management. Rapid economic growth througout Alliance; "consumer society," Keynsian economics. Naval, air forces emphasised. Anti-Draka sentiment increases steadily.

First fusion bomb exploded Bikini atol, February 1947 by Alliance project headed by Oppenheimer. Refugee German scientists working under direction of Alliance project headed by Dr. Clarke begin development of ramjet (later scramjet) suborbital missile to deliver "sun-bomb."

First integrated circuits, State of Ontario, 1949. Laser invented, U. of Buenos Aires, 1953. DNA identified, Tashkent Institute, 1951. Extensive Draka research into mid-altering chemicals, molecular biology, etc. First transplant of fertilized human ova, Alexandria institute, 1956. Recombinant DNA techniques developed, late 1950s.

Draka fusion bomb, 1949. Missile projects follow. Nuclear submarine, 1948.

Supersonic flight, 1947 (Draka). Earth-to-orbit turbojet-scramjet-rocket, Alliance Aerospace force, 1958 (unmanned). First Draka flight to orbit, 1960. First manned flight to orbit, 1959—Alliance, 1961—Draka. Alliance permanent space station, 1962. Draka, 1962. Alliance nuclear-pulse deepspace propulsion test, 1963.

1947 –   *S.L.A. Marshall elected president of U.S. O.S.S. begins clandestine operations in support of European Resistance. Switzerland surrenders to Draka after mass famine. Finland crushed, but becomes "hardship posting" due to extensive resistance. Mass deportations of Finns to east Asia.*

France, Belgium, Denmark, Germany, Ukraine declared open for Draka settlement.

1950 –   *Strategos Eric von Shrakenberg retires from
active list, appointed Senator, junior mem-
ber of Long-Range Strategic Planning proj-
ect. Publishes* The Price of Victory, *novel of
war experiences. Security Directorate fails
to have it banned, due to Senatorial immu-
nity, and it becomes a best seller, esp. among
young war veterans. Sweden, North China,
Korea declared open for settlement. Price of
unskilled European serf drops to 53 aurics.*

1951 –   *Draka Harmost of Loire Province (northern
France) killed with most of her staff by mass
poisoning at official banquet at Versailles
marking third anniversary of Provincial sta-
tus. O.S.S. "infiltrators" blamed; clashes be-
tween Draka and Alliance aircraft over
English channel. Ten thousand Parisians im-
paled along Champs Elysees in reprisal.*

1952 –   *Uprising in Barcelona overruns Security Di-
rectorate H.Q. Draka personnel evacuated
by helicopter and city destroyed by nuclear
bomb. Films, survivors shown over occupied
Europe.*

NOTES ON THE WORLD OF
THE DOMINATION

Military

War and repression are the raison d'etre of the Domination's state machinery; the Draka exist in a state of either war or serious preparation for same. The War Directorate itself owns a considerable share of the economy, and certainly not less than 20 percent of the total GNP is dedicated to military-related purposes.

There are essentially two Draka armies: the Citizen Force and the Janissaries. The Citizen Force is ultimately descended from the Loyalist volunteer regiments of the American Revolutionary period, and the militia units that conquered and held southern Africa in the late eighteenth century. Other influences included Classical history (notable in the military terminology), various European armies (particularly the Prussian) and native developments. The following description applies to the period of the Eurasian War, 1941–1946.

Training: Citizen children are enrolled in boarding schools eight months of the year from the age of 5. Military training begins almost at once, both physical and psychological. The aims are toughness, hardiness (ruthlessness and indifference to pain are emphasized), independence, leadership and cooperative teamwork.

*Robotic obedience is not encouraged; the Draka have
always been outnumbered, and cannot afford to blud-
geon their enemies to death. After 12, training becomes
more specific: marksmanship, fieldcraft, technical sub-
jects, small-unit tactics, wilderness survival, live-firing
exercises, etc.*

*Military service begins at 18 and lasts for four years
in peacetime. Since the conscript is already in fine
physical condition, and more than familiar with the
basics, "basic" training is actually more like an advanced
specialist's course. Leadership candidates are identified
during the first year, and qualification testing screens
applicants for NCO rank. All officers are promoted
"from the ranks," and then receive advanced training in
a number of specialized schools. After the basic four
years (longer for officers and NCOs) most Draka un-
dergo two months' reserve service a year; after age 40
most are transferred into second-line formations. At
full mobilization, 19.2 percent of the total Citizen popu-
lation is under arms.*

*Most units (the Air Corps and Navy aside) are terri-
torially based, with recruits drawn from a single area.
Great efforts are made to keep down personnel turbu-
lence, and the average Draka soldier spends his/her
military life with roughly the same group of faces. The
basic field formation is the Legion (roughly, a division);
Armies and Army Corps are plugged together from
these basic building blocks as need and opportunity
dictate.*

*In 1942, there are three types of Legion: Armored,
Mechanized, and Special—Airborne, Mountain, and
Amphibious. The Armored/Mechanized constitute about
95 percent of total strength. Organization is (roughly)
as follows:*

Table of Organization and Order of Battle
Citizen Force Armored Legion, 1942

Draka Unit Title	Commander's Title	Total personnel	Our Equivalent (approx.)
stick	monitor	4	
lochos	decurion	8	squad, sergeant
tetrarchy	tetrarch	33	platoon, 2nd lieutenant
century	centurion	110	company, captain
cohort	cohortarch	500	battatlion, major
merarchy	merarch	1,500	regiment, colonel
chiliarchy	chiliarch	4,500	brigade, brigadier
legion	strategos	13,000	division, general

At higher levels (e.g., Army Corps), formal rank
designation would be "Arch-Strategos"—roughly, Se-
nior General—with a functional qualifier to designate
role. Note that each grade would contain junior/senior
levels, and also that the Draka concept of rank is rather
flexible—ad hoc units under relatively junior command-
ers can be patched together at need.

At full strength a Legion of the Regular Line will
contain roughly 9,200 Citizen personnel and about 3,000
serf auxiliaries. These are unarmed support troops and
fill most of the lower-level noncombatant functions.
Thus, over 75 percent of the Citizen troops in a Legion
will actually be carrying rifles, driving tanks or stuffing
shells into guns; the percentage of auxiliaries increases
with distance from the front. (In the Air Corps, most of
the ground crews, etc., are auxiliary personnel.) The
percentage of officers is low (about 4.5 percent) and
"lead from the front" is an axiom. It is more dangerous
to be a company commander than a private. Given the
lavish state of their armament and high motivation, a
Citizen Force Legion is a devastating opponent; its weak-

ness is its lack of reserves. The Citizen Force is designed as a specialized instrument, an army-crusher, built for short-duration, high-intensity combat.

An armored legion has most of its infantry/armor teams integrated down to cohort level: two tank centuries, two infantry, one support and miscellaneous (medical, signals, etc.). (The model used here is the Archonal Guard Legion, 1st Armored, as of March 1st, 1942.) It would be organized roughly as follows:

Two three-tank lochoi plus a command tank to a tetrarchy. Three of these make a tank century. Two of these per cohort: total 40 tanks, 200 effectives. The tanks are Hond III, crew of 5.

Three infantry lochoi of one APC each plus H.Q. lochos: one infantry tetrarchy. Three of these to an infantry century. Two centuries per cohort: total, 28 APC's, 280 effectives. The APC's are Hoplite-class, modified Hond III hull, 8 infantry and 2 crew.

One fire-support tetrarchy, 7 Flail SP mortars on Hoplite chassis, 40 effectives. A 160 mm automortar, crew of 5.

The legion would essentially consist of six of these cohorts, plus several "pure" armor and infantry cohorts, giving a total of approximately 300 main battle tanks, 2,000 infantry (including APC drivers and gunners), the reconnaissance cohorts (amored cars and Cheetah light tanks), and a merarchy of SP guns—155 gun-howitzers and 200mm rocket launchers on modified Hoplite chassis, for a total of about 100 heavy-bombardment weapons. There would also be combat engineer, signals, medical and other units in proportion. Units larger than the cohort are "plugged together" as needed, but would usually consist of three merarchy-sized combat teams with supporting arms attached. Standard Draka practice (insofar as this exists) is "two up, one back."

A mechanized legion would be similarly organized, but with an armor/infantry ratio of 1/4 instead of 1/1. Independent chiliarchoi of varying composition also exist, to increase the flexibility of an Army or Army Corps commander. The reserve formations available to such a commander would include heavier artillery (200mm howitzers and 175mm guns, all self-propelled), engineers, and the support "slices" as appropriate.

The special-purpose units (Airborne, etc.) differ mainly in that they are foot-transported once dropped or landed. Their auxiliaries and mechanical transport are provided by the Logistics Corps as needed, and more of their maintenance and support units are Citizen personnel (which also increases their emergency reserve of infantry replacements).

Training cohorts are maintained for each legion, but in emergencies, individual "fillers" may end up in units outside their cantonal recruiting areas.

A notable feature of the Citizen Force is the attitude toward "discipline." In most armies, there is an analogy between social and military rank—the officer as gentry, the enlisted personnel as peasants; not least in the American Army (in both timelines). The Draka have no such tradition. Every private is an aristocrat, and military rank is regarded as equivalent to a medical degree—a technical qualification worthy of respect, but no trace of social awe. "Creative disobedience" is an honored tradition, and approved provided it works. Certain aspects of discipline—march and fire discipline, for example—are excellent, and the long training in teamwork provided by the Draka educational system makes for intelligent cooperation in the field. (Peer pressure tends to restrain barrack-room lawyers and congenital screw-ups, said pressure manifesting itself as anything from mockery to a grenade rolled under the bunk.) Formal military ritual is sparse everywhere and nonexistent in the field. Looting and rape, so long as they do not interfere with the mission, are officially recognized prerogatives of troops on foreign soil. Draka armies are notoriously atrocity-prone and utterly intolerant of attempts to restrain them in these matters.

The weaknesses of the Citizen Force are made up by the Janissary Corps. This is the serf army, commanded by Citizen Force officers and senior NCOs. Most Janissary legions are "motorized rifles"—strong in rifle infantry, antitank weapons, and towed artillery, but with considerably less heavy armor. Training and discipline in the Janissary forces are much more conventional and routinized than the Citizen Force, aimed at producing unthinking obedience. About two thirds of the Domination's infantry are Janissaries. Recruitment is by levy on private serf owners and the Combines. Given the privileges of even the lowliest Janissary private, volunteers are never lacking. The Janissaries are also extensively used for internal-security work in time of peace.

All services are united under the Supreme General Staff. In practice, this means the Army dominates, since the Draka are a continental power. Draka tactics and strategy both emphasize the indirect approach—overwhelming an opponent with movement and firepower rather than head-on battering: "Winning battles by attrition is to the Art of War as a paint-by-numbers kit is to the Mona Lisa." By the 1940's the armed forces of the Domination were not only of high quality, but also very large indeed. At maximum strength (early 1943) the Domination mobilized 4,200,000 Citizen Force troops, 6,500,000 Janissaries and 3,000,000 auxiliaries (not soldiers by Draka reckoning, but fulfilling functions that would absorb uniformed personnel in other countries), for a grand total of just under 14,000,000. And the Domination's war economy was capable of equipping them with the best weapons of the day, in any quantity needed.

Currency and prices:

The Domination's currency is gold-backed. The basic unit is the Auric (A), 1/10 of an ounce of fine gold, divided into 10 denarii (d) and 100 pennies. In 1942, an auric is rated at $3.72 U.S. (Geneva exchange rate).

Comparative prices:

Entry-level Citizen wage: A2,500 per annum.

Purchase price, Archona/Central Police Zone:

Standard unskilled serf:	A200
Machine tender serf (assembly-line):	A350
Skilled domestic servant:	A250 (up to 1,000 for fancy items)
Three-bedroom house in Archona:	A30,000, depending on neighborhood.
Dinner for two with house wine:	A1.5 (two-star restaurant)
Kellerman mini four-seat autosteamer:	A800 (will last 30 years if maintained)
Airship ticket from Archona to Tashkent:	A90.35
Walking shoes:	A6
Litre of fresh milk:	3p.
Kilo of sirloin:	25p.
Developed plantation in Police Zone:	A1,250,000 (includes labor force, manor)
10,000 hectare grant in New Territories:	Free, if settled and developed by claimant
Prime interest rate:	3.5% (Landholders League Bank)

Maintaining a serf in a large city, at accepted stan-
dards, would cost about A25 per year, not counting
housing.

Science and Technology:

The pure sciences are roughly equivalent to our his-
tory in the 1940s: Nuclear fission is near, the Bohr
model of atomic structure is current, the first applica-

tions of quantum mechanics are moving out of the laboratory. Biology is slightly more advanced; high-energy chemistry slightly less so.

Technology is somewhat more advanced than our 1942, and has developed along rather different lines. For example, vulcanized rubber and the pneumatic tire were developed in the 1820s, for autosteamers; natural asphalt from Angola and Trinidad was used for roads at about the same time. Steam engines of all types, particularly piston engines and small portable turbines, are more advanced than in our history. In this timeline, Africa is a "developed" region; accordingly, tropical med-icine and agriculture are more advanced, since they received concentrated attention. Problems such as bil-harzia, sleeping sickness, and river-blindness were over-come in the 19th century. By the 1940's the hydroelectric power of the Congo and the geothermal energy of the Great Rift were being harnessed, and the Sahara was in retreat before reclamation and afforestation projects. The Domination is particularly strong in civil engineer-ing, transport, weapons, and large-scale "process" indus-try, which are accordingly ahead of our timeline.

All this implies certain economic differences as well. The United States reaches far into what we know as Latin America, and the parts of Asia which fell under the Domination in 1914–1919 have been forcibly mod-ernized. Accordingly, there is less "Third World"; there are fewer and larger states, fewer tariffs, more trade, more surplus available for reinvestment (or war). World income per capita is higher up until the 1940's; urban-ization greater; birth- and death-rates rather lower. The world population is roughly equivalent in both timelines up until the 1940's, but the world of the Domination drops behind rather quickly after that. The low cost and early availability of air transport make remote regions more accessible. Tibet becomes a vacation center in the 1920's, for example, and Chinese fruit is air-freighted by dirigible to Europe in the same period.

Some Points of Difference

A. *Steam transport got under way about a generation
earlier than in our history, and steam cars have been
common since the 1820's, gradually improving. By the
time the internal combustion engine came along, so
much effort had gone into developing automotive steam
engines that they remained dominant in all but aero-
nautical and armored fighting-vehicle applications. Pe-
troleum or coal oil has been the dominant fuel for
autosteamers since the first Egyptian oil fields were
discovered (by teams drilling for water) in the 1810's.
Modern (1940) autosteamers have pressure-injected flash
boilers with high superheat, operating safely at 1,200
psi; the standard operating unit is a triple-expansion
uniflow with extensive electric auxiliaries. Heavy, artic-
ulated trucks are common, particularly in the Domina-
tion. The autosteamers of the 40's represent a "mature"
technology—fairly uniform everywhere, rugged, easy to
maintain and very long-lasting. Performance and price
are both lower than the equivalent internal-combustion
machines of our history, but reliability is greater. Since
they are relatively simple to manufacture, most nations
with any pretensions to modernity have an autosteamer
industry.*

B. *Air transport became a practical reality in the
1870's; the Domination's need for fast long-distance
transport provided the incentive. The first dirigibles
were steam-turbine powered, with laminated wood
frames and cloth hull coverings. By 1914, "metalclad"
airships were the rule (a thin metal hull providing gas
sealage, with an internal frame). Size had increased to
1,000 feet length, 250 feet maximum diameter, 8,000
mile range and 100 tons useful lift, burning a mixture of
kerosene and hydrogen as fuel. Heavier-than-air planes
were developed primarily to destroy dirigible bombers,
and did so very effectively. Transport dirigibles contin-
ued in use, and by the 1940's could carry up to 200 tons
for 12,000 miles at 90 mph. Long distance air freight*

dates from the 1890's (the decade of the first Atlantic crossing). The more primitive areas of the continental interiors were largely opened up by dirigibles: Yunnan, Tibet, the New Guinea highlands . . .

C. Urban mass transit got an earlier start, since the autosteamer could be employed on city streets. Monorails evolved from elevated urban railways—first pneumatic, then electric, then powered by linear induction motors. Autosteamers and trucks served as feeders to railways from the beginning, ousting animal transport very gradually over a period of generations—first in the advanced countries, and spreading from there.

D. "Modern" (Bauhaus) architecture never really got under way in the Domination's timeline; Frank Lloyd Wright practiced, but the German school was never born. Steel-frame and ferroconcrete construction are common, but the unadorned "glass shoebox" is reserved for industrial uses. Public and domestic architecture in the Domination is predominantly "Drakastyle"—an Art-Nouveauish version of earlier Classico-Mughal schools: lines are fairly simple, but with elaborately decorated surfaces (mosaic, murals, stained glass). Euro-American styles are variously historic, Art Nouveau-Art Deco, and "Mechanist." Skyscrapers are common in the larger American cities, but not much imitated elsewhere. Central air-conditioning was developed in the Domination in the 1850's, immediately after the invention of practical refrigeration, and spread rapidly to the tropical areas of the U.S.; small, single-dwelling units were available in America by the time of the Great War.

E. Clothing makes less use of synthetic fabrics, since the natural equivalents are much cheaper than in our history. Draka clothing adapted early to tropical climates; it is loose, light, and nonconfining. This has had some influence on general Western styles. Trousers for women were introduced for sporting purposes in the Domination in the 1860s, and for casual wear in "daring" circles by about 1900. The U.S. followed about a generation behind, and Europe still later. Hats remain common for both sexes past the 1950's; colors are usually brighter.

F. Social intoxicants have a rather different history in the Domination's timeline. Both the United States and the Domination are exposed to cannabis *on a large scale fairly early—the Draka from the North Africans and the U.S. from Mexico. Sporadic attempts at prohibition in the United States break down in the 1930's, with social acceptance (outside the Bible Belt) following during the Eurasian War. (In the process, ethnic Mexicans come to dominate organized crime in most major cities, much to the discomfort of the law-abiding majority of Hispanics.) Ganja is popular and legal in the Domination from the early nineteenth century; both countries launch occasional educational campaigns to prevent abuse. The first studies linking tobacco to cancer and heart disease are done in Germany in the 1930's and at first, widely discounted as Nazi propaganda. The U.S. is otherwise a spirits-and-beer country, with some wine-drinking enclaves. The Domination is a wine-and-brandy region with a minor key in (German and Scandinavian-influenced) beer.*

G. Solar-power units (glass circulating-water collectors, with underground pressurized-water heat sinks) were developed for isolated plantations in the Domination in the 1860's, and spread widely in high-sunlight tropical regions. By the 1920's most ranches and farms in the American Sunbelt have one.

H. Household appliances (vacuum cleaners, etc.) are primitive, and outside the U.S. rare.

Population: *world population 2,500,000,000 (approx.)*

Birth Rates per thousand, 1940:
Domination: Citizen 24, serf 30 (serf death rates are also higher)
Western Europe: average 17, lower in France and Scandinavia
U.S.: overall 24, Mexican states, 28, Philippines 37

South Asia: 38
China: 43
Japan: 32

In 1942, the free population of the Domination was 36,750,447, and the serf 501,792,544. Approximately 75 percent of the free and 38 percent of the serf population was urbanized. Of the serfs, 101,897,000 were owned by the Combines or the state; the remainder were in private hands. The African territories had a total population of 324,000,000 and remained the richest and most densely settled area of the Domination.

The population of the United States was 179,000,000. This included roughly 20,000,000 Hispanics and Asians (mostly Filipino) and about 11,000,000 blacks.

Race Purity Laws

Acts of 1836, 1879, and 1911 forbid sexual intercourse between Citizen women and unfree males. Apart from prohibitions on rape (of free women; rape of serf women is a civil tort actionable for damages by the owner) and molestation of free children, this is the only morals legislation in the Domination, and this has been (roughly) the case since the mid-nineteenth century.

Serfdom:

The institution of serfdom grew out of efforts to mobilize the labor of the native population of southern Africa, whose formal enslavement was forbidden by the British. While ordinary chattel slaves existed, prior to the British abolition of slavery throughout the Empire in 1833, they were never very common south of the Limpopo except in the Western Cape Province.

Instead, the natives were subject to a "poll tax." Since they had no access to the cash economy (and fairly soon after the conquest, no title to land) they were forced to accept employment as indentured servants, theoretically for a fixed term. However, the "wages" never equalled the charges for upkeep and the accumulated tax; hence, a servant could be legally forced to reindenture to pay off the debt. In theory only the debt and contract of indenture could be sold, but the distinction quickly became academic once the debts were made hereditary. Children of bondservants were automatically contracted to their parents' owners as they came of age.

Successive Master and Servant Acts subjected bondservants to restrictions more and more closely resembling those imposed on outright slaves. By the time slavery was formally abolished in 1833, the distinction had become very largely academic. In point of fact, the pretense of "contracts of indenture" was a legalistic farce almost from the beginning. Newly conquered populations were rounded up, culled and auctioned as property. The word slave was avoided for political reasons. "Bondservant" remained the technical and legal term until the 1880s, when the colloquial "serf" was introduced into Draka law.

In its classical form (after about 1840), Draka serfdom resembled that of Czarist Russia. Serfs were effectively personal property, and could be sold either as individuals (although there were restrictions on separating mothers from small children) or as part of an economic unit such as a plantation or mine. All persons born to serf mothers were serfs; serf status was unchangeable, with no manumission. Originally, the institution was also racially based: the free population was of European origin, the serf, African. Miscegenation and expansion into racially Europoid areas such as North Africa (and later the Middle East) tended to blur this, as did the decline of immigration and the hardening of the caste system.

In essence, the only restrictions on a master's rights over his/her serfs were those imposed by the Domination for police/security purposes—serfs had to be kept under effective supervision, could not be allowed to *wander at large, etc. Draka law held an owner responsible for torts committed by serfs, where negligence could be shown. A master who did not meet certain minimum standards of maintenance (food, clothing, etc.) would have control over their serfs removed and the serfs either auctioned or placed under a receiver. While there were no formal limits on physical punishment, informal administrative and social pressures tended to restrain the more bizarre types of sadism, at least when conducted in the public view.*

By law, serfs could own no property and make no contracts. Their testimony was not accepted in law courts, and their marriages had no legal validity. In fact, their status closely approximated that of a slave under Roman law: pro nullis, pro mortis, pro quadrupedis: "as nothing, as one who is dead, like a beast." The law forbade all education of serfs except under carefully regulated licenses. This was kept to the minimum necessary to manage an industrial economy, with a certain degree of inflexibility accepted as the price of security. Such education and training as was given tended to be as narrowly specialized as possible; e.g., serf typists would be taught sight-reading but have no knowledge of geography or history. Elaborate controls existed to prevent uncensored reading material from reaching literate serfs; as much as possible, training was conducted via visual media. Serfs were forbidden to carry any form of weapon, to travel outside their immediate place of residence or work without a permit, and were under a legal obligation of absolute deference to all Citizen adults.

Agricultural serfs generally lived in small villages near the manor of the plantation-holder. Others were usually housed in "compounds"—enclosed barracks of up to 10,000 individuals. The compound system was originally developed for mine labor, and gradually extended to manufacturing. Compounds are sited in convenient cleared zones in the industrial areas of Draka cities and towns, or at isolated enterprises in the countryside. Domestic servants, and certain types of clerical

*and service labor, live in their master's households. A
curfew, usually dusk-to-dawn, keeps all non-Citizens off
city streets unless operating under special permit. It
should be noted that there were classes within the serf
caste; priviledged elements—Janissaries, technicians,
strawbosses, etc.—that received better material treat-
ment and, in practice, protection from random brutality.
Also note that many of the compound-dwellers had very
little contact with the Citizen population, even at work.*

Economics and the Standard of Living

The Domination has three economies, separate but
interlinked: the command economy of the Combines—
huge quasi-monopolistic corporations usually partially
owned by the State; the bureaucratic/civil service econ-
omy of the free employees of the State and the Com-
bines; and a large "private sector" of small business,
which employs both serf and free labor.

Most town serfs are compound-dwellers. Their life-
style was described by an American visitor as "life
imprisonment in a cut-rate boarding school." Clothing
is a standardized uniform; rations (adequate and well-
blanced but dull) are issued in compound messhalls;
accommodations are clean but spartan dormitories. The
general tenor of life is of an unutterable drabness, with
virtually every non-leisure moment done by a mass
lockstep "time-and-motion" system. Religion, folk-culture
(e.g., song, dance, etc.) and a furtive black market in
alcohol and recreational drugs are the main outlets.
Compound serfs had no contact with the market econ-
omy, never touch money (and rarely even the compound-
scrip issued for bonus and incentive programs), and
often remain their entire life in the compound and its
creches. Each compound, therefore, tends to develop
its own subculture. There is a carefully maintained
gradation of conditions, so that transfer may be used as

a punishemnt/incentive; for example, some compounds are single-sex, others involve more disagreeable work, and so forth, until the mine-compounds of the Ituri and Kashgar are reached.

Plantation life is basically similar but much more informal, with more opportunities for personal choice but also more contact with the master-caste. Privately owned serfs in the towns are in a midway position. It is important to bear in mind that serfs are cheap. *They cost less both to purchase and maintain than an auto, since standardized, mass-produced ration and clothing packs are sold everywhere.*

The Citizen caste lives in a cross between a very comprehensive welfare state and a consumer society. The top one-tenth of the economy is reserved for Citizen labor, which has always been scarce and very expensive. Citizen employees are usually organized in guilds, which collectively own about a third of the economy. Taxes are relatively low, since the State derives much of its income from profits on investment and ground-rent (being the only landowner, in the strict sense). Education through university, medical care and much else is provided free of charge; no Draka Citizen is actually poor. Only those with severe personality disorders manage to fall below the general upper-middle-class minimum, and they are usually institutionalized. (And sterilized, under the Eugenics Laws.) Note also that the structure of Draka society gives the Citizen caste rewards that no amount of money could buy, and that personal service and its products are very cheap—servants are the largest occupational category in the Domination, and even children usually bring at least one with them to school.

The plantation aristocrats and other members of the Draka elite live in almost unbelievable sybaritic luxury—when not under arms in the field.

Constitution and Government

For the Citizen population, the Domination is a rather mild authoritarianism. There is an elected government, and a fair degree of freedom of speech and association. However, fundamental criticism (e.g., of serfdom) is not permitted, and the power of the Security Directorate has tended to gradually increase. Since there is a large degree of uniformity of opinion among the citizen population, this is not felt as much of a hardship.

Head of State and Government is the Archon, chosen for a 20-year term by two-thirds vote of the House of Assembly, the parliament. The Archon in turn chooses the heads of the Directorates (Transportation, Conservation, etc.) which manage sectors of the economy and provide services. The War Directorate is a special case, as its Director must be chosen from the General Staff and be approved by that body. There is a Senate, appointed by corporate bodies (the guilds, the Landholder's League, the Universities, etc.), which acts as a planning and coordinating authority; membership confers great social prestige. Local government is based on Provinces and Metropolitan Zones within the Police Zone, the pacified area, and under military/Security authority in the War Zone, where pacification is still going on. The Domination is actually more managed than governed, since over 90 percent of the population is property and, strictly speaking, subject to their owners rather than the State.

A noteworthy factor in the Domination's social system is the spread of overlapping ownership—many institutions which in the Western world would be supported by tax revenue instead own interests in the Combines, and thus have independent revenues.